Praise for Michael Savage's
New York Times bestseller

ABUSE OF POWER

"Power fiction, tinged with terrorism and intrigue, with an old-school, rough-and-tumble journalist as its hero."
—*Washington Times*

"A thriller sure to score a bull's-eye with its target audience. . . . Savage pulls off some neat twists as Hatfield and a handful of amateurs fight to prevent a disaster that certain officials choose to ignore or abet."
—*Publishers Weekly*

"An exciting, fast-paced story." —*WorldNetDaily*

"A fast-paced international thriller whose story spans the globe. . . . Dr. Savage has hit a home run with *Abuse of Power*. The story grips the reader and delivers the goods." —*Free Republic*

"Impressive." —*Media Matters for America*

ALSO BY MICHAEL SAVAGE

A
TIME
FOR
WAR

MICHAEL SAVAGE

St. Martin's Paperbacks

This is a work of fiction. All of the characters, organizations, and events portrayed in this novel are either products of the author's imagination or are used fictitiously.

A TIME FOR WAR

Copyright © 2013 by Michael Savage.

For information address St. Martin's Press, 175 Fifth Avenue, New York, NY 10010.

Library of Congress Catalog Card Number: 2012041267

ISBN: 978-1-250-03976-7

Printed in the United States of America

St. Martin's Press hardcover edition / February 2013
St. Martin's Paperbacks edition / August 2013

St. Martin's Paperbacks are published by St. Martin's Press, 175 Fifth Avenue, New York, NY 10010.

10 9 8 7 6 5 4 3 2 1

For Jerome (1946–1970)

Prologue

___

Tangi Valley, Afghanistan

Chief Petty Officer James Grand sat on the rattling red canvas seat among thirty-eight of his fellow SEALs as the CH 47-D Chinook slashed across the dusty valley. He didn't really see the men sitting across from him, wasn't aware of the white sunlight coming through the big windows, washing color from the cabin—save for the bright red, white, and blue of the flag stretched across the roof three feet above him. Some genetic part of him was always aware of Old Glory, wherever he was, wherever it was, however small or large, whether it was a grocer's lapel pin or high on a staff.

But right now, ferrying the quick-reaction team to a firefight, James Grand wasn't thinking of the present. He did what he always did when the uncertainty of the war closed in, when nothing was guaranteed but the present, this moment. He went back to his one pure and perfect time—the thirteenth of May 2010.

Spring was new and their life together was younger still. James Grand and Genie Bundy stood in her parents' backyard under a sharp blue Arizona sky, two dozen friends and relatives watching them marry. It was the last thing Chief Petty Officer Grand would do before shipping off to Naval Amphibious Base, Little Creek, in Virginia Beach, Virginia.

Joining the SEALs was a tradition begun by his grandfather in 1963, a year after the Navy's special operation force was founded. Taking a bride was part of that "big, holy deal," as his own father had once described it. You wed, you wore your country's uniform, and you served God by doing both. That was the proud Grand way, dating to the French and Indian War and Major Richard Grand of the Virginia militia. An only child of an only child, James felt a particular pride in being the standard-bearer for a generation.

The shrill, clipping sound of the Chinook's wings edged into his mind. Chief Petty Officer Grand willfully held on to the image of Genie in her simple white gown, like a little ray of sun given form and breath and a loving, trusting expression. As he spoke the vows and looked into her innocent eyes, life seemed full and complete, the future given form and clarity, the world made comprehensible. He smiled at the memory.

The smile lasted as long as a heartbeat. A moment later the Chinook made a sickening drop that kicked Grand's entire body up against the padded roof of the cabin. There were shouts, but they were just words: "Power . . ." "Down . . ." "Christ . . ." His body, along with those of the other men, didn't come down until the helicopter did, smacking the barren ground like a monstrous flyswatter, the fore and aft rotors springing earthward and then up before settling into ugly, still-twisting shapes as the cabin collapsed beneath them. Sand billowed from the impact zone, followed by a fanning array of sparks. Then they were swallowed by a massive red-orange fireball that punched from the olive-green chopper to both sides of the valley before the wreckage had even settled. The flames rolled back, seeking something to burn, as black smoke churned upward, driven by the dying turns of the rotors.

A Grand tradition perished in an instant, along with thirty-nine lives and countless futures.

Sammo Yang, the man nearest the explosion—the only man in this remote section of the valley—smiled.

He was behind a large rock, dead brushwood and gnarled juniper branches piled high on either side for camouflage. The Chinese national was still crouched on the balls of his feet, ready to retreat in case the helicopter was not traveling alone. It was difficult to be sure with the deafening echo generated by the twin Chinook rotors and visibility limited by winds that whipped up swirling dust devils the size of a mango tree. These windstorms were made visible by the dead foliage and sand they swept up.

The rolling heat of the explosion hit the boulder

like a silent scream blazing around him. When he felt the initial punch roll past him, the man pulled a billowing sleeve over the device strapped to his forearm. He looked over the rock, and did not see another helicopter.

A solo flight, as most of these missions were. Tandems typically came if there was a firefight and reinforcements were required.

The young man picked up the Type 56 assault rifle that had been hidden beneath the branches and slipped it over his right shoulder. Then he stepped sure-footedly along the rocky foothill, away from the blast. After four hours since his last break it felt good to stand, to move. He picked his way across a field with rocks the size of fists.

The short man was dressed in the *shalwar kameez* of the region, a loose-fitting, long-sleeved black tunic over drawstring trousers. He wore a beard cut in the short style of Tangi Valley tribesmen and his head was covered with a black-and-white checked *keffiyeh*. The sweltering Arab headdress was not requisite—a *topi* or *kufi* pillbox cap would have sufficed—but he did not want anyone to see his features or skin color. Though his superiors had selected a region that was rarely traveled on the ground, there were still roving Taliban and unaffiliated bandits. If seen, he would rather not attract their attention. The Taliban would execute you if you weren't groomed and dressed in accordance with Islamic law, and a *keffiyeh* was indicative of respect for tradition over comfort; the others would kill you if they thought you were an outsider carrying goods that could be sold on the black market. That included tribal messages about alliances with Americans, Pakistanis, Iranians, or local warlords; as well as American troop locations, temporary special forces outposts, and drone patterns. In war, information was as valuable as currency.

He had none of that. What he carried was far more valuable.

The young man rounded the edge of a bare, thousand-foot outcropping that stood jagged against the bright, late morning sky. A rugged slope spread before him. It was ten kilometers to the base: that was where he would meet his ride from Pakistan, an Aérospatiale SA 330 Puma. He didn't have to check the GPS device tucked in an inside pocket. He knew, from photographs, the precise geologic location of latitude 34 degrees, 41 minutes, 25.08 seconds; longitude 68 degrees, 23 minutes, 54.96 seconds—the outside limit of the helicopter's fuel capacity.

At least the trek home was downward, though he had to cross it before sunset. Satellite reconnaissance showed that the slopes—a popular route for drug runners and Taliban fighters—were rarely traveled during the daytime when the temperature was headed to a noontime high of 120 degrees. Even scorpions and marauders waited until dusk before stirring.

He ignored the perspiration that slipped past the folds of his headdress. He hooked a finger around the fabric and pulled it from his mouth so he could breathe the hot air. He ran the finger from side to side to expose some of his cheek to the hot wind. It let body heat out, and helped to keep him from overheating. He moved quickly, wanting to put as much distance between himself and the crash site as quickly as possible. It wouldn't be long before the Americans came to see what had happened to their chopper and to check for any survivors among the SEALs.

The young man moved across the rocks, their radiant heat rising up his pant legs. He left trails of sweat where he walked, but they evaporated quickly. He kept his eyes on the horizon, felt for footholds rather than looked for them, since the shadows and perspiration-blurred vision could be misleading.

He had trained for this mission in secret, in hostile environments, so he would be ready. The first part had gone exactly as planned. But it was just the beginning of a process that would end with an enemy broken forever and, more importantly, humbled. Economies can be restored, armies repopulated, and cities rebuilt. But "face," a nation's honor, was something not even the centuries could repair.

In less than a month, there would be only one world power.

PART ONE

The Beachhead

Chapter 1

Sausalito, California

". . . killing all thirty-eight Navy SEALs on board. . . ."

Jack Samuel Hatfield slapped off the alarm on his clock radio. The words hadn't quite registered as he blinked to clear his vision, tried to make out the luminous red numbers. He pushed the black hair from his high, strong forehead, dragged a hand across tired eyes.

"You're late, champ," he smiled, as Eddie bounded toward him from the foot of the queen-size bed. The four-year-old gray poodle, all tongue and forepaws and big brown eyes, usually woke him up a minute or two before the six A.M. alarm. Jack dug his fingers behind the dog's ears, and Eddie drew back his head and jerked approvingly.

Jack ended their morning ritual by pulling a well-worn chew toy from the drawer of his night table and flinging the toy to the floor. Eddie followed, landing on the rubber steak with a single, mighty leap and a whimpering squeak from the steak.

"Lie back and think of England," Jack told the chew toy. Then he groaned. He hadn't been awake two minutes and already England was back on his mind. Eddie had landed on the rubber steak like the full weight of Britain's blinkered bureaucracy had landed on Jack, who was still banned by the British Home Office from entering the United Kingdom, along with terrorists and criminals. Normally it never crossed his mind, but he had a lead for a story he was writing on the smuggling of illegal Chinese medicines. The lead was in London and London was off-limits.

Jack stood up, his body automatically adjusting to the gentle sway of the forty-ton *Sea Wrighter*. The cast-off bedsheet buried Eddie, who pulled his toy to safety and continued gnawing.

Jack Hatfield, Jack thought, *the defrocked talk show host and the last truly independent journalist in America, hounded by the il-liberal left and defamed worldwide, needs coffee.* But he still headed to his office-cum-video-editing station in the converted lower-deck stateroom before he made it to the kitchen. He clicked on the radio and started going through his e-mail.

"*. . . Prince William and the lovely Princess Kate will be touring. . . .*"

He turned off the radio.

"They probably spent sixty seconds on the Navy SEALs," he muttered, "but they'll spend a full five minutes on the vacation plans of royalty."

Every day he wondered, was his profession dead now? How about *now*? News channels were afraid to report anything that their audience might whine about, never mind topics that could scare them. Changing people's minds was serious, vital business, and nobody had the guts to do it anymore. Jack had received regular death threats when he was hosting his cable news talk show *Truth Tellers,* but they had never discouraged him. Instead, it had taken all the resources of a giant to swat Jack down, back when he posed one simple, rhetorical question to the panel on his show: "How would you feel if Muslim extremists got hold of a nuclear weapon?"

Within hours Media Wire, the leftist radical watchdog group funded by reclusive, Austrian-born billionaire Lawrence Soren, had organized a smear campaign. They had been looking for a hook on which to hang Jack like a slaughtered bull. He was labeled an Islamophobe, and the liberals gleefully piled on with the kind of manic indignation only aging hippies and ignorant youth could muster. By the time Soren was done, *Truth Tellers* had not only lost half of its sponsors but Jack was out of a job. And he was barred from the United Kingdom, due to his "radical and provocative statements" that were deemed "a threat to public security."

Eddie trotted into the office, the chew toy in his mouth. He lay down and sank his teeth into it.

Now Jack was freelance, but San Francisco had been quiet for weeks. The most promising story was the smuggling . . .

His phone rang. The caller ID said it was Max.

"I don't care if it's good or bad," he said into the phone, "as long as it's news."

"It's one of yours," she said, "so it's news."

Maxine Cole, twenty-seven years old, was a triathlete of Somali descent who'd moved to the United States when she was a kid. She'd spent her teens in the projects but got herself out by teaching herself how to shoot network-quality video. She'd managed to keep her street sense and her fearlessness, too, and the result was a coworker who could keep up with Jack in any situation, no matter how dangerous.

"The arrest of the state senator's son?" he asked her.

"Yes," she said. "I read your report." Jack had sent it to her for a few tweaks and some feedback. "Listen, Jack," she continued, "for ninety-nine point ninety-nine-percent of the world, this report is going to be exactly what we expect from you. But I have to say this. I think you're dialing it in. You're not fully in it."

Jack was silent for a moment. Then he said, "You're right."

"Just a tiny bit. Like I said, no one except me is going to notice. But I didn't feel right, not saying something to you."

"It's just . . ."

"It's just that it's not the smuggling story?" she asked.

"Exactly. It's a rich kid getting arrested for drugs. Meanwhile in China there are farms where bears are caged, lying on their backs with no room to move, with tubes in their abdomens to collect bile for so-called medicines. Some of the bears have actually committed suicide by starving themselves to death. And multiple smuggling operations are carrying the bear bile along with body parts from tigers and other endangered animals out of China to the rest of the world. I covered it on *Truth Tellers* until the network got too scared of offending their Chinese investors. Now I have a chance to break the story again and I can't."

"You have contacts in London, you can ask them to follow up on it, can't you?"

"Yes," he admitted.

"But it's not the same."

He didn't reply. She knew him well. It wasn't that he didn't trust his contacts to do a good job. He simply wanted to be the one doing it.

"I'm sorry, Jack."

"Don't be sorry for me, Max. I'm just frustrated."

"Well then, get over it," she laughed. She added gently, "And find a way to reconnect, OK?"

They said good-bye and hung up. Jack ran his fingers lightly over his computer keyboard. She was right; he needed to put his finger, not just a plug, back in the socket. He needed to recharge. And he knew exactly where to go to do that.

San Francisco, California

Standing just over five feet tall and "slight as a snow-pea," as her father put it, there was nonetheless something about twenty-six-year-old Maggie Yu that commanded the aisles of the Yu Market on Clay Street. It was partly her posture, erect and centered, creating a straight line from the top of her head to her feet. It was partly the serenity of her expression, her dark eyes never seeming to blink, her lips together in a relaxed line, her round face untroubled with lines or color other than the natural blush of her cheeks. And it was partly the unwavering focus she brought to the task at hand.

Maggie finished checking the inventory her father had brought in before dawn. There were fresh fish neatly arrayed on ice, vegetables harvested just hours before, sliced fruit he had cut himself and placed in plastic containers. The beverages, candy, and cigarettes had all been restocked, the floors carefully swept, and the mousetraps and fly strips cleared away. In her hand she held the clipboard with the receipts for all the goods, including the note he always left her—"I love you," he wrote in Cantonese on the topmost sheet before he went upstairs.

Taking a last look around, the young woman placed the clipboard on its hook beneath the counter. She removed the apron—it had belonged to her mother—checked herself in a hand mirror she had beside the baseball bat her father kept beneath the register, then unlocked the door and turned around the OPEN sign.

The century-old brass bell tinkled above the door. Maggie smiled as she welcomed her first customer, Mrs. Chan. The smile was sincere. Maggie felt blessed to be surrounded by three of the four things she loved.

One was her father. Johnny Yu had opened the grocery store in 1986, the year before Maggie was born. It was originally going to be named the Huangpu Market for the river where he used to sit as a boy growing up in Shanghai, his eyes on the ships that used to come and go—one of which, a freighter, eventually took him to his new home with his new bride. But Anita Yu did not want to be reminded of their old life: she insisted he name the grocery for his ancestors but also for himself and Yu descendants. He agreed that was a better idea.

Maggie's mother, Anita, died fourteen months after Maggie was born. All Maggie remembered of the woman was the hole it left in her father's life.

The second thing Maggie loved was the store itself. The checkout counter was straddled by a four-foot-tall dragon gate made of empty boxes of Chinese tea. It was held together by the flaps of the boxes, nothing more; it had survived the 1989 earthquake. There were three short aisles, each of which was lit by bulbs that reflected the contents: green for produce, red for condiments and spices, amber for grain. Small freezers and refrigerators lined the back wall. Mrs. Chan was pulling a bag of lime leaves from one of the freezers.

The third thing Maggie loved was the Chinese population of San Francisco. Today the community had over a hundred thousand citizens nestled between the Financial District and Nob Hill. The citizens were vibrant and resilient, hardworking men and women devoted to their families, their neighborhood, and their nation. They were patriots with affection for their ancestral land but a fierce love for their current home.

Sadly, there were also some—the fewest in number and certainly the least in moral character—who exhibited the kind of selfish ambition that tore the community apart a century before in a series of wars fought to control criminal activity. These people troubled Maggie. She saw them every day when they came into the store—usually young men, usually buying cigarettes, chips, or soda. They always looked out the door while they stood at the counter. There was something itchy about them, restless, as though they were about to do something or were preparing for something to happen to them. Eyes roving, shoulders rolling from time to time like a fighter before a bout, fingers texting or flexing or making gestures to other malcontents . . . but never at rest.

They just seemed ready to take. Not from her or her father; shoplifting was too small. Besides, the locals knew she was ready for them and there were security cameras behind the counter—one of the upgrades Maggie had succeeded in negotiating with her father. These misfits preferred to steal cars or electronics outside the community, so as not to embarrass family. They sold drugs or laundered currency to those who were not Chinese.

Until today.

The bell jangled again. A Chinese man entered the store as Mrs. Chan was leaving. He was in his early thirties and she had not seen him emerge from the black SUV double-parked outside, but there was no doubt it was his. The smoky windows were like his smoky sunglasses: secretive, out of place. He removed the glasses as he approached. He wore soft, tan gloves. It wasn't cold enough for that, not even on a chilly winter morning. The man was sharp, from the even lines of his buzz cut to the strong set of his square jaw to the rigid creases in his tan suit. He was short, only about five foot six, but the way he stood when he reached the counter, with his shoulders drawn back and his feet close together, made him seem taller.

"I would see the owner of this shop, please," he said, glancing about the store.

"My father is not here. How may I help you, Mr.—?"

"Lee." The man regarded her, his eyes very still. "You can help by telling your father I wish to speak with him."

Maggie did not believe his name was Lee; that was the equivalent of Smith or Jones in America. His schooled, noncolloquial English reinforced the woman's impression that he was not from around here. She guessed he was a Chinese national; his severe bearing, his neutral identity with personal nuance drilled away, suggested a military background. And he obviously wasn't here to sell her father anything: he wasn't carrying a tablet, a briefcase, or even a cell phone. *Protection?* she wondered. That was the enterprise of local thugs who knew better than to come here. Besides, the shop was on a block of mom-and-pop stores and restaurants. Shakedown money from all of them wouldn't pay for a week's worth of gas in his Escalade.

"Dad will be here in about three hours," Maggie told him. "If you want to come back—"

"My business cannot wait."

She smiled pleasantly. "I'm afraid it will have to."

The shop seemed unusually quiet, the street sounds more remote than usual. The man had barely moved since approaching the counter. Now he took a step forward. Several candy bars fell as he pressed against the child-high shelves in front of him. When he spoke, his voice was soft but firm.

"Call him, please."

Maggie continued to smile. This man—these men—whatever they wanted, it had been thrust on them. Something urgent.

"There are two things I can do for you," Maggie said, raising her voice. "I can give my father a message or I can sell you something. Which would you like, Mr. Lee?"

Lee smiled faintly; it was barely noticeable, but Maggie saw it. She knew he was about to grab her; she knew it from her twenty-two years as a fighter.

The fourth thing Maggie loved was kung fu. She had been training since she was four years old, first with their neighbor who held a black belt in the Nabi Su form, then at a martial arts school that practiced Jeet Kune Do, the hybrid style developed by Bruce

Lee. She had earned her black belt before she turned fourteen. The essence of both styles is that energy comes from the ground, from the air, from the world around the martial artist, who gathers it in his center and drives it forward. The attack often comes in a variety of animal styles, whose offense and defense were studied and adapted by the ancient Chinese. In the split second that the man smiled, Maggie planned her attack. She knew she had the size advantage—in kung fu, smaller is faster. She knew she had the counter to work with, to use as a barrier or maybe she could double him over on it. And she knew that she had quiet skills while he had pride and arrogance—the worst hobbles a person could have in a fight.

She also knew that she would only use her skills when it was her last resort—that was her training and she would never betray her *sifu*s' wisdom.

Just then her father appeared from the back of the store, accompanied by two women in white—mourning white. It was the death anniversary of Maggie's mother; the *jichen* ceremony was going to begin in a few hours, and Johnny had been getting ready for it.

"Everything OK, Maggie?" he asked.

"Not really, Father," she said. "This man wanted to speak to you—"

"Do I want to speak with him?"

"I don't think so," Maggie said.

Johnny fixed steady, unrelenting eyes on the man. "I don't believe you are welcome here."

The would-be attacker, denuded of all pride, took one look at Johnny and the two mourners. Maggie could see him calculating the odds in his head. He turned and hurried out of the store, the doorbell jingling on his way out. The street sounds were momentarily louder and the door slammed. There was a moment of silence followed by an angry squeal of tires. Then all was once again as it should be.

Maggie's father reached her. He could see in her face that she was shaken. He put his arms around her. Outside in the white sunlight, a crowd was massing, talking, pointing down the street in the direction the SUV had been facing.

"I'm all right, Dad," she assured him. He still smelled comfortingly of fish and cold dawn sea air.

He relaxed but didn't let her go. "What happened?"

She told him. He listened without comment, but was concerned and clearly baffled. Then he picked up the phone and called the police. As soon as he put the phone down he turned back to the counter. He pressed his hands together, bowed, and said, "Thanks to you." His remarks were directed toward one of the shelves, to a small spirit tablet nestled among the aspirin boxes. The red ribbon was inscribed with his wife's name in gold and was suspended over a small round candleholder.

Then he hugged Maggie again. "It could have been so much worse," he said.

A small group of onlookers collected in the street, though no one entered out of respect for the two. The arrival of a patrol car caused them to part as a pair of officers made their way toward the shop.

"Before I talk to them, there's one thing you should do," Maggie said.

"What is it?"

"That reporter, the one who helped when I found out about the Long Zai gang, when I was a kid?"

"Hatfield?"

"Yes," she said. "Call him."

"Why?" he asked.

"Something the man did told me why he was here, I think," she said. "If I'm right, we may need more than the police."

The black SUV ripped through the late morning traffic. Three Chinese men sat within it, all neatly groomed and well dressed in light-colored suits and fawn-colored gloves. The cell leader sat in the back, fuming about the girl in Yu Market. The man who was not driving sat next to him.

"You have embarrassed us," said the man next to the cell leader.

"You are not in a position to judge me—" he started.

"More importantly," the other man cut him off, "you have embarrassed yourself."

The cell leader, all of the fury he had swallowed in the grocery story raging forth, grabbed at the man next to him. "I didn't want to cause a scene!" he shouted.

The other man punched him on his right cheekbone with the full force of his body behind it. There was a dull, ugly snap below the cell leader's temple. The other man punched him again in the same spot. The cell leader shrieked. His jaw burst into pain. There was a moment of silence.

"You have no right to strike your leader," he whimpered.

"You are no longer the leader," said the other man.

The man with the broken jaw sat back with full realization of what that meant, and what would be coming next. Quickly he reached for the door handle of the moving car, but felt a knife tip in his ribs. His hand dropped. He was still.

The SUV was headed toward the Bay where an Angler V175 was waiting off Marina Green Drive. Every plan devised by Jing Jintao had an abort strategy. The SUV was disposable and untraceable, rented for cash with false IDs. Operatives, on the other hand, could not afford to be taken. The seventeen-foot, five-inch motorboat was their way out. The driver had phoned ahead to make sure the vessel would be ready to depart.

Gulls and pigeons scattered as the driver parked at the edge of the water, away from any security cameras. With Alcatraz poking through the morning mist beyond the sea wall, the three men emerged from the SUV. The last man to leave the car moved with aching effort, trying to keep his head upright. An empty water bottle clattered to the asphalt and rolled under the car. He left it. He had difficulty standing. The man was holding a wet handkerchief to the side of his face; it was the color of a rose petal, dyed by the blood trickling from his ear. He held the damp cloth gently. Any pressure, even the gusting wind from the Bay, caused him to wince.

There were two men in the motorboat. One of them reached up, took the injured man's other arm, and lifted him down. The other men jumped in. They sat the wounded man in one of the five ash-gray vinyl seats then half swung, half fell into the other chairs as the Yamaha engine roared and the boat sped away. No one spoke.

The motorboat raced from shore, the men sitting still as statues despite the strong wind. No one ministered to the injured man, and each bump over a new wake caused him to wince.

It quickly became apparent to everyone but the injured man that they were not heading to the staging area in Sausalito but were steering out to sea. The two men who had been in the SUV swapped knowing glances. Their eyes met briefly, then turned away like illicit lovers.

Every plan crafted by Jing Jintao also had a *diàn bèi*—literally a funerary mat, something on which to cast one's sins and misdemeanors; in colloquial usage, a scapegoat. These men had been with the Ministry of State Security for nearly a decade—four years in Beijing at the headquarters of the North American Intelligence Division; two years intensive training for deployment in the United States; three years in-country; and one year working directly for Deputy Director Jintao. They knew how he thought and how he worked. Failure was punished in ways that encouraged greater effort in others.

The operational hierarchy of the ten-man cell was always geographically divided. The leader went on the primary mission, his second ran the abort scenario, his third remained at the staging area. Activating the backup plan automatically put the second leader in charge. He had quickly and—judging from his blank expression—dispassionately made his decision regarding the injured man.

It was only when the shadow of the Golden Gate Bridge blocked the sun and threw a deeper chill into the boat that the injured man realized they were going west. He stiffened more against that reality than against the wind. The hand holding the handkerchief tightened. The area around his right eye was red and swollen but his left eye held the horizon briefly, then took in the rigid backs of the other men in the boat—their stiff necks and turned faces an obstinate statement of exile.

His left eye turned back to the horizon. They were heading toward another boat. The motorboat had been least likely to attract attention and it was as disposable as the SUV. Now they needed speed.

When they reached the thirty-eight-foot Bertram, no hand offered to help the injured man climb out of the motorboat. He awkwardly leaned forward, propped himself on one palm, and half fell into the yacht. Hard pain coursed through his jaw. The other men stood and watched. He realized they were waiting for him to enter the closed cabin of the Bertram. He did, and sat. They followed him in but turned their faces away again.

The yacht started up and his stomach slid. The boat was built for rough water, they were going to drive it fast, and now he would suffer the embarrassment of seasickness as well.

He shut his left eye.

He saw himself looking across the counter at Maggie Yu, wanting to slap her, to get her to listen, and teach her respect—

Every person commits mistakes throughout life. Most of them are small and instantly recognized as such. Those are actually the worst because they are fresh on the fingertips, still palpable but beyond reach.

The grocery store was still vivid in his senses. The old wooden floors on which he had been standing, the smell of the fish on ice out front, the way the morning sunlight struck the pale flesh of Maggie Yu, making her seem so fragile—

You deserve whatever is coming.

He had momentarily forgotten one of the guiding principles of their work. During two years of schooling, Jing Jintao had stressed the concept of *rěnnài*— perfect patience. The marshalling of purpose, the veiling of the self, the anonymity they granted. That idea had been nudged aside by his sudden, urgent desire to please his superior, to bend this woman to his will. And because of his impatient desires, the presence of Johnny Yu and the other two women had startled him. Had made him afraid. Had made him run.

His eye remained shut as the yacht hurtled forward. The pain in his jaw kept his body present while his mind punished him by replaying those moments. There was nowhere to turn for solace, save the strangely comforting thought that he would soon be free of everything including the worst pain of all—the shame of failure.

He didn't know how long they had traveled; the throbbing around his eye socket seemed to go on for hours. He was only aware when they stopped. He heard the engine throttle down, felt the bouncing subside. He did not open his good eye to look but rather, dragged the handkerchief in front of it, holding it across both eyes with a cold, unsteady hand. Now time was measured in moments. Each breath felt like the dearest gift a man could have. Savoring them was, tragically, the very soul of patience.

Two men grabbed him by the arms and pulled him from his seat, out of the cabin into the salt air. His handkerchief slipped from his eye, and he saw the skyline of San Francisco in the distance. He smelled a musty scent, like that of a dog come in from the rain. He heard throaty, clucking sounds and the splash of breakers. The men hoisted him up, and he turned, saw a raw, sharp, high outcropping of rock. There were elephant seals on the crags.

They're going to strand me here?

The movement sent a series of drill-like shocks through his head and, yelping, he clapped a hand on his jaw to hold it still. When he could focus his thoughts, he felt a sense of gratitude that they were going to give him time to make peace with his actions—

The man hit the water hard on his lower back. The impact folded him at the waist, his arms and legs shooting straight up as he went under. Water flooded his mouth, nose, and ears before he could right himself. As he flipped, the pressure of the cold sea shocked his wound, causing him to scream a strange, gurgling noise. His hands and knees came into contact with rough rock under the surface. He clawed at them until his face was above the surface. Through clogged ears he heard the muted barking of the seals, smelled their fur, the decay of their meals, their waste. He flopped on the slick rock, cried out as sharp edges punched his chest, then slid his forearms under him. He panted as he rested there. Behind him he heard the engine of the yacht, still idling.

Why are they waiting? To make certain I don't drown?

A wave caught him and shoved him roughly along the granite, scraping his chest. It was a strong breaker, pushing him several meters. He was raw from neck to mid-waist and his knee tingled.

As his brain was processing the pain and he realized he had to get up on the rock to keep from being buffeted again, he was dragged back, into the water. The tickling sensation became a fiery ache, as though it were being yanked across a field of sharp stones. When his open eyes went under he was disoriented; he did not see the green-gray water of moments before but a murky red haze. It was joined by amber

circles swimming around the edges of his eyes, by a
flame that shot along the outside and inside of his left
thigh, by a sudden intake of breath that filled his
mouth with something foreign and metallic-tasting,
that stuffed his lungs with a sense of spongy discomfort—

Located twenty-seven miles from the Golden Gate,
the uninhabited Farallon Islands are a nature preserve
with a large, seasonal seal and sea lion population
that attracts Great White Sharks. The predators mi-
grate there from as far away as Hawaii. Whales don't
bother them. Killer whales don't deter them. The Farallon Great Whites feed well on mammal flesh and
grow far beyond average, ranging from thirteen to
nineteen feet in length. Gang members call the 141-
acre wildlife refuge "The Pig Sty," inspired by the
Wild West practice of feeding murder victims to
herds of pigs.

Drawn to the man by the trickle of blood from his
ear, the shark pulled him from the rocky ledge. The
dying man's arms flailed spasmodically, involuntary
tics as drowning and blood loss caused his body functions to shut down.

He was gone up to the waist in the second bite and
all that remained after the third rending swallow
were a few stringy shards of flesh, sinking bone frag-
ments, and pieces of fabric. Even the bloody handkerchief was consumed.

In less than a minute the shark had moved on. The
occupants of the boat had watched without expression.
One of the men got out with a rifle and pistol. The boat

would return later with a tent, supplies, and a small runabout; now that the mission was under way, it would be necessary to have someone stationed here full-time. This was a place known to Jintao but not the others, who had only recently arrived. He had told the new cell leader that this would probably not be the last body that needed to be disposed of. A spotter would be needed to ensure that their actions were not witnessed. And, more importantly, to make sure that the final part of the plan was executed flawlessly. Every operation, especially one as ambitious—and deadly—as this must have a back door.

Once the man was safely ashore, the others sped away. Cormorants picked at the knots of sinew that bobbed on the foamy currents. When the black-winged birds returned to the shoals, all trace of the event had vanished—save in the memory of the four survivors. They would make sure that others heard of the ugly fate that had befallen the cell leader . . . a fate that awaited anyone else who failed.

Chapter 2

The de Young Museum always gave Jack what he needed.

Jack knew that artists didn't just capture moments of real life. They invested in those moments with their willpower and their most personal selves. They found meaning, then guided their audiences to it. Jack felt like they were passing him a bright, undying torch.

Sometimes he needed to stare for half an hour at the Herter Brothers' mantelpiece for Thurlow Lodge. Its wood carving was beyond fine. It was incredible. He could follow the chisel work of the bones and sinews of the hounds taking down a wild boar as if the marks were moving under his eyes. The craftsmanship did more than remind him of the importance of depth, details, and patience in his work. It re-created a feeling of proud diligence within him.

Other times, it was *Scene in the Arctic* that ab-sorbed him. William Bradford's painting showed a three-masted tall ship in the distance, stuck in the ice, completely isolated under a gray sky as impersonal as a judgment. The men on the ship weren't visible, yet the impact of their story was heavy in the paint. They had been sentenced to die in the cold. Their bravery staggered Jack and if his courage ever faltered from "full speed ahead," these dying men restored it.

Today, though, Jack needed *The Ironworkers' Noontime*, by Thomas Anshutz. It was an oil painting of nineteenth-century workers at a foundry. Though the men were on break, none of them were resting. Most of their lean musculature was still in motion, mid-action. The ones whose bodies were still, it was clear their minds were driving forward. They were all ready to get going and continue fulfilling their fierce mission—to build this nation.

"Break's over," Jack said to himself.

He was sure Max was right, that no one but her would have picked up on his slight distance from his work. But he knew. Now he was ready to reengage. His hand was tight around the torch.

His cell phone rang from his jacket pocket. His ringtone was "The Soldier's Song," the Irish national anthem. It reminded him that he wasn't the only one picked on by the British. He checked the caller ID, and the screen said it was Johnny Yu. Jack had a re-porter's instinct, and it wasn't like Johnny to phone and talk about the price of green tea. He took the call and walked toward a hallway where his voice wouldn't bother the other museum guests.

"Johnny, how have you been?"

"I've been well." Johnny's English was perfect. When Johnny and his wife moved here from Shanghai, they took language classes at the City College of San Francisco. They were among those immigrants who believed in embracing the language and ways of their new country. They were part of a culture that believed in real, practical knowledge—not just a document that declared you had been educated.

"What can I do for you?" Jack asked.

"May I come and see you?"

"I was about to—"

"Someone threatened my daughter," he said.

There was a crack in his steady voice. This was a man who had snuck up on drug dealers with an open cell phone line so he could send the conversation to Jack's tape recorder. It wasn't easy to shake him.

"Is Maggie all right?" Jack asked.

"She stared one of them down; he ran away and left."

Jack had gone to Maggie's black belt test when she was thirteen. He had been doing a report on highly disciplined youths of San Francisco, including members of Maggie's martial arts school. After the test, he had interviewed Maggie and her father for the article. A year later, they had called him asking for help.

"Was it the Long Zai?" Jack asked Johnny now. The Long Zai was one of the most organized and ruthless gangs in Chinatown, and they were the reason Johnny had needed help twelve years ago.

"I don't think so," Johnny said, "but the threat was not random. The men who came to the grocery wanted to see me. Maggie thinks she knows why. I'd like to tell you face-to-face."

Jack's reporter instinct was still humming. "Did you file a report with the police?"

"She's doing that now."

"Did she recognize any of them?"

"No," Johnny said. "And she didn't get a good look at the car. The police told me they will try to identify the man from the store surveillance camera."

"I'll tell you what," Jack said. "How about I swing by around two o'clock?"

"I would really appreciate that," Johnny said.

"See you then," Jack said. "And tell Maggie 'well done.' "

Johnny said he would do that. Jack ended the call.

It seemed that he had picked up the torch just in time.

The Consulate General of the People's Republic of China in San Francisco is a set of featureless three-story white buildings located at 1450 Laguna Street. A pair of fierce, squat, stone lions guard the stately six-panel chocolate-brown doors. These thick-maned guardians, known as *Shishi,* have traditionally stood in front of royal and governmental buildings for over two millennia. They always appear in pairs, signifying the propagation of the Chinese civilization, and are thought to have mystic properties that ensure survival.

Sixty-one-year-old Jing Jintao was nothing like the *Shishi*. He was a short, prim man with close-cropped, graying hair, a relaxed expression with a natural smile, and pale, penetrating eyes. The expression put people at ease; the eyes were invisible but missed nothing. He was the perfect diplomat: observant, perceptive, and expert at gentle flattery and small talk that revealed nothing.

To guests and even to his staff, Jintao seemed to be a man in repose. But unlike the *Shishi* whose bared but ineffective teeth greeted him every day, Jintao was constantly in motion, both mentally and by quietly and efficiently directing the movements of others. His personal thoughts were not informed by the past. He was a man of action, not philosophy. He knew only one direction, and he pursued it with a single-mindedness that would have been the envy of any Khan.

Born in 1952 in Wuhan, the capital of the Hubei Province, he attended the School of International Studies at Beijing University and worked his way up through the Ministry of Foreign Affairs. For years he had steadily progressed through increasingly more challenging posts—all of them in regions like Hong Kong and the Middle East where sensitive intelligence was collected, reviewed, and sent to the Ministry of State Security in Beijing.

Jintao was responsible for coordinating data from the many countries in which he had served to help spearhead a pair of cyber attacks on world computer systems. On March 28, 2009, he was part of Ghost-Net, a massive assault on government, corporate, and personal computers in 103 nations. The targets ranged from the U.S. Department of Defense to the Dalai Lama. He recruited talent in Europe, Asia, and the United States to launch a second cyber attack in December of that year. Operation Aurora targeted two dozen major corporations, including Google, raiding sensitive files and crippling operations. Investigating the operations, the U.S. National Security Agency discovered—alarmingly—that Beijing was taking a page from the jihadist playbook: talking to the loyal ethnic population in other countries and encouraging them, for pay, to help fight what Beijing called "imperialistic designs against the homeland with the goal of assimilating its population and culture."

Expatriates are reluctant to attack their new home, Jintao reflected, *but a few are willing to defend the old one.* The art of turning a displaced national was to locate those few, the outspoken in lunch spots and bars, in barbershops and in parks. It did not matter what they were saying, only that they were speaking their mind. The next step was to get close to them, speak in their native language, build trust, nurture a sense of injustice about their adopted country, make them believe that eavesdropping or applying for a job in a sensitive facility or allowing agents to live with them were vital and valid responses to some misdeed.

Agents, Jintao thought as he looked at the manila folder on the desk in front of him. A secretary had brought it to him with his morning tea. Beijing had hundreds of operatives in Western Europe, Canada, and the United States. Many were trained to infiltrate the transplant communities and disseminate information without the knowledge of the FBI or CIA plainclothes operatives who spied on virtually every embassy and consulate, both electronically and with eyes on the front door and carports. Messages were passed with cash after Chinese checkers matches in the park or in swapped iPods that were actually filled with photographs, scanned data, and other intelligence. No transmissions were done over the Internet or by cell phone—except for disinformation designed to make the Chinese seem plausibly naïve, tying up the electronic surveillance teams in nearby office buildings and mail trucks. None of the actual spy work was ever discussed or planned in rooms with windows, since the Americans had developed software to read the vibration of panes and transform them into speech.

That was the government's way of doing things. *"Cautiously aggressive"* was how Jintao would describe it.

But Jing Jintao had another way. He bypassed that bloated, inertial system entirely to do what he felt was essential.

His young male secretary, Shing Wei, brought him the intelligence dossier that the daily courier had brought from Beijing in the diplomatic pouch. Jintao had known from American news reports that bringing down the U.S. Navy SEAL helicopter in Afghanistan was a success. What he learned from the field report written by Sammo Yang was that the EMP unit had worked exceptionally well.

EMP—"electromagnetic pulse"—it sounded like a simple medical procedure, such as "CAT scan" or "sonogram." Originally discovered as one of the effects of nuclear explosions, virtually every country with a weapons development program had been working to create non-nuclear EMPs since the 1940s. The basic principle was to generate a magnetic field and an electric current simultaneously, then shape the resulting electromagnetic field into a pulse and direct its emission at a target. The pulse, upon encountering any electrical system within its range, would produce a surge in the system's voltage large enough to shut it down for weeks, if not permanently.

An EMP that disrupted an electrical system upon which human lives depended—such as a helicopter—certainly did have medical impact. Sammo Yang had also mentioned that the EMP unit he had built resembled a medical device. He would be arriving in the United States later that day with the unit, as part of the rotating Economic and Commercial contingent. These were the accountants and investors who helped to saddle the United States with added loans and increased debt. It was fitting that Yang accompany them.

Jintao went through the rest of the information in the dossier, mostly current names and addresses for operatives throughout the world. It was important for everyone to know where resources were at all times.

When Jintao was finished reading the update from

Beijing, he reflected upon his own operation, one that had nothing to do with the timorous Chinese leaders and their limited, even diffident EMP program. This morning had been a setback: the loss of a choice site and the sacrifice of a promising operative. Jintao had learned of the disaster at Yu Market. Upon hearing how the cell leader had failed to complete his mission, Jintao had condemned him without hesitation. The delivery-man had carried the execution order to the second-in-command. That accomplished two things: it removed a leader who had showed promise in training but impetu-osity in the field, and it warned the next leader that similar actions would earn him the same fate.

But a setback was only a defeat if he allowed it to be. That was not Jintao's way. He had spent decades watching the insular world and internecine clashes of the ruling State Council, the Politburo Standing Com-mittee of the Communist Party, and the People's Lib-eration Army. Beijing did not understand global politics in general or the character of the United States in particular. They did not grasp the need to act stra-tegically and proactively, rather than simply react sluggishly to world events or lash out in small, surgi-cal, punitive actions. His plan was one—the only one—that would guarantee the supremacy of Beijing before the year was out.

The cell was strong, resilient, and well trained by Jintao's colleagues in Shanghai. They would recover swiftly and move ahead.

Jintao informed his secretary that he was now ready

to begin the day's responsibilities of his office: coordinating local athletic and cultural activities, meeting with fellow envoys about interests mutual to their respective nations, and talking to reporters about matters pertaining to the Chinese community in San Francisco and Chinese policy in the Pacific Rim. The routine and mostly neutral and largely ineffective business of state.

No kind smiles and polite bows would change what he was doing in secret.

This stone lion was awake and nothing would stop it.

The table's wobbly," Abe Cohen complained good-naturedly.

"That's because you moved the cardboard," Bruno Spumante replied, pointing to the toe of the man's Nike. Four menus tucked under his arm, he bent to shove the cardboard back.

"That's real classy," Abe said across Bruno's back. Vegan-thin with a long-gray ponytail, Abe winked at Jack and Doc Matson.

"So says the man in the Rolling Stones sweatshirt," said Doc.

Abe Cohen was an unrepentant leftist hippie who owned a poster shop that catered to San Francisco's aging Flower Power population. Doc Matson, "older'n God," six foot two with granite eyes and a cowboy hat over his white hair, was one of Jack's oldest and dearest friends. They shared a love of wine and a distaste for doctrinaire leftists, but Doc and Abe disagreed with a vengeance on just about everything. Jack had met them for brunch at Spumante's, Bruno's restaurant in North Beach.

"Hey, this sweatshirt is vintage. From Altamont," Abe said.

"The prosecution rests," Bruno replied. He stood. His bald head glistening with perspiration under the warming sun and his lucky black vest showing its age—he had worn it every day since he opened his doors seventeen years before—fifty-year-old Bruno Spumante passed laminated menus to the three guests. They were seated at one of a dozen tables outside the restaurant. Because it was a weekday, brunch was not a busy time. Bruno didn't make money being open this early; he did it so his regulars could have coffee or melon. And also, Jack knew, so he would have an audience for his Mussolini-esque monologues.

Bruno smiled and bent to give Eddie a brisk rub on the head when he was finished. Jack knew that was probably the last smile Bruno would crack all day. The hardworking son of immigrants, Bruno was a fierce supporter of what he called American Truth, the nation's original compass settings, and he was chronically glum over the way the United States had become what he called "left behind"—and he wasn't referring to end of days but to socialism and a body part. Bruno's spontaneous, combative monologues had made him something of a tourist attraction in the Italian District.

"You hippies, you were moth-eaten forty-three years ago, when that shirt was new," Bruno said as a waiter brought water. "They were called 'conscientious objectors' in my father's day and 'cowards' in my grandfather's day."

"Your grasp of social movements is matched only by your understanding of how to properly fix a table," Abe remarked.

"This is an earthquake zone, *che cazzo*," Bruno snapped. "What you fix today will be broken tomorrow."

"What did he just call Abe?" Jack asked Doc. Doc knew how to curse in forty languages.

"A dick," Doc grinned.

Jack laughed. "By the way, Abe, I stumbled across an article about hippies," he added. "Specifically counterintelligence."

"That was the hippie movement, all right," said Doc. Matson's first military deployment had been in the bunkers under Lincoln Park and the Legion of Honor, his knowledge of which had made him invaluable in Jack's actions against the Hand of Allah. When the bunkers were closed, the young Matson volunteered to go to Vietnam before his officers had even formed the thought of sending him there. He was a paratrooper with the 101st Airborne, in a company full of "felons," as he put it—he wasn't kidding or exaggerating—before returning stateside for Special Forces training. He earned a medical degree in Guadalajara, too, but never developed a taste for the safe life. Instead of opening a practice, he had started working as a mercenary soldier wherever and whenever he was needed. He'd seen action in El Salvador, Haiti, Iraq, and—Jack was sure—more than a few places he couldn't mention. He had no patience for passive resistance, or passive anything else.

"The author of the article was calling it 'societal corrosion,'" Jack said. "Photos of hippies putting flowers into gun barrels and painting their faces with peace signs."

Doc sat back, his arms crossed on his chest. His index finger tensed as he pulled an imaginary trigger.

"The guy was arguing that if you neutralize the power of the military and police with pacifism, you declaw the state. Clever insurgents make themselves the equal of the state. That's about when I stopped reading."

"Like those 'Occupy' crybabies," Bruno said.

"Only the first wave was crybabies," Doc said. "The rest were outright anarchists."

"Amen," Bruno said. "And where did any of that get us, the hippies and the Occupiers?"

"It ended wars," Abe said.

"Bull," Doc said. "It stopped us from winning them, it didn't end anything. And it started wars at home. It turned the mainstream press into a mouthpiece for the Communists—"

"After they had been a mouthpiece for Joseph McCarthy and the witch-hunters," Abe said.

"They did lose their nerve," Jack agreed. "I've had some experience with media who are afraid to take unpopular stands."

"What's happening today is worse," Doc said. "Chicken hearts are bad, but Red Diaper doper babies are worse. You listen to the news this morning? A protest about a pipeline from Canada that would create thousands of jobs but might—might—threaten a few wild turkeys got as much coverage as a chopper full of SEALs going down in Afghanistan."

"Yeah, I heard the tail end of that this morning," Jack said. "What do you know about it?"

"Nothing," Doc shrugged unhappily. "No one does. There wasn't even a Mayday from the cockpit."

"A CEF?" Jack asked.

"What's that?" Abe asked.

"Catastrophic Electronic Failure," Doc replied. "That's what it looks like, though that's never been a problem with the Chinooks."

There was a moment of respectful silence for the fallen warriors. Then Bruno said, "God bless them. As for the Communist media, the protesters, their negativity, their entitlement, this is exactly why this stupid city, the whole country, are bankrupt."

Abe Cohen shook his head sadly. "'Do not be afraid or terrified because of them, for the Lord your God goes with you; he will never leave you nor forsake you,'" he said. "'The meek shall inherit the earth.'"

"I mean all kinds of bankrupt," Bruno said. "Financially, mentally, also spiritually. I mean these people who think the Bible is embarrassing, is an anachronism. They are unable to respect anything, to have respect. And this infected everyone. Look at how all the people communicate now. They tap on their phones like primitives banging little drums. There is no politeness. You know, I never hear the words, 'Excuse me,' here anymore. Everything, everyone, is cheap, is tasteless. Clothing stores full of crap from China. Coffee stores, the coffee is undrinkable, it tastes like battery acid. But here I find the strangest part, you know, is a society where mainly women are walking around with plastic bags and they're picking up dog crap. Imagine what this looks like to a Muslim woman fresh off the boat. She comes from a fanatical, third-world country, she sees us through that slit in her burka, she watches women bending over picking up dog crap with smiles on their faces. Only in America. Only in your America, Abe. And now, excuse me."

The restaurateur went back inside. Jack noticed a group of tourists staring at them. He couldn't believe how boorish they were, goggling like that. It was degenerative; they'd lost all concept of dignity or space. He could swear that the Chinese man at the table next to theirs was eavesdropping, too, but then, Jack did his share of that. A reporter had to, and the man was at least being polite about it, pretending to read a magazine. Jack set his attention back on his friends.

"Always an adventure with Bruno," said Doc, grinning. "He was a whole lot happier when his clientele was mostly North Beach Italians."

"Then the tourists found him," Jack said, "the food critics raved about him, the gays picketed him for things he'd say to customers, the government found new ways to tax small businesses, the waitstaff tried to organize, that Chinese clinic opened next door with screaming kids lined up outside—"

"Oh, you mean he couldn't deal with the rest of humankind," Abe joked.

"He couldn't deal with them telling him how to conduct his life and business, having their free speech protected while his was restricted," Jack said. "Believe me, I know something about that."

"My cousin Mickey Cohen felt the same way when they told him he had to stop killing people," Abe said. "You know, the famous gangster? First cousin once removed. He was an enforcer during Prohibition, helped build the Flamingo Hotel, which was the first one in Las Vegas, had no problem murdering anyone who cheated him in business or at cards. Spent time in Alcatraz," he cocked his head in the direction of the Bay, "which is how our family ended up here. He was still running things and we were all messengers."

"Which is why you can be a hippie-of-leisure," Doc said, clapping a hand on his shoulder. "When Mickey died in '76, he left his favorite cousin a nice little nest egg."

"That was only because he liked me," Abe said. "People tried to kill him on the Rock, people from both sides of the law. Lead pipes, shivs, strangulation, poison, once even a poison dart."

"Agents used to use poison darts," said Doc. "Not anymore. They've got an undetectable drug called succinylcholine now that can produce respiratory paralysis, creates a heart-attack verdict upon autopsy. Lose the dart and you've got—"

"Anyway," Abe cut him off, "I started publishing a

little underground newspaper called *The Bay Area Veritas*—"

"Nice try," Jack whispered to Doc.

"I wrote," Abe continued, "about conditions on Alcatraz and campaigned for prison reform. Mickey appreciated that—it helped get him transferred to the Atlanta Federal Penitentiary."

"That was about the same time I was putting M16 rounds into the heads of bad guys," Doc pointed out.

"But Mickey was called a gangster and you were hailed as a freedom fighter," Abe said.

"Context, brother Abe," Doc said. "Your cousin was blowing up honest businessmen. My targets were using babies for bayonet practice."

" 'Thou shalt not kill,' " Abe replied.

"How do you expect people to hear that, Abe?" Doc snapped. "In the context they live in, with all the other voices screaming for their attention? Can the Ten Commandments compete with the evening news? Can the warnings and exhortations of Job compare with MTV, or the blogs of those digital gossips who call themselves journalists? Look what the *Times* has become. One power-mad psychopath after another paraded throughout, with all the details of his or her personal wealth displayed so as to render the averagely successful reader impotent and hopeless by the time the sports page is reached. Can the epic of the Sulzbergers be compared with Ecclesiastes? No."

Jack could see Abe building up a head of steam to retaliate. "Deuteronomy 31:6, right?" Jack asked him. "Your earlier quote."

"Yup," said Abe.

Jack knew that Abe only quoted the Bible as ammo. In fact, he had once referred to its authors as "a collection of constipated poets, failed jewel hustlers, bankrupt sandal makers, whoremongers past their prime, child molesters, animal torturers, and other biblical age riff-raff." Jack didn't want Abe going off on that kind of pageant right now, and he didn't want Abe and Doc getting into a scrimmage, either. He was about to segue into something safe when the Chinese man at the next table leaned over.

"From the Greek *Deuteronomion*. It means 'second law.'" He answered their startled glances by saying, "Excuse me for listening in. I'm a doctor at the clinic. This was one of the more interesting conversations I've heard over breakfast."

"People don't debate the way they used to," Doc said.

"It's true," said the Chinese man. "That's why I come to Bruno's."

They all smiled.

"My family is of the Hui nationality, from China," the man continued. "We are Muslim Chinese. People forget there were Muslims in China before the People's Revolution. But after the revolution when mosques and churches were being destroyed indiscriminately, Bibles and Qurans burning in the same piles, the Muslims and Christians in my father's town helped each other. My father remembers reading the Bible as well as the Quran in secret, and he raised me on both. I wish I could introduce that required reading to the

Middle East, and any site of a religious war. I think that if we got to know the people we're supposed to hate, we'd find a lot in common."

Jack and his friends sat for a moment in silence, pondering that—the idea that tolerance and understanding should not only be self-evident but so easily accessible. Then Jack invited the man to join them, but his shift at the clinic was starting and he left after a round of handshakes.

"Hey, Doc," said Abe. "You know that old line 'Jesus saves, Moses invests'?"

"Yes," Doc said warily.

"How about this? Jesus saves, Moses invests, Buddha divests, Mohammad digests, and Krishna suggests."

"You're on a wrong tangent, Abe," Doc said. "Get off it."

Luckily the waiter arrived to take their order then, and Abe was easily distracted. Abe then talked about his poster shop—which Doc insisted on calling "a head shop in disguise"—until the waiter returned with sand dabs, risotto, lightly grilled potatoes, some of Bruno's specially cured Italian bacon from his famous "Prosciutto Room," and veal for Eddie. Bruno refused to introduce a brunch or lunch menu. It was the same offerings day or night, all served with a bottle of Bruno's own olive oil from the trees in his Sonoma hillside vineyard. Jack had once mentioned how he loved a particular brand of Spanish olive oil, and Bruno had been incensed.

"Spanish olive oil, what are you talking about!" he said. "I have the best olive oil in the world! We brought olive trees from Tuscany and our olive trees, they are Leccino, Pendolino, Moraiolo, Coratina, and Frantoio, the classical Tuscan blend. Olive oil is something sacred, God multiplied the world with olive oil!" Now Bruno gave Jack bottles of olive oil to take with him like a mother packing school lunches.

The rest of the conversation was relatively benign, except when Doc and Abe inevitably brought up the 1960s again. They were a microcosm of the era: the my-country-right-or-wrong warrior and the unreformed hippie. Despite the extremes, there was nonetheless common ground: the longing for an era when both sides still cared about the country, and put the well-being of the United States before their personal needs. That was gone now, swallowed by the sinkhole of entitlements and putting hyphenate interests before the best interests of the nation.

"America really is at a tipping point," Jack said at the end of the meal.

Bruno had come out to say good-bye to them. "The world is at a tipping point," he said.

"The world is always in peril," Jack said. "Americans are accustomed to disagreements and even a little chaos. But even the Civil War was between two big factions, big ideas. To feel the foundations of the country being undermined by countless little cracks and self-interests for the first time—that's new to us."

"There's no patching it," Abe said. "It's over."

"I don't believe that," Jack said. "As long as people of different opinions can be brought to the same table by common ground, as we do all the time, we will endure."

Suitland, Maryland

When the Office of Naval Intelligence was founded in 1882, its charter was to "evaluate" the navies of other countries. That was government-speak for "spy." After the attack on the battleship *Maine* in the Havana, Cuba, harbor in 1898, the ONI charter was expanded to include the "protection of Navy personnel and the ferreting out of spies and saboteurs." Its mission remains unchanged, and as the oldest such agency in the American military the ONI has a high degree of autonomy within the larger National Maritime Intelligence Agency, which is itself a part of the Defense Intelligence Agency.

Suitland is an unincorporated community in Prince George's County and a suburb of Washington, D.C. When Dover Griffith moved there five years ago after graduating from NYU, she told her parents that the town was famous for being the home of the Census Bureau and having the highest crime rate in the county. She found it darkly amusing that the murder rate caused residency data to fluctuate wildly, but her parents didn't see the joke. They worried whether their five-foot-seven daughter, with blond hair and blue eyes, was too easy a target.

Griffith had landed the job in D.C. when she was

thirty-one years old, just after she received her master's degree in journalism. During her final summer in New York, while earning tuition money at the sales counter of the Strand Book Store, she wrote a play called *Ops Attract* about a pair of spies who fall in love. It played Off-Off-Broadway as part of the Fringe Festival and was well reviewed; it was seen by the Director of Civilian Operations for the ONI, who asked for Griffith's résumé and offered her a job when she graduated. Since there were precious few jobs to be had in traditional journalism, she accepted the position. Dover's grandfather—a pilot in the Royal Air Force who was shot down by the Luftwaffe over the White Cliffs, hence her name—would have been proud.

"Except for the part about him risking his life and me sitting at a desk," she had told her parents when she returned from her interview in Suitland.

"It took people on the ground, in bunkers, to invent the radar that told him where to go," her father had said.

After a four-month training session at the National Maritime Intelligence Training Center in Virginia Beach, Virginia, Griffith took up residence in the sprawling 4-story, 226-acre complex at the Suitland Federal Complex where she edited the internal publication *Eyes On,* a traditional tabloid-size newspaper that was part news, part social calendar for all of the ONI. Because she was able to reduce complex ideas to a few digestible lines, Griffith was moved to the Current Events Bureau, which wrote the daily briefings for the Secretary of the Navy, the Chief of Naval Intelligence, and the Director of Naval Intelligence. Within a year of arriving she was giving briefings to representatives of foreign intelligence services. It helped that she had minored in Chinese at NYU. She was able to contribute a great deal to the ONI when it came to interpreting communications between Chinese agents and agencies.

The jobs were fun and challenging; having a high-security clearance made her Big News when she went home to Whitefish, Montana, for Christmas; and her dating life was rich: thirty-three percent of the population in Washington was single, and the men were impressed with her position.

Today the ONI was respectfully subdued but abuzz with the news of the SEALs' deaths in Afghanistan the day before. As rescue teams reached the remote region and data began to come in, and a news blackout was lifted—a cautionary move that gave local commanders a chance to see if military movements were being leaked by a mole—the data was circulated among everyone involved with intelligence analysis. The attack was what the intelligence community classified as "all eyes": everyone with appropriate clearance was asked to study and respond.

Griffith was surprised, then concerned that the initial reports cited zero communication from the downed Chinook; not even an automated Mayday. That kind of result came from running into a mountainside at high speed, which was not the case according to the first troops on the scene. There were no initial traces of an explosion—no obviously blown-out metal, no blast pattern on the surrounding terrain. The evidence pointed to an instant, catastrophic electrical failure, something that had never happened to this particular helicopter. But there was something that *had* affected it nearly three years earlier, Griffith found in her research.

In 2006, billionaire industrialist Richard Hawke founded a company called CelesTellia that would provide wireless Internet bandwidth using a new broadband technology. Within a few months, the American military discovered that CelesTellia's new technology was interfering with the GPS systems and electronics in some of its aircraft, including Chinooks. Pilots flying fighter jets identified the problem first. They would suddenly find their instruments going haywire, their planes unresponsive: total systems failure. In each case momentum brought the aircraft out of range quickly enough for the systems to recover before the jets threatened to nosedive.

However, CelesTellia had announced plans to make its wireless Internet bandwidth available around the world—remote locations as well as cities. This meant that navigable space, by air, water, or land, would be effectively booby-trapped by the broadband technology. The military objected, publicly and loudly.

Richard Hawke promised to shut down CelesTellia and abandon the broadband technology. The media furor continued for a few weeks, then faded out.

Four months later Hawke founded a company called Squarebeam that used the same broadband technology. However, the company was now offering a new line of separate products: electronic components that would shield electrical systems from the broadband technology. Supposedly a fighter jet with these electronic components installed would not experience electrical failure when flying through the range of a Squarebeam unit.

The military organized an investigation of Squarebeam, but it was shut down within hours—reportedly because Hawke had strong ties with the White House.

Griffith could find no further reference to the matter internally. Externally, however, she found a series of investigative reports from fringe journalists—and one mainstream report from an infamous journalist. There was a transcript of an episode of the TV talk show *Truth Tellers* from 2009. On that particular show were José Colon, a scientist from Caltech; Rebecca Walsh, the press officer of Squarebeam; and host Jack Hatfield. Griffith scanned the document to a section that had the gunpowder smell of a smoking gun:

Hatfield: Dr. Colon, you've analyzed the original CelesTellia system and the new Squarebeam system.

Colon: Yes, sir.

Hatfield: What differences did you find?

Colon: There are none.

Walsh: That's simply not true—

Hatfield: I didn't ask about the separate components your company is selling, which shield electrical systems from Squarebeam. Those components are a patch. They don't fix the actual broadband technology itself.

Walsh: They aren't a patch, they are integrated components—

Colon: Which have to be installed separately in all vulnerable electrical systems. That's not my definition of "integrated."

Hatfield: And that's a lot of fighter jets, battleships, tanks, and a whole army of other vehicles, which will need those components. Is Richard Hawke going to sign all those contracts by hand?

Walsh: The components are only a precaution for those who want it. The technology is safe.

Colon: It is not. Military aircraft passing through your firm's transmissions have had near-catastrophic electrical failures—

Walsh: Absolutely untrue.

Hatfield: These integrated components sound like the protection rackets run by the Mob. If you don't buy my add-on, the source hardware will kill you.

Colon: Exactly.

Walsh: Mr. Hatfield, it is irresponsible and insulting for you to compare our firm with the Mafia.

Hatfield: I'm sorry. You're right. The Mafia doesn't have connections with the President of the United States.

Walsh: Another unfounded allegation—

Hatfield: Ms. Walsh, I have here stock

certificates issued to the President when he was still a community organizer. He held over a thousand shares of stock in CelesTellia.

Walsh: Which he sold when he ran for public office, even though that was not required by law.

Hatfield: Yes, and Richard Hawke donated barrels of money to his political campaign for the Senate and then for the White House. And Hawke is still donating. My sources say a quarter million to the President last year and a quarter million to Congress.

Walsh: Mr. Hawke is a private citizen making legal contributions.

Hatfield: Mr. Hawke is making a lot of wheels very greasy. Those of you watching at home or listening on the radio: *Truth Tellers* will continue to investigate the dangers posed by the Squarebeam technology and its spin-offs—

Walsh: There are no dangers—

Hatfield:—and will tell you what we discover in a future follow-up segment.

There was no future segment. After inciting international fury over comments about Muslims, Jack Hatfield was off the airwaves. Griffith had read about that in a journalism blog.

She reread the *Truth Tellers* transcript. There was no question that Hatfield wasn't being impartial, but considering what was at risk and the weight of the corporation he was fighting, Griffith couldn't begrudge him his approach. In the end, the last public word on Squarebeam technology was still an open-ended one.

She turned to a quick search of the records on Richard Hawke. Hawke, already a communications mogul, had founded CelesTellia mostly on his own dime but with some funds from a small group of investors. He acquired the broadband technology when he merged with a small phone service company. CelesTellia's version of that technology was created and tested. Then CelesTellia ran into trouble with the military and Hawke shut it down. He reopened it as Squarebeam and—reportedly—used his relationship with the President to protect the new company and secure military contracts.

"When Hawke had Squarebeam ready to go, he got his old friend the President to drop the Top Secret curtain," Griffith muttered. "Behind the curtain he sold the military his technology, and then he sold them patches to protect them from that technology." She grimaced. "Hatfield was right. It's exactly like the Mob."

San Francisco, California

As Jack walked away from Spumante's, he thought about how much he loved San Francisco. The geography, the wind that blended the air of sea and land into something special, the bloodshot-setting sun, the streets, the sounds, the population, the melting pot that drove Bruno into a fury—they were an integral part of who Jack Hatfield was. The *Sea Wrighter,* the small apartment he kept on Union Street where he hid out and repaired watches and clocks as a kind of therapy, his close friends, even the anger he felt whenever he saw the GNT cable news network offices where he used to tape his talk show—they were all here. Their quirks, pricks, familiarity, challenges, disappointments, and comforts were part of the emotional gauntlet that kept Jack Hatfield alert and engaged. He didn't know who he would be, what he would be, how he would function without all of that. That's what is known as "home."

He looked at his watch. It was nearly two o'clock. He was on Clay Street now, the site of the first cable-pulled streetcars. Pedestrian traffic was normal, an equal mix of shuffling locals and stop-and-start tourists. Yu Market was located in the middle of the street with other storefronts and Asian restaurants around it. The buildings were mostly two and three stories tall with signs in Chinese and English. Jack saw a customer enter the grocery; the police were long gone and there appeared to be nothing out of the ordinary.

Jack felt a flash of nostalgia. He had first come to the grocery when he still had his talk show. Jack was old enough to remember the turf wars that had always been at a low simmer down here. They led to the founding of the SFPD's Asian Gang Task Force, which stopped most of the street violence. However, that did not end the lawless activities of the youth gangs. They went back underground and continued recruiting from high schools and pool halls, rewarding members with cash, women, drugs, and a sense of empowerment. Unlike the majority of the Asians, the gangs were scrupulously devoted to the idea of non-assimilation. Their idea of community did not extend beyond the boundaries of the gang. Chinese who did not support them were against them.

The struggle for control of the drug trade, gambling, the sale of knock-off designer goods, cock-fights, and fight clubs kept the gangs bickering among one another, unable to expand. Jack had once described it on air as "a local version of Iran and Iraq under Saddam, when they were so busy warring with one another they couldn't do much damage to anyone else."

The one area that did not apply was human trafficking. For years the Long Zai gang had transported young Chinese, Malaysian, and Thai women in cargo containers to Vancouver. Then they drove the women by van down to San Francisco, Los Angeles, and San Diego, ostensibly to work in restaurants. All the girls were forced into prostitution. Maggie Yu heard one of the gang members talking about his "ladies" at the martial arts school, where some gang members went for martial arts training. Maggie told her father, who was sickened by the thought that girls—some no older than his fourteen-year-old daughter—were being forced to sell their bodies. Johnny got in touch with Jack, who arranged for him to wear a wire while he watched his daughter train. Johnny picked up conversations that helped police break the Long Zai traffickers. Johnny continued to help Jack as an unidentified source in follow-up segments, and he was one of the few people who called Jack in support when he was fired from *Truth Tellers*.

The doorbell jangled on its steel ribbon as Jack walked into Yu Market. Johnny was behind the counter. He came around to greet Jack, his leathery face unfolding in a big smile that made him look twenty years younger.

"My friend," Johnny said, embracing the much taller man.

Jack noticed Maggie as she helped an elderly customer get something from a top shelf. When she was finished, the young woman hurried over. She gave Jack a warm, lingering hug as well.

"It's so good to see you again," she said.

"And you," Jack told her. "I hear you got to practice your mantra today: a martial artist must be gentle in life—"

"—and ferocious in combat," Maggie replied. "You didn't forget."

"When it comes to mottos and morals, my brain is like Velcro."

She broke the embrace and smiled up at him. "I remember when you arranged a studio tour for my college class, you and some of your friends were trading verses from the Bible," she said. "Do you still do that?"

"As often as possible," Jack told her. "Wisdom doesn't go out of style, even if it's in increasingly short supply." He stepped back and looked at her. "So. Are you sure you're all right?"

She nodded once. But there was uncertainty in her

eyes, in the way she fingered a silver charm bracelet on her left wrist. Her business with the intruder had come to a hard stop. That didn't mean it was over.

"Is it all right to talk here?" Jack asked.

"Yes, yes," Johnny said. He indicated the customers in the aisles. "We know all of these people."

"Tell me what happened," Jack said to Maggie.

Maggie told him. Her voice was calm as she described the man, their exchange, and his flight from the store when he saw Johnny and the mourners. Occasionally she pointed to show him where events had taken place. Johnny put his arm around his daughter as she talked.

When she finished Jack asked, "Your father said you noticed something unusual?"

"It was out of character with everything else," she said. "At first I thought he had come to try and extort money."

"A protection racket," Jack said.

"That's right. But when I told him I wouldn't get my father, that all I could do was sell him something—meaning groceries—he smiled. It was not an amused smile but something private, as though he knew something that I did not."

Jack considered this. "You're sure he wasn't a cop checking to see if you were selling drugs?"

"The police looked at the surveillance video," Johnny told him. "They said he wasn't one of their own."

"Maybe he was a dealer," Jack said. "He might've wanted *you* to sell for him."

"He looked too wholesome for that kind of trade," Maggie replied. "He didn't have the jewelry, he wasn't looking over his shoulder, he didn't have that dusty smell of a room with no windows."

Maggie was referring to the labs where drugs were sorted, cooked, or packed. Jack knew exactly what she meant. Men and women naked so they couldn't steal drugs, powder from the talc used to cut cocaine or heroin clinging to their skin, dryness from dehumidifiers that kept moisture out of the packets of blow or smack or pot.

"He didn't look like he was from around here and he didn't *sound* like it, either," Maggie said. "His English was very formal, and it had no hint of mainland gutturals. This was a schooled, educated man."

"A spy, recruiting?" Jack suggested. "That's how they do it. Guys come from the consulate, go out among transplants, look for people loyal to the homeland who might find a couple grand a week helpful. Maybe he hoped you would sell information."

"He didn't try and talk to me, get to know me—"

"It was your father he wanted," Jack reminded her. "They don't go after second generation, young people who have already assimilated."

Father and daughter fell silent. They obviously hadn't considered that.

"Did you see any of the others? Did anyone see them?" Jack asked.

"No," Maggie said. "I was ducked down and people in the street were looking at the speeding SUV. They couldn't describe the others."

Jack wasn't sure that recruitment was the answer. A "missionary," as consulate recruiters called themselves in the intelligence game, would not have tried to grab Maggie. He also wouldn't have had an SUV parked right in front of their store. He would have come downtown unobtrusively, made his rounds, talked to other merchants, come back some other time to talk to Johnny. Missionaries don't like to call attention to themselves.

Jack was out of ideas. "What do you think he wanted?" he asked Maggie. "You've obviously given this some thought."

"Until you said that about the spies, my belief was that he wanted to buy the store," Maggie said.

Jack looked at Johnny. "Is it for sale?"

"No."

"Do you know if he ever talked to other shopkeepers?"

"The police canvassed the block," Johnny said. "Apparently they came to see us."

"How many merchants own their properties instead of renting?"

"I own and so does the takeout next door and the cell phone shop on the other side," Johnny said. "I know the owners. The man didn't talk to them."

Jack looked around. His eyes went from the worn, green-tile floor to the embossed, rustic copper panels of the vintage ceiling. "What do you have that someone would want?"

"Everything," Johnny said.

"You lost me."

"When Chinese seek something, they never want just that one thing," he said. "It is like acupuncture. You put a needle in one spot, but it is really a larger wellness you are after."

"Someone wouldn't just want to buy your business?"

"Why?" Johnny asked. "It is a lot of work for little reward. But if, for example, you wanted to tear down the block and build an office tower, what better way to start?"

"But why build an office tower here?" Jack asked. "There must be something else."

The street was full of shops that were probably no better or worse an investment. A real estate deal didn't explain why Johnny had been targeted first, and the behavior of the intruder didn't fit with the typically smooth and stealthy tactics of developers and their lawyers. But no other explanation jumped out. If someone were just looking to launder money, the check-cashing business was better for that. Distributing drugs? There was the pharmacy, or the Asian movie rental store that catered to young people.

"Do you have a blueprint of the place? There was probably something attached to the contract when you bought it."

"Those are filed with my attorney," Johnny said. "What would that matter? And how would someone else see it?"

"Libraries, government offices—there's a lot of material available onsite and online," Jack said. "As for why it would matter, we won't know until we have a look. You have the two-bedroom place upstairs and a small basement, as I recall?"

Johnny nodded.

"I'd like to look at both, if that's all right."

"Of course," Johnny said.

Maggie went to check out a customer while Johnny took Jack upstairs. They looked out the window. There was nothing in the line of sight that stood out, no obvious targets for potential terrorists like flight paths or a police station. It wasn't like the old days when someone needed a neighborhood place for a stakeout. That could be done from a car, or even a laptop and a small sound amplifier from a park bench. They went downstairs. The cellar was unique for the street—there weren't a lot of basements in earthquake zones—but it was small and there was no back entrance. Johnny used the area for storage. Jack was a wine connoisseur, and his impression was that it would make an adequate wine cellar but not much more.

Nothing jumped out at Jack. No motive even suggested itself. They went back to the grocery. Maggie was chatting with a young man who looked to be about thirty. He was well dressed and buying an orange juice.

"I'll check with the few friends I've got left in law enforcement," Jack said, "see what they think. Are you going to be OK here?"

Johnny grinned. "We'll be fine." He cocked his head toward the counter. "That's one of Maggie's martial arts school brothers. He stops by every afternoon.

I'm sure that word will spread. They will make certain there are brothers and sisters coming in and out, walking by, available at the other end of the phone."

"Nice," Jack said. He used to have that kind of camaraderie at the GNT network. His staff, the other hosts, the news anchors and reporters. All he had now was his camera operator, Max. And she was freelance, only around when he needed her.

Johnny and Maggie thanked Jack, and they agreed to be in touch as soon as anyone had any information to share. Even though Jack didn't boast the kind of clout or access he once did, Johnny seemed relieved to have connected with someone who knew what to look for and where to look for it.

Jack decided to walk for a while and started down Washington Street toward the Ferry Building. He loved the new marketplace of stores nestled within the brick-and-ceramic arches carefully restored to look like the 1898 originals. The preservation of history kept it from feeling like a mall, and the smells from the bakery, the cheese store, the coffee shop, reconnected him with the city as a whole. San Francisco was a permanent friend and companion to whom unconditional, unwavering love was given and returned. Every street held a memory, every corner the promise of something new. It made him smile when nothing else did. Like now.

Jack found a corner of the marketplace that gave him some privacy but still let him smell the coffee from the coffee shop. He made two phone calls. One was to

FBI field director Carl Forsyth, whose very grudging trust Jack had gained after preventing the Golden Gate Bridge from becoming ground zero for a dirty bomb. He didn't mention the grocery in particular, just asked Forsyth if he had received any alerts regarding Chinatown or anyone who might have designs on businesses there, other than the usual thugs and punks. The answer was negative. Forsyth wasn't brusque with Jack; he just had nothing to give him.

The other call was to Detective Sam Jason of the SFPD. Jack had helped him back in 2009 when Jason, who was off duty, tried to apprehend a gang member for fare evasion at a near-deserted San Francisco Municipal Railway stop. The man told the officer he had a gun and tried to flee; Jason killed him with a single bullet to the spine. It turned out the man was unarmed. Jack found out that the dead man had been accused of rape six months earlier and might have participated in a holdup the year before that. His coverage encouraged a witness who had heard the victim say he had a weapon to come forward.

Jason looked up the report on Yu Market from the responding officers.

"They've got a photo of the Chinese guy from the grocery camera," Jason said. "No match in any of our databases. They found the SUV abandoned on Marina Green Drive, rented with falsified documents. The lab's got it now."

"Run-of-the-mill gangsters wouldn't bother with fake IDs," Jack said.

"Not likely. And they were smart enough to leave it where there were no cameras. I'll let you know if forensics comes up with anything."

Jack thanked him, hung up, and wandered out of the marketplace. Apparent outsiders, a singularly targeted location, and now forged papers used to rent an SUV. Plus a getaway site that was blind to the SFPD. There was something here; it was a wedge for something else. Whatever that was, it was well organized if initially overconfident. The men would be back.

Sammo Yang had never been to America. He spoke English adequately, having undertaken its mandatory study for seven years in primary and secondary school. But he knew nothing about America other than what he saw on the news or heard at the China National Space Administration, where he worked for his entire professional life. Now that he was here, the thirty-five-year-old Beijing native felt distaste pooling in the back of his throat.

His credentials as an attaché enabled him to pass quickly through Customs at the San Francisco International Airport. The diplomatic papers, on a China-based aircraft, would make it virtually impossible for American authorities to find out his true identity. He spotted a radiation detector tucked in a corner of the ceiling. He noted the security cameras, which would not help the Americans identify him. Though he had happily shaved the beard he had worn in Afghanistan, he had on a fisherman's black wool cap with a brim and sunglasses. He also wore a white windbreaker specially made with magnesium fibers for seam threads. The garment was highly reflective and created a lens flare that smeared the video image whenever he moved. The large plastic case he carried was not inspected, set off no alarms. He was met by a tall, efficient consulate employee who ushered Sammo to the van waiting curbside.

"Did you have a pleasant flight?" the youthful consulate worker asked.

Sammo didn't care that the question was banal. It was a joy to hear his language being spoken on the ground in this awful, arrogant land. Sammo's father had overseen a shoe factory for an American firm in Nanjing. When the firm got a better deal in India, they closed the shop literally overnight and Sammo's father was out of work. His parents had died within weeks of one another four years ago. They had both been in their fifties.

Sammo earned a degree in physics from Nanjing University with a doctorate in acoustics and engineering. He went to work for the CNSA in their top-security spy satellite program where he developed a method of intercepting secure wireless signals even in the vacuum of space. That brought him to the attention of the science office of the Central Military Commission. That brought him to Afghanistan, challenging himself in ways undreamed of, equipped with skills he had never expected to possess.

Now it brought him here.

Mistreating the citizens of the People's Republic of China was bad enough. It represented everything the

Chinese people had fought against, going back over a century to the Boxer Rebellion: the exploitation of hardworking citizens by foreign powers. But the actions the Americans had taken in the past six months had been intolerable. They would be made to pay dearly for that.

Sammo looked through the dark-tinted window at the airplanes riding gray plumes skyward while others seemed to float to earth. He looked at the towers of some city in the distance, at identical-looking stores offering food and electronics, at the occasional gleaming flashes of the waters of the Bay. He had read on the government's Xinhua News Agency website that Chinese banks effectively owned America. That did not instill him with feelings of pride but with revulsion: he did not want to own this place, he wanted to see it crushed and dismantled, the way his father had lost face for being unable to keep his factory, the way his family had been broken.

"This is the freeway called the 101," the consulate employee said helpfully. "We are headed north to San Francisco. That is the famous Bay on our right and just there," he pointed, "one can see Candlestick Park. That is the location of the San Francisco American football games."

Sammo's mouth twitched downward, and he snorted quietly. He had no interest in American sports madness. No longer listening to the consulate employee, Sammo sat with the case on the floor in front of him, his mind alert; he had slept well on the airplane, still exhausted from his trip to Afghanistan but exhilarated by the results. He was eager to begin the second part of the mission. Through intermediaries in Beijing, Jing Jintao had sent him a cryptic message that he wished to see Sammo as soon as he arrived, that there might be another way he could help his country.

Sammo was anxious to hear what the revered statesman had to say. He was willing to help in any way possible.

"Excuse me," Sammo said. "I was told that upon landing we would—"

The consular aide held a finger to his lips. He took a notepad from inside his gray blazer. That in itself told Sammo all he needed to know. They were being followed, and by a car with wireless surveillance equipment. If he tapped keystrokes on a laptop or numbers in a cell phone, they would be intercepted and read.

New arrivals are watched, he wrote. *We have standardized clothing at the consulate that helps to confuse—*

Sammo took the pen. *I need to see it now. Have the driver pull over with mechanical difficulty. Raise the hood. Be prepared to head toward the original target.*

The aide looked at him. Sammo removed his glasses. His eyes, his jaw, were hard-set. There was no confusing what he had written for a request. The young man understood and wrote instructions for the driver.

The driver read the instructions, and acknowledged

with a nod. He pulled off the freeway at the Grand
Avenue Exit and stopped at the curb in front of a line
of trees. He shot a questioning look in the rearview
mirror. Sammo nodded that the location was fine. He
had already set the case on his lap and was working
the combination lock.

The driver exited and raised the hood. The aide
watched silently as Sammo removed a device from
the foam padding of the case. It looked alien, like a
stiff, sectioned sleeve from a ceremonial costume in
the *Mulan of Mars* comic books he had read as a
child. Sammo removed his windbreaker and fitted the
device over his right arm. He had, in fact, made it
from a long universal arm brace that was jointed at
the elbow. He fitted one foam section over his bicep
and another over his forearm, adjusting them until the
bend in the device matched the bend of his elbow. He
tightened several screws so the foam wouldn't shift.
Then he slipped a hand strap between his thumb and
index finger and fitted a small cap over his thumb like
a thimble. When the entire unit was secure he removed its plastic sheath, revealing a tube on top of his
forearm that extended from the crease in his elbow
nearly to the knuckles at the base of his fingers. The
tube was cushioned on the forearm foam section and
connected by wire to the cap on his thumb. On the
underside of his forearm and wired to the tube attach-
ment was a fingerprint scanner. Sammo pushed his
left index finger against it. The tube hummed.

The scientist handed the case to the aide and put

his windbreaker back on. He was still wearing his cap
and sunglasses. He pulled a pack of cigarettes from
his pocket, opened the van door, left it open, and lit
the Hong Mei. Sammo did not smoke as a rule, but it
proved useful as a signal at night or a distraction, as
now.

He casually walked to the front of the van. He pretended to be interested in what the driver was doing.

"Where is the vehicle that was following us?"
Sammo asked.

"It is an Escalade SUV. He continued past and
turned right at the corner. He will circle and come
back, then probably stop toward the end of the block.
There." The driver pointed to an open space behind a
brown delivery truck. There was a stop sign; Sammo
recognized the shape and color from his training. The
Americans would have to wait before turning.

"You are ready to get back on that freeway?"
Sammo asked.

"Yes, sir."

"You know the original destination?"

"I do, sir."

"Tell me when you see him coming up the side
street," Sammo said. He faced away from the spot,
leaning against the van, looking idly at the trees.
Smoke curled from the cigarette. He enjoyed the
smell. That, too, reminded him of home.

The driver stood on the street side of the van, looking
around the open hood. He moved his hands idly among
tubing and caps, his eyes on the end of the block.

"He's coming, sir."

"Close the hood, get back in the van. We will be going north."

The driver obeyed.

Sammo drew back his right hand sleeve so the tip of the tube was exposed. There was no sight; he didn't need one. He had practiced the differential like a circus marksman who had to shoot from the hip. The Escalade pulled up to the stop sign. Sammo pressed his index finger to the top of the thimble. There was a sound like compressed air escaping.

The Escalade did not move from the sign. The electromagnetic pulse from Sammo's device had disabled every electronic system in the SUV.

Sammo jumped back to the door, pulled it shut, and the van sped from the curb. He kept the cigarette, after grinding it out in an ashtray; there was no reason to leave even a partial fingerprint or his DNA. The van was back on the 101 headed north in under a minute. Sammo looked out the window, back at the exit. The Escalade was still at the corner. One of the FBI, perhaps CIA, agents had emerged. He was shouting into a cell phone.

"He doesn't seem happy," the aide remarked.

"He has no reason to be," Sammo said. "His car is dead. And his cell phone is not working. Would anyone else know our vehicle plate number?"

"The consulate has three vans and one limousine that travel to the airport," the aide said. "I'm certain the license numbers are all on file." It had taken him a few moments to gather his thoughts. He still wasn't quite sure what he had witnessed.

"How are they able to track us going forward?"

"The only license-reading devices are on the bridges so that is not a concern. It is possible they may try to spot us using helicopters—"

"I don't think so," Sammo said. "Not when they begin to consider what has just happened."

The aide knew better than to ask what *did* happen. He was still sitting with the case on his lap.

Sammo removed his windbreaker, shut and unstrapped the device, and nestled it back in its padded container. He did not smile, did not show the satisfaction he felt at having met American overconfidence with something new, something he had helped to create.

Something that would show these people what it was like to interfere with Chinese progress, something that would cause them to lose what his parents had lost—dignity, face, and their very lives.

Chapter 3

Suitland, Maryland

Dover Griffith had reread the *Truth Tellers* transcript a dozen times. Even though it was clear that Jack Hatfield was right about Squarebeam and Hawke, she couldn't figure out how this might have impacted the Chinook in Afghanistan. The military would have been aware of any Squarebeam technology being used there. The Tangi Valley was not exactly a hot spot for development anyway. It wasn't impossible that the technology could have shown up there and *"whatever remains, however implausible, must be the truth,"* she remembered, but there was a reason why Sherlock Holmes refused to be an employee of any government agency. Dover couldn't pass a *what if* up the chain of command.

She set the transcript aside and concentrated on

sifting through the data coming from the crash site. She was still studying the horrifying, heartbreaking photographs of the wreckage when her computer pinged an alert. It was from the Intelligence Coordination Center of Homeland Security. This division made certain that all data collected the Defense Intelligence Agency, the CIA, the FBI, the National Security Agency, INTERPOL, and other intelligence-gathering services was "cross-pollinated"—shared among appropriate departments. Because of her background in Chinese, Griffith received the alert from the FBI. It was a report filed by the San Francisco Field Office less than ten minutes before:

At 1:46 P.M., Pacific, an FBI vehicle with a two-man complement was on a routine SFO-to-San Francisco tail of a Chinese consulate van with one unknown passenger and a single carry-on case. The van left the 101, ostensibly with engine trouble. Agents followed, circling the block. Upon renewing visual contact the pursuing vehicle suffered complete electronic failure, including all forms of communication and GPS. The van quickly departed, headed north.

Griffith reread the report and sat back.

"Catastrophic failure," she murmured. Not just of the car but of the cell phones within the car. That in itself was disturbing and had earned the incident a Level Two tag at the field office: INVESTIGATE UTMOST URGENCY. That allowed for the assignment of additional agents and any civilian resources. But the idea that it had happened twice within a thirty-six-hour period, a world away, was more alarming still.

Griffith idly rolled her mouse back and forth, not seeing the cursor or the screen but contemplating the incidents. It made no sense that China would be in Afghanistan to knock down a Chinook. But maybe that was not the way to approach these matters.

She clicked on her internal address book, accessed the drop-down menu, and sent a secure instant message to Dr. Doug Jane in the Advanced Electronics Research Division. She didn't want to set off any alarms until she had more information, so she had to watch what she said:

From DGriffith: Thoughts on Chinook?

From DJane: Electromagnetic pulse.

From DGriffith: External?

From DJane: No. Chopper abt 2K' high. Means 4K' blast diameter. Geosynch satellite wld've noticed.

From DGriffith: Got it. Do you know if vehicular GPS units are powered by main battery?

From DJane: Not. Wldn't help if they were stranded for a few days.

From DGriffith: Right. Thanks.

So they were going on the assumption that a device of some kind was snuck on board. That would be one reason for the information blackout that occurred after the crash: complete home-base lockdown until the actions of everyone could be accounted for. The search would be expanded now, to include anyone who had access to the Chinook as far back as they'd need to look.

Griffith felt a burning in her gut. She was by nature a calm, easygoing woman, but what the ONI called "Potential Heightened Alert Situations" did not typically land on her desk. She wasn't the one who made connections; she interpreted or reacted to the findings of others. If these two incidents were related—and that was still a substantial *if*—then Dr. Jane was wrong. The hypothetical EMP source *was* external.

Griffith went to the Pacific Gas and Electric website. She saw no notices of outages in the area. She checked the cell phone carriers, routed herself into their online help center, saw no one complaining of any sudden dead zones. There was absolutely no mention of collateral damage beyond the FBI tracking vehicle.

It could be a coincidence, she thought. The car died. An agent's phone charge ran out. But the GPS ran off its own power source, probably charged by the car battery. That couldn't be a coincidence.

She looked up EMP data in the ONI online library. She found a short overview of portable shock wave generators. They produced a targeted burst of acoustic or electromagnetic energy that shattered kidney stones and other small, local objects, or disrupted the stability of microprocessors. The current state of the art was that they could be linked imprecisely and ineffectively to antennae, dishes, conic arrays, or directional horns to produce non-local results. The bulk of the research in that area was being undertaken by a handful of private firms with the object of civilian applications such as high-speed chases. The big impediment was that existing technology was only effective against plastic or fiberglass. It was useless against any form of metal container, which disbursed and weakened the wave. The military did not have any research-and-development programs in that area, but were underwriting some efforts in the private sector.

Griffith ran a quick check of firms involved in the military-funded research. Nothing controlled by Hawke was on the list, but after all, Hawke had already demonstrated that he didn't work and play well with the military. The list of firms doing research without military funding didn't include any Hawke companies, either.

Still, Griffith couldn't get the impact of the original Squarebeam technology out of her mind. Squarebeam, or something like it, could have crashed the Chinook. The incident could have been an accident. Perhaps the Russians had been testing a wireless system in Afghanistan. But Squarebeam or something similar could also have disabled the FBI tracker vehicle. Again, that could have been accidental. But the two incidents together added up to a coincidence. Griffith had been suspicious of coincidences ever since she started studying journalism.

She wanted to run these events past a pair of knowledgeable, outside eyes. Someone who didn't have the step-by-step mind of an intelligence analyst. The Department of Homeland Security coined a term for individuals who until recently were grouped under the heading of "Conspiracy Theorists." People who suspected their government of misdeeds were still called that. But people who believed that corporations or other governments were out to get us were back-handedly legitimized as "Assets with Paranoid Vision."

Jack Hatfield might not exactly qualify as APV. But, except for herself at this moment, Hatfield was the closest Griffith could think of.

She decided to look him up.

Sausalito, California

The two men closed the trunk after securing the package, then left the small shipping company on Humboldt Avenue in Sausalito and entered the Audi parked out front. The five-year-old firm, Eastern Rim Construction, did brick-and-mortar work. They did not advertise and did not seem to do a great deal of business. But they made enough money working with the Chinese community, shoring up pre-earthquake-code buildings, to cover the rent on the five-hundred-square-foot cinder-block building they rented. They also made money lending out copies of blueprints from their library, a nearly complete collection of building documents pertaining to Chinatown. These were used for restoration projects and landmark evaluation hearings.

They had a white van for construction materials. The men were not taking that vehicle now.

The rented black Audi attracted no attention in a city where that make of car was plentiful. The Chinese agent had picked it up earlier, from a different company than the one at which he'd rented the abandoned SUV, using a different set of IDs and credit cards. The latter was a number picked up by a Chinese waiter using a handheld card swipe device. The waiter quit after making the theft. He was a member of Jing Jintao's cell. He, too, had used a false ID to gain employment and could not be traced.

The Audi went unnoticed on its northward route through the start of the rush hour traffic. It was headed to Stockton Street in San Francisco.

It would not be unnoticed for long.

After leaving the Yu Market, Jack Hatfield went back to his office on the *Sea Wrighter* to check up on local, national, and international news. His emphasis was on the local, since that was the meat-and-potatoes of his freelance news work. He looked at police blotters, legal dockets, even celebrity news sites to see what events and fund-raisers were in town. Then he did an online search for the history of the buildings on Clay Street, in case a real estate deal for Yu Market somehow made sense, but after an hour nothing had turned up. Eddie's big brown eyes gazed at Jack from where the poodle had flopped on the teak floorboards.

"Let's get the hell out of here," Jack said.

He grabbed a khaki vest from a hook. Eddie ran in

front of him to the parking lot nearby and Jack let the poodle into the passenger seat of his 2010 twelve-cylinder S600 Mercedes, midnight blue. Then he took the driver's seat.

"Afternoon, Wilhelm," he said as he turned the key.

The Mercedes was a luxury, admittedly, but it was more than just Jack's middle finger to the world when he bought it after *Truth Tellers* was canceled. Owning the sedan was a way of reconnecting with his days of racing D-Jags at Laguna Seca when he was in his early twenties. *Truth Tellers* was wrecked; he needed to find a new pedal and put it to the metal. And do it fast, before the rage and anxiety of the wreck induced paralysis. The Mercedes had embodied silent power, a necessary phase for Jack as he planned his post-show career and embraced the possibility, now the necessity, of being a freelancer. Once that brief phase of silence had passed and Jack was turning out reports at a steady clip, he simply loved to hold the steering wheel of work well done. Dedication to craft was a disappearing virtue.

Jack didn't want to be alone right now. He had a feeling his thoughts would turn radioactive. He decided to drive not to the apartment where he kept his collection of clocks in various states of repair so that he could tinker and think, but to Spumante's, where he was known and had friends. Maybe Bruno would be in a pugnacious mood and they could kill some hours with a good debate, maybe change a few eavesdroppers' minds for the better.

Spumante's was more than that, though. It was on the route he used to take to go to Justin Hermann Plaza, where they created a skating rink similar to the one in Rockefeller Center in New York. Two years ago when Jack had broken up with Rachel in the fall, he had faced a lonely Christmas season. Since he didn't have a wife or family of his own, he would go to the rink and hang on the rail at night and watch the children with their mothers and fathers, skating around the ice like little fledglings learning to walk beside their parents. He would watch with vicarious contentment as a mother would place her little daughter in-between her legs, pushing her around the ice with her knees turned in to prop her up. Jack marveled at how much it was like the animal kingdom. At some point, though, he would usually have to turn away, thinking of his own mother and how she had taught him so much—how to walk, how to dance, how to tie his tie, how to talk to a lady, among other things. Like most strong men, Jack never talked about her. What could he say that wouldn't sound sentimental and false? But her life had enriched him beyond calculation, and her death had hit him like a fist in the gut.

Just after Jack crossed the bridge, he paused to call Doc Matson to see if he could meet him at Spumante's. Jack wanted a sane, unsentimental voice in his ear.

Happy to come," said Doc into his phone, "if you're buying. See you in a few."

Doc hung up and took a sip of his Diet Coke. It was

one of those special just-after-rain moments in San
Francisco, and he had been walking down Broadway
toward the Bay, which was a china blue that ordinarily wasn't seen in September, only in late winter or
early spring. Only the boaters and knowing locals
would note that particular hue. Doc took in the limp
flags on the becalmed sailboats, Coit Tower smirking
over the scene, the red-brick buildings that dated to
the days of the Barbary Coast. As he turned the corner of Sansome and Jackson, an energy force almost
knocked him off the sidewalk. She was so powerfully
built and so stunning in appearance that most people
just ignored her. Her expression said: *You are dirt, I
am goddess, my father was general in Russian military, go away.*

Doc's head snapped as she strolled past him. He
was tempted to run after her and pitch to her: *I'm perfect for you. I spend half my life on boats and planes.
I know how to treat a woman, and I love your rear
end.*

He said nothing and continued on his way. She, in
her insular self-love, missed a gemstone for her crown
of thorns that rare beauties wear.

Jack left the car with the valet who parked it in front
of the restaurant, and walked with Eddie to the table
where Doc was already sitting. The sunlight was different than it had been four hours earlier. It was ruddy
and tossing oblong shadows across the streets. A wind
blew in from the Embarcadero, carrying the smell of
saltwater and fish. There were more people about

as businesses closed and restaurants prepared for dinner. The line outside the Chinese clinic next to Spumante's was gone as doctors and nurses who worked dawn to dusk saw their final patients.

"Free medical care promised by Mao," Doc observed, "but not delivered. And here it is on a silver platter from Uncle Sam. Medicaid mills being broken all across South Florida, but they're untouchable here. We should ask that doctor whether he's noticed any abuse of the system, next time we see him here."

"Hi, yourself," Jack said, sitting down and setting Eddie under the table. "It looks like even Wilhelm can't beat you."

"I cheated," Doc said. "I jogged. Got here a few minutes ago." His walk down Broadway had been preparation for a run.

"A merc has to stay in shape," said the sixty-five-year-old who looked about forty-five. That was one reason he was a vegetarian. The other reason, he maintained, is that he often had to survive in the wild on what he called "fruits and roots." That was not a diet one wanted to come to suddenly. "Not when fiber-induced flatulence can give away your position," he once told Jack.

It was good to see the man again, without Abe to stir up trouble. Doc had a quick smile, though in this case he greeted Jack with something more like a smirk.

"I ordered you a Bruno's Sauvignon Blanc, though I held off on the pan-roasted halibut," Doc said. "Wasn't sure what you'd be in the mood for."

Jack wasn't sure himself, though Doc couldn't have gone wrong with the wine. Bruno, inspired by his youth in the Molinara, Benevento province of Italy, had purchased hills in Sonoma—in the same parallel as Italy, the 38th. When Jack first visited him there in 1993, Bruno was working like an ox to clear the trees and brush alongside the Mexican workers he hired. All of his cuttings were en route from Montalcino, and they were hurrying to prepare for them. Later Bruno had walked Jack over the vineyard, pointing out the rocky volcanic soil, the southern exposure, everything that made up the terroir. "Wine is made in the vineyard; it's not made in the cellar," Bruno had stated, "and the terroir determines the taste of the wine." He had been right, of course. His micropicked estate wines were perfection, and he was the first vintner to create a Brunello Sonoma. He eventually became a sponsor of Jack's show and when Jack was fired, Bruno sent him a case of the Brunello.

Eddie shifted under the table and sat on Jack's foot. Jack was reminded of Bruno's old dog, Emma. Unlike other vintners, Bruno didn't check the sugar content before he picked the grapes. He just fed a grape to Emma, and she'd spit it out if it wasn't ripe. But when Emma herself ate the grapes right off the vine, that's when Bruno called the winemaker, and they'd pick the grapes that day. *Just like a story,* Jack thought. The best stories have to unfold naturally in their own time. When you've got a ripe one, be ready to hustle. Until then, try not to go nuts with the waiting.

Jack looked at Doc's big fist, which enveloped a can of Diet Coke.

"No more cervezas? Trying to forget El Salvador?" Jack said.

"Been a while since I was down there shootin' alongside the Contras," he said in his gravelly voice. "Might be in danger of forgettin' those days."

"Inactivity will do that to you," Jack said.

"Actually, periods of inactivity suit me," Doc replied. "I'm older than you. I like longer spaces between my suicide runs." He took a sip of his Diet Coke and leaned back in his chair as far as he could go.

Jack grinned. Doc invested himself wholeheartedly in every assignment or mission he had undertaken. To do that, he needed to be able to rest in whatever downtime he could find. On his earliest missions he had run on beer and adrenaline. On his downtime it used to be beer and a smoke. Then it was just beer. Now it was Diet Coke. Doc never went in for weed. He grew up in the counterculture community of Bolinas, nearly thirty miles northwest of San Francisco, where homegrown weed was the relaxant of choice. Today, just smelling it on a beach or in a park took him back to a time when people were deluded enough to think that luddite isolationism was the solution to everything that ailed humankind. You could only get to Bolinas on roads that weren't marked and in some cases weren't even paved; if you happened to find your way in, you weren't encouraged to stay.

"You know how crazy your own family can sometimes make you?" Doc had once asked Jack. "Imagine if your family was an entire community of potheads who were a little nuts *before* they got high."

As a boy, Doc had seen military aircraft flying overhead and wanted to know more about them. As soon as he was of age, he enlisted.

Adrenaline and beer, Jack thought. *Shoot or don't shoot.* Sometimes he envied Doc the simpler choices that governed his life.

Bruno came out with Jack's glass of wine. Noticing the silence at the table and Doc looking out at the street, Bruno shot a sharp glance at Jack.

"You've got trouble?" he said.

Jack took a sip of his wine. "It's great, Bruno," he said.

"I know, it's a good wine," Bruno said. "Listen, when I was a little boy in Italy and we had nothing but trouble, my grandfather told me, 'Everyone has a cross to bear. Lucky is the one that can keep the cross in his pocket.'"

Jack and Doc both smiled, and for Jack, it was a genuine smile, not a polite disguise. Nobody could restore perspective the way Bruno could.

"And now," Bruno said, "I'm going to teach you how my grandfather taught me how to taste wine when I was six years old. He said to me, 'Bruno, you take a small sip of wine, you put it on your tongue. Don't move anything. And count to eight and let it go down from the side of your mouth.' Most of the time I choked to death."

They all laughed.

"But you know, when I did it, I experienced." He

stretched out the word. "Because the side of your mouth is the most delicate part of your mouth. I experienced something incredible. The wine goes all the way down to your throat." Bruno motioned under his chin. "My grandfather used to say, 'You know, when you do that, you take the pants off the wine and you really see what is there.'"

Jack and Doc chuckled again. Bruno sat down, and Jack realized that he was going to watch Jack taste his wine properly. Just then a Middle Eastern man, about sixty, approached and greeted the restaurateur. Bruno stood and clapped both hands on his shoulders, smiling, then introduced him to the table.

"Jack, Doc, this is Asif, he owns the Persian restaurant around the corner. You'll like him. You know what he says to me one day? He says—hey, Asif, you tell it, about the starving Muslims."

Asif grinned and said, "It's an old story, just that when the Jews don't eat, the Muslims starve to death."

They all broke out laughing.

"Because," Bruno explained, though he didn't have to, "in the days of the Jewish holidays, the Jewish people don't go to restaurants!"

They laughed some more, and Jack felt the last of his tension drain away. Bruno and Asif disappeared into the restaurant and a small silence fell on the table.

"What are you thinking?" Doc said.

Jack looked at him. "About the lamb chops," he grinned. He almost always ordered fish or pasta. "What does lamb chops *scotto dito* mean?"

"It means 'you'll burn your finger.' But don't let that stop you, I've heard it's phenomenal. And Pasta Bruno for me. So," he put aside his menu, "you've been down lately."

Jack shook his head. "Between you and Max, I have no private life."

"I'm not worried about you, it's just something I noticed."

"Max wasn't, either. My focus slipped a bit, that's all."

"Here's how I see it," said Doc. "You played cat and mouse with the FBI, snuck into a country that's forbidden you from entering, then climbed the Golden Gate Bridge, and saved a good chunk of San Francisco. Any normal person would plant his tired rear end on a Caribbean beach after that. You didn't. You let yourself get debriefed by the FBI, by the DHS, by the SFPD, and probably a few others that you're not allowed to mention."

Jack's smile told him he was right. The Mossad had also had a long, long chat with him.

"And how many interviews did you do with news media? A dozen?"

"At least. You know what the hell of it was? I spent so much time talking to other people about it, I never actually got to do my own report."

"Brother, you'd make a terrible merc," Doc said. "Journalism 101: the news is free. Stories are what you do for pay."

Jack chuckled. He took a swallow of wine and noticed a pair of women looking at Eddie on their way into Spumante's. Eddie, of course, was mugging for their attention.

"Try the poodle," Jack told the ladies. "It's the best in the city."

The women weren't sure whether to laugh and hastily entered the restaurant. Doc and Jack grinned at each other.

Suddenly Jack felt as though a pair of boxing gloves punched him on both sides of his head and stayed there. He heard his jaw pop; heard an intake of air through his mouth. At the same moment something pushed against his back and knocked him forward. The table shook, the wine spilled, and Eddie howled, then scooted out the other side. The poodle was standing, barking, but Jack couldn't hear him. Jack saw Doc, who was across from him, rock backward, catch the edge of the table, then throw himself to the tiled patio. Behind him, the sun seemed to go backward, rising instead of falling, as the restaurant and the buildings and the sky itself turned a murky crimson.

The flash, the noise, the impact, were all over in an instant. But the shock lingered another few moments.

Doc was the first to recover.

"Bomb!" he shouted, looking past Jack.

Jack couldn't hear him, but he could read Doc's lips and his expression. He was just realizing on his own what had happened. He turned and looked toward the clinic. It was now a flaming, smoky shell.

Car alarms and shouting began to penetrate the thick hum that filled his ears. He saw wicks of flame moving against the larger inferno—people who had been caught in the explosion, their arms and torsos afire. He threw aside the chair and ran toward the small white building. Doc was a few paces ahead of him. Jack looked back. Eddie had jumped onto one of the chairs and was watching. He knew the poodle wouldn't be moving.

Crowds were converging from all directions. Some were trying to help the injured. Others were breaking car windows in the street, shifting the gears where possible to roll them from the fire. Jack himself went as close as he could to a black car, possibly an Audi, that looked like it had been ground zero for the blast. The heat was fierce, like someone had opened a giant oven. He didn't see anybody inside. It wasn't a suicide attack. The hood of the trunk had been blown into the middle of Stockton, and the bottom of the chassis had ceased to exist. That was where the explosives had been, triggered either by a timer or a remote detonator; probably the latter. Rush hour traffic was too risky for a ticking clock.

Fire sirens penetrated the remaining dullness in his ears. Their flashing lights were reassuring, a sense of functioning infrastructure, of capable men at a moment of chaos. Jack lingered near the Audi, wanting to make sure that the crime scene was preserved as much as possible.

His ears had cleared enough so he could now hear sobbing. Family members who had been waiting for patients stood clustered outside, held back by pedestrians who refused to let them rush in.

Chinese families. A Chinese clinic.

Jack did not know why, he did not know how, but his nagging reporter's gut told him that this was not unrelated to what happened on Clay Street that morning. He took out his cell phone and began shooting video of the car—not to have a record for the police but because it was news and because it was research.

He had found his next story.

Chapter 4

New York, New York

It was nearly five P.M. when Richard Hawke left the Midtown Manhattan building he owned to get into the stretch limousine that would carry him a dozen blocks to the private helicopter that would shuttle him to his luxury jet, the revolutionary, new Quiet Small Supersonic Transport.

The sixty-two-year-old telecommunications titan did not look the part of a three-time *Forbes* Person of the Year. He was a short, emaciated man who always wore sunglasses but was pale as a domino. He had recently beaten throat cancer and was not quite at the halfway point of being clear for five years. He bought the clinic that treated him in Germany, just in case he needed it again.

His cancer was the result of a profligate youth

spent in this very neighborhood, when he stole from food vendors on Ninth Avenue for breakfast and lunch, helping to stretch the small income his parents earned in the Garment District—his mother as a seamstress for a nonunion shop, his father as the operator of a label-cutting machine.

Their apartment on West 45th Street no longer existed. That was the site of the Hawke Building, a fifty-three-story tower made of dark glass and shaped like a geometric rocket, flat and tapering. There were many who said that, standing among the lower-lying structures, it looked like a large, extended middle finger. If so, not even his critics begrudged him bragging rights. Richard Hawke was the definition of "self-made." When, bored and restless, he barely graduated from high school in 1969, a friend got him a job working the spotlights at one of the few surviving burlesque houses on 42nd Street and Tenth Avenue. Watching the strippers and naked contortionists night after night, it occurred to Richard that there was money to be made by filming the acts. He arranged a royalty payment for the artists; those women taught him the art of hardball negotiation. When you had something that someone else absolutely needed, you charged a premium. Of course, when you had all five performers on board you learned the value of counter-negotiation: you threatened to cut each one out individually until, without the others knowing it, everyone had reduced their fee.

The deals made, he bought a used 16mm camera, set it up beside his lights, and then arranged private showings for underage kids in the backroom of a soda shop down the street from his apartment. He cut the owner in on the profits. When home video started making noise with the introduction of Betamax in 1975, Richard released his library—with a musical accompaniment—on his own label, Hawke-Eye Cinema. That earned him his first million dollars, which he used to buy his parents a big waterfront place in Sheepshead Bay, Brooklyn, now a favorite neighborhood for Russians. Producing all-new, hard-core narrative films for Hawke-Eye earned Richard his second and third million. His next big purchase was the lot where his apartment and the adjoining apartments sat.

Upon the advice of his attorney, Hawke diversified into more legitimate businesses. In the early 1980s, he had been fascinated with the early adoption of mobile phone technology by pimps to warn hookers on 44th and Broadway when the cops were headed their way. He bought the company that made the phones, infamously renaming it PMT—Pimp Mobile Technologies—and expanded by purchasing small microwave networks and nascent fiber optics companies and merging them into a communications empire. In the ensuing three decades, there was not a month when any company in any part of the world had more cutting-edge technology available for the marketplace. If they did, Hawke bought them. That was something he learned from Bernie Michaels, who owned the burlesque house: it was ultimately more economical to buy your competitor's talent than to try to grow your own.

Richard had always had more energy than any two men around him. When the cancer was diagnosed after a long, lingering sore throat—squamous cell carcinoma of the tonsil—it was the first setback Hawke had ever encountered. He took some small solace from the fact that it had been caused by the sexually transmitted human papillomavirus. He had either gotten it from the showgirls or streetwalkers he hung out with as a young man, or the $2,000-an-hour escorts he hired as soon as he could afford them.

However it had happened, it wasn't recent. Richard hired escorts now to play different games. His favorite was an enactment: two prostitutes, one woman, one very well-hung man, having sex with each other while Richard pretended that the woman was a friend who had rejected him because of the size of his penis. He was only ever her friend, never a lover, and the two of them had agreed to this bargain, he imagined. Somehow this reverse fantasy, this sexualized double business arrangement, could bring Richard to orgasm. His constant anxieties about his penis size had only increased with age and every other approach to satisfaction usually failed. Business was his vitality; financial conquest, his virility.

As a bonus, this particular need of his meant relationships were out of the question. Richard didn't like relationships. He didn't like to share anything; he liked to own, even if it was just for an hour or two. As for children, he had been known to comment, "Either you pay for it by the hour, by the day, by the week, or for the rest of your life. . . ." But mostly he just wanted to avoid the question of an inheritance. He would leave behind billions, surely, but he wouldn't be obliged to. Obligations were for cowards.

After the initial shock of the diagnosis, he met the throat cancer head-on. The tumor itself was surgically removed, cutting a diagonal scar into his throat. He underwent an aggressive regimen of radiation. As the diseased tissue was eradicated in a daily dose of fire and pain, Richard focused on each step, just as he had done in business. Get through the session. Put on the narcotic patch. Work on producing saliva. Rest. Repeat. Accept that the feeding tube inserted into a cut in his side and strapped to his shoulder was an experience, not a weakness. How many men had poured high-caloric cocktails directly into their stomachs? He focused on the fact that the feeding tube was allowing his throat to heal. Besides, the concurrent chemotherapy made even the thought of solid intake nauseating.

When he had beaten the disease, he found that his taste buds had essentially ceased to function and he wasn't able to put on much of the thirty-odd pounds he had lost. But that was the price of victory. And he *had* won. If necessary, he would win again. That was what Richard Hawke did.

The Agusta A109 twin-engine helicopter was ready to take off when he arrived. It was gleaming white, with the blue silhouette of a hawk in flight on both sides. Hawke climbed into the private passenger cabin. He selected one of the five big, white leather seats on the port side and looked out the large rectangular window as the helicopter rose over the Hudson River. He looked down at the thick traffic on the West Side Highway. He felt good not having to be a part of that madness. He had risen above it literally and figuratively, by the efforts of his mind and will. He looked at Manhattan as he rose to the equal of his tower and then the larger buildings. He had succeeded in one of the toughest markets society had ever birthed, a city that crushed more ambition every minute of every day than any anvil in human history. That was a source of unending pride. And then to beat cancer as well—

It wasn't enough.

He had realized that when he returned from Germany after receiving his last treatment. He flew home, to his triplex apartment on 57th Street, over this city, over *his* city, and knew he needed more. He had always thought like a teenager trying to get out of Hell's Kitchen. He had matched the achievements of the greatest entrepreneurs from Andrew Carnegie to Steve Jobs. But that was like being at the top of the historic "B list." He had impacted culture but not the course of civilization. During his recuperation, Hawke read biographies of men like Julius Caesar, Napoleon, Lenin, and Mao Zedong. These men were like the treatments he had received in Germany: they cut out every sickness, every impediment to their vision. As with radiation and chemotherapy, that process was not gentle or sentimental.

And it doesn't always work, he thought. The mortality rate among stage four oral cancer victims was less than forty percent. The mortality rate among despots was even higher. But the theory was sound: big problems require powerful, targeted solutions. Lying in the clinic in Bad Mergentheim, he reasoned that there had to be a better way to impact the course of history, especially for a man with his resources.

He believed he had found that.

The helicopter reached JFK International in under ten minutes. Within a half hour of leaving his office Richard Hawke was on his jet. The sleek white aircraft had a Concorde-like design, improved for speed and silence with two small forward wings and rear diagonal struts that ran from the top of the tail to the rear center of the swept-back wings. He would be on his yacht off Saint Martin in less than two hours. He wanted to be away from the office, away from the United States for a while. He did not want to hear the melodramatic whining of newscasters and colleagues as events expanded and intersected and became something that even the visionaries or the tyrants had never imagined.

Sausalito, California

Jack Hatfield slept poorly.

What clung to his nostrils and ears, eyes and mind, was the carnage he had witnessed at the destruction of the Chinese clinic.

Jack had stayed at the bombsite until well after midnight. He had called Max and she had biked to the site with one of her smaller digital cameras on her back, in case the police were going to block car traffic.

Max's footage of the aftermath would bracket the cell phone footage Jack had taken.

After a few hours of sleep, Jack got out of bed shortly before six A.M. to look at footage on his computer and mark a few edits for Max. The phone beeped while he was making coffee. Caller ID showed a 240 area code. He had no idea where that was or who "Dover Griffith" might be. He let it go to voice mail and went back to the edits.

Max was one of the new generation of photographers. To her, everything about the medium—*hell, everything about the world,* Jack thought—was digital. Instant, disposable, fixable. He missed the days of watching film and, later, video on a machine built for that purpose. The sense of anticipation, waiting to see if you had captured the experience in a brief bit of footage or a still image, if your eye had found something in a moment that you had missed in the mad flow of events.

He finished his video notes, sickened by the high-definition video Max had recorded. Her zoom had found powerful images in the inferno that he had missed. Dolls and books. Immolated chopsticks. A medical school diploma. Jack wondered about the Hui Chinese doctor who had sat next to them at Bruno's that morning. His shift probably hadn't ended by the time the bomb exploded. He was probably dead.

Jack rubbed his temples, then went to the galley to pour himself a cup of coffee. He had walked and fed Eddie and made coffee when he got up, but as usual he got immersed in what he was doing and forgot to drink it. He made himself a tuna sandwich while he was up, and as his bagel toasted he listened to the message from Dover Griffith.

"I hope I have the right Jack Hatfield," the caller said. "I, uh—I work for the government, and I'm looking into something you reported about on *Truth Tellers* a few years back. If you could call me, I'd like to tell you a little more and get your thoughts. Thank you. 'Bye."

Jack sat at the table with his breakfast, scrolled to the number, and pushed the call button. Griffith picked up on the second ring.

"Mr. Hatfield—thanks so much for calling back! Hope I didn't wake you."

"No," Jack said. "I was up. Who are you and what can I do for you?"

"Off the record?"

"OK." It was amazing to Jack that a reporter's "OK" in that regard was taken as an oath. He didn't know any other profession outside of being a mobster where the handshake rule applied.

"I'm an analyst with the Office of Naval Intelligence," Griffith said, "and I want to talk about Squarebeam technology."

Jack didn't know if she had paused for dramatic effect, but the result was the same: letting the words hang there brought back all kinds of unpleasant thoughts for Jack. There were smugly reassuring sound bites from that patronizing autocrat Richard Hawke, interviews with fighter pilots whose controls went AWOL when they passed through the unfriendly

Squarebeam skies, and scientists who warned that the technology was cutting edge of the wrong kind: one had described it as a technological headsman's axe.

"There's a subject that doesn't send a thrill up my leg," Jack said.

"I know and I'm sorry, but it may be like one of those mutant cockroaches that adapts to the latest formula of bug killer."

Jack liked the metaphor. Griffith had bought herself some more time. "Go ahead," Jack said.

"Two complete, apparently targeted electronic system collapses on different days, different parts of the globe," Griffith said.

"What's the second?" Jack asked. He didn't have to ask about one of them. The woman was ONI. It was probably the SEALs Chinook in Afghanistan.

"An FBI vehicle in your backyard, off the 101."

"What were they doing?"

"Routine tail to the Chinese consulate."

China. Again, Jack thought. "I can find out about that," he said. "What makes you think this is Squarebeam-related?"

"Nothing," Griffith admitted. "Except that it's the only technology I've come across that can do anything like this. I guess I want to rule it out."

"So you've got a hunch, is what you're saying?"

"I don't know," Griffith said. "What's a notch or two below that? An apprehension?"

Jack spread the tuna on his bagel and took a bite. He liked Griffith. It was a rare intelligence analyst who could maintain a sense of humor in the face of the awful potentialities that crossed her desk every day.

"Let me make a call and I'll get back to you," Jack said. "You civilian or military, Miss Griffith?"

"Civvie."

That explained it. Jack had been a bit of a kidder, too, in Iraq. It just came out, in response to the stoicism of the military personnel around you. Maybe you went in the opposite direction to maintain your identity.

Griffith thanked him, gave him her private number, and hung up quickly, like she had been embarrassed to go outside the ONI for help—or was afraid of being overheard. That kind of fear, at least, was something Jack had never experienced.

He finished his tuna sandwich and gave Eddie the last of the bagel. Max arrived then, having slept a little better than Jack. She reminded him that she spent her early childhood in Mogadishu, where bombings were a daily occurrence, as government and antigovernment forces all but destroyed the nation in general and the capital in particular.

After calling Johnny Yu and making sure that there had been no further disturbance at the grocery, Jack went up on deck to phone his semi-buddy Carl Forsyth at the FBI field office.

San Francisco, California

The FBI's San Francisco field office is located on the thirteenth floor of a blocky white tower on Golden Gate Avenue. Forsyth was not superstitious. FBI agents dealt with facts, not fantasy. But the brawny six-foot former USC linebacker—who joined the FBI after being passed over in the 1988 NFL draft—couldn't help but wonder if maybe one of his former wives was jamming pins into a Carl Forsyth voodoo doll. Last month there was the car bomb they failed to intercept. The assassination gambit involving the President. And finally Jack Hatfield, of all people, saving him along with the city of San Francisco from an Islamic bomb plot. *Jack Hatfield.* The guy who the *Washington Post* once described as "the most incendiary man on television." Forsyth couldn't confirm or deny that; he'd never seen the man's show. It used to be on at ten P.M. He was asleep by then. But Hatfield had an annoying habit of showing up at crime scenes before anyone else, asking questions no one had the guts to ask. Most reporters knew that if they annoyed the cops, annoyed the FBI, they lost access to sites, personnel, and press conferences. So they lobbed softballs. Not Hatfield. He was never put on "access" lists, but he *still* showed up and got inside, still asked questions that he knew officials couldn't or wouldn't answer. Because to someone with Hatfield's experience the truth was apparent in any response, even "No comment."

The thing of it was, after sparring with Hatfield for the nineteen months he'd had this job, Forsyth admired the way the man ran over or around him. The man was free to follow a hunch to his target. He wasn't bound by policy and protocol the way Forsyth was.

Right now, Hatfield's beeline involved the dead FBI vehicle.

"I can't confirm or deny what happened," Forsyth said. "You know the drill."

"I do," Jack said. "You just confirmed it by not denying it."

Carl Forsyth made a face. He was about to contradict that but realized that anything he said would probably compound the lie.

The forty-year-old was sitting behind his small desk in his small, sunny field director's office. To his right was a cup of strong black coffee, his third of the morning. On his computer was a report from the vehicular forensics engineer whose lab was in a walled-off section of the parking garage. The checklist-style document detailed the condition of the field car that had been following the Chinese consulate van. All that mattered was the final line containing the engineer's analysis: *Complete electronic failure. No internal fault discovered.*

"Where are you getting your information, Jack?" Forsyth asked. It hadn't been on the news.

"You tell me who the two agents were, I'll tell you how I found out."

"You know I won't—"

"So there were two," Hatfield said. "That means this was a routine tail, you weren't expecting trouble, no need to ramp up the complement. One agent stayed behind the wheel trying to get a visual on the dashboard camera—which wasn't working. The other got out to eyeball. What did he or she see?"

"Jesus, Jack."

"Let me try this another way," Jack said. "I could

go through the morning's arrivals and figure out who they'd be routinely tailing—Russians, Mexicans, Arabs, Somalis. But that doesn't matter."

Forsyth allowed himself a little smile. At least Hatfield didn't have that.

"But let's say for the sake of argument they were Chinese," Jack said.

"Why would you say that?" Forsyth asked. The field director quietly damned Hatfield—and himself for having gotten cocky.

"Because there were two incidents yesterday, one of which you probably don't know about," Jack said. "Both involved Chinese."

Forsyth was about to sip his coffee. He stopped. "The clinic and—?"

"*Were* your guys following the Chinese?"

Forsyth caught his sigh before it became audible; he might be about to give in, but he sure didn't need to sound like it. A simple information swap would save time and more aggravation from Hatfield. "Off the record?"

"Yes."

"They were," Forsyth said. "And it was a routine tail." He swallowed some coffee, set his blue FBI mug down, and opened a window on the computer, preparing to type. "The other incident was?"

"SFPD has a report," Jack told him. "Chinatown, Chinese outsider threatened the Yu Market."

Forsyth accessed the report. It said little more than what Hatfield had just told him. "Reason?"

"Not sure," Jack said.

"What do you *suspect*?" Forsyth asked. Two could interpret non-answers.

"Maggie Yu, the daughter of the owner, thinks they wanted to buy the place. But no one knows why."

"They?"

"One guy inside, two guys in an Escalade. They drove off after the front man ran out of the store."

"You know more than the cops seem to."

"They deal in facts, Carl. That's never the whole story."

Forsyth's mouth twisted unhappily. Again. *Hatfield hunches, voodoo fears—what was this, a to-hell-with-facts morning? Or was it a trend? What next: would someone in D.C. suggest reviving Project Cassandra, named after the Ancient Greek prophet, the experimental use of psychics?*

"I recall you having some issues with the Chinese," Forsyth said.

"What, you mean the way Beijing is full of vampire politicians who act like aristocrats then drain our blood when we're not looking?"

"I remember you used a line like that on your show. Drew some angry words from the consulate here."

"My neck bleeds. My heart doesn't. Look," Jack went on, "the Yu Market and even the clinic may not be the big story here."

"What is?"

"Your car. That the Chinese killed it from the outside."

"Anything's possible," Forsyth said.

"But that's the one that scares me, and it should scare you," Jack said.

"Why?" Forsyth asked. "Honestly, Jack, I just got the forensics report. We're not even at that point yet. Do you know something about this?"

"*Honestly,* Carl, I don't," Jack said, throwing his own "honestly" back at him like a challenge.

"Right. You just happened to hear about the car?"

"Actually, I did," Jack said. "And I'm wondering aloud here if that's ground zero for these other incidents."

"That's a leap," Forsyth told him. "You know as well as I do that the Chinese *and* the Russians *and* the Iranians always have a lot of balls in the air."

"I do know that," Jack replied. "But I happened to be next door to the clinic last night when the car bomb went off."

Forsyth was very attentive. "And?"

"Faint smell in the air, like bananas," Jack said.

"Christ."

"Yeah. Not your average kitchen-made terrorist bomb. That's the stench of nitro. That was TNT—a lot of it. Enough to blow the car, most of the building, and all of its own components to hell. It's going to take an electron microscope to find traces of high explosives. You got any reports of dynamite being stolen?"

"Not that I'm aware of," Forsyth replied. "But it could have come from anywhere—"

"I know. Doesn't matter. Lone wolves wouldn't risk that kind of theft, wouldn't have the resources or cash to pull it off. We are dealing with something that has organization."

"I know," said Forsyth. "We wondered about the neo-Nazis. The system is helping immigrants and leaving red-blooded Americans in the cold, that kind of mentality, they decide to take out a piece of the system."

"That's a stretch," Jack said.

"I'm aware," said Forsyth. "You'd have to be a nut to take out a clinic, but nuts don't organize well on a large scale."

"That's thinking locally. Globally, you want to go over the list?"

Forsyth chuckled, the kind of chuckle when it isn't really funny.

Jack continued, "I don't know if Maggie Yu or your dead field car are a part of this but—"

"But we have to assume they are," Forsyth said. "Thanks, Jack. I'll let you know if I hear anything."

The field director hung up. For the first time in nineteen months it didn't hurt to say that. The guy was a pain in the neck but he knew his business. He was also right about one thing. Forsyth had better be concerned about a bigger picture. Not when they had a chance to do more studies of the car; not after they had a meeting about the agent debrief that was done when the agents were picked up after they called from a local restaurant; he had to worry *now*.

Forsyth called the dispatch desk.

"Eva, I want you to pull details from the other con-sulates. Have them follow every vehicle that leaves the Chinese consulate and stay with them until they return. I'll get you the order in fifteen minutes."

"Yes, sir."

"And make sure the agents are carrying change," he added. "In case they need to use a pay phone."

"Yes, sir."

Eva's voice had a little laugh in it. She'd obviously heard what happened to the other agents. She probably assumed their cell phones simply died. She also assumed Forsyth was making a joke. He wished he were.

It had taken the terrorist attacks of September 11 to get the intelligence agencies talking to one another with a real sense of cooperation. The nation had benefited from that. It had taken the Golden Gate incident to get Forsyth to talk to Jack Hatfield. Even if this turned out to be nothing, he had a sense that the nation would gain from that relationship, too.

It was a shame, he thought, that it took tragedy rather than a sense of the common good to get people— including himself—to cooperate. But it was definitely the right thing to do. He had to acknowledge that he was the one sticking pins in the doll and no one else.

Fairfield, California

Located nearly 3 miles east of Fairfield, California, 46 miles northeast of San Francisco, Travis Air Force Base encompasses nearly 6,400 acres and is home to the 60th Air Mobility Wing, a major component of the Air Mobility Command. With a workforce of 14,353 military members and civilian employees, it is also home to branch divisions of the Department of Defense, the Department of Homeland Security, and other government agencies.

With over 200 surveillance cameras, 30 radiation detectors, and over 1,000 security personnel, Travis is one of the most physically secure facilities in the United States. But like so much of the United States, an assault on the body was not the gravest threat. Chinese agents had been planning, testing, and executing cyber attacks on American systems for nearly a decade, starting in 2004 when hackers in the Guangdong Province code-named "Titan Rain" by the FBI retrieved sensitive information from military facilities, NASA, the World Bank, and other institutions. Two years later another Chinese team cyber-invaded the U.S. State Department, which enabled them to access computers in American embassies worldwide. That same year the Bureau of Industry and Security at the Commerce Department had to get rid of all its computers when it was learned the Chinese had compromised them. That did more than inconvenience a government agency: it literally shut Commerce down for over a month.

There were over a dozen other attacks ranging from small targets to large, from the Naval War College in Rhode Island to senatorial offices to the top secret files of Lockheed Martin's highly advanced F-35 fighter program to the already legendary GhostNet assault in 2009, which compromised over 1,200 systems in more than 100 nations.

Now the Chinese were launching a new front with

Sammo Yang as their trailblazer. There was a message to be sent to Washington, one that they would hopefully begin to receive and understand when he was finished here.

After escaping the tail, Sammo had intended to reconnoiter along the southern perimeter of Travis Air Force Base, confirming the usability of the attack position he had already selected based on satellite photographs. Then he would have returned to the consulate to stay. It would have required a few hours at most. But an environmental reclamation project unknown to Chinese intelligence had changed the flight paths of all the aircraft taking off from or landing at the air base. Now Sammo needed to find a new position. He was going to have to spend more time in Fairfield than he had planned.

He booked a room near the air base at the Cordelia Respite Inn, using the fake Taiwanese passport he carried. After signing in, he selected a few brochures from a rack, then sat in the lobby and pretended to read them while he assessed whether anyone was likely to pay attention to him, or to anything unusual. There was no doorman. One bellboy was more interested in the girl at the counter than he was in any cars that pulled up outside. Another bellboy stood in a corner chatting with a guest, a soldier. Sammo watched as a car stopped to drop off passengers. The soldier peered out, shook his head, resumed his talk. He was obviously waiting for his family to arrive. Neither bellboy went outside to help the arriving guests.

Perfect, he thought. None of them felt any need to be observant. His maneuvers would go unnoticed.

Sammo went out to the pool and sat for a while, ostensibly checking e-mails on his cell phone, but actually taking pictures of aircraft. His successful test on the helicopter in Afghanistan had confirmed that the EMP device required a direct line of sight that was no more than two thousand feet away from the target. None of the jets he was currently observing were suitable. They were not flying low enough and they appeared to be commercial flights, which meant the collateral damage would be severe. Beijing was targeting the military, not civilians. He needed a military plane specifically.

He returned to his room and got online to see if the air base organized any visits for civilians. He ran the language translation program on his computer and discovered that there were tours every Thursday for groups of twenty-five to forty people. However, the notices of heightened security protocols meant that it would probably be very difficult for him to wander away from the tour to get to the southern perimeter.

The situation was frustrating. The base had been selected because of the proximity of the southern fences to public properties—easy access. And there were no buildings in the way—direct line of sight.

Sammo tried to access the Federal Aviation Administration website to see what flight lanes were restricted to military use and if any of them were lower than two thousand feet. The FAA information was password protected, and he didn't have time to bounce the information back to Beijing.

Instead, he did a general word search of air space restrictions in the larger area of Solano County and found something promising: minutes from a Suisun City Board of Supervisors meeting that referred to a land development problem because the proposed building was in the approach pattern for Travis. It referred to a parcel of land off Highway 12 between Suisun City and Fairfield. Sammo looked up the filing from the developer. He didn't need a translator to recognize the logo of the Mother Hen Toy Company, an international corporation that had started out making chicken hand puppets in a British factory. They were looking for a height exemption to construct a North American distribution center.

"The lowest-flying aircraft will be more than eleven hundred feet above the four-story structure," said the proposal. "The sound concerns that affect general construction along the corridor will not impact this building, which will only be inhabited by day workers, only a few of whom will be assigned to the automated upper floors."

A four-story structure would be about sixty feet high. That would put the military aircraft approaching the air base well within range. All Sammo had to do was find a position along the flight corridor from which to operate the EMP device. He was sure there would be multiple suitable locations.

Sammo called the consulate to have a car sent for him. It would take about an hour, during which time he would have lunch in the hotel dining room.

The meal was delicious—he had assumed it would be, in a coastal town—and Sammo savored the taste of the fish, the tang of the capers, the rich crunch of the lettuce. It was useful to have nothing to do, at least for a short while. Not to relax but to acclimate. It was difficult for a foreigner not to stand out physically, far more challenging for him not to call attention to himself behaviorally.

Sammo used this time to observe, mimic, adapt. He watched tourists argue over their maps. Mothers with babies having lunch. The soldier who had been waiting in the lobby, now seated at a table with his family, taking pictures. Loud teenagers who were school age, yet not in school. Sammo adjusted his behavior in several small ways, not least of which was learning how to watch without staring, a mannerism that caught the attention of one or two people, albeit briefly.

The mannerism of a child, he reflected.

But the single-minded purpose of a child had to be partnered with adult skills. Those were qualities the American agents following Sammo did not possess. He knew the agents would try to find him. He knew how they would try. He knew they would already have begun.

And he knew he would be ready for them.

Sausalito, California

A day after the explosion, Jack still had a dull hum in his ear. In Iraq, IEDs would explode with a *pop* or *crack.* This one had been a *pow,* and it had settled somewhere inside his inner ear. He was recovering, but slowly. Jack had to crank up the sound on his cell phone, his computer, and he found himself actually looking at lips when he spoke with people. He used to complain about how noisy the marina was. Never again. When he got back to the boat and walked Eddie, bells that he knew were crisp and sharp sounded like dull gongs. He couldn't even hear some of the more distant gulls.

Back in his workspace, he sat on the stool by his editing computer and shifted his jaw from side to side in a useless effort to clear his ears. Giving up, he put the phone on speaker and called the personal cell phone number Dover Griffith had given him.

"How are you, sir?" she asked with a buoyant flourish.

God, Jack thought. This deep into the day back east and she was still chipper. Either Dover Griffith was a special human being or they were breeding them differently in her generation. When he was fifteen years younger, Jack was already being described as a curmudgeon—and that was by his friends.

"I'm good," he said, "except that the FBI doesn't know what killed their tail car. And I believe my guy. He's in a position to know and—well, interviewing people for years, you kind of know when they're telling the truth."

"Hence the name of your old show, *Truth Tellers*."

"Right. You have anything?"

"Not really. By the way, I've been watching some of those episodes on YouTube. Or rather, listening to them while I researched this. You didn't take any prisoners."

"Never. Someone comes on my show with an agenda, wants to attack me, they better be able to defend their position. It's a tactical choice, too. Naysaying is a great way to get windbags to articulate."

"And it makes good TV," Dover added quickly. "That wasn't really a criticism, just an observation. I loved the animal rights activists you had on."

"The one who didn't want eyeliner tested on bunny rabbits?"

"That's the one."

Jack grinned. The woman, who was in her fifties and twice widowed—once by a suicide—had actually suggested that new makeup formulas be tested on convicts instead of on animals.

"With the added benefit that these guys will look great in the showers," Jack had replied. His glib response ticked off the woman and PETA but earned him the first positive comments he had ever received from the gay community.

"Enough about me," Jack said. "Getting back to your 'Not really'; did you find anything at all?"

"Well, I can't tell you more than this, but over the past two years there has been extensive, direct contact between Richard Hawke and high-ranking officials of the Chinese government."

"You can't tell me because it's classified?"

"No," she said. "I can't tell you because we have nothing about those dealings on file. I got that information from *The Economist* and *Forbes,* and that's basically all they said. Though it was interesting," she added. "One of them openly wondered if the old Squarebeam technology was responsible for inadvertently bringing down that drone spy plane over Iran in December of 2011."

"Where would you be without the Fourth Estate?" Jack asked. That was no joke. Since 9/11, more than sixty percent of actionable intelligence came from journalists and ordinary citizens. "I suspect there are no files because Hawke has friends at the ONI, the CIA, and everywhere else in D.C."

"Most people at his level do," Dover replied.

Jack didn't want to say more in case either of their phones was being monitored; being harassed by the government was not pleasant, especially if they recruited the IRS and local police in the project. He'd known targets who were fined for disturbing the peace every time their dogs barked. But he had seen that kind of relationship before. One way intelligence agencies got personnel in-country was as ride-alongs with business entourages. He had witnessed secret deals with Saudi businessmen to gain access to Libya before the civil war, and pacts with Russian black-market tsars to get agents into Iran. In order to benefit from Hawke's access to China, the Department of Defense would certainly have agreed not to track or interfere with his business activities. It was simply assumed that no American in Hawke's position would do anything treasonous by design or stupidity.

"Did you do that research on your office desktop?" Jack asked.

"Yes," she said.

"You *do* know that those searches are stored and filtered for keywords, don't you?"

"I do. In fact, I'm counting on it. If my superiors tell me to stop, it means Hawke is under our protection, as you suggest. *That* means he's invisible to us, to the FBI, to the CIA, to Homeland Security, and to everyone else. And that leaves him or his people free to take any potentially unlawful, off-grid actions they want. I hate to think the worst of people, but it comes with the job."

"The rich and powerful aren't immune to bad political judgment," Jack said. "Charles Lindbergh was a racist and Nazi sympathizer. Lucille Ball was a registered Communist. So let's assume you're still worried about Squarebeam. What then?"

"I file a report about my concerns. The higher-ups are aware of the dangers of this technology, but they may not realize it could be adapted and abused. Hawke himself may not know."

Jack felt she was being dangerously naïve. It was also possible the ONI or one of the other agencies had helped to develop the technology and someone fed it to the Chinese for a lot of cash. But maybe innocence was also Dover Griffith's shield. The ONI might not be inclined to dismiss a valued analyst who was simply pursuing a reasonable lead. Not without first firing a shot across her bow.

"Maybe." "Might not," Jack thought. Those were not words that inspired confidence. If any of this was true, then coming down on Griffith, the ONI would also find him. And he had no facts, no protection of any kind, nothing to bargain with. He had to move this along before it made its way through channels in D.C. Besides, this was more than a matter of information being power. It was also news, and that's what he did for a living.

"So," Dover said, "before I talk to the other agencies, is there anywhere else we can go for information?"

"I was just thinking about that," Jack said. "There is one thing I can do."

"What's that?" Dover asked.

He told her, "I can call Richard Hawke."

Vancouver, British Columbia

On January 1, 2008, after existing separately for nearly a century and a half, three Canadian entities—the Fraser River Port Authority, the North Fraser Port Authority, and the Vancouver Port Authority—were joined to create the Vancouver Fraser Port Authority, popularly known as Port Metro Vancouver. Located on the southwest coast of British Columbia, Port Metro jurisdiction spanned over 600 kilometers of shoreline from Point Roberts at the U.S. border to Port Moody and Indian Arm, east along the Fraser River and north along the Pitt River. It is one of the largest tonnage ports in North America, with twenty-eight major cargo terminals and three rail lines. Port Metro is a trade hub for over 160 world economies, handling nearly 130 million tons of cargo each year.

Security at Port Metro met or exceeded the standards set by MARSEC—the U.S. Coast Guard Maritime Security system—which was a collaborative between all hemispheric ports and the Department of Homeland Security, the Homeland Security Advisory System, the National Terrorism Advisory System, the Commandant of the Coast Guard, and their corresponding Canadian institutions. The port maintained round-the-clock high-definition video surveillance, secure card-gate access, sophisticated gamma-ray screening equipment, radiation detectors at all terminals, hands-on passenger and baggage screening, and random tracking of personnel who passed through Customs. MARSEC euphemistically referred to this as "visa support inspection" and "foreign personnel studies," when it was, in fact, profiling. Any foreign individual whom agents felt was potentially suspicious earned a tail at least as far as the bar or motel they visited.

Among the visitors who received the least attention were those who entered the port without cargo. Lone Wolf fears were mostly centered on homegrown anarchists like radicalized Muslims or misguided Occupy Wall Street puppets. It was presumed that terrorists entering North America were doing so increasingly through the porous Southwestern border of the United States, typically under the protection of Mexican drug cartels; or via plane or boat that snuck in under the radar, quietly in the small hours of the night; or occasionally on private jets or yachts owned by oil sheiks who were happy to take American money but detested American morality and "multiculturalism"— a catchword that actually meant Christians and Jews.

The vessels whose personnel received the least attention were those that carried paying passengers. Among those were the 66,000 deadweight-ton freighters of the French *New Wave* fleet: the *Godard,* the *Chabrol,* and the *Truffaut.* Each working vessel provided simple accommodations for up to six paying guests. It was a comparatively economical way for travelers to visit multiple ports of call or even circumnavigate the globe.

The three-hundred-meter *Godard* was the freighter that made the round-the-world voyages, though passenger Liu Tang came aboard very late in an eastbound journey whose midpoint was Tangier. He joined the trip at the Port of Chiwan in Chiwan, Guangdong, China, having been detained by business. He had, in fact, applied for a partial refund— which, by the terms of his contract, could not be provided.

As he knew full well. Liu had never intended to go around the world. He merely wanted it noted that he had attempted to disengage himself from this voyage. That fact would show up on the manifest provided to MARSEC. It would suggest he had no urgent reason to be in Vancouver. He was coming to visit a half-brother in San Francisco—John Lee, of which there were over one hundred. That would immediately place him under low Level Three scrutiny: a border crossing that did not come with a ticking clock or imminent departure date. In short, it implied that he represented no timely terror threat.

The opposite was true. The threat was both real and immediate.

That was the problem with security measures, he thought as he gathered his things in his modest compartment. *They were designed to spot aberrations.* All Liu had to do was not stand out.

Part of his strategy was to establish a routine in which the slightly unusual was done in sight of all and seemed normal. In Liu's case, that was playing chess. He had a small board with plastic pieces that folded into a neat leather carrying case. He had a pair of books with illustrated games and tactics. He had videos he watched of classic games. He played by himself on deck and carried his board with him at mealtimes, even if he had no intention of using it.

The other part of his strategy was an ivory chess set, which he proudly displayed to the crew and his fellow passengers, telling them he had purchased it for his brother. The pieces were large and ornate, manufactured before international regulations banned the hunting of elephants for their tusks.

"Very rare," he told everyone in the limited English he had been taught.

But the real value of the chess set lay in how it would be wielded, like a chess piece in a game. Liu was going to use it as a false aberration—a distraction.

Having left the ship with the crew, Liu brought all his belongings through Port Metro Customs. He had one bag and a separate, expensive case for the ivory chess set. The inspecting agent, a big man with a big mustache, asked about the chess set. Liu winced and gestured that he didn't understand.

One of the deck boys standing behind Liu explained, "It's a gift for his brother in the States."

The agent handled one of the pawns and frowned. "This is *ivory*," he told Liu. "Contraband. No-no. Unless you have a certificate of antiquity, I cannot allow this into the country. The Americans won't let it in, either."

"Sorry?" Liu said.

"Elephants," the agent said. "Killing. It's illegal." He spoke loudly and slowly as if that would make the English understood.

Liu grew anxious. "Sorry? China."

"Yes, China is very lax about this sort of thing," the agent said. "We are not."

The deck boy grew restless. "Hey, can't you cut the guy a break?" The young man was in his twenties, Tasmanian, on his first voyage. He was eager to get to the city. "He's some kind of grand master. Always has his board and books."

"I don't care if he's the Queen's own tutor," the agent replied. "I can't let this in."

The deck boy made a face. "How about the rest of his stuff?"

The agent put the ivory chess set aside and went through Liu's bag, examined the lining, smelled his

toothpaste, gave a cursory glance at the chess books
and videos and plastic chess set, and pronounced the
bag fine.

The line behind Liu was growing longer. There
were several unpleasant remarks from the back.

"We're going to have to move this along," the agent
said.

The deck boy nodded and looked at Liu. He pointed
to himself. "Listen. I send to your brother." He pointed
at the ivory chess set, then made an arcing gesture
with his hand to indicate mailing. He asked the agent,
"You'll keep it here until I come back?"

"Safe and secure."

The deck boy made an OK sign to Liu and gently
pushed him forward. "It will be fine. Let's go."

Liu moved forward reluctantly. The deck boy wasn't
carrying any baggage, and the agent passed him
through quickly. Liu reached back longingly toward
the ivory chess set.

"It's OK," the young man assured Liu, moving him
along.

Liu's passport was still in his hand. With gestures,
the deck boy asked to see it. Liu handed it to him. The
young man took out his cell phone. "See here?" he
said. "I'm going to take your address—" he stopped.
"Oh. It's in Chinese. Right. Never mind. I can take a
picture and—"

Liu snatched back the passport as the young man
went to take the picture.

"No!" Liu said.

"Hey, I was just trying to—"

"Thank you," Liu said, pointing ahead. "Man here."

It took a moment for the young man to understand. "Someone is meeting you? Oh. I assumed you were flying down."

"No. Friend."

"Great," the deck boy said. "Then he—or she," he winked, "can deal with it."

The young man clapped Liu on the shoulder and then left the small, impersonal shell of a Customs building. Liu waited until he was gone, then stepped into the morning sunlight. The smell of the sea was strong as the harbor winds wrapped around him.

That could have been a disaster, Liu thought. *It would not do to have a record of my fake passport.* It would have been ironic after his strategy had worked so well. The inspecting agent had fallen for the distraction completely, stirring up trouble over a relatively harmless ivory chess set when the real threat was hidden inside seemingly innocent plastic chess pieces, which easily passed hand inspection by anyone who was preoccupied.

That was one reason the team had selected Port Metro after months of dry-run passages along the west coast of the continent. The trips had shown Vancouver to be the most predictable in terms of security: nothing ever happened here so the routine was always the same. In Seattle, Tacoma, Portland, and other U.S. ports, occasional efforts to smuggle drugs and guns—as well as use-it-or-lose-it federal anti-terrorist funds—had resulted in an ongoing FBI presence and random, intense security checks. There was also a rising animus between Americans and Chinese to consider. That was based on the resentment of how much American debt was held by Chinese banks.

We are the new Muslims, Jintao had warned them, speaking of the rise in hate crimes that had come to the attention of the consulate. The cell did not want to risk a vendetta crackdown at a port or air terminal in the United States.

Liu walked to the parking lot where a blue sedan was waiting for him curbside. There were four men inside. The mission did not require a team of that size except for something that must take place at the Peace Arch border crossing.

Liu looked back at the harbor as the driver paid the parking fee and headed out the rolling gate. He smiled before settling back into his seat. The smile was partly relief that things had gone as planned, but also because of the irony of what had just transpired. Port Metro was also one of the most environmentally responsible maritime facilities in the Western Hemisphere. Liu could not help but wonder what the board of directors would think if they ever discovered what had just eluded the system and entered the country.

Chapter 5

Suitland, Maryland

At the start of her junior year at NYU, Dover Griffith was an education major. Her interest in teaching was an outgrowth of the dinnertime debates her father and her surviving grandfather had around the dinner table every Sunday in Whitefish, Montana. Her grandfather had served with the U.S. 2nd Battalion of the 119th Regiment during the Battle of the Bulge. Her father had served in Vietnam. In the fall of 1967 when the North Vietnamese shelled the U.S. Marine outpost Con Thien, her father was a spotter that helped to direct the air counterattack during Operation Neutralize.

Each man had an identical view of war, that it was an unfortunate but necessary way to achieve peace. What they could not agree on was who started them.

Her grandfather maintained that it was the military prodding the politicians to get them in the game, while her father believed it was all the work of politicians.

"If they said the right words to one another, war would never be necessary," he said.

The debate went on for years, like war itself. Ideological ground was taken, surrendered, retaken. It changed with the seasons, was colored by world events, was supported by this history book or that, which the men had read and bookmarked and brought to the table. It was fascinating but frustrating. Like religion, there seemed to be no absolute, undeniable truth. Dover wanted to learn more with a vague idea of becoming a teacher. She wanted to be, to a lake of youthful faces, what her father and grandfather were to her: "incoming," as her grandfather called it with a laugh. An artillery barrage of ideas.

Dover returned to school her junior year with a suitcase full of new clothes she and her mother had bought at the outlet stores in Clinton, New Jersey. But they hadn't found any belts she liked, so she took a short subway ride downtown one morning to buy some at the Century 21 clothing store. The doors were locked when she arrived so she went across the street to Burger King to have coffee and read the *Village Voice* while she waited.

She was just sitting down when American Airlines Flight 11 plowed into the north tower of the World Trade Center. The impact rocked the floor, killed the chatter, and dropped a gray shroud over the sun. The

initial, hollow bang—"like someone tossing a fire-
cracker into an empty trash can," as she later described
it—was followed by an odd assortment of clunks,
pings, grinding, and then cries.

Still holding her coffee, she followed the other
breakfast patrons outside. The impact zone was on the
opposite side of the tower, but they could see the
smoke rolling skyward, saw the glitter of glass falling
in the morning sun, heard shrieks as large shards of
the glass façade struck asphalt, concrete, and pedestrians on the corner of Vesey and Church Streets. A
man ran toward them with his hand across his face,
his eyes wide, blood streaming down his chin onto
the topknot of his tie; the rest of his face had been
cleanly severed. It appeared as if the man's nose had
been slashed away.

Dover looked around, saw a newsstand on the corner of Liberty Street, and bought his entire supply of
five disposable cameras. She took pictures of people.
She stopped when a second, more ferocious explosion
followed a roaring directly overhead, as United Airlines Flight 175 smashed into the south tower. Dover
backed over to Zuccotti Park until she could see the
shattered face of the skyscraper. She did not turn her
camera up to the ragged scar, to the people standing
on jagged girders, to those who could no longer endure the heat and choking black cloud. The sound, the
physical impact, the impossibility of the images rolling out in a kind of slow motion had paralyzed her
torso. Later, when she had the pictures developed, she
saw that she had continued to snap photographs—of

her feet, of papers landing on the street, of other people's legs—everything below knee-level.

She continued to move backward through the park and reached Broadway, where police officers were starting to block streets, to push people to the east. Dover moved with them, hearing snippets of people who were talking on cell phones—she did not yet own one—and crackling sounds from radios as she passed police officers and firefighters. She reached the East River, where there were herds of business people incongruously mingled with joggers and merchants from the Fulton Fish Market. The burning towers were visible over the tops of the low-lying structures. The Brooklyn Bridge was behind her.

And then the north tower fell. The moan from the mass of people was a sound of such pain as she hoped never to hear again. But it brought her back to life. She still had three unused cameras. She resumed taking pictures of faces and the shared horror and the longing to be in contact with their neighbors. She did not see anyone praying, which she thought was strange. Then she realized the conflict: who could believe in God at a moment like this? That would come later, when people sought meaning in the incomprehensible.

I need to be a part of that process, she remembered thinking then. That was the moment she turned from the idea of educating a classroom to educating the human race.

With speed born of a strong, sudden epiphany, she literally ran the two miles back to NYU. Before the university offices shut down so out-of-town employees could get home, she gathered up the papers needed to change her major. Then she found a pay phone and called home. Her mother was tearful and relieved to hear from her.

Her father said quietly, gravely, "Now three generations of Griffiths have been to war."

That was a fact. Her legs gave out as she stood at the pay phone on University Place. She fell to her knees, crying hysterically, and had to be helped to her dorm room by an off-duty campus security guard.

Dover had not regarded the job at the ONI as a logical fit with her experiences on September 11, 2001. It made sense on a certain level: evil men had attacked the nation, and she was helping to hunt for other evil men. But it did not satisfy her soul the way taking those photographs or writing about the experience for her hometown newspaper had. The power of journalism was made clear and poignant by the dozens of belts that were sent to her mother's house with notes thanking Dover for her front-page article. She missed that connection with readers, and in a strange way it had given her conversation with Jack Hatfield an unexpected misting of melancholy: she had to imagine that he missed it, too, more acutely than she had. Protecting a San Francisco landmark and thousands of lives as he had saved his city from Islamic terrorists was not the same thing as digging into minds and sparring with words and testing your belief system against that of another. She saw how lost her father was when her grandfather died. It wasn't just the end of making memories. It was the end of a certain, very personal kind of sharing. The same kind a passionate man like Jack Hatfield developed with his listeners.

Dover was not surprised when she received a phone call from administration.

So Hawke is protected, she thought. Someone inside the government was aware she was investigating and wanted her stopped.

What surprised her was that she was told to report immediately to Commander Carrie Morgan, Protocol Administrator. She had never met the woman, who was several leaps above the officer she reported to in her chain of command. Either she had hit the research jackpot or stepped in "deep doo-doo," as her mother put it.

Dover hurried to the ground floor executive wing, which she had never had cause to visit. She followed the signs, found room 112, and did not have to wait. Her gut burned with anticipation. Not the good kind, like the night before Christmas, but the principal's office kind. As she walked through the inner door she knew this was going to be a dressing-down. She had seen naval personnel relaxed, and she had seen naval personnel in engagement mode. Sitting behind her gunmetal desk, surrounded by three walls of proud citations and photographs with senators, vice presidents, and one president, the fifty-something commander was looking at a brass-framed iPad, a secure unit made especially for the military.

Dover was not invited to sit. She stood in a civilian

imitation of "at ease"—her hands behind her back, her spine as straight as nerves would allow, her lips pressed together.

"We're putting you on an open-ended unpaid furlough," Commander Morgan said, still scanning the tablet.

"Wow."

The commander looked up, her eyebrows arched. "I'm sorry?"

"That's—I'm sorry, ma'am, but that's Guantanamo-Bay-speak for 'You're fired.' And for what? For doing my job? For trying to find out if—"

"Stop!" Commander Morgan said.

Dover's mouth clapped shut. That was her dad talking, Master Sergeant Griffith. Her response was reflexive.

The officer set the tablet aside and folded her hands. It was a classic, formal, military, how-dare-you posture. "You have been in contact, on ONI time, on ONI premises, on ONI business, with a hostile source. As per your employment contract, Human Resources will review the matter with your superiors to determine the correct course of action. However, your file will be amended to include that last comment, which I find personally repugnant."

"Wait—what?" Dover said. She was still working on the first part of the commander's statement. "What 'hostile'—?" She was utterly confused.

"Jack Hatfield," the commander said.

Dover smirked. She couldn't help herself. "Do you mean that calling a journalist who has limited media access is more of a threat than finding out if a billion-aire international industrialist is playing on an enemy team—a tycoon who has the resources to hire an army to topple a third-world government or buy an election?"

"Your investigation of Richard Hawke is not the matter on the table," Commander Morgan said.

"Ma'am, it *should* be!" Dover said.

"If taken up at all, the question will be dealt with by appropriate staff in appropriate departments at appropriate levels," the commander said. Her gaze was fixed on Dover. "You know the protocol for contact with outside sources. You check to see if they are on a no-go list before you send an e-mail, place a call, or have a drink with them."

"Right, but I never thought a guy who saved a city would be *on* that list!"

"Saved by vigilante, unilateral action, the way he does everything," the commander replied, rapping a knuckle on her tablet. "Jack Hatfield is an inflammatory, anti-authority voice whose help we *do not* solicit and whose favor we *do not* nurture."

"Ma'am, if you'd heard the call, you'd know I said some of those same things to Mr. Hatfield—"

"We did not listen to what you had to say, nor is the tone of your contact the issue."

"I understand, but I'm only trying to explain the *reason* for my call—and that reason is important—"

"We're finished here, Ms. Griffith. You will be contacted within a week as to the final disposition of this matter."

"Commander, *please* let me finish. I'm worried that Hawke technology may have taken out our chopper *and* an FBI vehicle."

Commander Morgan regarded the young woman flatly. "Do you have evidence to support your claim?"

"Well, no. That's what I've been trying to explain. Our files are bare. I contacted Hatfield to see if *he* had specific information about Squarebeam technology interfering with electronic systems."

"Did he?"

"He did not," Dover admitted. "He was going to check with FBI contacts."

"Did he do so?"

"Yes."

"What did they tell him?"

"Nothing," Dover said—though she knew she was doomed. "They—they said they were going to look into it."

"You're aware that we have FBI contacts," Commander Morgan said. "Pretty good ones, in fact. Director Steve Russell. You've heard of him?"

"I have."

"You grasped, to some degree, that Mr. Hawke is a person of considerable influence in both governmental and military circles. One who might not appreciate being investigated."

"I did."

"You knew something of Mr. Hatfield's reputation as a loose cannon who has a vendetta against people like Richard Hawke and Lawrence Soren."

"Ma'am, I wouldn't put them quite in the same category—"

"And that Mr. Hatfield has been banned from travel in Great Britain, one of our closest allied nations, whose Royal Navy Service Police provide us with a substantial flow of useful data."

"Yes."

"Yet in light of all that, it did not occur to you that contacting Hatfield might be reckless and irresponsible, given the fact that your search is not only largely outside your job description but involves a man who has security clearance far in excess of your own."

"I was focused on trying to understand a problem that killed thirty-eight SEALs," Dover said, exasperation in her voice. "Before it could kill again."

"A *potential* problem," the commander said. "A hypothetical link. One that I suspect even you would not have classified as Red Level Urgent."

"No," Dover said. "Not yet."

"'Not yet,'" the commander said. "We are in the business of connecting dots, not drawing free form. And we have people on the ground in Afghanistan researching the problem. We have top analysts in Washington studying all possibilities. You have created a needless manpower distraction by raising a red flag. The door is behind you."

Dover stood there. She had that same paralysis she had experienced at the World Trade Center. Something wrong, destructive, and completely unexpected had shaken her world and her confidence. She didn't know where to turn or how to get it back.

A hot, impatient look from the officer got Dover moving. Her body turned and her legs moved, but her brain was still looking down at the woman's hard expression, turning the words over and sideways. She was able to comprehend the logic. Don't jump to conclusions. But as they had learned in events ranging from Pearl Harbor to 9/11, sometimes the ladder is missing rungs. If you don't leap, you stand still.

Because she was being sent home pending a departmental review, Dover did not have to suffer the indignity of being escorted from the complex by armed MPs. She was allowed to get her bag from her desk—under the cross-armed, unsympathetic gaze of her supervisor, Lieutenant Commander Ward—and nothing more. None of her coworkers in adjoining cubicles looked up as she passed.

I guess they connected the dots, Dover thought bitterly.

She walked to her car, got in, and sat there. She was too angry to punch the wheel. She might damage it. And crying wasn't her style. Watching fellow human beings jump from windows of the World Trade Center was something she'd wept over when it hit her as she called home that dark day. This was simply enraging.

The ONI would still be monitoring her personal calls—which, it occurred to her, was probably the main reason she had not been fired, so they would still have a legal claim to her privacy. So she could not call Jack Hatfield from her cell phone or send him an e-mail. But that wasn't going to stop her.

The last time Dover had a lot of downtime, between

customers wanting to know where to find a book at the Strand, she had written a play. This time, she intended to do something more ambitious.

She was going to see if her suspicions about Hawke were right.

San Francisco, California

For Maggie Yu, the basement of the grocery store was more than just a storage area. It was a temple in which she revealed her soul and connected with those that stretched back nearly 1,500 years.

The cellar was just four cinderblocks, a cement floor, and two central, rusted iron support pillars that reinforced the beamed ceiling against earthquakes. The only construction Maggie's father had added was a small oak closet in which they kept the cleaning supplies. Lit by two bulbs hanging at either end and slightly longer and wider than a trolley car, the basement was filled with ever-changing columns of wooden crates and cardboard boxes, all of them piled and arranged haphazardly to create a maze-like space. Those aisles were barely wide enough to walk through, which is why Maggie liked them. In the back of the basement was a Diebold safe Johnny had purchased at auction when the 1989 Loma Prieta earthquake forced the condemnation of a warehouse in Santa Cruz. Something had told him to buy the knee-high iron box: researching the serial number, he discovered that it had originally belonged to a failed Chinese bank in the 1880s.

Maggie came down here every day in the afternoon, took off her shoes and socks, changed into the traditional white *gi* that hung on a hook beside the closet, donned her well-worn black belt, and spent a half hour practicing her kung-fu forms. Barefoot, she did not stop if she stepped on an apple stem or crate splinter or nub of concrete. In combat, one could not afford to be distracted by the unexpected. She would simply shift her weight slightly to minimize the discomfort. It was a philosophy that applied to life as well as to combat.

Each day there were hundreds of different moves and combinations of moves to execute, all of them replicating the animals that first inspired ancient Shaolin monks to create a weaponless form of combat. Maggie loved kung fu not just for its effectiveness and the balance it gave to her life, but also its universality. Eagle, snake, crane, monkey, tiger, scorpion, even snail—there were styles to suit the age, temperament, and physical makeup of every human being. This unity of body, spirit, purpose, and community had enabled men, women, and children to build towns that outlasted kingdoms.

Maneuvering through the tight alleys of goods and perishables, bent at the knees to remain poised and flexible, Maggie drove through imaginary foes, moving up, ahead, down, backward, turning in tight screw-like moves, shouting a *kiai*—a triumphant shout with each blow that helped to unnerve an adversary and focus one's own energy. Her voice filled the space bordered by crates solidly packed with cans and bottles, cellophane bags and Styrofoam containers. Physically and psychologically she owned the space through which she moved.

And Maggie knew this space better than her own bedroom because she was so focused here. She was familiar with its every structural nuance and sound, the dry smell beneath the fresh vegetables, its seasonal temperature shifts. She knew from the sound in the pipes whether a bath was being run or a toilet flushed above or to either side. She could feel the larger trucks that rumbled by outside.

It was because her energy so completely filled this space that Maggie was able to feel when there was something wrong. It literally stopped her in mid-form, as she was moving from side to side in the sinuous, lizard-like dragon style. Somewhere beyond the crates there was a faint buzzing sound, like a fly inside cupped hands. She moved forward silently, on the balls of her feet, listening. It was coming from the closet. She walked over, laid a palm on the door. It wasn't vibrating; the hinges were secure. She opened it, crouched, tucked her head inside.

A dustpan hung from a nail on the back wall. She rose and touched a fingertip to it. The humming stopped. She rotated it aside and placed her palm on the back of the closet. There was a barely perceptible movement in the wood. The movement was steady and sustained, not like distant jackhammering or paving.

Like an aircraft turbine, she thought, remembering her last flight to China to visit relatives.

She wondered if any of the other shops or restaurants felt it. Probably not; she hadn't heard it upstairs. It was most likely the subterranean wall picking up the sound through the earth. Whatever it was, it didn't seem to be coming closer. Maggie would not let it concern her. She resumed her workout, closing the closet door with the heel of her foot as she pivoted 180 degrees. Her *sifu*s had taught her that all of life is training, from walking down the street to brushing your teeth to making love.

At least you've got two of those going for you, she thought with a self-deprecating laugh. She made her way back through the stacks of groceries with her arms raised, hands drooping, praying mantis style. That was the price of being a celebrated black belt: there weren't a lot of men, even martial arts school brothers, who saw the sex appeal of a woman able to drop them with a finger pressed to the side of the nose.

There was nothing Maggie could do about that. The universe would provide the right man or not. That was something else kung fu taught her: she did not need anyone else to complete her.

Sausalito, California

Jack went on deck to call Richard Hawke. This wasn't a call for confined spaces: he needed sun and sea and the strength that came from knowing he could go anywhere in the world simply by pointing his boat outward. The sea could take him anywhere, from

Canada to Antarctica, from Osaka to London. One needed only fuel, supplies, and the fearlessness to go. Without realizing it, Jack had conducted his life that way. He had run his talk show that way.

Don't be afraid of what's out there. Just *go*.

Jack sat on a deck chair facing the ocean and called Hawke Industries; the main number was on the website. He asked to be transferred to Mr. Hawke's office. A woman answered. She introduced herself as Bahiti.

"This is Jack Hatfield," he said. "I'm a reporter. I'd like to speak with Mr. Hawke."

"He isn't here, sir. May I help you?"

"Being there or not doesn't really matter these days, does it?" Jack asked pleasantly. "You can forward the call."

"He isn't receiving calls at the moment. May I be of assistance?"

"OK," Jack said. "I'll play the game. I believe Hawke technology is being used to murder Americans. Can you assist me with that?"

The woman was silent for a long moment. "Mr. Hatfield, I'm going to transfer you to our press department."

"Bahiti, if you do that I'm only going to hang up and call again," he said. "I've got an open schedule and unlimited minutes—I can do this all day."

"As I said, Mr. Hawke is not taking calls. If you like, I will pass along your number."

"What I'd *like* is to talk to Mr. Hawke within the

next few minutes, before I put my suspicions on the airwaves and cybernets." He was bluffing, of course, but Bahiti would not know that. And he was betting she didn't want to be the last person he spoke with. "My report will make a great follow-up to the coverage of the Navy helicopter that went down in Afghanistan. Knocked out, I believe, by Hawke technology."

The woman was silent. Bahiti was an Egyptian name. He pictured her on the other end of the phone, his journalist's mind imagining her backstory. If she stood up to him, figured out how to deflect him, put him on permanent hold, she was older, experienced. If she came back—

"Please hold, Mr. Hatfield."

—then she was younger, a beauty for the front office, just the first line of defense. Jack expected that he was being passed along to an executive assistant of some stripe.

"Mr. Hatfield?" asked a high, youthful voice. "Phil Webb, executive assistant to Mr. Hawke."

"Hi, Mr. Webb."

"Just Phil, please."

"OK, Phil."

"So—are you the Jack Hatfield of *Truth Tellers,* the man who saved San Francisco?"

"Well, I saved a part of it," Jack said.

"The Golden Gate Bridge is more than 'a part,'" Webb said.

"Right. I also kept Alcatraz safe for tourism." Jack could tell when he was being *schmoozed,* a butteringup that stopped ever so slightly short of being patronizing. He liked that less than he liked outright stonewalling. "I assume Bahiti passed along my request to speak with your boss?"

"Yes, and for the record Mr. Hawke considers his employees to be partners and coworkers, not subordinates," Webb said. The young voice had a sharp little rebuke in it now.

"My apologies," Jack said. "So you're his partner in taking down American choppers?"

There was the briefest hesitation; Jack had been expecting it.

"Mr. Hatfield, Bahiti passed along your request along with that rather alarming accusation. It is extraordinarily wrong."

"I'm not surprised to hear you say that, Phil. Your saying so also carries no weight whatsoever."

"You are as plainspoken as I've heard."

"I find it saves a lot of time."

"And made you few friends, I bet."

"I've got all the friends I want," Jack said. "What I need is information. Are you going to transfer the call or do I leave a big hole in my story filled with a very small 'no comment' from Mr. Hawke?"

"That would be untrue," Webb told him. "Hawke Industries absolutely and vigorously denies your statement."

"I didn't say 'Hawke Industries,'" Jack pointed out. "I said there would be a 'no comment' from Mr. Hawke."

Another short silence. Phil Webb obviously wasn't

used to volleying with someone who had a strong backhand, just corporate counterparts with loud, threatening forehands at best.

"That, too, would be untrue," Webb said. "He will give you a personal statement."

That one caught Jack off guard. "He'll talk to me?"

"That's what you asked for," Webb replied.

"Great. When?"

"You're still in San Francisco, Jack?"

His mind growled, *It's Mr. Hatfield to you, punk,* but he answered, "Yes. Why?"

"He will be sending his private jet to San Francisco International to collect you. It should be there in about five hours."

"To 'collect me' for what?" Jack asked.

"To talk," Phil said. "That *is* what you wanted?"

You were just played, Jack thought. The talk with Phil had been a stall. Hawke was either in the room or his flunky coworker was texting him as they chatted. In either case, he had underestimated the kid.

"That's what I want," Jack said.

"Very good," Webb said. "I'll text you the specifics as soon as I have them. At this number?"

"Yep."

"Excellent. We'll be in touch. Oh—you have a valid passport, do you not?"

"I do." That was a dig, Jack felt. The guy obviously knew about his troubles in the United Kingdom.

"Bring it with you, please."

"Why? Am I leaving the country?"

"You'll want an ID other than your driver's license."

Phil hung up. Jack ended the call.

"Now what the hell was that all about?" he wondered aloud. His first instinct was that Hawke was guilty as hell and wanted to offer him a bribe, face-to-face—or else to Squarebeam his own plane with Jack on board. *No,* he thought, *that would be too high profile. If he wants me dead, there are quieter ways to do it. A mugging, an engine fire while I'm asleep, food poisoning at Bruno's.*

Whatever it was, whatever little trace of puzzlement the industrialist had thrown into him with that curve, he felt energized. It was good to be a working journalist in the thick of it.

He was about to go inside to make lunch when the phone chimed. It was a D.C. exchange, caller ID: "Washington Metro." He had an idea who that would be.

"This is Jack," he said.

"Hey, it's Dover," said the caller.

"Pay phone?" Jack asked.

"Yeah. I'm being monitored. And I've been furloughed. Not because of Hawke, though."

"Oh?"

"No, because of you. You're *persona non grata ad absurdum.*"

"That's a lot of Latin for an ex-TV talk show host," Jack said. "Though now that I think of it, I guess I've been cursed at in most languages."

"Which is kind of ironic," Dover replied, "since it's our English friends you seem to have pissed off the most."

"Ah. ONI is worried about their alliances."

"Exactly."

"Well, I'm sorry about your being collateral damage," Jack told her. "But if we can pin this down, maybe they'll reconsider."

"Why, you got something? You spoke with him?"

"Not yet," Jack said. "He's sending a jet to 'collect me,' as they put it."

"Wow. Like a trophy," Dover said.

"More like garbage," Jack replied, still smarting from Webb's respectful condescension. "As long as I get to talk to him, who cares?"

"You don't really think he'll tell you anything, do you?"

"Not in words, no," Jack said. "But if he's bad, I'll know it."

"Right. The 'interviewing people for years' B.S. detector thing."

Bringing up the reference, Jack did not detect any cynicism or doubt in her voice. Dover was letting him know she'd heard what he told her earlier and understood.

"Hey, I've got an idea," Jack said. "If you have nothing to do, why not come out here and work with me on this?"

"You mean compound my sins by actually collaborating with the enemy instead of just talking to him on the phone?"

He was looking out at the ocean. "Pretty much. The benefits suck, but the view is terrific."

"I should probably think about that."

"What for? 'Furlough' in D.C. means 'You're being fired through due process.' Like I said, if we tie Hawke to something rotten, you'll probably get a raise and a civilian commendation, maybe even an office instead of a cubicle."

"How did you know I have—had—a cubicle?"

"You were talking low. You didn't have a door to close."

"Nice," she said. "Actually, there's something out there I want to have a look at. How far is Murrieta?"

"In Riverside County?"

"South, yes—the Temecula Valley."

"About seven hours by car," Jack said. "There's an airport pretty nearby, though. Ontario. Pretty big place. You might even find a direct flight."

"All right. Screw it. I'm coming. Where and when?"

He gave her the name of the boat and where it was docked, told her to wait until tomorrow.

"In case I don't come back from wherever he's flying me, at least you won't waste the airfare."

"Wait—you don't know where you're going?"

Jack smiled. "Dover, you may find this difficult to believe, but that's been the story of my life."

San Francisco, California

The throaty hum of the generator rolled across the rubble of the destroyed Chinese-American Free Clinic. The generator had been hauled from the Eastern Rim

Construction van as soon as the police gave the all clear for recovery crews to enter the site. It was powering two different searches.

One search was for any outlets and electrical systems that were still functioning. The excavation and repair crews could run their lights and equipment more easily on internal electric lines than on the generator. The team members could conduct this search with handheld equipment.

The second search was for structural integrity, specifically looking for rooms in the remains of the clinic that were safe to send team members into. To conduct this search, one of the Eastern Rim workers was using his laptop to maneuver a robotic crawler through the half-collapsed shell of the clinic. The crawler had been purchased with Department of Emergency Management funds and was usually used after earthquakes. It was the size of a red wagon and had four wheels, as well as a 360-degree omnidirectional radar system that would pick up hidden structural flaws.

That's what the crawler and its human handler should have been searching for. In actuality, the operator was using the crawler's video and radar images not to look up or around the rooms of the clinic, but to look down. He was studying the floor for something that blueprints of the clinic had revealed.

He was searching for a section of the building that would be the key to the next phase of the cell's operation.

Sausalito, California

"It's not only freakin' crazy, it's disgusting, man. You're what Nixon was to Cambodia. You're creating the carbon footprint of a small army!"

Abe Cohen was responding, with eyes wide and mouth even wider, to the news that Jack would be taking not just a gas-guzzler jet to see Richard Hawke, but a supersonic gas-guzzler jet. Jack was sitting on a deck chair, waiting for the text from Phil Webb and drinking a Beck's. He had been reading about Hawke on his iPad and enjoying the tranquility before Abe and Doc popped over separately. Abe had motored in on his own boat, a Defever forty-nine-foot pilothouse, which he used for getaways when the stress of the city got to be too much.

"You should talk," Doc Matson said as he pulled over a chair and flopped down. Doc had been at the marina having lunch with an old friend, Lieutenant Commander Ben Mabry, Chief of Waterways for the Coast Guard's Vessel Traffic Service, Sector San Francisco. He happened to come by just as Jack was telling Abe about his upcoming trip.

"What do you mean?" Abe asked.

"Even your softened hippie brain should realize you're not doing the environment any good with your weekly trips halfway to Japan in that diesel-burning monstrosity you sail," Doc said.

"Which I had refurbished, at great personal expense, to burn ultra-low-sulfur diesel," Abe fired back. "My boat has literally been blessed by a priest who works with the EPA. Plus, diesel engines get better fuel economy than gas. The Farallons are less than a fifty-mile round trip, which means I'm probably producing less CO_2 than either of you two clowns."

"Not me," Jack said. "I mostly keep the *Sea Wrighter* where she is and I bike wherever I can."

"Except every time you drive your Mercedes to the city."

Doc cut in. "What Jack has is called a 'job,' Abe."

Abe grimaced at Doc. "And I guess your 'job' requires a vintage Mustang and your Piper whatever-it-is?"

"Piper Cherokee," Doc said. "Like your hybrid car is helping the world."

"What's wrong with *that*?"

"You run it on electricity generated by a nuclear power plant—which you've picketed, I'd like to remind you."

"I use about one electron of power," Abe protested.

"You shouldn't be using any," Doc said. "It's hypocritical."

"You're insane, Doc," said Abe.

"I would describe him as 'prone to charming filibuster,'" Jack grinned.

"You're *both* being idiotic. I'm a visionary and you just can't accept that."

"Yeah. I wish to hell I was a visionary like you," Doc said. "A product of what your generation did to our universities. You started calling yourselves visionaries to justify how you hounded out your legitimate professors, the older ones, the ones who deserved to be authorities because they had the sense and the knowledge to teach, as opposed to the airheads you replaced them with who think that knowledge of a subject consists of how they *feel* about it. That's who's running the universities now. They hardly deserve the term 'universities.' They've become plunder of graduate students' labor. The plunder of all lost ideals everywhere and in all time since Abraham tried to slay Isaac but was saved by a counter-hallucination. The administrations sought out for admission, scholarships, hiring, promotions, those who are anything but white males. Liberalism is the stereoisomer of Nazism and its obsession with racial purity. The universities prove that. They stopped gauging skill, talent, even work ethic. They fostered a generation of incompetents not seen in the history of the Republic, incompetents who created their own fields of study to justify their lack of productive scholarship in the real fields of learning. Those fertile fields which once blossomed with a flora so vibrant and diverse, reduced in size and offering to 'women's studies,' 'black studies,' 'Chicano studies,' 'lesbian studies,' 'gay studies,' all non-sciences created by jingoists with tenure desperate for attention and respect and as much getting laid as they can get along the way."

"The yuppies made those distinctions, not the hippies," Abe snapped. "My friends and I were products of our own visionary imaginations. You should wish you were me! We need soldiers for progress, not soldiers for war."

"It was three or four subterraneans like you who destroyed all that was decent in America," Doc said. "Allen Ginsberg, Timothy Leary, William Kunstler, and Bella Abzug."

"They are my cultural heroes," said Abe.

"Leary popularized LSD and destroyed the minds of thousands who then destroyed the thinking of millions. Ginsberg pretended to be a Jewish prophet when he was a Communist pervert who preyed on young boys. Kunstler perverted the law and rode the freedom buses south to get laid. While Abzug with her pseudo-liberationist rants against men twisted tens of thousands of young women's minds, making them into man-hating harpies."

"What we need," Jack interrupted, "is to ease up a little. The problem is nobody's listening to anyone else."

"Because they're mostly talking nonsense," Doc said, thrusting his chin toward Abe.

"I rest Jack's case," Abe replied. He was pacing, working out his perpetual agitation.

"You once did some fancy math on a cocktail napkin, told me how many future generations I'd destroyed because of all the people I'd killed in my life," Doc said. "I agreed with you. And for the record, I hated every bullet or blade I put in a man. But you didn't do the math about how many generations I'd saved by getting rid of genocidal lunatics. I'm still waiting for that list."

"It's impossible to know," Abe shrugged. "Some of those people you saved may have grown up to be killers."

Jack looked at him. "Abe, did you really just say that?"

"Statistically, it makes perfect sense," Abe told him. "Each year, there are nearly nineteen thousand homicides in the United States alone. Surely a few people Doc saved would be responsible for some of those."

Doc and Jack stared at Abe, then at each other. Jack leaned over, put his hands over Eddie's ears, and said, "Don't listen now, dear. I'll tell you about it afterward."

Doc laughed. He recognized the reference, the story of how during a screening of *Oliver Twist,* Winston Churchill had put his hands over his poodle Rufus's eyes when Bill Sykes was about to drown his dog.

Abe thought they were laughing at him. "Fine, have more fun at my expense," he said.

"What other reason is there to keep you around?" Doc asked.

"Apparently none," Abe said. He stopped at the gangplank. "I will take my leave."

"That's a military term, you know," Doc said.

"What about 'up yours'?" Abe asked.

"Only if you say, 'Up yours, sir,'" Doc said.

Abe frowned and left. The insults never stuck: whatever the beatnik-hippie-revolutionary's flaws, he did not hold a grudge.

Doc and Jack chatted briefly about Hawke—Doc knew nothing of the man, other than the Squarebeam controversy—after which Doc left.

"I need to go for a long run," he said. "I love meeting friends when I'm in town, but I always overeat."

"*Why we fight*," Jack joked, quoting the title of the famed World War II training films. "So Doc Matson can stay trim."

"Hey, Abe might argue that obesity is a bigger killer than combat."

"He might be right," Jack said. "Certainly the tarts and swells in Hollow-wood would agree with him."

"Yeah, a man totally unaware of his own hippie food pyramid: the opioids food group, the cannabinoid food group, the alcohol food group, and the deep-fryer food group."

"He's still sneaking french fries?"

"Can you believe he thinks I can't tell?" Doc smirked and departed.

Jack turned back to his reading. Less than two minutes after he left, Jack received a text from Phil Webb, Hawke's executive assistant:

Fixed Base Operator Terminal,
North Access Road, 6 p.m.

Jack texted back:

I will be there.

Abe Cohen was texting while he guided his quarter-century-old boat out into the Bay, headed for the Pacific. He was still arguing with Doc Matson, as they had been for years, via evolving forms of technology—

first mail, then phone, e-mail, and now texting—about what Abe saw as the tragedy of America's dilution. Doc, who actually traveled the world and witnessed it firsthand, saw the change as the globalization of American values.

So they argued, endlessly, neither man giving ground.

Abe felt that Doc was happy because he always had a war to fight, somewhere. But Abe, the old hippie, mourned his long-gone free-love era, when men wore nothing more feminine than beads and women went topless, and they had normal, recreational sex with each other.

How can you say that, you hypocrite? Doc had texted early that morning. *Freedom is freedom! That's why I fight—to help make people free.*

Abe had replied, *True freedom is without structure . . . it is not organized, state-approved segregation, which is what we have now! The marketers and banks all support it. They carve out ethnic groups, financial groups, sexual orientations. It helps them target their buyers and sell more goods.*

That got Doc started on the need for capitalism, investment cash as the engine for economic growth, all the things Jack Hatfield used to promote on his talk show.

So Abe replied with, *You're a tool of the Man, Doc.* Then he was out of cell phone range.

Peace at last.

Doc wasn't wrong about everything, Abe knew that. Abe remembered the end of the free-love era vividly, how freedom and love had mutated into something ugly, how every little need and aberration sought legitimacy, choosing to control and be controlled. It started with the Gay Liberation Front at the tail end of the 1960s, with its promulgation not just of male-male sex but everything that went with it: makeup for men and the "manscaping" of bodily hair, domestic partnerships and the adoption of children, and finally homosexual marriage. That was not the free love he grew up on. It was the institutionalization and proselytizing of a way of life. The kind of thing that gnawed at the foundations of society. As if that wasn't enough, there was the concurrent plague of feminism, which turned so many women into castrating aggressors and then into lesbians. Who, as it turned out, hated the gay male population for introducing AIDS to the world. Then there were minorities fighting for their share of attention, their permissive legislation. Illegal immigrants. African Americans. Muslim Americans. Hyphenates of every damn stripe. It had reached the point where an old singer's transgendered offspring had been attacked as being misogynist by another fanatic actor couple's child who had it chopped off—or was it sewn on—to become their new son or new daughter.

Liberalism was no longer a progressive ideal. It had become a mental disorder.

Now, the latest annoyance. They were all banding together to fight a new enemy, capitalism, under yet another banner: the vague, messy, annoying Occupy Wall Street movement that only compounded the noise.

More loud, shrill voices demanding immediate action from someone about something.

He missed the days when everyone chilled and went with the flow. That's why these weekly getaways were essential. He loved his store and its ties to the glory days of human freedom, when Haight-Ashbury was literally in flower, and he loved his old-school, radical clients—the true anarchists, the Libertarians. They didn't want to erect new rules to govern new pockets of entitlement. They were all about taking rules down.

Abe typically went out to the Farallon Islands to watch a society that managed to function without rules. He envied the elephant seals. They lived for about twenty years, most of which time they spent eating, swimming, and having sex. It was just like the 1960s. And there was the risk factor that reminded him of the old days. Just as he and his communal friends had to watch out for the cops—*the fuzz*—the elephant seals had to watch out for the sharks.

He throttled down as he neared the southeastern tip of the island group. He looked out the window of the pilothouse, couldn't see clearly because of the spray, and went out to the foredeck. He leaned against the rail, fished a pack of Camels from his shirt pocket.

He was about to light one when he saw something drifting in the water. He turned, unlatched a boat hook from the railing. He stretched it forward, snagged the object that was eddying around the prow.

It was a piece of tan blazer; part of a sleeve, it seemed. With blood on the soggy cuff. He started to bring it aboard, at the same time looking around for any other detritus—

Abe felt a punch in his left thigh, just below the hip. He heard a crack in the distance, quickly forgot it as his torso went left, his legs went right, and he literally bent sideways in the middle. He dropped the boat hook in the water and fell on the deck on his right side, his mouth tense and chest heaving. He was distracted by a terrible, pulsing heat where he'd felt the punch. He turned his eyes toward his legs, saw his jeans staining brown with red drops forming quickly and dripping onto the deck. There was a ragged hole in the middle of the stain.

"What the hell?"

He extended his left arm toward the hole, wincing, his hand trembling. He thought, absurdly, that he'd been bitten by a bug or a seabird or that he had somehow caught the hook on his leg without realizing it.

Then he remembered the sharp report he'd heard. He looked through the port side railing, saw someone running toward him. It was a man in a blue wetsuit. He was carrying a rifle in his right hand, a pistol in the other. It made no sense. Someone had *shot* him?

"Hey!" Abe said, intending to shout, but his voice sounded like a rough whisper.

His vision started to swim. Blood continued to flow from the wound. He pawed at it, had an idea that he'd better stanch it with a handkerchief or maybe a sleeve or a sock—

The man was on board now. He went below. Abe's head was lying on the deck. He heard the man's footsteps through the flooring. Then they were on deck and coming toward Abe. He looked at the interloper. The man was Asian. He was still carrying the weapons. He set them down near Abe, then knelt beside him. Abe smelled gunpowder.

OK, he thought. *I've been shot. By accident. The man's going to help me.*

Abe cried out in pain as the man picked him up roughly under the arms.

"C-care . . . ful . . ." Abe croaked. His head was swimming now. The stabbing, hot pain in his leg was all that kept him awake.

He felt himself being hoisted up. Pushed against the railing. He thought the man was trying to get him onto his feet so he could take him below.

The world turned round as Abe was pitched headlong over the rail. He splashed hard on his back, in the water, the sea filling his lungs as his arms made a brief, spastic effort to keep him from sinking.

His eyes were open as the blue-green darkness was tinged with red. He sank, thinking he should text Doc about this, wondering where his phone was, his fingers clutching for it, and then the water suddenly feeling very, very solid.

He was being pushed against something, sideways. Someone was holding his leg, trying to pull him out. Then he spun and was facing down, the pain in his leg spreading to his waist. He felt a sharp, electric jolt across his belly and right thigh.

Abe did not know he was dead below the waist. Mercifully, he did not feel the shark muzzle that buried itself in the cavity of his lower body, eating him from the inside. He did not feel the other sharks close on him, tearing at his arms, his torso, his face.

Abe Cohen was already dead.

The Chinese spotter went below and stomped the heel of his *tabi* boot on the floor. The flexible knee-high boot had a ribbed rubber heel for maximum gripping on the shoreline rocks slick with saltwater, animal waste, and blood from combat between the bull seals.

The hull was solid fiberglass.

The young man quickly checked the pilothouse for any kind of log, any indication that someone knew where he was. There was nothing. The spotter wasn't surprised. The American had looked like a rogue, someone who did not live a structured life.

He went back to the ladder, climbed into his motorboat, left the long-range rifle and pistol, and opened a backpack. He removed a brick of C-4 explosive, used a pocketknife to cut a piece from the corner, selected a timed detonator, and returned to the stateroom. C-4 cannot be detonated by a shock or bullet and will not explode when set ablaze. It can only be triggered by a combination of the simultaneous heat-flash and concussive force of a detonator. Flame alone will simply cause it to burn; the spotter used small quantities of the plastic explosive for heating his meals in the small, camouflaged tent he had on this desolate rock. That was a trick he had learned during survival training as a commando in the People's Liberation

Army Ground Force. Though he knew it was a possibility, the young man did not expect to have to shoot any of the boaters who came by or use the C-4 to sink ships. If the American had not found the remains of the former cell leader, this would not have been necessary.

With his motorboat lashed to the ladder, the spotter steered the larger vessel to deeper waters some two hundred feet to the north. He would set the timer on the detonator and head back to shore. Below deck, the explosion would not cause a flash that could be seen from shore or by satellite. The influx of water would quickly put out any fires, smother any smoke. The boat would sink quickly.

The spotter stopped the boat and scanned the horizon for any vessels close enough to see it; if there had been any, he would have waited. There was nothing but a tanker some forty miles distant and moving away. He pressed the small triangle of plastic explosive to the floor, far enough from the fuel tank so there wouldn't be an oil slick on the surface, something that might draw the attention of one of the Coast Guard vessels, tour boats, or environmental study ships that came by every day or so. Then he set the detonator for five minutes and hurried back to his idling motorboat. A Great White, drawn by the few drops of blood that had dripped from the main deck, nudged his little boat as he was about to enter. The spotter waited until the shark passed. The eleven-footer might not intend to knock the boat over, but there was no reason to risk it. Not that there was a lot of time to waste. He had to be back on shore before the C-4 exploded. The shock wave would travel through the boat to the water; moving perpendicular to the existing currents, it would give the motorboat quite a rattling.

The motorboat was already hidden in its cove on the windward side of the eastern island, the spotter safely ashore, when he heard the deep, muffled pop of the explosion. The sounds of the sinking boat were lost among the breakers crashing along the rocky coastline and the trumpeting of the elephant seals. It wasn't until he had reached a small promontory that he saw the last of the flybridge going under. As he had calculated based on his study of local nautical charts—there was precious little else to do on the island—the water was deep enough to swallow the boat entirely. And the sea was murky enough so that, unless an aircraft was looking for it, they might not see the pilot-house.

At least, not within the few days needed to finish the mission. Even if they found it, the wreckage would tell them nothing.

Feeling good to have served a purpose to the great Jintao and his cause, the spotter returned to his tent to contact Sausalito on his high-end encryption *ying xiong* "hero" radio. He briefed one of his comrades, then went back to the rock where he had left a pair of high-powered binoculars and watched the distant city, a city that would soon be as vacant and dead as it appeared through the haze.

Blaine, Washington

Located between Blaine, Washington, and Surrey, British Columbia, the Peace Arch State Park—the Peace Arch Provincial Park on the Canadian side—is the most heavily traveled U.S.-Canadian border crossing west of Detroit. It is named for the monument that stands in the wide grass median that lies between Interstate 5 and Highway 99, the north-south roads. Topped with the flags of both nations, the sixty-seven-foot-tall ivory-white arch was built in 1921 to commemorate the Treaty of Ghent, which ended the War of 1812—the last conflict in which the two nations were adversaries.

The crossing never closed, and the noncommercial traffic tended to move quickly with an average wait time of five minutes.

Liu Tang lit a cigarette as the car neared the border crossing. The other men in the car did likewise. They kept the windows rolled up. The fan was turned on, spreading the smoke through the vehicle. As they slowed and joined the southward-headed queue, Liu drew heavily on the cigarette to calm himself.

This was the last possible impediment. The Canadian cell was to bring him legally across the border where he would be turned over to members of the American cell. From there, it was an easy drive to San Francisco. The Canadian cell would stay in Seattle for two days, so as not to arouse suspicions by an immediate turnaround.

Liu opened his plastic chess set and handed the

strategy book to the man sitting next to him. The base of each chess piece had a magnet that covered a carefully drilled hole in the plastic. The board was arranged in the penultimate set-up of the Kasparov-Topalov match from 1999. Liu's companion knew nothing about the game in general or that match in particular. Only Liu was aware that, fittingly, this was considered the greatest attack match in recorded chess history. As they had planned, the two commenced a spirited argument about the game in Chinese.

Driving through the border, overt security consisted of guards checking vehicular undercarriages and trunks, primarily for nuclear devices. Because explosives were easily manufactured in terrorist kitchens, agents did not spend a lot of time on each car, van, or truck. Especially if the license or make was not on a watch list. Guards looked in the windows on both sides. Occasionally they asked to check random, specific items in the vehicle like dolls or computers or cups that might have false bottoms.

Liu knew that the real work at this and many international border crossings was "extreme racial profiling." Unofficially and illegally, more and more checkpoints had adopted the approach of Israel's El Al airline, which, despite being a prime target, had been free of terrorist attacks for three decades. Encountering a person trying to enter the United States who was of Middle Eastern, East African, or Indonesian descent, agents would follow the Israeli model. They would ask personal questions drawn entirely from passport, visa, and driver's license data. If a person knew the serial number of the document or instantly recalled the second or third or tenth stamp in its pages, chances were good they'd stupidly memorized a fake passport. Most terrorists were uneducated, living puppets given a seductive sense of importance by attentive radical leaders. These individuals were not capable of extemporizing. They had to commit data to memory. Guards also acted like human lie detectors, asking a series of innocuous questions peppered with pointed inquiries about social and political beliefs. Most people hesitated, crafted a careful response, said something personal but innocuous about party affiliation or support of a particular candidate. They tried to be truthful but safe. Terrorists, on the other hand, tended to have quick, rehearsed responses. Queried about militant movements, most passengers disavowed them. Radicals did so immediately and almost always with a dismissive little laugh. Personnel were trained to notice not just the speed of a response but changes in expression, a rise in the voice, sudden hand motions, nervous swallowing indicated by movement of the Adam's apple, averting the eyes, or an unblinking stare to avoid the appearance of anxiety. That earned follow-up questions that were harder, more aggressive, and invariably earned the subject of the interview a strip search and complete baggage deconstruction.

Crossings at the Peace Arch rarely reached that level of engagement. Moreover, no one at the border spoke any Asian languages. The cell had checked. They had also profiled several shifts of personnel. The Chinese all smoked because these dry runs had proven that the younger guards in particular didn't like it. That made the process go very, very quickly.

And, of course, there was the unspoken belief that China would not attack the United States. They had too much invested in the nation to want to see it brought down.

That was the problem with people who thought fiscally instead of ideologically, Liu thought, as he faced the chessboard but watched their approach from the corner of his vision.

The van reached the border. Guards approached from the front driver's and passenger's sides. They motioned for the driver's window to be rolled down. A third guard examined the outside of the vehicle.

The agent on the driver's side was of Asian heritage: Japanese, from his rigid bearing and humorless expression, Liu guessed. He didn't flinch as the cigarette smoke rolled out.

"Passport, please," he asked, pointing at the driver.

The driver had been holding his cigarette. He jabbed it in his mouth and removed his passport from his shirt pocket. He handed it to the agent. The young man examined it. He looked at the driver. The driver smiled thinly, nodded politely.

The agent flipped through the passport and handed it back. As he waited for the guard inspecting the vehicle to give it an all clear, he peered through the back window. Liu made a move on the chessboard. His opponent sat back, bemoaning his situation.

"Checkmate," the border agent said.

Liu looked at him. Slowly, he took the cigarette

from his mouth and smiled. The agent smiled back and waved them on. The men in front rolled up the windows. The van entered the United States.

Liu did not realize how tense he had been until the constriction suddenly lifted from his chest. He finished his cigarette and ground it in the ashtray. It was luck. Maybe fate was with them. In any case, they were here and there was nothing to stop them. What had taken place back in the Vancouver Customs building would soon be enacted on a massive scale.

Distraction—followed by an attack that would collapse a nation.

Fairfield, California

The consulate car reached the hotel just as Sammo was finishing his lunch. He had been watching for it through the amber-tinted window. As instructed, the car just pulled to the curb and waited, a spotlight of sun bouncing from its black roof. It was in plain view of the traffic on Central Place.

And the traffic was in plain view of Sammo.

Less than three minutes after the consulate car arrived, Sammo saw a particular vehicle drive by in the steady traffic. It was the same make of car as the one he'd shut down outside of San Francisco. He watched as the vehicle swung past again less than two minutes later at a modest rate of speed. He leaned toward the window for a better look. He saw the car make a right onto Lookout Hill Road. That was a dead end. They weren't making another circuit. Sammo went to the pool, which faced the side street. The car had turned around and was parked facing Central Place, ready to move.

As Sammo had expected, officials had responded to his unexpected attack by following all the cars that came from the Chinese consulate, sometimes with regulation vehicles and sometimes with others more nondescript.

Minus one, he thought with a private grin. The car he had hit would not be going anywhere for days. Not until all its electrical systems were replaced.

Sammo did not fault them this response. Until now, the bulk of Chinese activity had been to meet and bribe government employees or sabotage the Internet. Without a precedent to follow—like al-Qaeda or other terrorist groups with known patterns and member-types—it was virtually impossible to prepare for a man like himself and what he had done to the car. The task of quickly ferreting out cells or contacts was especially difficult in a region like this with a vast and geographically diversified Asian population. It wasn't the same as looking for a single, surly, swarthy man in a crowd of shoppers or commuters.

Sammo went to his room and waited. At exactly two P.M., the house phone rang. It was one of the men from the car, calling as ordered. Sammo had wanted any observers to see a man get out and a man get back in, unable to ascertain whether it was the same man. The tail would have to follow the car. He also did not want the American authorities to have surveillance access to his own cell phone.

The communication would consist of one word, in the event that anyone had followed the man in and was listening through the switchboard. *Yī*—one— meant that Sammo would be joining them. *Èr*— two—meant they were to get back on the highway and travel north without him.

"*Èr*," he told them.

"*Èr*," the man in the car repeated, then hung up.

Sammo went back to the lobby. The sedan was gone. He strolled to the pool. The other car had left as well. Pleased at having lost the FBI tail, he selected a local map from the rack in the lobby and returned to his room. He would not be able to use any online map service for the same reason he did not call the car on his cell phone. He could not be sure of the security of any wireless activity.

Somewhere in the distance the sound of an airplane rumbled, like the challenge of a distant animal. He looked at the map. Central Place paralleled Highway 12. Following it, he would have no problem reaching the site of the Mother Hen Toy Company facility.

He felt like he did when he was in Afghanistan. He had expected he would be able to blend in here, but that was clearly not an option. He was back in undercover mode. It was not what he had expected to be doing here, and he had to make sure that he had an exit plan from the site. But he was ready for it just the same.

Sammo set his phone alarm to ring at five-thirty, then removed his shoes and lay down on the bed.

During training, he had learned to fall asleep quickly by reciting poems he had committed to memory. In the field, it was necessary to take whatever rest one could. Especially when he needed to be alert on both fronts.

Offensively and defensively, it was going to be a taxing and very busy night.

Agent Al Fitzpatrick was not dressed like a G-man. He wore the lunchtime sweats that he used to work out in the bureau gym. When Field Director Forsyth gave them their assignments, he told them to disguise themselves as best as possible in case it was necessary to track anyone on foot.

Watching the front of the hotel, it seemed as if the same man had gotten back into the Chinese consulate car as had left. But Fitzpatrick and his partner, Agent Meadow Wood, could not be sure. They agreed that he should get out and watch the hotel while she followed the car. He slid from the driver's side, which couldn't be seen from the hotel side, and waited behind an oak tree. When both cars were gone, he jogged up the street to the main road. He entered the hotel, went to the registration area, showed the clerk his credentials.

"The man who came in from the black sedan," he said. "Did the same man leave?"

"Yes, sir," the young clerk told him.

"What did he do?"

"He went to the house phone around the corner."

"Do you have a record of who he called?"

"No, sir," the young man said. "It does not go through the switchboard."

"Just circuits."

"I guess so, sir."

"Are there any Chinese nationals registered at the hotel?"

"Sir, you'd have to ask the manager—"

"Never mind," Fitzpatrick said. If someone had requested the car, he probably hadn't registered using a Chinese passport for exactly this reason. Perhaps he hadn't registered at all. There might be no one here. For all Fitzpatrick knew, the hotel manager might have been bribed. Or perhaps the chain was Chinese-owned. He would have to check. "Back doors?"

"Only one and it leads to the pool and parking lot," the clerk said. "They're fenced in."

"Security cameras?"

The young man nodded.

Agent Fitzpatrick considered whether to ask to see the footage. The playbook said yes, but he decided against it. An enemy operative might be waiting for him to do just that—to create a window of several minutes, a blind spot, to leave the building without his knowing and tie up another FBI resource. This entire exercise, triggered by an innocent tail from the airport, might be nothing more than an attempt to stretch FBI resources for some reason, or to challenge them to see their response.

Fitzpatrick told the clerk he was going to wait in the lobby, and the clerk was to simply ignore him and say nothing to any of the other staff. The young man agreed. The agent went to a yellow vinyl, cushioned seat facing the elevators. He texted Division, told them he was on Level Four Stakeout, which meant it was a low-priority watch that could not, however, be avoided. He told them where he was.

And then he brought up *Angry Birds* on his cell phone and waited.

San Francisco, California

Jack made arrangements with Max to watch Eddie until his return. The poodle didn't mind the camera operator, though she was often running out for free-lance assignments and didn't give Eddie quite the attention he obviously thought he deserved.

I know how you feel, Jack thought after dropping the dog at her apartment on Howard Street. There hadn't been a woman in his life who gave him her full attention, either. Not since his sainted mother. It wasn't a case of being a mama's boy and it might not be politically correct, but Jack believed it was OK for women to dote on men once in a while. He once had that debate with a feminist on his show. She had written a memoir called *The S & M Society: She Must Be Mute*. Jack had disagreed with her thesis.

"No one's telling you to be quiet," Jack said.

"Men are," she had replied. "It's what men do."

"Some men," Jack corrected.

"Isn't that what you're doing to me?" she asked. "Telling me to be quiet?"

"No," he said. "I'm disagreeing with you. That isn't

the same thing. I'm also telling you that you really shouldn't be complaining when men ask for attention. It shows that we need you."

"What you need," she replied hotly, "is to get away from the teat, to stop breast-feeding."

"You," Jack replied, "obviously have one kinky private life."

She walked off the show.

Before heading to the airport, Jack stopped at his apartment on Union Street. None of his friends knew about the place, which was located on the twentieth floor of a twenty-two-story, sixties-era complex right off the Embarcadero. It was his secret haven just a block from the Bay, a touchstone with sanity in an insane world. It wasn't the most beautiful building in San Francisco, but it held a singular appeal for Jack: there were four or five entrances and exits on various floors. Back in the day when he was an incendiary talk show host, it would have been difficult for any of the nutjobs or corporate powers who had threatened him over the years to stalk him.

Jack steered Wilhelm into one of his two underground parking spaces. His Mercedes, dented and dirty from the explosion at the clinic, looked even worse next to the pristine Mercedes SLR McLaren in the other parking space. The McLaren belonged to Rachel, the former model who had been married to Jack for ten years and divorced from him for two. Her boyfriend, a tax attorney, had a twelve-car garage to keep the McLaren in, yet Rachel parked it at Jack's place. She said it was for convenience, but she hadn't touched the car since she drove it here, and just sent Jack a check occasionally for the parking space fee. She'd even left her keys, which Jack had taken up to the apartment and tossed in a drawer. He suspected that she wanted to force him to look at the car, to be reminded of her. She didn't want him, but she didn't want him to forget her.

No question, it was a beautiful car—all black, even custom black rims and black glass. The "Batmobile" was how Jack thought of it each time he checked that its trickle charger was plugged in and charging. He wondered if the tax attorney had bought the whole car for her or if they'd gone halvsies.

The last time he had gone back to his house, before Rachel had sold it so she could move in with the attorney, Jack had been picking up some of his stuff. He'd noticed that Rachel was uncharacteristically light of spirit, nothing like the depressed, angry Rachel Jack had lived with for years. The tax attorney was there—very tall, very fat. Jack hadn't known how serious the relationship was. He took Rachel aside and said, "Either get him out of here or I will physically remove him myself. He's only after your—our—property, our money."

Rachel stared back at him coolly. "First, I doubt you could physically do it yourself. Second, he doesn't need anything of ours, believe me. And, Jack, you and I were in a graveyard together. I'm getting older. I can't control my aging body. What I want, what I need, I have a right to find and keep."

* * *

Jack opened the door to his apartment and walked straight to the window. He needed to clear Rachel and her boyfriend out of his thoughts. The spectacular view did just that. Facing north, the window looked out across the Bay. Just beyond the Richmond Bridge he could see the East Brother Light Station, a small island lighthouse that—earthquakes and fires be damned—had been in that spot for over 133 years.

Jack walked over to his favorite clock, the walnut German Berliner with a winged angel embossed on its brass face. It had been weeks—far too long—since he rewound it. He listened to the rings as he wound, taking care not to overwind, and a little order was restored to the world, as it always was when he came here. This apartment was one antidote to Jack's mild case of Asperger's. The other, when he was on the *Sea Wrighter,* was video editing. His boat was full of the tools of his trade, his mission, so the rest of his life was here, stored in objects and books, photographs and mementoes that had meaning only to him. He jokingly thought of it as the Museum of Jack Hatfield, not as a repository of some inflated sense of self-worth but as a place of understanding and reflection.

There were some of his childhood toys: his favorites were a vintage 1940s Indy 500 racing car and a gas-powered model airplane that still had the same wooden propeller he had watched spin when he was seven years old. There was an old red-and-white fireboat that he used to play with in the bathtub. The hoses still fired an impressive stream of water. Now and then he tried it in the kitchen sink with a smile as big as he could remember. Here and there were the track and football trophies he'd earned in high school. A bowling ball he'd once rolled down Filbert between Leavenworth and Hyde—a teenage prank that had mercifully not struck any cars but had earned him one hundred hours of community service.

On the walls were his journalism and broadcasting awards, scattered among paint-by-number art pieces his mother had done with him and portraits of deer and fishermen. Country landscapes bumped frames with his small collection of nautical scenes by nineteenth-century painters that he had inherited from his father. He paused by the marine paintings, entranced by the clear pale sunlights, the blushing clouds and taut white sails, the sheens on the sides of the tall ships. His gaze was drawn to his prize, a William Coulter of a three-masted ship trying to veer away from the rocks of the Farallon Islands. Judging by the strength of the waves, the torn sails, and the broken rigging, the ship wasn't going to make it. Next to the Coulter was another unknown masterpiece, by Gideon Denny, an American who was born in 1830, died 1886. *Steam Sailer off the Golden Gate* presented an orange sky and a ship nobly plowing through storm waves, and this ship was going to survive the journey. *"Even man's greatest works pale in comparison with the immensity of God's creation,"* had stated the brochure that convinced Jack to buy the painting.

Jack knew that he was going to see luxury beyond belief when he was in Hawke's territory, but he doubted he would see an ounce of the careful beauty that these painters had added to the world, and the respect they had paid to the work of God.

On a shelf below the Coulter was the helmet Jack had worn in Iraq, with shrapnel rents that reminded him of how close he had come to dying there.

Sometimes Jack came to the apartment to hide. There was no computer, no phone, no television. He turned off his cell phone and sat at the small desk and repaired watches. That—and sex—were the only things that cleared his mind of all other concerns. He sat down now with a Hamilton Model #3 two-tone pocketwatch that he had pulled out a few weeks before to repair. A rare part had come in, but he hadn't even opened the mailing package. Now Jack brought out his father's repair tools, but he wasn't at work half an hour before he felt a kind of inner pressure. Working on the watch would not calm him if he was avoiding something vitally important—if he was hiding from himself. He needed to face the near future and get centered.

He rose from the desk and sat in an old armchair, looking out the window. Philippians 4:8 came to his mind: *Finally, brothers, whatever is true, whatever is honorable, whatever is just, whatever is pure, whatever is lovely, whatever is commendable, if there is any excellence, if there is anything worthy of praise, think about these things.*

He did think about them. He thought about them because, for some reason, there was something about this trip to Hawke he found unsettling. Part of it was the fact that he had no idea where he was going. Jack didn't mind flying blind, as he had often done in Iraq or pursuing a story in some remote spot of the globe or even in a dangerous alley in West Oakland. But at those times he was on the ground and able to change course or duck. There was an exit strategy. Not here. Another part of the equation—a larger part, now that he thought of it—was the sense that he was about to put himself in the hands of someone he'd practically accused of treason. If Hawke couldn't convince him of his innocence, the billionaire might well cause Jack to disappear. He needed to shake the feeling of dread before he got on board. Confinement would only make it worse.

How do you do that? he asked himself.

There was a copy of the Bible on a rickety wooden stool beside the chair. Jack used to sit on that stool, in a corner, as punishment, when he was a kid. He once had a distinguished child psychiatrist on *Truth Tellers* who had written a book called *Cruel and Unusual Punishment.* The Harvard-educated $400-an-hour New York–based highbrow thirtysomething childless woman maintained that forceful discipline of any "person of youth" was wrong.

"Were you punished as a child?" Jack had asked her.

"Never," she said. "I was spoken to as an adult."

"Did you understand what was said to you?"

"Some of it."

"I see," Jack replied. "That would explain *this* conversation."

The memory of her angry reaction—effectively, a childlike tantrum—made him smile. He felt some of the tension go away.

He laid his hand on the Bible as though he were channeling its wisdom, running the words through his brain, searching for something that would put him entirely at ease. The Psalms were about courage, and he mentally picked his way through them.

I observed the prosperity of the wicked . . . Arrogance is their necklace, and violence their clothing . . . Their prosperity causes them to do wrong; their thoughts are sinful . . . They speak as if they rule in heaven, and lay claim to the earth . . . They say, "How does God know what we do?"

"He knows," Jack said. "And he empowers those who would challenge you."

Jack wasn't convinced that God would shield him or welcome him with an embrace if he fell. But he did believe there was a right and there was a wrong. The universe wasn't ordered to suit Jack Hatfield, and whether he liked it or not he was suddenly one of the gatekeepers of justice. Those words of Benjamin Franklin he had once quoted came back to him: *Those who would give up essential liberty to purchase a little temporary safety, deserve neither liberty nor safety.*

"OK, Jack," he said, giving the Bible a pat and rising. "Get over yourself and go do the job."

Before he left the apartment he went looking through his desk drawers. Then, downstairs in the parking garage, the gullwing doors of the SLR McLaren opened upward for him. He roared into the late afternoon traffic. Somehow the machine felt like camouflage as he prepared to enter Hawke's field of vision.

The rush hour drama on the way to the airport barely dented Jack's consciousness. He was wondering whether he should call Rachel and tell her he was driving her car, which he knew was just shadowboxing before the main event—confronting Hawke. The drive down 280 was therapeutic—the throaty roar, the black glass, the overwhelming sensation of 638 HP. He was momentarily aggravated by the bottlenecked traffic at San Francisco International, but he wasn't going to any of the main terminals in the big, snowflake-like design.

Jack parked in the ultra-secure parking facility of the private terminal, which was a three-story, pale-gray structure that seemed more window than wall. He grabbed his small overnight bag and walked in. The bag contained his computer and also a change of clothes he did not know if he'd need. He knew damned little, in fact. But there was something exciting about that. If Jack had wanted life to be predictable, he would not have gone into journalism, to Iraq, or into television. In reverse order, those were three of the least routine arenas on the globe.

Jack did not have to go to the counter. A flight attendant rose from one of the chairs when he walked in. She was dressed in a black suit and black tie. The only thing that gave her away was a silver Hawke logo on her breast pocket.

"Mr. Hatfield?"

"Yes."

"Welcome. My name is Martina." The young woman stepped forward and offered her hand. She was about five foot six, blond, and blue eyed. Austrian, Jack guessed from just the trace of accent in her voice.

"Hi, Martina."

Jack looked past her. Through tinted windows he saw three jets on the tarmac. Jack knew at once which belonged to Hawke. It wasn't just the logo on the tail fin; it was the fact that Jack had never seen an aircraft quite like it.

"Would you come with me?" Martina asked.

"Sure. Where are we going, by the way?"

"The pilot has that information," she said.

"Don't you?"

"I do not," she replied. "My duties are the same wherever Mr. Hawke sends the aircraft." She reached for his shoulder bag.

"It's OK, I've got it," Jack said.

"Of course," she said, backing away instantly with an obedient little nod.

The woman was deferential to a fault and not nosy. Just like Bahiti. Jack imagined that every employee in Hawke's personal circle had those qualities right at the top of the job description.

They walked toward the door that opened onto the tarmac. As they crossed the otherwise empty building Jack felt the anxiety of the trip return. He needed to shake that and noticed a small help-yourself concession counter to the left.

"Hey, I'd like to grab some popcorn before we go," he said.

Martina seemed mildly confused. "We have Almas caviar on board, Mr. Hatfield—"

"Yeah, but that's not popcorn."

"No, it isn't," she agreed.

"Right, and I'm guessing that must be some damn fine private jet terminal popcorn." He jerked his head to the stand. "I'm gonna grab a bag. Want some?"

She smiled sweetly. "No, thank you."

"OK. Be right back."

Jack hurried to the stand. He took a tall, narrow bag from the lamp-heated glass case, shook some of the contents into his mouth, enjoyed the crunch and the taste, but most of all, the momentary respite. He was determined not to slip back into that state of mild anxiety. He stood there, thinking about the one sure place he could visit to get his mental feet under him.

Jack thought back to his father's death. He remembered when he was five years old. His father had driven him to a mountaintop where, his arm folded around the boy to keep him warm against the brisk mountain wind, he pointed to a lake below and taught him the word "shimmering." He had him repeat the word.

"Shimmering, shimmering, shimmering," Jack could still hear himself saying in his little boy voice.

Later in life, as they would hike in the mountains, his father would point to the quaking aspens in the west.

"Remember when I taught you the word 'shimmering'?" his father said the last time they were up there. *"Look, Jack. The leaves are shimmering."*

As Jack's father lay dying of cancer, he had a request for his son. They were the last words he ever spoke. He wanted to go back to that spot on that mountain and look down upon the lake where he had first taught Jack the word "shimmering." Against the advice of his doctors, Jack took him from the bed in his home and drove him to the spot that meant so much to them both.

A few days later Jack's father left the earth.

Jack felt the anxiety ease. Sometimes a little independent action, a little quiet reflection, was all it took. Remembering his friends, his mentors, his heroes. Thinking of them, and turning his attention to the job at hand. He had to start doing his job.

Jack returned to Martina's side.

"Is it everything you expected?" she asked.

"It's not Abe Cohen's homemade kettle corn, but it's not bad. You sure you don't want any?" He inclined the bag toward her.

"Completely," she replied with a patient smile. "Are you ready now, Mr. Hatfield? We do have a schedule."

"Yes, sorry." They resumed walking. "I was just thinking—Almas caviar. That's Iranian, isn't it?"

"I believe it is."

"Pretty expensive," Jack said.

"I would imagine."

"Why would you 'imagine' that?" Jack asked.

"Because everything Mr. Hawke does is first class."

Jack didn't have to imagine the cost: he knew. He had seen the caviar offered in a catalogue from a London dealer at $25,000 a tin.

"Have you worked for Mr. Hawke for very long?"

"We work *with* him," she corrected him. "And yes—nearly three years."

Jack had to admire the "coworker" ideology that seemed to permeate the Hawke staff. It was a smart way to empower employees and generate loyalty.

They went outside, Jack letting Martina walk ahead. In addition to her other qualities she had a nice sway. That little distraction also helped him to relax.

A slight wind kicked up dust from the field, causing Jack to shield his eyes with the popcorn bag. Fueling was just being completed. The white skin of the jet looked like orange Mylar in the setting sun. It resembled one of those helium balloons Jack saw on party boats, only in the exact shape of a swan. The jet had a long, arched neck, big swept-back wings with a gentle upward bend in the center, and two cylindrical engines tucked underneath like legs. The tail feathers were smaller wings in the rear.

"Supersonic?" Jack asked as they reached the ladder.

"The Quiet Supersonic Transport flies at Mach 2 with a range of four thousand miles," she said, and gestured for him to ascend first.

Jack obliged. His first thought was, *Four thousand miles. They could be going halfway around the earth in any direction.* His second thought was that private plane pilot Doc Matson would be seriously envious when Jack told him he'd flown on this aircraft. *Assuming you ever see Doc again.*

Passing through the oblong door, Jack had to remain bowed slightly because of the low ceiling. The first thing that struck him as he entered the jet was the smell of leather. It was like new car smell, only deeper. The seats were thick and white, with a dull orange cast from the sunset. The cabin seated twelve and was neither very high nor very long. To travel as high and fast as the jet did required certain sacrifices to size and weight. But the trappings were clean and elegant. There were four seats in the forward section, two on either side facing one another. An open door led to an area in which there were two facing pairs of seats on the starboard side, a sofa across from them, and two more sets of two seats beyond. A small wet bar, white with a black burl top, was tucked in the back by the rear emergency exit. The carpet was black with a charcoal-gray zigzag pattern that made the cabin seem wider. The lines were repeated in embossed white up the center of the chairs and also across the sofa. Handmade pillows made of black leather added decorative interest if not practicality. The seat belts were black with white plastic fasteners. There were small HD monitors in the front of the cabin and across from the lavatory in the front was a closet for bags. The low, sloping ceiling did not allow for overhead storage.

Neither the pilot nor the copilot emerged from the closed-door cockpit. Jack placed his bag in the closet—along with the popcorn; he would feel uncouth putting salty fingers on the leather—and was instructed to sit wherever he liked. He chose the seat nearest the door, even though it was facing back. He had once flown backward in a C-130 Hercules in Saudi Arabia. It was an interesting experience, feeling the force of takeoff from behind. It was a memorable flight for another reason; he happened to be sitting next to then-Secretary of Defense Dick Cheney, whom he was interviewing for the *San Francisco Chronicle*.

"Have you ever gone backward?" Cheney asked Jack.

"No, sir, it's against my nature," Jack replied. "That's one reason I'd never go into politics."

Cheney chuckled. It was not an amused laugh, but a knowing one.

Martina shut the door, notified the flight crew that they were ready, then selected the seat opposite Jack. Her smile was professional rather than warm; her eyes turned out to the large, square window. The sun was nearly down, and her face was in shadow. Yet at that moment he thought he saw the real woman: relaxed, briefly off-duty, reflective.

"What are you thinking about?" Jack asked.

She regarded him, surprised by the question. "That I have never been to this city."

"That's a shame. It's special."

"So I have heard. How long have you lived here?"

"My entire adult life," Jack said.

The plane began taxiing almost at once. The engines sounded like a long note played on a bass cello.

"What about you?" Jack asked.

"Vienna, Paris, New York," she replied. "That is where I am based now. I used to think of myself as worldly, but, you know, one cannot truly know a country until you are outside the big cities. I so rarely get that chance, either."

"No, I'm guessing Mr. Hawke doesn't stay in one place for long."

She only smiled in response. She turned her eyes back out the window. Obviously, in mentioning her boss, Jack had gone where even angels fear to tread. That was telling. It was not a reaction of respect but fear. That actually helped Jack get past his own concerns. A woman in danger—even if it was just a vague, intuited psychological jeopardy—was always a strong motivator for him.

The plane was on the runway. Jack heard the cello string rise an octave. The jet picked up speed quickly, much faster than a commercial passenger jet and certainly faster than the C-130. Jack was thrust forward more than he had expected. He gripped the calfskin armrests.

He looked out the window at the city as it dropped away at a sharper angle than he was accustomed to and in a different direction. He fell in love all over again with the familiar sights and the emerging lights and the ribbons of traffic, red moving away, white coming toward him, every driver the center of his or her own cosmos but *his* people. How much in love he was became clear when the plane banked west past the Golden Gate, Point Diablo and Point Bonito were lost to view, and only then he remembered there was a beautiful woman sitting across from him.

She rose when they leveled off. They were at roughly ten thousand feet and still climbing.

"Mr. Hatfield, would you like your carry-on?"

"Please." He didn't offer to get it. He would let her do what she was happily accustomed to doing. Sometimes that, too, was chivalry.

She brought his bag and set it on the floor. She held the popcorn, unsure what to do with it.

"You can toss that," he said. "I only wanted a taste."

She did not react with curiosity to what was clearly a lie. The human contact was clearly over.

"Would you care for anything to eat or drink, perhaps some of that caviar I mentioned?"

"I'll take a Glenrothes single malt if you've got it."

"Would a Jameson eighteen-year-old Limited Reserve be acceptable?"

"That would have been my very strong second choice," he smiled.

She walked past him, and Jack turned his head slightly to watch her go. Martina fit perfectly under the low ceiling. In the muted white light of the cabin he realized that her uniform had been color-coordinated with the interior of the jet. There was even a faint zigzag pattern up the back of her jacket. A design element, perhaps. It struck him more as a subtle brand, a sign of ownership.

He booted his computer and looked up the stored files on Hawke. He still had a lot of reading to do before he got to wherever he was going. He had read about the man's background, about how the company was started. He already knew about the Squarebeam debacle. He started in on the company's current assets.

Martina returned with his drink. He didn't bother folding down the computer screen. No need to insult her intelligence. She could have guessed what he was doing. He sampled the whiskey. Martina hadn't even waited for him to acknowledge it so; she had gone on to the cockpit. The drink was warm, spicy, nutty, rich. He savored it as it warmed his throat and chest, then put the glass back on the table. He was going to nurse this one for a while. Otherwise, he'd be drinking more of it than he should.

Reviewing the material, Hawke was global in every sense of the word. He had offices in twenty-eight nations and homes in many of those same places, according to a *People* magazine profile from two years earlier. Jack narrowed his examination to the man's American holdings. He wanted to get some idea which lab—domestically or internationally—might have the capability of designing or producing an advanced EMP device.

His eyes locked on one name in the list of Hawke laboratories.

"Aw, Christ."

One facility jumped out like a coiled snake: HITV Labs. Hawke Industries Temecula Valley. It was a large industrial complex located on Nutmeg Street, just north of the intersection of Interstate 15 and Interstate 215.

The address was in Murrieta. The town Dover had said she wanted to visit.

She wouldn't go there alone and start asking questions, Jack told himself. *She couldn't be that naïve.*

But a desk jockey could be *exactly* that green, he decided. And that curious. And that eager to redeem herself.

His damsel-in-distress glands were pumping out large doses of adrenaline. He was on a jet heading at just under Mach 2 in what he had determined to be a southeasterly direction, while his nominal partner in this was headed for potential trouble back in California.

He logged onto the jet's wireless system. Hawke might well be eavesdropping on all communications as a matter of course but that couldn't be helped. Jack sent Dover an innocuous e-mail. He got an away message that said she was taking a few days off with limited Internet availability. He tried to call on her cell phone. The ONI would definitely be listening and wouldn't appreciate that, but he was the one placing the call, not her. It would not add an extra black mark to her record. Not that it mattered: he got voice mail. She was probably on her way. He left a message for her to call, though if he were leaving the country there was no way of knowing when he might get it.

Shit.

Jack thought about how he had felt a little helpless contemplating this trip. That was nothing.

Considering his options, he could think of only one. He sent a vague text that he hoped would make sense to the person who received it. Then he sat back with his whiskey and nursed it, waiting for an answer to his message.

PART TWO

Resistance

Chapter 1

————

Murrieta, California

Dover Griffith arrived in the middle of a massive dust storm. What bothered her was not that in itself: it was that she had been sure, after the way it began, the trip was only going to get better.

Dover had an apartment in a three-story brick complex in Suitland, 5601 Regency Park Court, building number seven. She phoned for a cab to take her to the airport, then went down to meet it. As she got there—with the number of the taxi on her cell phone—she saw an older man just getting in.

"Hey!" she yelled. "That's my taxi!"

"Sorry!" the passenger waved. "Mine will be along shortly, I hope."

"You hope? God*dammit,* that's my ride!"

Dover had enough time to call and complain to the

cab company before the man's taxi arrived. The cab driver gave her a hard time because her name was obviously not Toby Dickles. She wished the other driver had been more thorough.

She made it to the airport with little time to spare and got through security with even less time to spare. She sat less than five minutes before the plane took off.

Her seat was right next to Toby Dickles. They did not speak. Except for a moment of alarm on her part and dim, dawning recognition on his, they exchanged no looks, no words. Dover was on the aisle. Every time Mr. Dickles had to use the bathroom—which was every half hour or so—he simply rose, without a "pardon me" or "excuse me," and she had to get up. The one time she hesitated, he undertook to shimmy around her. When Mr. Dickles finally fell asleep— with the volume on the earphones turned way up, so she could literally sing along with Italian opera—he snored.

At the car rental facility in California, off Haven Road at the eastern end of the airport, she picked up her car—a Kia Rio, which came fully equipped with a CD player and nothing else—and swung onto 10. She took it a short distance to Highway 15, headed south, and ran right into the storm.

The dust was like a thick sheet of tawny-gray gauze pulled over the windshield. She could see a few yards in front but nothing else. It stretched up as far as she could see. Dover pulled over, along with most of the sane people on the freeway, turned on the radio, and found a local station that said it would pass through the region in about a half hour.

"This is part of what comes with living in our big, beautiful Inland Empire," the newscaster said. "You get the great temps year round, you get the recreation, you get Las Vegas and San Diego and Los Angeles a couple hours in any direction. And sometimes, yeah, Mama Nature reminds us she's alive and well with a trembler or a wildfire or a wall of desert sand a thousand feet high."

Dover turned off the radio. It was more fun listening to the wind bellow, cars poking by with drivers leaning into their horns, and the scratching sound of countless silica bits blasting across the windows and chassis. She didn't want to waste her cell phone battery so she left her phone in her bag and pulled a map from the glove compartment. The good news was her destination was about forty-five minutes straight ahead, the Clinton Keith exit on 15.

The cloud passed suddenly. There was no announcement, like the trailing off of a rainstorm or the bowling alley rumble of retreating thunder. The dust storm had rolled through and simply ended.

Now, of course, there was a careless starting up of traffic, with lurching, uncooperative moves from cars parked two rows deep on the shoulder and dismal bottlenecks where 15 and 60, then 15 and 91, crossed to the south.

Welcome to California, she thought.

The last time she was here was before her freshman year at NYU. Her best friend, Christina, wanted to become a movie star so they took a trip to Los Angeles. They stayed at the Sheraton Universal and took the tour, where Christina fell in love with their tram guide. They hooked up, stayed hooked up for nearly a week—while Dover did the tourist sights, including Disneyland, mostly by herself—then broke up. Her friend was devastated and never went back to California. Dover hadn't been impressed enough with anything, either, especially the traffic. Now it was even worse than she remembered, thanks to a county full of people who required big, brawny trucks to get from place to place instead of little VW Beetles.

Though if there were a Beetle, Toby Dickles would probably be driving it and doing fifty-five in front of me, she reflected. Mercifully, an offspring or nephew had met him at the terminal and hustled him away.

By the time she reached her exit, Dover wished that she had rented one of those trucks. Some of them literally created a mild shock wave as they passed, causing her to wobble, and all of them were high enough from the road so the drivers could actually see past the truck in front of them. Dover spent more time looking at rear fenders and taillights than she did watching the road. She didn't realize how tense she was until after she pulled off the freeway and stopped at the light. She was literally squeezing the steering wheel.

It was after five P.M. when she arrived. She had made a reservation at TemVal Motel on Whitewood Road. It looked nothing like the photographs online, which showed a freshly painted, neat little roadside motel with a kind of cowboy charm. In reality it was the kind of seedy place most people avoided.

But it was inexpensive, it was near to where she had to be, and all she intended to do there was sleep. There was a woman at the counter, which put her at ease. She was pleasant enough and apparently surprised to see someone actually staying for the night. Dover checked the lock and the sheets. They were fine. She took her wallet but left her bag in the room, plugged in her near-dead cell phone, and went out. She wanted to get her bearings by driving past the industrial park that was the home of Hawke Industries.

The game plan was to be up-front, just like Jack Hatfield. Commander Morgan and Lieutenant Commander Ward had always admonished their teams to be aggressive in the pursuit of intelligence. The mantra was "Nation before self." As far as Dover was concerned, the ideals of national security were no less true whether she was behind her desk or in the field. Like her grandfather, she couldn't be afraid just because the enemy was out there, somewhere in the dark. If her fears were valid, this was absolutely worth pursuing—the ONI's repudiation of Jack Hatfield be damned. As long as she didn't misrepresent herself or reveal classified information, there were no restrictions on what Dover could ask or say. She didn't expect anyone to reveal any secrets. But she expected that a smart corporate representative would be as curious to find out what she knew, or suspected, as she was about them. This could be mutually beneficial. What American company, privately owned by an

American, wouldn't want to know if their technology had been appropriated and was being used to kill Americans? They might even offer her a better job than she had in D.C.

I might even buy a truck, she grinned.

As for the ONI, she had nothing to lose. What were they going to do, fire her? On the other hand, if she was right and could bring back even the hint of evidence to back her claim, then she might get her job back, the Hatfield connection notwithstanding.

Even if I have to push it up the ladder, past the commander, she thought. Reading about Hatfield she had come to realize this much: you don't get ahead by being afraid. Not only was Dover surprised to find herself calm, she was actually energized. She had processed the fieldwork of others often enough. The prospect of doing her own was exciting, challenging.

The Hawke complex was across the street from a gas station, a fast-food restaurant, and a Starbucks, which had obviously been built there for employees: they were linked by a new pedestrian foot bridge. The Hawke facility itself was a series of charcoal-gray buildings arranged in what looked like a zigzag pattern. There were solar panels on the roof and, in the distance, air turbines that towered about two hundred feet and caught the Santa Ana winds that—she had read in the in-flight magazine—blew seasonally from the desert. There was no gate, no guard, no swipe-card access that she could see: just an open parking lot beyond marble columns topped with bronze statues, about a dozen feet high, of large hawks in flight.

What do they do out here, she wondered, *work on the honor system?*

She knew that couldn't be true. There were probably sensors of some kind in the eagles, along with video cameras. Glancing at the cars nearest the gate she noticed windshield stickers. They were probably embedded with ID chips.

Workers were just beginning to file out in the twilight. Tired from the trip, Dover was planning to wait until tomorrow before trying to talk to anyone. But it occurred to her that she might be able to set up an appointment for the morning, at least find out who she needed to see to start this matter working up the chain.

She hesitated. The moment of truth was more frightening than it had seemed back in Suitland.

But you've got to push yourself, she thought. *You're not in school or behind a desk. Courage, risk—that's how things get done out here in the real world.*

She turned into the parking lot. Painted on the asphalt was a series of white arrows with a small white label painted at the top: GUEST PARKING. She followed the arrows to a small lot on the west side of the complex, under the shadow of the wind turbines, away from where employees were leaving. The lot was empty. In the back of the complex she saw the area where delivery trucks were parked and, beyond that, an area marked SECURITY. Pulling in near a door that said VISITORS, she walked over. There was another, smaller bronze hawk above the door. She appreciated the bird-of-prey irony since these birds were also most likely for surveillance.

The scrutiny suddenly gave Dover reservations about what she was doing. She felt exposed, unprotected. Maybe that was the subtle effect of the hawk iconography. To make ordinary citizens feel a little like field mice.

Don't go there, she told herself. *What's the worst they could do to me? Deny my request? Have a security guard escort me from the complex? Call the ONI and get me refired for doing my job?* She didn't relish any of those prospects, but she wasn't afraid of them, either. She didn't think there were any legal reasons she couldn't be here. It wasn't as if she were going to break into the place. *You've got to think more like Jack Hatfield.*

She entered the reception area and was momentarily distracted: it was like stepping into a museum. There were framed photographs of Hawke with heads of state going back to Ronald Reagan, as well as a row of relics in glass cases resting on marble columns—not just models and mock-up memorabilia from Hawke projects but also, according to brass plates fastened to the marble, prototypes by Thomas Edison, Samuel Morse, and Alexander Graham Bell. And standing to the right of the opaque glass doors beyond the reception desk was a full-size, moving figure of Hawke. It reminded her of the American Presidents attraction in Disneyland, only more lifelike. As she neared the desk, however, Dover saw that the figure cast no shadow. It was, in fact, a hologram, seemingly solid and complete in every detail—fascinating, a little freakish, and uncomfortably self-worshipful. The eyes watched her as she approached, the expression changing from austere to welcoming.

There was no greater tribute the man could give to himself than hagiography using the kind of technology he championed.

A young woman sat behind a desk that consisted of a glass top and four legs, with what looked like an LED display built into the glass. The receptionist was dressed in a white suit and black tie that had a white zigzag pattern. A nametag said CHENOA. She seemed oblivious to the presence of her "boss."

"What a lovely name," Dover said as she approached.

"Thank you," the woman smiled.

"Native American?"

"Yes. It means 'dove' in the language of the Pechanga," she replied.

Dover grinned. "There's kismet. My name is Dover."

The pretty woman smiled back. It was a neutral smile, unmoved by the synergy. "How may I help you, Dover?"

"This is the lab that ran the Squarebeam research. I'd like to make an appointment with someone about that. Specifically, the status of the technology."

"May I ask your affiliation?"

Dover took her ONI ID from her wallet and passed it to the woman. She felt gutsy and justified.

The woman did not react as she entered data from the ID into her desktop—literally, by touching a keyboard that was apparently built into the desk. "Are you here on official business?"

"Yes," Dover lied.

After looking at the desk for a long moment the woman said, "I see that no one from your office has contacted us."

"That's correct."

"Then this is *not* an official visit?"

"It's part of an investigation," Dover said. "I'm afraid I can't say more."

"You want to talk to someone—in what department? Scientific? Public relations?"

"How about International Relations?"

"We don't have a division by that name."

"What's the closest?" Dover pressed. "What department makes technological deals with foreign customers?"

"Global Sales and Logistics?"

"That sounds right," Dover said.

The receptionist touched the desk. A blue light came on in a small device in her ear. "Fay, there is a Dover Griffith from the Office of Naval Intelligence at reception. She would like to speak with Mr. Siegel whenever it is convenient."

"Tomorrow, if possible," Dover said quietly.

"Tomorrow, if possible," Chenoa repeated.

Dover could hear nothing of the other side of the conversation. It wouldn't surprise her to learn that the Bluetooth was custom-fitted with zero sound leakage.

"Thank you," Chenoa said. "I'll let her know."

A finger tap on the desk and the conversation was over.

"Mr. Siegel has a few minutes to see you now, if

that is convenient," Chenoa said. "He is Vice President of Business Development, GTL."

"Perfect!" Dover said. "Thanks."

"Follow the lights. They will lead you to his office."

Dover had no idea what the woman was talking about until the thickly frosted glass door clicked open behind her. As Dover passed through the door she saw small squares of light on the floor. They literally traced a path through the maze of offices, each one vanishing as she passed. It was functional, showy, and a little intimidating. As fast as technology was infiltrating normal lives, there were obviously levels to which the general public had not yet been exposed.

Like portable EMPs, she reminded herself.

Dover walked slowly, gathering her thoughts as she walked. She hadn't been prepared to see anyone now. She wasn't dressed for a meeting, hadn't made her mental list of bullet points. *Knock it off,* she told herself. *You're in. You should feel good about that.*

During the short walk, Journalism 101 came flooding back. *Start an interview conversationally. It's a chat, not an interrogation. Convince your subject you're a friend, an ally.*

The path ended at another glass-topped desk outside an office. The young woman, presumably Fay, welcomed her with a quick look.

"Go right in."

Another click and another glass door opened behind her. Dover entered the Spartan office. It was mostly windows on one wall, looking out at the landscaped hill to the east. Siegel had the same glass-topped desk as the women, though the office did have two personal touches: framed, antique, global maps on the wall and an MBA from Harvard Business.

A tall, lantern-jawed man came from behind his glass desk. "Dick Siegel," he said. He had short salt-and-pepper hair and a Boston accent.

"Dover Griffith," she replied. "This is quite a place."

"You've never been?"

"No." She grinned. "You obviously have a thing for hawk sculptures."

He smiled. "Most people assume it's just an iteration of the corporate logo, but the truth is they keep away the owls. Otherwise, the darn things hoot down the vents and disturb the night crew."

Dover gave herself a mild reprimand. The bronze birds might well represent Hawke and conceal surveillance equipment, but they also had a very practical function.

Therein lay the undoing of many journalists, she thought. *Jumping to conclusions.*

Siegel did not ask Dover to sit. "I only have a minute, but you have questions about Squarebeam."

The man seemed to hesitate a little when he said the word. Or maybe it was just Dover's imagination.

"Concerns, actually," she said. "There have been two incidents recently in which vehicular electronics in different parts of the world have been one hundred percent shut down. I'm trying to rule out the idea that Squarebeam technology was involved."

"May I ask what these incidents were?"

"I'm not at liberty to disclose that," she replied. "But there is some concern that the technology could have made its way into foreign or private hands."

"Concern by—?"

"Several of us investigating the matter."

"All of our technology is strictly protected by patents which are vigorously enforced," he said. "And as you are probably aware, that particular resource has been retired."

"Officially, yes," she said. "But is there any way someone could be using it unofficially?"

"We have many, many safeguards to ensure that our research and blueprints are secure. We have never been hacked. It's been attempted."

"What about someone on the inside downloading and transmitting information?"

"Impossible," he said. "Each department has only portions of any given project for R and D. Only Mr. Hawke's inner scientific circle has access to what we call 'full picture' technology."

"And those people are—"

"Beyond reproach," Siegel said. "Look, I have a conference call with our Taipei office, but why don't I do this—I'll make sure all the old Squarebeam systems and components are accounted for and then give you a call. Is there a number where I can reach you?"

There was that hesitation again, as though he was watching what he was saying. This time Dover was sure of it.

"I'm staying in the Valley tonight. Would you mind

if I stopped by in the morning?" Dover remembered another journalism adage: keep your foot in the door.

"Sure," Siegel said. "We'll have breakfast in the executive dining room. Maybe I can pry more information from you then, and we can figure this out together."

She gave him a "good luck" smile.

"Come by at nine?" Siegel said.

"I'll be here," she said. "Thank you."

Dover left, the little light road illuminating her way back. It occurred to her as she walked that these were little square beams. A coincidence, no doubt.

She felt good about the meeting. She did not feel as though Siegel were hiding anything or trying to mislead her. He seemed sincere. With luck, a second, longer session would prove more enlightening. Hopefully she would be able to talk to Jack before then, see what pointers he might have, learn what he might have picked up if he'd met with Hawke himself.

She did not notice the eyes upon her as she left. They were not the eyes of a hawk but the eyes of a pair of men in a black Mercedes in an area of the parking lot marked SECURITY.

Dick Siegel checked his watch as he sat at his desk. The meeting had been unexpected and alarming. It was not company policy to see anyone who walked in off the street, even if they were affiliated with a national security organization. There were security issues, first and foremost. There were also liability issues: this *was* a lab. There were occasional "work from home" alerts when radioactive materials were being brought in or tested. Just a week ago they had an "inert bug" brought in from the Centers for Disease Control in Atlanta. The buzz was that they had brought smallpox. The rumor was, Hawke Industries was creating a capsule to store them—in space, where they could be replicated automatically, safely, and dropped on any nation that failed to respond to diplomacy. People were told to stay home. Siegel didn't always know what these experiments entailed, only that whenever he had contact with their insurance representatives he found them to be an unusually skittish group.

The CelesTellia debacle had been in full bloom when Siegel went to work here. The newspapers were describing the broadband technology as Hawke's Albatross, his first big failure, his first public embarrassment, and Hawke hadn't come back swinging with Squarebeam yet. That was when Siegel learned just how dedicated Hawke was to his inner circle: as disastrous as CelesTellia had proven in terms of several lives being lost and tens of millions of dollars of military aircraft destroyed—not to mention Hawke resources tied up and ultimately wasted—Richard Hawke accepted the full blame, passing it to no one, dismissing no one.

However, CelesTellia and Squarebeam had become unmentionable around HITV, the way Jack Hatfield was to the media. If a conversation led to Squarebeam, talk suddenly stopped and took a different course.

Which was why, when someone came to Hawke Industries and actually said the word, he had to see them. Though it had taken a little bit of psychological gearing-up, with a self-imposed gag reflex to overcome, talking to an outsider made it seem all right.

None of which addresses the reason for her visit, he reminded himself. As soon as he got off the Asian call he would talk to Mike Alexander, head of internal security.

Siegel touched the Bluetooth, was about to phone Taipei, when an incoming call stopped him. Calls at HITV were not announced with a tone but with a number. This number was 884. Siegel knew who that was.

"Mike," he said. "I was going to call you in a few minutes. I have a call to make—"

"I won't keep you long," the caller said. "What did Dover Griffith want to know?"

"She is with ONI," he said. That was a purely defensive remark. He knew that Mike would already know that. Siegel wanted him to know that he wouldn't have received "just anybody." "Ms. Griffith was looking into a couple of electrical shutdowns, wanted to make sure none of our technology was involved."

"Why would she assume it was?"

"There were total systems failure in specific vehicles," Siegel replied. "We have a pretty public track record there. It would be a reasonable stop on anyone's search."

"Except that she was suspended from the ONI and has no official standing," Alexander said.

"She presented credentials at the desk—"

"I saw them. I checked. This reckless investigation is what got her sidelined."

"I see." Siegel felt a low-level burn in his belly. "Well, all I told her was that it's not possible we or any of our proprietary technology was involved. I said I'd look into it, though I know what I'll find. She's coming back tomorrow. I had intended to confirm that this is a dead end. That will be the end of it."

Alexander's silence on the other end told him this was not the case.

"The woman is apparently a radical in league with other radicals," the security chief said at last. "I'm instructed to tell you to have no further contact with the woman, to leave this matter with security."

"Of course," Siegel said. "I want you to know that this was strictly a fact-finding meet on my end."

"I'll pass that along," Alexander said.

"Thanks," Siegel said. "Sorry if I was a little over-ambitious."

"I'm sure it's fine. That is what I'm here for, Dick. To make sure the lab, its interests, and its personnel are safe."

Alexander clicked off and Siegel sat for a moment, feeling used and stupid. And the word "Squarebeam" once again had the quality of a malediction, one that was not only unuttered but unthought. The burning was replaced by a big, lonely hollow in his gut, the feeling that his bad call would come to the attention of Hawke himself and stall him in this office for years.

Another victim claimed by that damned technology, he thought, as he sucked it up hard to make the call.

Fairfield, California

For most people, night evoked an image of quiet, restful darkness. What Sammo Yang had discovered over the past few weeks was that only at night did the personality of a place or individual truly emerge. And night was different wherever he went. Night in this small city in Northern California was nothing like night in Afghanistan, which was nothing like night in China. It was not quite ideal for the activity he was planning.

Dressed in jeans and a dark sweater with bulky sleeves, he went out at seven P.M. He headed north on Central Way. According to the minutes he had read and crudely translated online, air traffic over the city was terminated at nine P.M. The last few hours of every flight day were always the busiest as cargo, loaded in the morning, arrived at Travis.

There was no sidewalk so he crossed the parking lots of shops and businesses that lined the main artery. Traffic was still heavy as people went home. He tugged the right sleeve of his sweater every minute or so; the device caused it to ride up. The fabric had been specially treated so as not to generate even a mild static shock, something that might upset the delicate circuitry. He moved toward storefronts, where there were other people and he was less conspicuous. He watched them going about their business, unaware of the holocaust he was about to unleash. It made him feel important, powerful, godlike, this knowledge that he alone possessed: that he was going to change their lives, in some cases end them.

It was a harsh price, but a necessary one. If Sammo did not believe that, he would not be here.

As he crossed the parking lot he became aware of someone crossing diagonally behind him. Sammo waited. The chill of the Northern California night had begun to descend. He pulled at his sleeve. He looked to his right. The man walked back toward the road and waited by a light to cross. Did he know he was being watched?

Sammo continued on. He saw the man cross and then continue in the same direction Sammo was headed. He was almost certainly a tail. But why?

The low buzz of an engine came from somewhere in the distance. Sammo scanned the skies. It was still too distant for the bright wing lights to be visible. He did not know how often the big planes came in. But if someone was following him, he knew that this incoming plane—still not visible—was his best option, perhaps his only option.

He walked more briskly. He wondered if he had underestimated the FBI. They might not have fallen for him sending the consulate car away.

No matter, he thought. *Whoever that man is, he's only observing. So far.*

That changed suddenly. The man was even with Sammo and moving more rapidly. In moments he was a few paces ahead. If the tail was watching for an attack, he probably figured he was safe for the next few blocks since there was nothing but homes and empty lots here.

What if he's concerned about a rendezvous with a consulate car? One that was unmarked, not being followed? He would want to be ahead of it, in the direction traffic was going.

Sammo kept going. The man was nearly jogging now. Evidently he had it in mind to cut back across the street and intercept his prey before he reached a populated area or side streets where he could lose himself. The man could not know what Sammo's target was, only that it was probably better to stop Sammo sooner rather than later.

Sammo could be wrong about all of that. And he had his consulate credentials in Chinese and in English.

He continued forward. The other man was well ahead of him now and did as Sammo had anticipated: he came back across the street, this time not bothering to wait until he reached a traffic light.

The man can do nothing to you, legally, Sammo told himself. But this was a dark patch of road and accidents can happen.

If Sammo turned back now, the man might think this was a dead-end pursuit and go away. Or he could use the delay to summon assistance—perhaps the local police, whose cars Sammo had seen drive by. They could watch him in shifts, pen him in.

The sound of the plane was much nearer. To reach it now, Sammo would have to pick up the pace. If the man interfered, Sammo would have to get past him. That meant using his knife.

What are you prepared to do? he asked himself.

The man was ahead of him now, leaning against a tree, touching buttons on his cell phone. Maybe he was texting; maybe he wasn't. He was clearly there to see what Sammo did next.

Sammo had been schooled in diplomatic protocol. The local authorities could not prosecute him, even for murder, but they could detain him. Doing so, they would find the device.

He could not allow that to be taken.

When he had been hidden in the Tangi Valley, waiting for the helicopter to pass within range, Sammo had learned the importance of patience. He recognized the sudden deflation of spirit he experienced, as though an OFF switch had been thrown in his muscles. But that was as much a part of the job as courage and flexibility. The attack on the plane would have to wait.

Sammo made a show of pulling back his left sleeve and looking at his watch, as though he had been out for a constitutional and time was up. Then he turned into a pizza restaurant just past Lookout Road. He ordered takeout by pointing. He had no idea what he had asked for; it didn't matter. He would return to the hotel with his dinner, go to his room, and slip out as soon as he could. If he were being followed, he could not risk staying there. He would go out via the pool area, pick his way through the dark, tuck himself behind a bush or a Dumpster all night, and try again the next day.

But not like this. They had interfered with his plan. Walking back, running the plans of the air force base through his head, he decided on something a little bolder and much bigger.

Something so grand it wouldn't matter who followed him.

"He turned back, chief."

As soon as Agent Al Fitzpatrick saw his target walk into the hotel with the pizza he'd picked up along the way, the agent got on his phone and went out back to the hotel's pool area for privacy. Upon establishing the Chinese Consulate Detachment that morning, Field Director Carl Forsyth had added a directive ordering that he be contacted directly if anything unusual happened. The presumed diplomat's twilight run seemed to qualify.

"What do you make of it?" Forsyth asked.

"The subject was definitely working," Fitzpatrick said. "I think he was probably trying to hook up with the people who came by today. What did they do?"

"They took your partner up to College City, drove around the town, then went back to the consulate. He's been watching the consulate. The car hasn't come out again."

"Sir, I've been sitting in the hotel wondering if this whole thing is just a ploy to tie up manpower. Except for Travis there are no high-value targets here, and if he was scoping out the base he was going in the wrong direction."

"Does he know you're there?"

"No doubt," Fitzpatrick said. "I wanted to get ahead of him, watch for a make and tag if he was picked up. We were the only two people on foot. No way I could slip that one past him."

"You think it's worth staying with him?"

"I do," Fitzpatrick said. "There's something off about the guy."

"All right. Do you have a picture?"

"Took some cell phone shots," Fitzpatrick said. "Sending now. They're dark and grainy but maybe Tech can make out something useful."

"Good work," Forsyth said.

Fitzpatrick ended the call and went inside for a much-needed trip to the bathroom. The target would probably need at least five minutes to eat his pizza dinner.

Murrieta, California

It was dark and the area around the door was illuminated by just a single dull bulb in a bug-filled lantern above the threshold. Dover didn't notice the black Mercedes until she heard it pull behind her car in the motel parking lot. She was just putting her key in the door of the one-story building when the vehicle stopped perpendicular to her car, the passenger's side at her trunk.

Her first thought was that she should go inside, shut the door, and call 911. She turned the key, popped the lock, but stayed outside waiting to see what this was about.

Both doors of the Mercedes opened and two men emerged. They were stocky, dressed in black suits, their hair cut short, marine style. Their expressions were unsympathetic, their eyes steady. The driver remained where he was. The other man came over. Dover's heart rate quickly doubled.

"Ms. Griffith?" the man asked as he approached.

He wouldn't have asked if he didn't already know the answer. She said nothing.

"I'd like to talk to you about your interest in Hawke Industries," he said.

"I'm kind of tired," she said, backing into the room. "Can this wait?"

"I'll only need a minute," the man said.

"Maybe tomorrow," Dover told him. She stepped inside quickly and shut the door.

From which you forgot to remove the key.

The young woman heard the key turn. The curtains were drawn and it was dark outside. She switched on an unsteady floor lamp. There was no rear exit and there were no windows in the back. She hurried to where she had left her phone plugged in on the night table. She activated it as the man entered.

"Please put it down," he told her.

"I'm calling the police."

"The sheriff's office is about a half hour from here," he informed her. "You might get a deputy who is already on the road and can be here in ten or fifteen minutes—or he may be off in another direction entirely."

"I don't care."

"Ms. Griffith, it doesn't have to be this way." The intruder's hand slipped inside his blazer and remained there, behind the lapel. "Please be reasonable. I only need a few minutes."

Dover hesitated. The man had left the door open. His associate had moved from the driver's side and was standing just a few paces behind his partner.

"What do you want to know?" she asked. Her mouth was dry. The words sounded like rice paper.

"Put the phone down and we can talk," he said.

She continued to hold it. He remained where he was, his hand inside his jacket. She didn't think he would shoot her, but her odds seemed a little better if she cooperated. Slowly, she laid the phone on the table.

"All right," she said. "Talk."

He removed his hand and stood with his arms at his side. "We would like you to leave Murrieta tonight and end your investigation into Hawke Industries."

She stood there, dumbfounded. Dover had clearly crossed more than the Rockies on her way out. She had gone back in time about 150 years.

"You have no right to make those demands," she said. "I haven't done anything wrong."

"You misrepresented yourself as an investigator with the ONI," the man said.

"No, that is the truth."

"You are a civilian analyst with the Current Events

Bureau, current status 'suspended.' You are not authorized to initiate, conduct, or contribute to field investigations. We have a text from Commander Morgan confirming this."

It had been a little more than a half hour from the time she reached HITV and returned to the hotel. In that time, Hawke Industries had used professional contacts and influence with the military to obtain private information about her. That abuse of access was worse than anything she had done. Dover was angry now, and indignation that deep had a way of trumping fear.

"What you just said is bullshit intimidation," she told the man. "If I worked at the Starbucks down the street, I would still be *allowed* to stay at this hotel. I would be *allowed* to walk into your building and ask to see whoever I wished. Are you really going to shoot me for that?"

In response, the man reached into a shoulder holster and withdrew an all-black TASER X2 gun. He raised it with both hands and came around the bed.

"Ms. Griffith, you are going to be leaving the premises."

Dover backed against the wall, into a corner, because there was nowhere else to go. The bathroom was to her left but too far to get to. She guessed from the heft of the weapon and the two long, narrow paddles attached to the front that he would not have to be very close to reach her. She picked up a wastebasket, the only thing that was handy, intending to throw it. Holding a metal object probably would not have afforded her much protection from an electric charge.

She heard a grunt outside. The intruder turned suddenly. Because Dover was no longer in line with the door, she could not see what had happened outside. An instant later the driver of the car half-flew, half-stumbled into the motel room, followed by a foot. The foot belonged to a powerfully built man who kicked him in the kidneys and knocked him hard into the side of the cheap desk. The attacker entered the room. He was dressed all in black, including a wool cap, and held an automatic weapon that swept the room and landed on the man with the TASER. He used his heel to kick the door shut.

"Put your left hand up, throw the weapon into the john, then put your right hand up," the newcomer said to the man. While he spoke he walked up behind the driver, grabbed the collar of his jacket, and twisted. The driver gagged. The newcomer did not relax his grip.

"Whoever you are, you better let him go and leave while you can," the man with the TASER said.

"Aim for the toilet," the newcomer said. "I like it when they sizzle."

The man hesitated while his companion gagged.

"Your friend runs out of air in twenty seconds," the newcomer said. He extended the weapon at arm's length toward the man with the TASER. "He'll be conscious enough to hear you die with time to spare. And the lady and I will be gone long before those wandering sheriff's deputies get here."

With a face that reminded Dover of a dragon mask she'd seen in Chinese language studies, the man raised one hand and tossed the TASER in a long arc toward the bathroom. He missed the toilet.

"Back to bad guy boot camp for you," the newcomer said. "OK. Cell phone next. Left hand, two fingers, on the floor in front of you."

"I know the drill," the man said.

"Just making sure," the newcomer told him. "Not that I had anything to worry about, the way you throw."

The man took the phone from his belt using his thumb and index finger and let it fall to the worn beige carpet.

"Kick," the newcomer said.

The man kicked the phone into the corner where Dover was still huddled.

"Jacket," the newcomer said.

The man held it open to show that he had no other weapons. The newcomer released his grip slightly on the other man. He hoisted him to his feet and pushed him forward. Both hands on his automatic, the newcomer ordered the gasping man to take off his jacket. He had a Glock 21 in a shoulder holster. His partner was ordered to remove it and the man's cell phone with the same two-fingered grip. They both ended up in the corner with Dover.

"Grab a pillowcase and put 'em in," the newcomer told Dover.

She did as he'd instructed. Then he motioned her over. She stood behind him.

"OK, boys," the man said. "Your tires are punctured on the driver's side. You call for a ride from here and your number shows up on the lady's phone bill. Enough for her to prove charges for unlawful entry. You can walk back, though I wouldn't advise it. That rabbit punch-kick combo to the kidneys is designed to bruise the gluteus medius. Walking could tear it." He used his head to motion Dover to the door. She opened it. "The keys are still in the ignition," he said to her. "Get it out of the way, then rev up your rental."

She nodded, grabbed her handbag and suitcase, and left.

The newcomer glared at the men in silence until he heard Dover's engine turn over. "You guys could use more extensive training, what we in the military call 'Deep Offense,' " he said. "If you want to make me an offer, just call on your cell."

Flicking the safety back on and slipping the gun into his belt holster, the newcomer stepped through the door.

"Go to the Starbucks across the street from Hawke," the man said as he climbed into the passenger's side of the rental.

"I don't think you need the caffeine," Dover said.

"I may want a biscotti," he deadpanned.

Dover didn't know if he was serious. She didn't care. She swung the car onto the road and sped north toward Clinton Keith.

"Thank you," she said as she drove. "I hope."

"It's OK, you're in good hands," her passenger said. Dover had placed the pillowcase on the backseat. The man retrieved it and put the guns in the glove compartment. "My name's Doc Matson. Jack Hatfield asked me to fly down and keep an eye on you."

"How did Jack—?" she began, then clapped her lips shut as she replayed the conversation with him in her head. Of course Jack would figure out why she was coming to Murrieta.

"Our mutual friend is a pretty clever guy," Doc said. "Though I have to say, for an intelligence agent—I was eavesdropping, sorry—your breadcrumb trail is more like a series of loaves."

"I've got a lot to learn. Clearly."

The traffic on Whitewood was sparse. It thickened when they reached the main road. Fortunately the Starbucks was only a short distance from the intersection.

"So I'm guessing you have a car at Starbucks?" she ventured.

"A cab," he informed her. "I took it from the airport, figured we'd drive your car back. I was watching for a rental driven by someone who matched your description. When you left, I had the driver follow you back to the hotel and drop me off. I waited behind the ice machine to see if anyone from Hawke did the same." He shook his head. "What a pair of morons. One of them should've been watching the street."

"Those tires were pretty flat," Dover said.

Doc slipped a Bowie knife from a sheath under his left arm. It had a nine-inch blade and a faint, oily smell. "A little grease, slide it deep, the oil keeps it from hissing when you pull it out."

"Where did you learn that?"

"A greased blade? Cutting rebel throats for the Russians in Chechnya," he replied. "Men try to breathe through the wounds if you're holding their mouths— which you do to keep them from shouting. You need to keep the air passage quiet, too."

Dover felt her chest tighten. She forced herself to concentrate on the road, on the traffic, not to picture what her passenger had just described.

"The cab's waiting in the parking lot so he can jump on the freeway headed south," Doc said. "For a hundred bucks he's going to drive the cell phones away from the direction we're headed. The GPS will put him somewhere in Fallbrook while we're on the way to Ontario."

"What happens when they find him?" Dover asked, trying and failing not to picture a dying rebel.

"The driver plays dumb, says his fare must've forgotten his pillowcase." Doc grinned. "I'd love to see those guys' faces when they catch up to him."

"That's why you removed the guns," Dover said.

"Bingo. I don't want him to have trouble if they call the cops."

The car reached the Starbucks. Dover was driving on automatic. She saw the sign, swung in without thinking. Doc jumped out. The young woman's head felt like it was along for the ride: it had stopped trying to process anything that was happening. She was amazed she had figured out why he'd taken the weapons from the pillowcase.

Doc came running back. "We're good," he said. "Back to the Ontario Airport."

"I'll have to see if I can change my reservation," she said as she spun back onto Clinton Keith Road. She made the light, was no longer afraid of the fast left lane as she headed north on 15.

"You won't need a ticket from here," Doc told her. "I flew down."

"As in, your own plane?"

He nodded. "It's the only way you can get your own guns into or out of a country."

Her passenger was sending a text, and Dover stopped talking. There was nothing else she wanted to ask. She was done thinking about anything except getting to the airport—and one thing more.

Someone at Hawke Industries had a secret to protect, one she had jeopardized. One for which they were willing to TASER her and kidnap her to get her to the airport. She didn't know if she would ever be safe. She knew that her bridges at the ONI had not just been burned, they'd been blasted. The only way through this was straight ahead.

Whatever concerns Dover had about the profession of the man sitting beside her, drumming his knees and humming Sousa's "The Thunderer," she was grateful to have Doc Matson and Jack Hatfield watching her flank.

Marigot, Saint Martin

Of all the places Jack had thought he might end up at the flight's end, the Caribbean was not on his short list. Only the sign on the distant terminal told him where he was, in Saint Martin; Martina was still mute on their destination. Even as they were making their final approach.

And then it hit his chronically suspicious brain: *You should have expected something like this. Maybe it was a long-planned getaway or maybe Hawke is just staying out of the country in case this investigation goes south for him.*

Hawke's jet came in so low over Maho Beach, Jack could see the faint sheen of wet sand in the moonlight. He thought about the sunseekers who would have thronged the beach that day. Veterans would have ignored the low-flying aircraft; there would have been panic in the eyes and gestures of newcomers.

Imagine how the Arawak Indians felt when they saw the ships from Spain, he thought.

It was strange to think of toned, near-naked ladies playing volleyball and the crew of Christopher Columbus on this same clear stretch of waterfront. It was possible that the Indians were wearing even less than vacationers, which was the only backward step he could conjure up. He thought of those men crossing the ocean in a slow-going, wind-driven chamber pot while he flew here faster than the speed of sound. He thought of the diseases that had ravaged the civilization in the Leeward Islands over half a millennium ago and the medicines that prevented them today. He thought of the slavery introduced by the Spanish and the freedom paid for in blood by American soldiers who fought oppression at home and abroad in war after war.

As the jet crossed the chain-link fence and *plip-plopped* onto the tarmac, he turned his thoughts to Richard Hawke. The man was somewhere on this island. As he recalled from the *Fodor's* he'd read before going to Antigua, this region used to be inhabited by hereditary chieftains, not self-made lords. That, too, was different. Whether for better or worse remained to be seen.

A white stretch limo was waiting on the tarmac. A swarthy Customs agent with a pencil moustache and a pinched grin came out to meet the jet after the steps were lowered, but he did not bother to check Jack's bag. He did confiscate the popcorn, however, saying that foreign grain was not permitted. Jack didn't believe that. He just looked like a man who needed a snack.

Jack said good-bye to Martina. They shook hands. It had been a strange and singular experience being around a woman who was so beautiful without inhabiting or enjoying that beauty. She was only the marketable shell of Hawke's machine.

The limo was equipped for a party. There was a digital jukebox, a forty-inch HD TV, Dom Perignon on ice, and a refrigerator with more Iranian caviar, fresh slices of expensive Yubari melons, and the world's most expensive pie from the Fence Gate Inn in Burnley, Lancashire, England. It was made with two bottles of 1982 Château Mouton Rothschild red wine, Wagyu beef from Kobe, Japan, matsutake mushrooms, and a crust with gold-leaf topping. Jack knew all of this because the car also came equipped with

Utako, a stunning young lady who also, by coincidence, came from Kobe. She explained it all as they rolled through the airport gate. She wore the same uniform as Martina and had the same aloof manner. Not that there was time for Jack to try to get to know her any better than he knew Martina. He spent less than ten minutes in the car as it took him not to some mountaintop estate, as he was expecting, but to the Daniel Dutch Marina on Simpson Bay. There he boarded an Aquariva speedboat. Except for its fiberglass hull, the sleek vessel was almost entirely mahogany from the cockpit to the decks, with Gucci print fabric upholstery—waterproof, Utako informed him as they boarded. The pilot, dressed in a tailor-made black suit with the now-familiar Hawke logo on his seaman's cap, immediately revved the two quiet 380 HP Yanmar engines and they took off, planing at 35 knots.

Jack did not have to ask where they were going.

Through the forest of moonlit masts belonging to small pleasure boats, he saw the side of the yacht: it was like a brushstroke of gleaming white across the darkness. It bore the name *Hi-Lite* in bold, black letters.

Utako must have noticed Jack staring.

"The lengths of yachts have grown exponentially in just the last decade," Utako said, loud enough to be heard over the hum of the massive diesel engines, the rush of the wind, and the slap of the hull against the water, "culminating in the launch of *Eclipse* at five hundred and thirty-three feet. On the list of the world's largest yachts, which includes royal and state ships, Richard Hawke's yacht at four hundred and thirty-nine feet is ranked only number eight. But it has very rare features. Built under an extreme blanket of secrecy by Blohm and Voss shipyards, she is one of only two private yachts that are ice-classed. Featuring over forty-eight thousand square feet under air, she has seven decks, including twelve guest cabins, twin master suites, a hangar, several pools, and two helipads, one of which, on the aft deck, is hydraulically retractable. She can accommodate up to twenty-four guests and has a live-aboard crew of twenty-seven, including three security men who were formerly Russian *Spetsnaz*."

What Utako did not mention, of course, Richard Hawke thought as he eavesdropped on their conversation through a computer chip on the young woman's uniform, *was that* Hi-Lite *was equipped on all sides with components of the Squarebeam technology.* The gun-like devices could deactivate the electronics of any threatening vessels as well as emit a blinding light that rendered any opponent incapable of seeing the yacht as Hawke sped away from danger.

Back on the speedboat, Jack was amused that he had merited the information about the former *Spetsnaz.* Hawke had a high opinion of his abilities, apparently. "How many guests are there now?" Jack asked.

Her short, black hair blowing behind her, the young woman said, "I believe you are the only guest."

Jack had not expected her to answer. That meant Hawke wanted him to know they would be alone except for his loyal crew. Make him alert, guarded, worried, defensive, carelessly offensive—any number of small, destabilizing reactions.

"The yacht was especially designed by Mr. Hawke for dining on the topmost deck," she went on. "That assures privacy from other vessels, from the dock, and also from the crew, and maximizes views from the finished wood alfresco dining table and wraparound seating."

Which means we're having dinner, Jack thought. *A courtesy or a coercion?*

They arrived aft of the large white vessel in five minutes flat, climbed the few steps to the main deck. The captain was waiting for them.

"Russ Browning," the uniformed man introduced himself, smiling.

The captain was about forty-five with salt-and-pepper hair showing under his hat. He had a rich tan, a big smile, and perfect teeth. He stood like a seaman, legs slightly apart for balance, spine ramrod straight. Captain Browning radiated the same kind of formal perfection as the Hawke women. Jack wondered which came first, the perfect captain's bearing or employment by Hawke.

"Would you care to visit a cabin before meeting Mr. Hawke?" Browning asked.

"I did everything I needed on his plane," Jack said, looking around. "This is quite a setup, too."

"She is the loveliest vessel in the water," Browning declared.

Jack had no way of knowing whether or not that

was true. But based on just the mini fridge in the limousine, he was not about to question the captain. At the same time, he thought of the *Sea Wrighter*. It was small by comparison, cramped, and you felt every buck and heave of the water. But it was home. It was personal. He suddenly missed it very much.

They made their way through the main salon, which was the size of his Union Street apartment. It had a wet bar, a spotless white carpet, big picture windows, more black-and-white leather sofas, and a pair of Renoirs on the wall. The lamps were by Tiffany, the captain mentioned. Jack didn't think he meant the singer.

They continued up to the bridge deck, all the while Jack feeling less and less as though he was on a boat. Even when he saw the bay, he felt like he was in a beachfront hotel. The sway was that minimal, the trappings so unboatlike.

Jack wanted to ask Captain Browning about his experiences before joining Hawke—they might bond over their love of smaller boats that one could actually pilot, and that relationship could prove useful—but he didn't think there was time and he wasn't sure the seaman would be any more forthcoming than the women had been. It wasn't a life Jack aspired to, but he could imagine workers not wanting to leave surroundings like the jet and yacht if they didn't have to.

From there they went to the sundeck, where Richard Hawke was lying on a black hammock with an e-reader and a clip-on light. The hammock was clearly custom-made, with a wide base made of what looked like matte-black carbon. There was a strange, pinched joint in the middle of the head and foot supports; on the head rail of the hammock was what looked like a photoelectric sensor. The captain explained that the unit "read" the sun, communicated with small, silent motors in the two joints, and kept the hammock facing the sun at all times. It was still oriented to the western horizon and would reset in the morning.

Jack was overwhelmed rather than impressed.

Hawke was dressed in a white robe and reading glasses. When he rose, Jack was surprised how stooped and thin he was. He had read about the man's battle with throat cancer. Even the best doctors and healthiest sunshine could not undo the pallor of what he had endured. As his host walked around the six queen-size sunning beds built in a large marble well, Jack noticed the Hawke logo embroidered on the back of his robe in black and gold.

Like a fighter's robe, Jack thought.

There was a point at which excess became comical self-mockery. The hammock had come indulgently close; the robe crossed the line.

"Mr. Hatfield," Hawke said quietly as he approached.

"Call me Jack," Jack said.

"Like Ishmael?" Hawke replied.

"Helluva question to ask on a boat," Jack said.

"Why?" Hawke said. "Ishmael survived."

Hawke offered his hand, and Jack shook it. The man's grip was firm enough.

"It's odd we've never met," Hawke remarked.

"We don't exactly move in the same social circles," Jack pointed out.

"True, but we're nearly neighbors."

"Your place in Carmel?"

"I come to a lot of public events in San Francisco," Hawke said. "The kind you used to attend."

"You mean, when I mattered."

Hawke laughed. "Your modesty is unexpected."

There was a false, frustrating informality to the greeting. Part of that was the awkwardness of any first meeting; part was the fact that this was bound to be adversarial. Jack had expected that. But it made Jack wonder if anything about the man was real, honest, off-the-shelf. Jack had always been able to put his TV guests at ease with a few jokes and his naturally easygoing style. But then, most of them were tense about going on TV and wanted to be relaxed. Hawke was guarded but he did not seem tense. And he had the home court advantage.

"What would you like to eat, drink?" Hawke asked.

"Nothing, thanks."

"Just the facts, ma'am," Hawke laughed.

"I *am* a reporter."

"So I was just reading," he held up the e-reader and wigwagged it. "Your articles on the Hand of Allah. Fascinating."

Jack thanked him. Hawke said that if his guest didn't mind he'd like to go to the dining room. Jack agreed and followed him down a different set of stairs from the one he'd come up.

The dining room was gently air-conditioned.

"We don't get much of a breeze this side of the island, and that sun cooks the roof for the entire day,"
Hawke said, waving a hand at the ceiling. It was covered with a Renaissance-style mural of great inven-
tors and their creations, in the guise of saints. "What
do you think of my faux Italian masterwork? It was
painted by the gentleman who was arrested five years
ago for creating fake Michelangelos."

Nothing real, honest, off-the-shelf . . . Jack thought.
"Did you commission this before or after?"

"After," Hawke admitted. "I paid for his defense
team. Talent like this should not be doing chalk draw-
ings on a prison wall. He got six years, served three.
This took him two years. I didn't bother him the way
Pope Julius kept after Michelangelo. Art can't be bul-
lied."

Ironically, the mural was probably not much
smaller than the Sistine Chapel ceiling.

They sat at a corner of the Louis XVI dining room
table.

"This is not a re-creation," Hawke tapped it as he
sat in one of the matching, cushioned chairs. "It was
made for Versailles but never delivered. Marie Antoi-
nette felt it wouldn't be large enough for the room she
had in mind." He pointed to a painting behind him.
"That is she, in hunting attire. It's by her portraitist,
Joseph Krantzinger. She didn't like the background,
insisted he do the whole thing over."

"Royalty," Jack said as he sat. "What can you do
with someone who has so much power?"

Hawke smiled as water was poured by a young

male steward. "Behead them, of course. But you never know what will take their place. Was Napoleon any better?"

"No," Jack agreed.

"Was Lenin an improvement over Tsar Nicholas II? Did Cuba fare any better under Fidel Castro than it did under Batista?"

"Those are either-or situations," Jack said. "Not everything is so black or white."

Hawke took a long drink of water as he sat back in his white chair. He didn't answer.

He didn't have to.

The industrialist smiled. There was something unhealthy in his expression. Not just in the flesh but in the poison that lay beneath it. Like a snake trying to hypnotize prey.

"Do you own one of these?" Hawke asked, holding up the e-reader.

"I just got a tablet a few weeks ago," Jack said. "I'm not an early adaptor."

Hawke continued to smile. He spoke one word, quietly. "Pierre."

A young man trotted silently up the staircase. Jack just now noticed a small bulge in the frame of Hawke's glasses, just over each ear. An embedded Bluetooth, he surmised. Pierre was carrying a plastic cylinder, which he handed to Hawke. The way the young man bowed to make sure his boss didn't have to reach far for it, or even look over, reminded Jack of a bas relief he had seen of a quaestor presenting Tiberius Caesar with a writing tablet. Pierre removed the e-reader and remained by Hawke's elbow.

The cylinder was actually a flexible display nearly two feet across. Hawke spread it on the desk with both hands. The display remained flat.

"Our latest commercial application of proprietary military technology," Hawke smiled. "The tablet you purchased is already obsolete. This device utilizes our own patented semiconducting material with eight times the current modulation rate of existing organic thin film transistors." He smiled triumphantly. "Instead of employing electronics based on conventional solid chips in archaic plastic containers, we've created a display driver just twenty microns thick and integrated it into the pane itself. Only dedicated Hawke electronics function on board the *Hi-Lite*."

"You mean I had myself wired up for nothing?"

Hawke laughed, but not at the easy victory. It was an expression of joy. The man seemed prouder showing off that little screen than he did his jet and yacht.

His legacy is more important than what it has bought him, Jack thought.

Hawke gestured toward Jack. Pierre brought him the display screen, laid it out before him, tapped an icon on the plastic sheet, then left.

"You will recognize this, I think," Hawke said.

Jack looked down at the surprisingly bright and lifelike image. It was an episode of *Truth Tellers* from 2010, the one with Dr. José Colon of Caltech and press officer Rebecca Walsh of Squarebeam. The audio came from speakers that were hidden in the ceiling and walls around the table. It began at the point when Jack was saying, ". . . what you were describing sounds a lot like the protection rackets run by the mob."

"I don't need to see or hear it," Jack said. "I remember what I said."

"Do you remember every show you've done? Or just that one?"

"A call from the Vice President of the United States tends to stick in one's memory," Jack told him.

"What did he tell you?"

"That's between me and the Vice President."

"Do you know the definition of a lonely man, Mr. Hatfield? A man of ideals in a selfish world."

Jack shrugged a little. "I'd call him a beacon."

"Like a solid old lighthouse or a candle in the window," Hawke said with a flourish. In the process of saluting them he mocked them.

"I would say more like a pole star," Jack said.

"Of course you would," Hawke said. "You know, though, that pole stars are true *only* at the poles. And they change over time." He leaned forward. "The Vice President told you that you were overstating the danger of Squarebeam technology. He informed you that we were on the verge of making a significant deal with the Chinese government that would provide work for my laboratories in Connecticut, in Florida, and in California. He suggested that the President would like to be able to talk about the thousands of jobs and hundreds of millions of dollars this relationship would bring to America. Does that sum it up?"

"Except for one thing," Jack said. "He didn't answer my question about what kind of technology you were selling to China."

"Did you expect him to? What is your security level, Jack?"

"The word of a journalist is the only security level he needs," Jack said. "That's why the public never heard about D-Day before June 6 and Joe Voter did not know about JFK's back pain or mistresses."

"Ideals again," Hawke said.

"They always come back, just like spring," Jack said. "Why do you hate them so much?"

"Because they lack any connection with reality, any use in an evolving society. They are the ultimate form of narcissism."

"Not this?" With a sweep of his hand, Jack moved from the flexible display to the boat. "Everything in your colors, black and white. Everything with your zigzag line cutting through it. Your predatory bird logo on every employee."

"You must learn the difference between vanity and uniformity," Hawke said. "I don't announce to the world, as you do, that my ideals are correct. These trappings—and that's all they are, accessories to a life—are proof that my judgment is correct. I understand what people need, from ordinary citizens to government leaders."

"And when they succumb, you brand them," Jack said.

"You're wrong," Hawke said. "It's a partnership."

"So your employees keep telling me. Each of them

stamped from your mold, articulating your dogma, surrendering self for comfort and access."

"You make 'comfort' sound like a dirty word."

"Not at all," Jack said. "I happen to love it myself, though I wouldn't trade my bike for your tinted-windows limo. I'd miss too much of the world."

"You have it before you, right there," he pointed to the display.

"Data, not experience."

"That depends on the kind of experience one wishes to have," Hawke said. "Does a woman want the pain of childbirth or the child itself? Does a man want the pain of dentistry or a radiant smile? When you ride your bicycle, can you play the piano? Can you paint, read? Drive an SLR McLaren? Everything in life is a trade-off, Mr. Hatfield."

"Not freedom," Jack replied.

"*Yes* freedom," Hawke said. "You are not free to rape or burn down a house of worship."

"That's where ideals come in," Jack said. "Without them—a Bill of Rights or a church, for example—nations crumble."

"A moral anchor," Hawke said dismissively. "Something other than an iron will to unify people. To you it's one or the other."

"Isn't it?" Jack asked. "That's one reason the Soviet Union didn't make it. Uganda under Amin. Iraq. Suppression and corruption are no substitute for a code of honor."

"You have a high school student's view of the

world," Hawke said. "Have you actually spent time in Russia, in Chechnya, in the other republics? I have. The Soviet Union failed before it began because the Tsar, the leader the masses despised, was executed and thrown down a mineshaft. Civilizations don't rally around morality; they rally around hate. Did the Confederacy rally around slavery because it was moral? No. They were united in their strong, universal dislike of being ordered to change their way of life, to make the needs of the state subservient to the whims of the nation. Despite being better financed, better armed, and with more men, the North took four bloody years to subjugate the Rebels. When was this country more united than after Pearl Harbor or 9/11? Joseph Conrad argued that what truly changes the world for the better are acts of 'ferocious imbecility.' Who can argue that humankind's response to that has always been shoulder-to-shoulder unification? Look at the Crusades. To this day, many Muslims condemn them. When President George W. Bush dared to say— on September 16, 2001, when our nation was still bleeding—'This crusade, this war on terrorism is going to take a while,' he was widely criticized for using that word. Yet what made his words necessary? What caused the original Crusades? In the eleventh century, as in 2001, it was an act of vicious aggression by radical Muslims—in that instance, cutting off access to Jerusalem. Hate, Mr. Hatfield. Hate unifies. Hate inspires. Hate of poverty, of degradation, of endless, difficult choices. *That*, Mr. Hatfield, is a third option."

Jack saw where this was going, and it frightened him. He imagined Hitler and his war against the Jews turned loose in some way he had yet to figure out. But a good journalist never lets opinion or ego get between himself and information. He lets his subject think he is the smarter of the two. That keeps him talking, explaining.

"At the risk of being sent to detention," Jack smiled, "how does that have anything to do with why I'm here?"

"You told an associate that you believed my technology was being used to murder Americans," Hawke said. "Is that accurate?"

"I did."

"May I have your evidence? If you need to use a computer to open a file or database, the touchpad on the screen before you is linked to my corporate system through the Hawke-B satellite. You can even open any number of ONI files, if you need them—though I would have to give you my password."

Jack did not react to Hawke's latest demonstration of access. He looked down. He typed a few commands into the touchpad. It was impressive. "I don't need a computer," he said, "just an answer. And, if necessary, an explanation." Something else a good journalist did was to never become the interviewee.

Hawke laughed again, this time with a little less enthusiasm. "I rarely watched your program when you had one, but I see why it was successful. You believe that pushing and bullying is the way to get information."

"It saves time."

"Is that how you seduce your women as well?"

Jack was not intimidated. "You wouldn't believe the lures I throw at women."

"Like a fly-fisher?" Hawke smiled.

"More like that than you would imagine," Jack said. "Seduction is not my style, Mr. Hawke. Women are pretty smart. Either they click with you or they don't. You're pretty smart. Either you answer my questions or you don't."

"If I don't," Hawke said, "what then?"

"The main part of my business here is through."

"The main part," Hawke said.

"I'm pretty sure that someone with your 'proprietary technology' is up to no good," Jack said. "But I'll find that out on my own."

"Not with the help of Ms. Griffith," Hawke said confidently. He indicated the flexible display.

Jack looked down, saw security footage of a woman entering and leaving the Murrieta facility.

"She learned nothing," Hawke told him.

"Sure she did," Jack said.

"What was that?"

This was one question Jack was happy to answer. "That she's not alone. The two clowns you sent to chase her away? Didn't turn out too well for them." Jack had learned that by reading the text message from Doc on Hawke's flexible display.

Hawke had survived too many boardroom battles and Congressional committees to be thrown by a sideshow setback. What seemed to wound him—and

Jack had followed his eyes carefully as they went from Jack to the flexible display then back—was the realization that his own device had just been used against him.

"What is your other business with me?" Hawke asked. His voice was unworried, but his expression was slightly guarded, his eyes were wary.

"You're guilty of something," Jack said. "You've told me that by your lack of curiosity about what I suspect, what I may know. An innocent man would have asked."

"You think too highly of yourself," Hawke said. "You're a conspiracy theorist, nothing more. You lucked out once, with the Hand of Allah, and you're desperately trying to do so again. On my back."

"Do you have anything else you want to share?" Jack asked.

"Just this." The veneer of graciousness vanished, like harsh sunlight breaking through mist. "I flew you down here to sit across the table from the man who called me a Mafioso, a level of attack that even heads of state have never dared."

"They're afraid of you," Jack said. "I'm not."

"They're wise," Hawke replied. "You're not. I wanted to tell you, face-to-face, that the sound of Jack Hatfield's voice no longer matters. Who has come running to the Hero of Golden Gate? Where are the offers? Where is *The New Jack Hatfield Show*? You were always a fringe voice, but now you are a discredited one as well. A freak who chased down a radical freak, nothing more."

Hawke tapped his glasses, paused, smiled.

"You and Miss Dover Griffith—a man on the way down leading a girl who has lost her way. I'm informed that you sent a bully as your proxy, a rogue coyote. He attacked two security men who were merely escorting the young lady from a dangerous situation. *That* is your contribution to society. Verbal and physical thuggery. That is your flexible display screen, your contribution to the world. Fortunately your wife left you. There is no one to hear you except a poodle, a mercenary, a pizza maker, an aging hippie, and now a frustrated journalist. You come here and piss on *my* people? You and your circle are pathetic."

"Are Americans pathetic, Mr. Hawke? Are the Chinese better than us?"

"The Chinese again," Hawke said. "You're like a journalistic abattoir, you know that? You examine every part of the animal, over and over, to make sure it is used for something. I already told you, my activities are at a level of security—"

"I didn't ask about your activities," Jack interrupted. "I asked about the Chinese."

"You'll have to be more specific," Hawke said, amused and apparently intrigued. "They are no more monolithic than Americans."

"What do the leaders want?"

"Personally? Globally? Domestically?"

"Dealer's choice," Jack replied.

Hawke thought for a moment. "There are two kinds of Chinese leaders. Egalitarian—those who believe in the Maoist ideals of widespread equality and work tirelessly to achieve it—and the elite, aristocratic Chinese—those who believe in equality, but also that their nation is more equal than others. They detest what they perceive as American arrogance."

"You mean, the fact that *we're* proud, too? The fact that we beat them and practically everyone else on the planet to every important scientific and cultural step forward."

"The Chinese had gunpowder, what they called 'fire medicine,' in the ninth century, when North America had more buffalo than Homo sapiens."

"Yeah, but since then? Since the Europeans came over and created a new breed of can-do people?"

Hawke smiled. "There. You see? American arrogance. Jingoism. We didn't create Beethoven's *Ninth Symphony*. The Sistine Chapel ceiling. The Parthenon."

"No, but they only would've been heard by Aryan ears without us," Jack pointed out.

"That victory is aging like Chinese gunpowder," Hawke said.

"No, it's part of an ongoing series," Jack said. "We drove, we flew, we telephoned, we split the atom, we went to the moon, we invented PCs and wired the world. Even you—there was a time when you were about the thrill of discovery. Americans may not have invented the idea of crossing new frontiers, but we made it our own. The Chinese have followed, in our shadow. They're not angry at us. They're ashamed."

"Well, you seem to know all there is to know

about the Chinese," Hawke smiled. "Why did you ask me?"

Jack had let Hawke talk because that was what journalists did, he had reminded himself—even as each blow landed. The man was no amateur; he knew just what bruises to press. But there was a point at which even journalists had to go on offense to get results.

"I ask you because I think you're doing what the Chinese do, Mr. Hawke, these 'elite Chinese' of yours. The Chinese can't beat us unless they break our spirit. So they play corrosive games, the same way you do. I talked about this on my show. To them, a psychological victory is more important than a tactical or logistical one. Even when we discovered and rooted out their cyber attacks, exposed their artificial currency deflation, they withdrew and looked for another way in. Like you said, they haven't done anything significant for over a millennium. The only way they catch up is by making us doubt ourselves, by causing us to undermine ourselves."

"And you see me that way?" Hawke asked.

"You flew me here, didn't you? For what? Not to inform, not to educate, and I'm guessing not to try and bribe. You just wanted to play."

"Remarkable," Hawke shook his head. "Apart from overstating your market value, you see me and China as all that is bad, you and America as all that is good. What was it Cervantes said? 'So educated, but so misinformed.' "

"I wouldn't know," Jack said. "I'm more of a Bible man myself, and I hold dear Proverbs 3:7—'Do not be wise in your own eyes; fear the Lord and shun evil.' I don't run my life by whim or presumption but by evidence. We're all a work in progress. That's why *I* agreed to come here." Jack rose. "Mr. Hawke, I want to thank you for your hospitality and the fifty-thousand-mile checkup."

Hawke's expression was as dark as the sky outside. "You're not a 'work in progress,'" he said menacingly. "You're finished. Pierre!"

The young man appeared at the top of the stairs.

"Pierre, see that this self-styled vox populi gets as far as possible as quickly as possible." He looked at Jack for the last time. "If the water here weren't just ten meters deep, that is the direction I would choose to send you."

Jack rose. "That's OK. I know how to swim. Incidentally, what you just told me was the other business that brought me here." He looked down placidly at the hostile face of the titan of industry. "I wanted to look in your eyes, know for certain that you'd kill to get your way."

"Only people I know," Hawke said. "I want to be sure I'm doing the right thing."

"I'll make sure you get another chance," Jack said.

"Not advisable."

"But we're not finished."

"I think we are."

Jack grinned. "Then I guess you *don't* really 'know' me."

Hawke's body was tense as he stood and turned from Jack.

"This way, sir." Pierre was at Jack's side, between him and Hawke. His arm was extended toward the staircase.

Jack walked ahead, the aide following closely like a mobile quarantine unit.

The Aquariva speedboat was revved and waiting for him. It sped away at once. Utako did not acknowledge him, other than to wait until he was seated before instructing the driver to depart.

The night air was decidedly chilly. Yet that wasn't what caused the goose bumps running up his arms. It was the personal power this man had amassed and the certainty with which he used it. Unlike Hitler, he didn't need ministers and foreign allies and a compliant British prime minister. He had technology that put his influence everywhere, from outer space to government offices to individual cell phones—his own, now that he had read that text on Hawke's flexible display.

He never doubted that Hawke could kill if it suited his design. He had nearly said as much during that segment of *Truth Tellers*. The questions that bothered Jack were: What *was* his design? Are the Chinese involved and, if so, how? To what end?

Jack felt he had an answer, of sorts, in the Hawke employees he had met so far: Bahati, an Egyptian.

Utako, a Japanese. Martina, an Austrian. Pierre, a Frenchman. It wasn't just an eclectic group, an enthusiastic young rainbow culled from his offices around the globe. To Jack, it said something more.

It said all nations made one.

Under Hawke.

Chapter 2

Fairfield, California

Sammo returned to his hotel after stopping to purchase a pizza. He went to his room and changed into jeans and a Travis AFB sweatshirt he had acquired in the hotel gift shop. Then he went to the hotel counter, carrying his box of pizza. The lobby showed no sign of the man Sammo had encountered on his walk. Sammo said one word to the night receptionist: "Bicycle."

"Yes, sir, there are a number of places you can go," she said before Sammo shook his head to indicate he didn't understand what she was saying. Nodding, the woman held up a finger then began typing on her computer. When she was finished, she rotated the flatscreen monitor toward the guest.

"Bradbury's Bike Shop," she said. "The address is

2222 Rockwell. They are open until eight." She brought up a MapQuest route and pointed to *B*. "It's a little over two miles. Do you want a cab? A taxi?"

"Yes, please," he said.

While the clerk made the call, Sammo reflected on the wisdom of having been taught just a minimal amount of English. He knew the key words and phrases, could recognize enough writing to read signs and enunciate the names of roads and cities. But brainwashed American liberals became more solicitous, embraced you more readily, when they thought you needed help. It was much easier for an agent to enter a society when he was invited by "nice" people.

The clerk printed out the map and circled the destination for Sammo. She made sure he had bills small enough to pay for the ride. It made him feel all-powerful to know that in just a few hours this woman would be broken with horror, awash with tears and a crushing fear for the future, that her life would never again be safe and normal.

Sammo gave the map to the driver and sat back, the pizza box on his lap. He was reminded, as the cab passed a church, of the ancient god Tian, who was synonymous with the greatness of the cosmos. The deity was depicted in writing with the script character 天 that resembled the Christian cross he noticed atop the steeple.

We are all one in every way, from our basic faith to our instinctive terrors, he thought. Our basic needs are the same as well, though Americans have never understood that. He had learned how the nation was built, by individuals in wagons, on homesteads, panning for gold. Despite the name, they had never truly united except to fight wars. Sammo felt the kind of pride and sense of belonging that were worth any sacrifice, any risk.

Mao's Revolution made us communal in nature, equal in purpose and resolve. We move as an unstoppable mass and not as arrogant, aggressive individuals.

That was why the Chinese would always be victorious, he thought.

Traffic was still heavy, and Sammo probably could have walked the distance in the time it took to drive. The box on his lap was beginning to cool but that didn't matter. The contents didn't matter. It was merely a prop.

He could not tell if he was still being followed. He could not see a taxi behind him, though he noticed that the driver had a GPS computer. Presumably law enforcement could follow Sammo that way.

Those efforts wouldn't matter, either. All he needed was proximity and his cell phone.

Renting a bicycle required more time and documentation than Sammo was prepared to give, so he simply purchased a used model for cash, one with a wire-frame basket in front. He also bought a helmet and a large canvas notebook bag. The shop was empty and the sales personnel ignored him as he crouched on the floor and put the takeout inside the bag. The edges of the box stuck out. That was fine. He wanted the contents to be visible.

Donning the helmet, he pedaled south along Rock-ville Road to Rio Vista, which ran east and west. He took it east, hearing the distant drumbeat of the power-ful transport engines and the occasional whistle of a fighter. He was enjoying the exercise, the way it reminded him of getting around Beijing, and was grateful his original plan had not worked out.

This was a better one.

It was nearly nine P.M. by the time he reached his destination, the southern entrance to Travis Air Force Base. The guard post was unexceptional-looking: a booth, mostly glass, with a large framework that covered the two-lane road. An iron gate-arm blocked the way. None of that mattered to Sammo. All that con-cerned him was the floodlit structures beyond.

He parked his bicycle outside the gate and walked toward the booth. There were two uniformed young men inside. Both wore disinterested expressions. One pressed a button.

"Can I help you, sir?"

Sammo held the black notebook bag with the edge of the box facing the guard.

"General," Sammo said.

The young man asked. "General who? Are you saying a general ordered a pie?"

The two airmen laughed.

"This has got to be a gag," one of them said. "What's the general's name?"

Sammo appeared confused. He held up a finger and laid the bag on the bicycle basket. He took his cell phone from his pants pocket and pretended to make a call. He spoke in Chinese, loudly and with agitation, all the while watching the two men. And as they watched him back, amused by his flustered chatter, he was busy snapping flashless pictures of the base. He faced one way, pacing, then turned the other way. Then he stopped and faced forward. When he was finished, he shut the phone, shoved it in his pocket, apologized with a few words and bows, then rode off.

Back at the hotel, Sammo checked the hotel lobby again. There was a man nodding off in one of the out-of-the-way corners. He might have been the same man who had interfered with Sammo's earlier plans, but it didn't matter enough for Sammo to check closely. Sammo had alternate plans now.

He went up to his room, parked the bicycle against the foot of his bed, and used a digital ruler to measure it from front to back. Then he ate the cold pizza while he booted his computer. He loaded the photos from the phone's memory stick; he did not dare e-mail the images over the wireless network in case the FBI was monitoring his activity.

He brought up the photos and dropped them into a 3D modeling and analysis program. The spatial point orientation function allowed him to accurately measure distances in two-dimensional images. This was achieved by measuring the lines of perspective in relation to a known object: in this case, the bicycle that Sammo had placed against the gate. He input the size of the bicycle into the computer and the program did the rest.

The main area of interest was the control tower. If

that was within range of the gate, he could return with the EMP device and shut the tower—and whatever aircraft were within range of his device—down during peak traffic hours.

The initial findings were not promising. The top of the tower was just under two hundred feet, but it was set back a half mile—too far from the gate. He went to the online map of the air force base and examined the perimeter. He needed a direct line of sight or ran the risk of the electromagnetic pulse being disbursed or absorbed by any number of dense materials, from certain types of wood to iron.

The northwest region looked promising. He enlarged the image and studied it more closely. The juncture of streets labeled Peabody Road and Air Base Parkway put him at a point that was slightly out of range of the tower—but only just. He could not tell from the map whether there was a military fence at that corner. He couldn't take the chance.

But it appeared to him that if he traveled east along Air Base Parkway he would pass close enough to the tower. He wouldn't be able to stop there, but he wouldn't have to. All he needed was a clear shot at the tower.

I will require a vehicle for that.

Sammo felt he was still safe from personal interference, having done nothing to justify a move against him. If the man who had been following him felt a threat was imminent, he would have done more than simply show himself. Still, summoning a consulate car would only bring more American agents to the area, agents who might decide to detain them on some pretext. Sammo had to find a way to swing past the base without attracting attention. Since Air Base Parkway was a main thoroughfare, the bicycle was not an option.

He could probably take a bus that traveled that route, but his route would be known and, if they saw him tonight, the FBI might not want him near the air base a second time. Moreover, he would be trapped in a bus or even a taxi after the event, easily captured.

But there may be another way to go about it, he thought, remembering the display case in the lobby. Deleting the photographs from his computer and camera, Sammo went to the lobby and selected several brochures. He glanced around the room, saw a number of guests, none of whom resembled the man he had seen earlier. That meant nothing. The agent could be out front smoking a cigarette, in the parking lot watching his window, or even in the room next to his eavesdropping. He would learn nothing from that or from the brochures Sammo had selected. Sammo chose several so the agent would not know which—if any—was the one that was important to him.

He spread the brochures out for the young woman behind the desk, who dutifully called the numbers and made the appointments.

She started with the only one that really mattered to him. "Is eight o'clock in the morning all right?" she asked Sammo.

"Yes," he replied.

She booked the appointment and looked at the next brochure.

When Sammo returned to the room he sent an e-mail asking for a car to come for him at seven A.M. He requested a driver and a male secretary of his acquaintance. It did not matter who might intercept the message. It wouldn't do them any good.

San Francisco, California

The excavation at the bombed-out clinic proceeded slowly.

The location and force of the blast did enough damage so that engineers with the Department of Building Inspection demanded that the remaining structure be torn down. That had to wait for the inspection and preliminary report from a team of structural analysts with the insurance company.

While that was going on, the team from Eastern Rim Construction picked their way through the ruin, gathering whatever files and equipment could be salvaged for the temporary clinic that had been established in the Peter and Paul Church north of the site. Preceding them each step of the way was the robotic crawler, though the only data that interested the men was the subsurface data recorded by the radar system.

It was on the day after the explosion, when the building was still off-limits to everyone but the Eastern Rim team and the investigators, that the crawler found what they were looking for. In fact, it was the reason they had planted the bomb in the first place.

The spot was marked on the blueprints for the original building that had stood on this site, a boarding house that had survived the earthquake and fire of 1906. It was demolished in the 1950s to erect a small office building that became the clinic. The target was located in the records room—or rather beneath it, under a layer of concrete that sat atop an old oak trapdoor. The small team made a point of informing the Department of Emergency Management liaison that they were going to focus on recovering the records for the doctors. He was very supportive of their efforts and impressed by their courage. His praise was the height of political correctness, a pat on the back for Chinese who were risking their lives to help their own kind.

Hu Kai and his fellow workers were not impressed. The patronizing attitude here—historic toward the native Chinese in San Francisco—was one of the reasons they were, in fact, putting themselves in harm's way to achieve their objective. Hu, a fifty-seven-year-old native San Franciscan, remembered the stories his grandfather used to tell, not just about the Angel Island Immigration Station that was opened in 1910 to process—and detain, often for months—Chinese immigrants. There was also the enduring injustice of the Federal Chinese Detention Act. It wasn't until 1943 that the laws were repealed, but even then the Chinese people were not as free as other Americans. Relaxed immigration laws allowed criminals to come to these shores, especially from Hong Kong, and that brought increased police scrutiny.

That brought tension, Hu thought as he watched the laptop in what used to be an examination room. *It fostered resentment. It gave us the desire to fight for the same pride in heritage that was given so freely to African Americans, Muslim Americans, Gay Americans, to every hyphenate that had done less to forge this nation than the Chinese who built the railroads and worked the silver mines and panned for gold and both planted and harvested crops across the plains.*

Hu felt a profound sorrow for the men, women, and children who had perished in this clinic—seventeen in all. But they were the first victims of a toxic social system that had to be destroyed. And they would not be the last.

Because the surviving structure was so fragile, the team did not employ jackhammers to break through the floor. They employed chisels and hammers, working precisely where the enhanced radar image told them. Hu could watch their progress in real time on the laptop, the chisels showing up as solid black silhouettes against the white background. He redirected anyone who started to move away from the trapdoor.

As they were working, Hu received a call on his radio.

"This is Hu."

"This is Officer Valigorsky," said the caller. "There is a Mr. Tang to see you?"

"I will be right out," Hu replied.

He motioned to one of the men with the chisels to replace him while the others continued working. Dusting off his coveralls, he walked toward the exit. There had been little cleanup, only whatever was necessary to get through the broken walls and ceilings, crushed furniture, and smashed equipment.

Hu smiled as he saw the short, slender man standing outside the blue sedan. The car was parked on the other side of the yellow police tape. Liu Tang stood beside the passenger's side door, smoking a cigarette.

Hu ducked under the tape and bowed. "It is an honor," he said in Chinese.

The other man crushed his cigarette as he bowed a little more formally. "We have a delivery. We went to your office, but I have been instructed to give it to no one but you."

"I understand," Hu said quickly. "We had to change our own plan. Except for a secretary, we have all been here."

"Is everything all right?" Liu asked.

"Very much so. We have located what we were seeking."

Liu bowed again slightly, but for a longer time, acknowledging the other man's resourcefulness and expressing joy for his good fortune. It was a more respectful gesture than the previous bow.

"I suggest we go back to the office where a secure system has been prepared to your specifications," Hu said.

Liu Tang agreed. Hu radioed his associates in the

clinic and told them he would be back later. The men in the backseat of the sedan made room for Hu, and he instructed the driver how to get to Humboldt Avenue.

Knowing that he was just a few feet from the package gave Hu a feeling of profound humility. That such power was being entrusted to him reinforced his resolve to succeed. He could not wait to get back to the clinic, to resume his work there.

Of all the things Dover Griffith had never done, riding in a small plane and leaving the airport on the back of a Harley could now be checked off the list. As she headed into San Francisco, clutching Doc's leather jacket, she wasn't sure which was the bigger shock to her normally deskbound system.

The flight was like riding an airboat—which she *had* done, once, during a family vacation in the Everglades. Instead of a big fan behind her, on this flight there was a big propeller in front. Instead of a wool cap to keep her hair from blowing, she was wearing headphones so she could communicate with Doc. Instead of racing across murky waters that caused the boat to bump and sway, she rode a deceptively solid ocean of air that sent every current and eddy up the mainframe, through the seat, and up along her spine.

"It's not as bad as sailplaning," Doc assured her with a little laugh.

"You mean hang gliding?" Dover asked, trying to appear at least peripherally knowledgeable.

Doc shook his head. "A glider aircraft," he said. "Pull you up with a towline from a motored plane, cut you loose, then you ride the thermals as long as you can. Once the heat stops rising, it becomes more difficult to stay aloft. Until you can't, and then you plunge. Hopefully you've picked your landing spot before that. Otherwise—" He made a downward motion with his hand. "That's real flying," he went on. "Used it to sneak into Chávez country once."

"Where?"

"Venezuela," he said. "We were running a merc operation to recruit anti–Pink Boots on the ground in his hometown of Sabaneta, Barinas. The previous administration was channeling money to us through the Office of Foreign Disaster Assistance of the U.S. Agency for International Development. Our motto was 'Let no natural disaster go uninfiltrated.'"

Griffith didn't need that explained. When she first came to ONI, undermining the so-called Pink Tide was one of the greatest concerns of American intelligence. It was a growing movement in Bolivia, Nicaragua, and Venezuela to form governments— and alliances—based on the model of Fidel Castro's Cuba. Some of Dover's coworkers believed that the United States should be included in that list, given the Marxist philosophies of its president. Dover had always thought they were overreacting until she started getting smaller paychecks while her unemployed journalist friends got larger ones.

Doc laughed. "Four of us, in two planes, glided into a field of sugar cane. That stuff is high, twice as tall as any of us. Swallowed the gliders completely, hid them long enough for us to make our way into the village."

"How did you get out when you were finished?"

"Took a fishing boat across Lago de Maracaibo to a sub in the Gulf of Venezuela. I was there four months. That was six or seven years ago. Last I heard, the twenty or so guys we recruited were still working for us and had brought in another half dozen. It's slow work but effective."

"Did they believe in your cause? Is that why they stayed with it?"

"I couldn't tell you," Doc replied. "All I know is that the solution to stopping socialism is cash. Not handouts, like we've been doing more and more in the States, but payment for services rendered. I don't care whether it's lawn mowing or car repair or running a small business. Make a person feel useful, instead of like a beaten dog who can't or won't come out from under the bed, and you've got a prosperous nation of eager, happy capitalists. The other way? The Pink way? That's not for the people. That's for the megalo-mania of the puppet masters who are running the show, the Stalins and Mao Zedongs and Barack Obamas. Did you ever think we'd have a power-mad Leninist in the White House?"

Doc Matson was different from anything on Dover's Everglades vacation as well. He was different from anyone she had ever met. He piloted the plane with a casual strength, like a cowboy who had long ago broken a wild horse. The controls were in his muscle memory. His attention seemed to be on the mission: the rescue of Dover Griffith and her integra-tion with the world of Jack Hatfield.

During the course of the two-and-a-half hour flight, she heard about Jack and Abe Cohen, Jack and his "home boat," and perhaps the most important member of Jack's entourage, his gray poodle.

"Only a handful of us are allowed to dogsit Eddie," Doc laughed. "Actually, let me put that another way: there's a handful of us that Eddie will condescend to stay with."

It wasn't the veteran merc talking now, with scars in his memory and a world-weariness in his voice, but a man who was proud of, amused with, and challenged by a dear friend. A friend for whom he would do anything—witness dropping everything to fly to the Inland Empire and bail her out.

Through it all, Dover saw California pass twelve thousand feet below her. That was much closer to the ground than she had ever flown, and it gave her a new appreciation for the glorious patchwork that was this state—and, by extension, all of America. They flew over multicolored deserts where she could pick out cotton-puff sandstorms like the one she had driven through. There were lakes, foothills, bursts of life in isolated villages, larger towns, small cities, and then stirring metropolises. The snow-capped peaks of the Sierra range to their east lifted her spirits. Imagining the pioneers, the early ranchers, she could see the faces on the old daguerreotypes she had pored over in books about the Old West. She felt a sudden burst of affection for the two oceans that had helped to keep her country safe from serious physical invasion. At the same time she felt a raw anger at the people who took that safety for granted, who used it as a foundation for nothing but rapacious self-interest—the Richard Hawkes of America.

Despite the risks, she felt prouder, happier, more alive, more heroic, being allied with Jack Hatfield, a scrappy provocateur, rather than serving an arrogant dictator comfortably but helplessly—like the people she'd met at HITV.

The plane ride ended with a lumpy touchdown. Even as Doc was putting the wheels on the ground, he had warned her that the Cherokee wasn't a 737 and she was going to feel the landing.

"It'll feel like your car hit a pothole," he smiled.

He was right.

They landed at Hayward Executive Airport, which was twenty-six miles from San Francisco. While Doc secured the plane, Dover walked off the flight. She still felt as though she were swaying, just as she had the few times she went out sailing.

"It'll take time to get your land legs back," Doc told her as he grabbed her suitcases from the cockpit. "Weird how the muscles take time to readjust to 'normal.' Makes you realize how adaptable humans really are."

She did not have time to appreciate that as they roared along 580 East. Her bags lashed to a chrome-plated luggage rack behind them, her head tucked tightly in a matte-black, three-quarter open-face retro helmet Doc had brought for her, Dover was busy acclimating herself to the new vibrations beneath her, the new instability. He had assured her that the Ultra

Classic Electra Glide with its Screamin' Eagle Twin Cam 110 engine would give her the smoothest, most comfortable ride on two wheels.

That may be, she thought, as they ripped and swayed through the fading daylight. But she found herself wishing, devoutly, that she had not eaten the candy bar he had offered her before they left Hayward. And every time Doc accelerated she thought of a friend of hers, an ER resident doctor, who called these things "donor-cycles."

Her cell phone told her the trip to the marina took just an hour. It felt longer than the plane flight. Then again, with limited peripheral vision and the back of Doc's helmet eating up most of the view, and nothing but the constant slap of the wind in her ears, Dover's brain had had nothing to distract it.

She was relieved to get off the sleek machine, even if it was for yet another unfamiliar environment, Jack's sixty-two-foot yacht.

Doc had a key that let them on board.

"There's food in the—"

"No thanks," Dover interrupted. She didn't even want to talk about it. She sat on a sofa in a room. She didn't know anything about boats. She didn't know what the room was called or where it was, exactly. All she knew was that while the gentle rocking was different from the jostling of the Piper Cherokee, different from the racing momentum of the Ultra Classic Electra Glide, it was no less foreign to a body that was used to the motion-free ground of Suitland, Maryland.

Doc came over with a landline phone, which he put on speaker. He set it on a small inlaid coffee table. He drank a Diet Coke as he stood beside Dover.

"It's Jack," Doc told her.

"Hi, Jack," the young woman said. She looked slightly away from Doc so she couldn't see him drinking.

"I hear you've had an adventure," said the voice on the other end.

"It has not been the kind of day I was expecting," she admitted.

"Those are the best kind!" Jack enthused. "Doc's going to be leaving to pick up Eddie—you're not allergic to dogs, are you?"

"Only cats and llamas," she said.

"Llamas?"

"Petting zoo when I was a kid," she said. "I had hives for a week."

"I'm that way with mealworm beetles," Doc said. "They're all over South America."

Dover tried hard to focus on the call. "Where are you, Jack?"

"I was in the Caribbean," he said, "on Hawke's yacht."

"Blow it up?" Doc asked.

"Sorry, my C-4 was confiscated at Customs. Anyway, I'm somewhere over the Midwest now. You think Bruno will still be up, Doc? I could swing by."

"Wow, you're ambitious," Doc said.

"What do you mean?"

"I'm thinking you'll be near burnout by the time

you're wheels-down. Why don't I have him send something over?"

"You may be right," Jack said. "Can you stick around? Join us?"

"I've got a bunch of work to catch up on, fun though the day has been. Want me to see if our other buddy is free?" He said in a stage whisper to Dover, "Abe Cohen. That's someone you definitely want to meet."

"Go for it," Jack said.

Dover did not tell either man that the mention of food still put her off.

"More important, how are you two?" Jack asked.

Dover told him about her trip to Murrieta, and Jack listened silently. Doc contributed only a few comments, remarking on her courage and resilience and on the impertinence of the Hawke security guards.

"Sounds like you taught them manners, Doc," Jack said when Dover was done. "And good job, Dover."

"Doc did all the heavy lifting," she said. "How did things go with you—or are you not able to talk?"

"I can talk. I wouldn't be telling you anything I didn't say to my host. But I'd just as soon wait until I've had a chance to process all of it. Doc—"

"I'm on my way," he said. "You know how Eddie loves the Harley."

"Thanks, buddy. For everything."

Doc ended the call, finished his soda, and made sure Dover didn't need anything.

"Actually, I'm going to take a nap," she said.

"Make it a power nap," he warned. "I'll be back in

about forty-five minutes, and Eddie is a handful. He's like his boss. Suspicious of men but he instantly loves the ladies."

"Where will you be if I need more protecting?" she asked.

"At home, studying satellite photos of Victoria, Texas," he said humorlessly.

Dover knew enough not to ask for details. In just the few hours they'd spent together she learned that Doc was charmingly loquacious when it came to things he wanted you to know and mute when prudence was required.

Doc had texted Abe while he was speaking, was surprised not to get a response.

"OK, I'm outta here," he said, putting his phone away. "If you need anything, I'm number two on Jack's speed dial."

"Who's number one?" she asked.

"Not for me to say," he grinned as he left.

Dover leaned back on the couch and closed her eyes, but that just brought back the queasiness. With her eyes open she thought she could see the yacht sway, which didn't help. She needed something to distract herself while her inner ear and her gut adjusted to the new motion. She grabbed the nearest printed material, an op-ed written by Jack Hatfield for *USA Today*.

Don't Punish Brave Marines

Most of the "men" in the news media—the same journalists orchestrating the attack on

Marines who allegedly urinated on Taliban terrorists they killed in battle—have never even been in a fistfight, let alone a firefight. And yet here they are, piling on the real men who have the guts to go into combat against fifteenth-century radical Islamist throwbacks.

The piling on our Marines has done far more damage to the morale of our fighting men than our soldiers' actions. And yet we hear Marine Corps Commandant General James Amos calling the act "inconsistent with [our] high standards of conduct," then whining about our commitment to "upholding the Geneva Conventions, the laws of war and our own core values."

This in the face of Taliban atrocities—car bombings, beheadings, the murder of women and children—that flout the Geneva Conventions and yet are routinely ignored by the media and our military higher-ups, who also downplayed the Fort Hood massacre by Major Nidal Hasan.

Our fighting men must be supported at all costs at a time like this. How can we in good faith ask them to put their lives on the line against the vilest, most extreme of enemies while at the same time we attack them in the press at every turn?

I'm not saying that what these Marines did isn't a violation of military code. But unlike murderers who are granted appeal after appeal, these Marines have already been tried and found guilty in the media.

The desecration of war dead is universally condemned, but it is as old as war itself. These boys are not the devils. The Taliban fighters are the devils.

Our Marines are heroes. They should be rewarded for having the guts to go into combat, not punished for stepping over the line. It's the latest attempt by the liberal news media and the increasingly timid military brass to destroy the few, the proud, the brave, the Marines. Remember, "to err is human, to forgive divine."

Dover thought about that last sentence. She decided that if Jack was right about Hawke and Square-beam, she would rather not have that sentiment forefront in the minds of a jury.

Maggie loved teaching white belts.

It was the privilege of senior belts at the Market Street Martial Arts Academy to instruct newcomers on the basic forms of the discipline. Most students came into the storefront school with the idea that they were going to go back in the streets after a few weeks as "total badasses," an expression Maggie heard more times than she could remember. Most of those students left after two or three lessons when they realized that the first step to becoming a martial artist was absolute discipline of body and spirit.

She had studied at the school with *Sifu* John Qishan since the death of *Sifu* Kuhl when she was just seven years old. Now eighty-three years old, *Sifu* Qishan was born and raised in Chinatown. His mother, a poet, was one of the founders of the Chinatown Public Library in 1921. His father was a hatchet man for the "Highbinder" Tongs, criminals who specialized in vice. *Sifu* Qishan honored his parents with a shrine in the back of the school.

After training an early evening white belt class, Maggie waited for *Sifu* Qishan to finish with his beloved black belts. She did not fall in with them as she usually did but sat on a wooden bench just beyond the mats. The class ended with a bow from the *sifu*. It was not a hard stop but an easing away, like receding tides. The black belts stood with their eyes shut then slowly allowed their own worlds to return. There was a tangible dissipation of energy that always made Maggie a little sad.

Short and thin with white hair pulled into a ponytail, *Sifu* Qishan stood at the edge of the mats and watched them go. Maggie knew not to approach him for several minutes. His eyes were also shut as he visualized everything that had taken place during the class.

"If you see it, you possess it," he often told all his students, explaining the concept.

She waited with her arms at her sides until he opened his eyes. He saw her and smiled.

"Your energy was low today," he said.

"Spirits have been with me," she said.

His eyes showed concern. Neither the Qishan family nor the Yus believed in ghosts in the traditional sense. It had been a topic over many dinners shared with close friends and schoolmates; spiritualism was not a subject outsiders took seriously. But Maggie knew that the life force of one's ancestors, the energy of those who had lived and moved around you, endured after death. These forces survived not as identities but as the essence of what a person was—good, evil, strong, fearful, generous, introverted. The essence lived on in the air, the ground, the buildings themselves. It was nourished or repelled by the energy of those who moved through it. But it could never be destroyed.

"When did this start, and where?" *Sifu* Qishan asked.

"Yesterday, in our cellar," she said. "All the years I have been down there I never felt anything. But there were noises while I did my forms."

"From beyond the walls," he said.

"Yes," she said.

"That is troubling," he said.

"Why, *Sifu*? What is there?"

"Physically? Just emptiness . . ." his voice trailed off.

Maggie's students and fellow senior belts departed, each bowing deferentially to *Sifu* Qishan as they left. They did not interrupt the conversation. The white-haired teacher acknowledged them with a gentle bow. Soon he and Maggie were alone.

"Please tell me, *Sifu*. Do you know what is making the noise?"

"I do not," he told her. "But I know the history of what went on there."

"Where?"

He looked around the empty school for a long moment as though he were seeing people, places, another time.

"When I was a boy and my father was a member of the Tongs, I heard him speak with his confederates of the alleyways that were connected to cellars—which were linked one to the other by a network of tunnels."

"These still exist?" Maggie asked.

"To my knowledge they do," he said.

"How did one get to them?"

"There were trapdoors in the floor," the master replied. "Many of these exits had been put there after the great earthquake and fire, as escape routes. Through these, the hatchet men could flee the scenes of their crimes unseen. But that was not their primary function. The Highbinders used these passages to smuggle young girls from the holds of ships to houses where they would serve out their indentures."

"They were brought from China?"

"Beginning in 1912," he said. "That era was a time of peril for young women. The Qing Dynasty had fallen and the Republic of China was founded with Sun Yat-sen as the leader. Young women, some only twelve or thirteen years of age, fled to escape attacks from the soldiers—and from dishonor in their homes and villages."

"Dishonor? They were victims, *Sifu*!"

"Who survived," the older man said. "Many chose death or mutilated themselves to avoid the unwanted attentions." He drew an imaginary slash mark across his chest. "Few knew what lay ahead on these shores. They were aware of the hard sea journey in an airless hold with little food or water, and the abuse they could expect from sailors. They were not naïve. But they were assured that any 'problems' would be taken care of by doctors in America. To them, America was a place of miracles."

"They were not wrong, Master," Maggie said. "My parents are evidence of that. *I* am a free Chinese woman."

"You are not wrong," *Sifu* Qishan replied. "Even today, our people there are tortured for their faith, imprisoned for demanding freedom. Then, the women were exploited for just one commodity, used by their own countrymen, passed from Chinese merchants of the sea to Chinese merchants of the Barbary Coast. From 1848 through this period when my father was active, the area within Montgomery Street, Washington Street, Stockton Street, and Broadway was hell for these girls." He smiled a hollow smile. "And do you know what these girls did when they were not working in the brothels?"

Maggie shook her head.

"They served *zá suì*, 'assorted pieces' of pork, eggs, bean sprouts, and celery."

"Chop suey," she said.

He nodded. "It was the bait that hooked American high society from coast to coast, a fad that became a staple. The girls caught the eyes of rich and influential Americans. They were delivered to apartments kept by these men—not through the tunnels but in car-

riages. Like ladies, so the men would not be shamed.
Yet I have heard that the women were more disgraced
by the pretence. Many were Catholics and Protestants
who had been criminalized for their faith by the Dao-
guang Emperor. The women were especially targeted for the chastity they prized—virtue that was
now mocked with finery and the trappings of purity,
white gowns and veils."

"It's the spirit of these girls I feel in the basement,"
Maggie said gravely. "Their pain is what I feel. They
are coming to me for peace?"

"Or revenge," *Sifu* Qishan cautioned. "This may be
bigger than you. I urge you to leave it alone."

His advice was sound. She would be alone in this.
Her father was a pragmatist who did not believe in
spirits. He believed in things he could see, count, and
sell. He had always dismissed her sensitivity as being
the naturally excitable state of a woman.

"Your mother was the same way," he would tell
her, and laughed when he recalled how they used to
attend services at the old Zen Buddhist Church of San
Francisco on Eureka Street. *"She would leave an offering of food at the shrine and slip into a state of
elation or depression—sometimes both, which is also
uniquely female. She said she felt the hopes and sor-
rows of all who had been there.*

"Myself?" he said. *"I could only marvel at how
many groceries I had personally sold, which ended
up at the feet of the great teacher."*

The sound of a car alarm brought Maggie back to
the present. *Sifu* Qishan regarded her, gave her hand

an encouraging squeeze. "Stay away from the basement until this passes. Go to the park or come here to do your forms."

Maggie was silent. It wasn't just the spirits that troubled her. There was a practical side to the matter as well. Someone had come to buy the grocery, someone who knew about the tunnels underneath the store. What did they hope to find there? Or what did they hope to use the tunnels for? She had to be sure before she involved her father or went to the police. The only way to do that was by moving shelves that had been there for decades, seeing what lay beneath.

She regarded her *sifu* with an expression that was well known to him. Her father had bandaged her scraped knees. He had been there through romantic heartbreak and shared loss. The Yu father and daughter worked together and had common goals. But *Sifu* Qishan was the one she turned to for confession, enlightenment, spiritual security. Her expression showed that level of love and trust.

There was no hiding her intentions from him.

"Be careful," he said to her as she stepped away.

"I will," she said as she went to the small women's dressing room to change.

Tomorrow was her father's mah-jongg night with other Grove Street merchants. She would do it then.

Before leaving, she lit a stick of incense in front of the small Buddha by the door of the school. She knelt in prayer—not for herself but for her mother, who did not have a teacher like the *sifu* to turn to.

I salute your strength, she thought. *Please watch*

over me as I ignore my sifu*'s advice and shock my father.*

With a final bow she left the sanctuary to join the noise and chaotic energy of the San Francisco night.

Sausalito, California

In the news business they used to call it "tired but wired." It was a transitional state before complete collapse that occurred when you had been covering a story without sleep for twenty-four hours or more. Your brain was still running, albeit a little slow, and your body was drained, but functioning, and your senses were compensating by being overenergized.

That's how Jack felt when he arrived at the *Sea Wrighter.* After he drove about fifteen minutes away from the airport, he had pulled over at a parking lot to call Carl Forsyth. He ran down the basics of the Squarebeam technology, and Forsyth was suitably shaken. But the call took the last of Jack's brainpower and he was too wiped out to stop at his apartment to switch cars. Rachel's Batmobile was just going to have to sit in the parking lot in the Sausalito salt air. He didn't give a damn.

Eddie greeted Jack in the pilothouse with a volley of jumps, leaping up at him as though his tail were a spring and his legs were little pistons.

"Hey, boy!" Jack said, scooping the leaping toy poodle in his arms and letting him air-lick his face from cheek to cheek. "You like that Caribbean smell? A little spicy salt air?"

While Jack cradled the dog his eyes went to the blue-eyed blonde standing behind him. Maybe it was his overtired mind, but there was a dreamy quality to the young woman. She was wearing an NYU sweatshirt and jeans. She was barefoot. Her open face had a friendly, welcoming quality that put him instantly at ease; it wasn't until then that he realized how tense he still was.

"Dover," he said. "Hi."

"Hi, Jack." Her smile was small but sincere. It occurred to him it was the first real smile he had seen since he left San Francisco. "I hope you don't mind, but I took a shower."

"I don't mind."

Her scent reached him then; something fruity. Apricot. Apricot and woman.

A yip from Eddie informed Jack that he had stopped scratching behind his ears without permission. Jack's fingers resumed their massage.

"Greedy little guy," Jack explained.

"We just had a nice nap," Dover told him. "Doc dropped him off, and he fell asleep on my stomach. After a long belly scratch."

"He lets you know what he wants," Jack said. "Speaking of which—I need food. Did Bruno deliver?"

"Personally, with instructions on reheating each entree," she said. "He was very particular."

"His food is his art," Jack said.

"Why don't you do whatever you need to?" Dover said. "The table is set in the main salon. The food's been sitting out for a while, but I'm ready to microwave."

"Food is actually a priority," Jack said. "I didn't want to accept the hospitality of Hawke's cuisine on the plane. That would have been wrong, considering he probably bought it with foreign money."

"Well, we can talk about that later," she said. "Let's get you fed."

Jack put Eddie down and, true to form, he deserted his master for the woman. Not that Jack blamed him. Considering everything she'd been through since waking up in Suitland, Maryland, her composure and alertness were remarkable.

There's a reason our intelligence community hires the people it does, he reminded himself. *The people in the bullpen of intel-analysis had to be able to take mental, psychological, and bureaucratic punches and keep their wits about them.*

Bruno had sent over Jack's personal favorites. Petrale sole with a light pomodoro sauce, roasted sliced potatoes, and sautéed broccolini from his ranch. Of course there was a monster order of pasta marinara with shrimp and, for Eddie, a grilled veal chop, no salt or pepper.

"Bruno said you would have the wines to go with—?"

"Actually, I'm going with a beer," he said. "You?"

"Sure. Whatcha got?"

"Beck's, Pilsner Urquell, Corona."

"No microbrews?"

He could see she was teasing. "No microbrews,"

Jack grinned. "All too hoppy or sweet. I stick with hundreds of years of trial and error. Do you know the difference between the beers?"

"Haven't a clue."

"Beck's is very tart. Pilsner Urquell is maybe the best beer in the world. It's very hoppy. Corona is kind of mild."

"I'll take a Corona," she said.

"You'll like it," he said, heading for a small stainless steel cabinet. He squatted and opened the door. There was nothing but beer inside.

"You have a fridge just for beer?" Dover marveled as she went to the counter where Bruno had left the printed-out instructions.

"No beer lover has the right to call himself that unless he owns one," Jack said. "Hey, you're a journalist. Have you ever come across a term for a beer lover?"

"You mean like 'oenophile' is for wine lovers?"

"Exactly."

"Other than hophead?"

"Yeah, something a little more elegant." Jack placed her bottle on the counter where she was carefully draping the plates with cellophane wrap.

"I think the Latin for beer was *zythum,* or something like that," she said. "So—zythumophile?"

"Sounds like a bacterium," Jack said. "Let's stick with 'hophead.' " He clinked the bottom of his Pilsner against her Corona. Then he checked his cell phone. It was dead. He went and got the power cord, plugged it in beside the coffeemaker, then sat heavily at the teak table. The microwave hummed busily behind him, then beeped. The sole was ready, followed quickly by the pasta, and the aromas took his mind off everything else. They ate in silence for quite some time, Dover evidently waiting on Jack's lead. He was too tired and hungry to do much of that, at first.

"This is damn good," he said when he became aware of the silence.

"Very damn good," she said.

He realized he had been staring at his plate. He looked at her. The world outside was dark, giving a strong sense of home to the golden light in the room. He thought of the sterility of Hawke's yacht and felt a deep sense of being grounded. He missed being on TV, but he loved the scrappy life of a freelance, old-style journalist. He had a good life, and he knew it.

"I really have to thank you for covering me," Dover said. "I never imagined Hawke would be so *obvious*."

"About booting you from his town? It was inevitable. Guys like that, who are surrounded by so many layers of yes-people, lose sight of anything that isn't 'theirs.'"

"I don't understand. Then why did he let you *in*?"

"Power play," Jack said. "Bring me all that way in a gilded cage to slap me around, send me home."

"Did he really think that would work against you? I mean, you climbed the Golden Gate Bridge to kill a terrorist."

"Physical risk, an adrenaline rush, those are different from putting fear on a man's radar, forcing him to watch everything and everyone more closely, think before he goes out, or speaks, or even turns out the light at night."

"Terrorism," Dover said. "Of course. Osama bin Laden didn't exactly invent that concept."

"Anyway, you're welcome. We actually did Doc a favor."

"Oh?"

"If he sits on the shelf more than a few days, without someone to rescue, he gets sarcastic. I'll bet he was in a good mood the whole time you were together."

"Very."

"You see?"

Jack finished his beer and went to get another. Dover was still working on hers and declined a second. He shot a disapproving look at Eddie, who was curled by her feet. The dog ignored him. Jack knew that Eddie was giving the lady some attention, as usual, but he was also guarding her. Jack and the poodle had that tendency in common.

He checked his recharging phone as he passed. There was a text from Doc.

Nothing from Abe. You?

Jack scrolled through his messages, wrote back:

Nada.

He sat back down.

"Can I ask you a personal question?" Dover said after another lengthy silence.

"Shoot."

"Who's number one on your speed dial?"

Jack stopped chewing. "Why? Did you hit it by accident?"

"No, no—before Doc left he told me he was number two. So I was just wondering. Not that it's any of my business. You don't have to tell me. *Obviously,* you don't have to tell me."

Jack smiled. "It's my former wife."

His face must have registered the discomfort he felt, because Dover flushed slightly.

"Sorry," she said. "That was stupid of me—"

"No, it wasn't," he insisted. "It just was not a question I expected."

"Please forget I asked it," she said. She washed the statement down with the rest of her beer, then went to get another.

"I'm not going to do that," Jack said. He sat back, sipped his second beer. "My relationship with Rachel was—is—complicated."

"*Please,* you don't have to tell me—"

"I want to," he said. "Doc, Abe, all our friends—they're tired of hearing me be confused. You're a fresh canvas. And you're smart. And curious. And you analyze data. You may see something the rest of us have missed."

She relaxed slightly.

"We were married for ten years. It ended two and a half years ago. It probably ended long before, but that's when we pulled the plug. She was a model, five foot nine, green eyes, black hair—a real night owl. We met while I was doing a segment for *The World of the Runway Model*. She segued from that to flipping houses.

One of those planners who had a real estate license 'just in case' her modeling career ended. She was—*is*—good at being prepared. Tastes change, anorexia is in, hips are out—you never know. Also, she would get bored with things real quick. She bagged college after six months, took up modeling, sold houses, studied nutrition so she had something else to do when the housing market collapsed. Always a step ahead. She's got a terrific practice now, training vegans in Tiburon—that's across the bay in Marin County."

"Alone?"

He grew wistful. "She's living with a big-shot tax attorney. I resent him."

"Because—?"

"I wish I knew," Jack admitted. "He treats her well, he makes her laugh, he's been cordial to me the two times we've met—even if it's this 'I'm a Harvard grad' noblesse oblige, like he's just a little bit better than me. Anyway, what about you?"

"I dated in college, a lot. There were trust-fund kids, bad boys, scholars. I date in Suitland. Career military, career diplomats, career bureaucrats. I always got along best with the guys who can put their work aside and concentrate on me. Do you ever use number one on speed dial?"

"Never have," Jack said, "but it's the only human connection I've got left with her." He stood suddenly. "Let's take our beers on deck. I want to see if I can learn this relaxing thing."

He wasn't sure if that was a "move" or if his guard was just way down. Whichever it was, Dover rose and smiled and seemed happy to follow his lead. Maybe she was just tired, too.

They went out onto the flybridge, followed by Eddie. It was chilly, and Jack offered her a blanket. She said she was used to the cold, actually enjoyed it. He showed her to the helm seats but she remained standing. So did Jack.

"I'm not sure it's working," he said. "All I am is tired. But my brain's still working."

"Look up," she said.

Jack turned astern to view the stars. They were unusually bright and he realized why. It was past four A.M. He wasn't usually out at this hour. The lights of the city did not throw as much light in the sky as he was accustomed to.

"Does that relax you?" Dover asked.

"Frankly, it bores me," he said.

"Hmm. That's not what we're going for."

"I don't get philosophical about the stars, eternity, the cosmos. I tend not to think about the things I can't impact."

"So what do you think about?"

"When I'm not thinking about work?"

"Yeah," she smiled. "That's the drill."

He looked across the water. "I think about now and a little beyond. Don't get me wrong. I *enjoy* things, like wine and beer and good company. And I can appreciate the dynamics of what's going on around me—like the harbor and the life that's under it or on it or above it. I like interaction, sparks, surprise. I guess that's why I don't think past the moment. I've learned we don't have a whole lot of control beyond that. I can plan for a TV show and—*bang*. I'm suddenly off the air. I can plan to walk down a street and—*bang,* literally. A car bomb goes off. I can be infatuated with a woman, and she's gone. I can be angry at all women, and then one shows up who makes me forget that I was mad. I live in the moment, because that's all I'm guaranteed."

"That's fair," she said. "A little grim, but fair."

Dover was watching him with eyes that sparkled with reflected lights from the city, from other boats. There was a moment he liked. They were far more interesting to him than the stars.

"What about you?" Jack asked. "What do you think about?"

"I'm still optimistic enough to look ahead," she said. "I think about the big things. The usual, I guess. Eventually having a relationship, a family." She laughed. "I guess I'll also have to think about a new job, a new career."

"I'm not convinced of that," Jack said. "I still think there's something big we can pin on that—"

"Uh-uh," Dover said. "That's not relaxing. That's work."

"Sorry," Jack said. "It's involuntary. We were talking about you—"

She drank a little beer, leaned with her back against the rail. She was a dark silhouette against the darker waters.

"I also find myself thinking about how hopeless things seem at times," she said. "The world, I mean.

Some of the reports I see, about atrocities, genocide, tribal warfare—it's enough to make me want to find a Tibetan mountaintop or South Pacific atoll to retire to. But that's not me, either. So I guess I kind of punt. I get reactive instead of proactive."

"Until you didn't with this whole Squarebeam thing," Jack pointed out.

"Until I didn't," she agreed. "And it got me thrown into a maelstrom."

"Do you regret it?"

"I don't know," she said. "Ask me again when we find out what happens next."

"What do you want to happen next?" he asked.

That did not come out the way it had sounded in his head. Spoken, it was less a question than an invitation. The time between his asking and her answering seemed uncomfortably long.

"Bed," she said, finishing the beer.

That was no help, Jack thought. He looked down at the dog. "How about it, Eddie? Are you ready for sleep?"

Dover smiled. "I didn't say sleep."

Jack grinned boyishly. "I wasn't sure I heard correctly."

They went below, and whether it was mutual exhaustion or conviction that moments were worth seizing or Dover being more shaken and afraid than she had let on, they slipped into each other's arms. They remained standing in an embrace that surprised Jack with its intimacy. This wasn't a woman jaded with life experience and looking to escape for as long as she could. This was a woman who still had questions, and dreams. He didn't just feel her need, he felt her trust in the way she kissed him, held tight to his shoulders, let him prop her up just a little. She made him feel like Jack, not just any man. Rachel had done that, too, but it was not always a Jack that either of them liked.

This one was. The hero, the mentor, the winner. Every man needed to experience that now and then.

He literally waltzed her toward his stateroom as they kissed; he leading, she following. He cradled her carefully as he lay her on the bed, still kissing. The smell of her was stronger now, even more enticing, and when his fingertips touched her arms through her blouse she shuddered and sighed, a small taste of the much deeper desire he would quickly discover.

Not being promiscuous and not having had a sexual encounter in a while, Jack was somewhat shy and intimidated, especially since Dover was so much younger than him.

Their first kiss changed all that. Like teenagers in the backseat of the family car their tongues did all the talking without many words. Applying the New Age technique of "friends first" Jack asked Dover if she'd like a back rub, both knowing where this would go.

He told her to lie on her front side, her back to him. Mounting her, still fully clothed he straddled her buttocks and began the deep-tissue massage of her all too tense upper back all women seemed to love.

Dover told him how good his hands felt, not mentioning the stiff center prodding at her parts with each thumb press on her upper and lower back. Jack initiated the next step in the sequence asking the lovely, long-legged blonde girl to remove her sweatshirt so he could better massage her.

His shirt off, he faced one of the most erotically charged sights known to man. A half-naked beauty completely submissive on his bed, the straps of her brassiere asking to be pulled.

Being Irish, her cheeks turned a deep pink. Being Jack, he removed his pants.

Knowing all men feared they were not large enough or hard enough, Dover said, "Your thing is nice." Jack was taken aback but pleased. He didn't know what to say . . .

Naturally this encouraged him, and excited the blood rush making him even more potent and more vigorous.

The sun was just illuminating the skyline from behind the city when they fell asleep. The lovers were cuddled, beyond exhaustion, but they were closer and much, much richer for the moment they had seized without any thought of the future.

Fairfield, California

Agent Al Fitzpatrick spent the night in the hotel lobby.

Though he hadn't been on a stakeout since his rookie years, the ten-year veteran slipped back into it like he'd never been away.

Except that you're six years older, he reminded

himself between snatches of sleep and short breaks outside to check the pool area.

He had arranged with the night clerk to hit the front-desk bell if their Chinese guest came down or seemed to have visitors. The first bell had rung after the target had picked up brochures at the front desk, then returned to his room. The second bell rang at seven A.M., when Fitzpatrick was drinking a complimentary cup of coffee from the continental breakfast bar.

"We offer this service free to any law officer who safeguards our establishment," the manager had said with a trace of sarcasm when he'd poured the coffee a half hour earlier.

Fitzpatrick had a cab waiting. He had called the previous evening and agreed to pay $150 for it to stay until nine A.M., when the driver's shift ended. He had a feeling it would be needed. Fitzpatrick had also obtained the names and addresses of the local attractions for which the Chinese guest had made appointments. The agent assumed he would be following the man.

As the night clerk rang the desk bell, a black sedan pulled up at the front door. Fitzpatrick didn't see an FBI tracking vehicle on the main road. Less than a minute later the man Fitzpatrick had tailed the night before entered the lobby from the hotel. He was wearing a red windbreaker with bell sleeves and a hood, sunglasses, and blue jeans. Fitzpatrick didn't bother taking a picture of his face; there wasn't enough of it to be seen, even if he didn't mind being obvious about it.

The man was carrying a camera case, several brochures, and nothing else. He greeted the hotel employees with a clipped "Good morning" and a little bow. He got in the sedan and shut the door.

The sedan just sat there.

A few minutes later the man emerged from the sedan with another man, this one wearing a business suit. They reentered the lobby and came directly over to Fitzpatrick. The man in the red windbreaker stood behind the man in the suit. The agent rose so he could see them both.

"This gentleman says you have been following him," the man in the suit said. "He would like to know why."

"He is mistaken," Fitzpatrick said. "First, to whom do I have the pleasure of speaking?"

"I am Yan Hua of the Chinese consulate in San Francisco, and this man is our guest." He removed a small leather folder from his inside pocket and made a point of showing Fitzpatrick his credentials.

"Mr. Hua, I assure you I have been here on other business entirely."

From the corner of his eye, Fitzpatrick saw the sedan pull away. He looked back at the man in the windbreaker. He wasn't sure it was the same man. What the hell were they up to? Pinning him down?

"Excuse me," Fitzpatrick said. "There's something I need to take care of."

The men remained where they were as the agent went out to the cab. He looked at the man's license that was affixed to the passenger's side visor. Then he gave the driver a $100 bill and his business card.

"Mr. Enslin, I need you to stay with the black sedan," Fitzpatrick said. "Call and let me know where it goes."

"Mister, there are restrictions on where I can go—"

"I'll smooth it over, whatever it is," the agent told him. "Please."

There was urgency in the speaker's voice, and the driver finally looked down at the card. Then he looked back at Fitzpatrick. "You've got it, sir," he said, and drove off.

The agent turned back to the lobby, peered through the dark windows.

The Chinese were gone.

Fitzpatrick ran inside, asked the clerk where they went.

"To the room, I believe," the clerk told him. "At least, they went in that direction."

"Get someone to open the door and check."

"Sir, I—"

"Now. *Now!*"

Fitzpatrick ran out back, looked around the pool area, ran along both sides of the hotel. He didn't see them. But that didn't mean they couldn't have gotten away in the surrounding trees or ducked onto one of the side streets. If the Chinese plan had been to stretch the FBI's resources to the point where there were too few agents and too many consular people in motion, they'd succeeded brilliantly. If not—

He came back to the lobby via the small workout room. They weren't there, or in the bathroom.

"Housekeeping reports that the room is empty," the clerk told Fitzpatrick.

"Where else could they have gone?"

"I called the dining room," the clerk said. "They aren't there. I have the bellmen doing a top-to-bottom search."

Fitzpatrick thanked her as he stepped outside. He called Forsyth.

"Sir, I think we may have a situation in Fairfield," he said.

"That doesn't surprise me."

"Why?"

"A fire in a Chinese dry cleaning van clogged the entrance to the Bay Bridge right after the consulate car got on. They delayed our tracker by about ten minutes. We weren't too concerned, because we figured we could make up most of that time."

"They didn't need very long," Fitzpatrick said bitterly.

The agent explained what had transpired since his last report at two A.M. The objective was obviously to isolate him from assistance and get his eyes off the target. He didn't know the reason for that, either, and requested immediate local assistance. The Chinese might be doing nothing more than gauging the FBI's response to this situation, gathering tactical information they could use as currency in dealings with Middle Eastern or Far Eastern nations. However, the Field Office couldn't take that risk, not after Jack Hatfield had planted the reality of Squarebeam in Forsyth's brain.

"You'll have every resource we can bring to bear," the field director told him. "I'm looking at primary and secondary targets in the area. We've got Travis on the A-list. The only other high-priority assets are the Monticello Dam and hydroelectric plant at Lake Berryessa. Unless the Chinese are doubling back to San Francisco or heading to Sacramento, we need to get eyes on those."

"I've got a cab watching the sedan, driver Eric Enslin, Fairfield Livery and Limos," Fitzpatrick said. "He's got my number. Can we get a police chopper up?"

"Already requested, and I've sent a red alert to the air force base. We'll get the bastards, Al."

"Yes, sir. I'm going to try and find the two who were on foot. One question, sir. Why didn't they shut down the tracker car electronically?"

"I've been wondering that myself," Forsyth said.

There wasn't time to consider that now. Fitzpatrick hung up and jogged out to Central Place, headed toward Lookout Hill Road and Travis Air Force Base.

Suddenly Fitzpatrick heard someone calling "Sir! Sir!"

He stopped, turned. A bellman was running toward the street. Fitzpatrick started running back toward him. When they met, the young hotel worker was out of breath.

"The . . . two . . . Chinese men . . . are . . . back," he gasped.

"Where were they?" Fitzpatrick started walking briskly back to the hotel.

"In . . . the meeting . . . room," he said. "It was open . . . for a local . . . union breakfast."

So their move was *a feint. This was all about getting the sedan away.*

"But, sir?" the bellman panted. "I was . . . here when . . . the guest first arrived."

"Let me guess," Fitzpatrick said. "The man in the red windbreaker isn't the same man."

The young man was openly impressed. "How . . . did you know?"

In response, Fitzpatrick only gave him an appreciative slap on the shoulder. But as they hurried back he thought angrily, *Because everything they've done since the son of a bitch arrived has been about getting him away from us.*

San Francisco, California

Politically, Carl Forsyth was not a brave man. He had risen through the hierarchy of the FBI due to a combination of hard work and caution. To him, "Cover your rear" was not a shameful act. It was a necessity, one that everyone practiced.

But there was a duty to country that ranked higher than a duty to self and to career. That was why, after considering the broad rules of deployment involved in a high-level security alert, he made the call to Colonel Arnold Pretto, Commander at Travis Air Force Base.

He was put through after a brief routing process that ate nearly two valuable minutes.

"Director Forsyth, we received your alert and have gone to modified lockdown. No one in, only essential personnel out."

"I think you need to do more," Forsyth said. "We have reason to believe the base may be subjected to a powerful electromagnetic burst."

"Air launched?"

"From the ground, strong and directed, possibly line of sight. You should minimize available, active targets. I advise you to ground aircraft or land them elsewhere. I also suggest that you block all public roads surrounding the base with armed, not motorized, personnel."

"Barricade public roads? I don't have the authority to put armed men out there without a declaration of martial law—"

"Commander, we may only have *minutes*." Forsyth began typing an e-mail. "My recommendation is coming, in writing. I'll assume responsibility."

"I appreciate that, but I'll make this call. Thank you, Director."

The commander hung up, and Forsyth dropped the secure landline back in its cradle. He went to a Mr. Coffee in the corner of his office. He wasn't sure caffeine was a great idea—he noticed his hand trembling slightly as he poured—but he needed to do something. He paced with his mug, sipping slowly, wishing he were onsite but content—no, proud—for having made the proper command decision.

As he walked, Forsyth asked God for two things.

First, that he was wrong about all this.

And second, that if he was right, he was also in time.

Fairfield, California

Sitting in the backseat of the sedan, Sammo Yang listened to the nearby sound of aircraft rumbling to a landing or screaming into the skies at the air base. Before long, those sounds would be swallowed in a conflagration of unimaginable power.

He reflected on how this game with the FBI had become a fascinating challenge—one that was about to intensify, one that he had no doubt he would win.

The American resources were spread over a field that was too wide and too unpredictable. He had spoken with Jing Jintao very early this morning on the hotel telephone, confident that the man in the lobby would not intercept it. Even if the staff listened in on his instructions, none of them spoke Chinese.

"We have fielded enough vehicles now to spot those that are routinely following us," Jintao had told him. "We have engaged an outside resource to make sure the car en route to you is delayed several minutes."

"I need no more than three minutes to make the switch," Sammo had told him.

"You will have that," Jintao had promised.

Sammo almost felt bad for the FBI agent who had remained in the lobby. He was a dedicated man who

was clearly surprised by a maneuver that was old
when the Chinese nation was young: Sammo switch-
ing places with a secretary he had met at acclimation
classes in Beijing. Sammo liked winning, but he enjoyed it more when it was a challenge and not a simple exercise. In this case, he had left himself several
options.

He had made reservations at various tourist attrac-
tions in case the FBI tracker car made it across the
bridge and it was necessary for the consular car to
tie them up. Sammo had watched YouTube videos of
the stunt plane ride and the hot air balloon trip. Both
operated just north of the base and would have afforded Sammo proximity and an elevated vantage
point from which to hit his target. The plane would
even have given him a route of escape. He carried a
small knife hidden inside a key, which had never been
detected in any security checkpoint he had passed
through. A blade to the pilot's neck would have given
him a ride to any local airport of his choosing.

"There is confusion ahead."

The voice of the driver drew Sammo to full alert.
He looked down the wide road. Vehicles were slow-
ing. It appeared that foot soldiers were leaving the
base. He lowered the window and looked out.

They were armed soldiers, not vehicles. And they
were apparently blocking the road. With the window
down, Sammo heard the distinctive *rap-rap-rap* of a
helicopter coming along the thoroughfare from behind.

Perhaps he had congratulated himself too soon.

The car stopped along with the rest of the traffic. Sammo opened the door and stood on the seat so he could see ahead. Traffic was being stopped in both directions. No one was being permitted past the air base. He shielded his eyes and looked up. Air traffic seemed to be holding above the base.

So, he thought. *They had figured* something *out. Something close to the truth.*

This was the challenge he had wanted. He knew it would not be long before his clumsy but obviously dogged adversary was upon him.

Other motorists were getting out of their cars, trying to find out what was going on. Sammo got back inside. He raised the window.

"Leave the vehicle," he told the driver.

"Sir?"

"Get out and go anywhere, it doesn't matter—just away from here. Leave the engine running."

The driver acknowledged and got out. He walked toward a shoe store at the side of the road. Sammo took out his key knife and began ripping up the seat. He pulled the padding out, strewed it along the floor. Then he gutted the back of the seat, tearing out as much of the padding there as he could. He took his cigarette lighter from his pants pocket and broke it, spilling the contents inside the gutted backrest. He squeezed into the front seat, cut the cushions there, and pushed in the cigarette lighter. He turned the fan on full and directed the vents toward the back. When the cigarette lighter popped out, he ignited the padding front and back, then flipped it into the hollowed-out seatback in the rear of the car. The lighter fluid ignited with a breathy sound.

Flames rose quickly, and the fans blew them toward the back. Sammo exited the car and headed in the same direction as the driver. Other motorists began to notice the charcoal-gray smoke curling from the sedan. They shouted, left their cars, and ran in every direction. Sammo turned as he reached the shoe store parking lot, saw the helicopter coming closer to investigate. It crept ahead cautiously, not wanting to get too near the burning car. Sammo figured it would be another minute or so before the fan-blown flames reached the fuel tank.

Sammo walked on, toward the helicopter, as a thickening crowd of people raced around him. There were words he couldn't understand, cries that were universal. He looked behind him, saw soldiers on the edge of the line straining to see what was causing the smoke.

Sammo looked back at the helicopter. It was inching forward.

With a sense that his personal journey had come full circle, he raised his right arm toward the single-rotor aircraft.

He pressed the button on the device he wore.

Mr. Fitzpatrick? We're all stuck in traffic."

The voice of driver Eric Enslin of Fairfield Livery and Limos reached Al Fitzpatrick as the agent was running along Suisun Valley Road headed toward

Interstate 80. Fitzpatrick was not surprised by the message.

He had phoned the police department to request transportation to Travis, which was about seven miles away. He was told there were no cars available, that they were all headed toward Air Base Parkway. With traffic going northeast already starting to back up near the entrance, there was no point commandeering a vehicle. He reached the on-ramp and started running around the slowed traffic.

"I see smoke," the FBI agent said into the phone.

"Sorry? Can't hear you—"

"Smoke!" Fitzpatrick shouted, wishing he had brought his Bluetooth. He slowed to a brisk walk so he could be understood. "Do you see smoke?"

"Yeah," Enslin said. "Hold on, there's a chopper overhead. I can't hear a damn—"

The sound reached Fitzpatrick over the phone before it came rolling across the city. It was a crackling pop that accompanied a flash above the freeway. The flare came from the ground up, under the smoke. The sound he heard thundering down the road was an explosion.

Fitzpatrick was running again. He got onto the freeway, saw the helicopter in the distance and fire on the ground ahead of it.

"Mr. Enslin?" He looked at the phone. The call had not been disconnected. "Mr. Enslin?"

"*Jesus*! I'm gettin' out—that car just—"

The call ended suddenly. Fitzpatrick watched as hills of fire rose, one after another, from the site of the first explosion. The booms followed immediately thereafter, blending into a mass of sound as smoke, flame, and shards of metal tumbled skyward. He barely heard the screams of motorists around him who had stopped their cars, got out, and were watching the holocaust unfold.

Fitzpatrick was still moving forward, shouldering through cars and pockets of onlookers, when the helicopter went down. It was well above the smoke and flame, and did not appear to have been struck by debris because there was no struggle to control it, no lopsided moves of a rotor that had been struck and bent.

It just fell straight down.

There were more cries of horror from the crowd as the aircraft threw off a spray of yellow-orange flame that was quickly consumed by churning black clouds. It reminded Fitzpatrick of an upside-down atomic bomb, with the mushroom cloud on the roadway. It was difficult to gauge, but it looked to him as though a half mile or more of Air Base Parkway had been swallowed in the series of explosions.

Conflicting feelings of urgency and outrage, despair and guilt fought for control of Fitzpatrick's mind. He had to push them aside and focus on purpose. There was no question in his mind about what had happened to the chopper and who was behind this. The tracker car on the Bay Bridge hadn't been "killed" because the killer was here, waiting to strike.

Finding that man was his purpose.

There was no point in continuing ahead. He turned back to get to a hotel landline. As he ran, he thought of the cab driver he had inadvertently sent to his death—and of all the others who had died because of him. It was his caution, his passive surveillance, his falling for that simple bait and switch that had allowed the terrorist to get away.

This is on you, he told himself. *You could have prevented it.*

He ran harder, hoping the effort would somehow shut down his thinking. If there was any consolation, it was that they had apparently prevented a larger disaster at the air force base itself. He could not even imagine what would have happened if a huge C-130 transport—taking off, loaded with fuel—or a squadron of fighter jets or *all* of them had gone down over the city.

You did that much, he told himself through a sudden rush of emotion. *You and Forsyth made the right call.*

As he ran, Fitzpatrick tried to call Forsyth to report what had happened. His call did not go through. He wondered if the airwaves were jammed or if power to local towers had been cut to keep the perpetrator from communicating with *his* superiors.

It didn't matter. Forsyth would know soon enough.

As he raced back along Suisun Valley Road, he flashed back to his college days, when he first learned of the 9/11 attacks and the immediate, temporary shutdown of American airspace. That enactment of

SCATANA, the Plan for the Security Control of Air Traffic and Air Navigation Aids, lasted only until September 13.

Having a terrorist on the loose with the ability to bring down aircraft from the skies? God only knew the impact that would have.

Fitzpatrick's small, sole hope was that God would find time, among these larger concerns, to forgive him for the job he hadn't done well enough.

PART THREE

Counteratta

Chapter 1

San Francisco, California

Doc Matson woke early after a restful night. He always slept well after biking, flying, and doing damage to bad guys.

He had planned to spend the day researching the U.S.-Mexican border outside of Victoria, Texas, where he'd be headed in a few days. But after checking his cell phone and computer and finding no messages from Abe Cohen, he decided to go out for an early morning ride to Abe's shop in North Beach.

The old wood-structure shop on the corner of Bay and Taylor was closed. That didn't surprise Doc: it was not quite six A.M. But the mail from the previous day was still lying on the floor where it had been shoved through the slot and the drain pan from his ancient dehumidifier was nearly overflowing. *What an environmentalist,* Doc thought as he emptied the pan. *The air's a little damp for Abe's taste, and he slaps an electricity-sucking machine on it.*

Doc went around back. Abe lived alone in a second-floor apartment. The mail was still in the box. No one answered the bell. Doc forced the door easily with a push. Abe didn't have anything worth stealing and didn't bother with security—or a lock that was younger than the sixty-seven-year-old door. Doc felt for the wall switch, turned on the light, looked around the apartment that smelled from a blend of weed, unfiltered Camels, and roasted Brussels sprouts. Abe was always igniting some leafy thing or another.

The bed wasn't made, but Abe wasn't in it. Doc went to the bathroom, felt his toothbrush. The bristles were dry.

What the hell happened? Doc wondered as he walked back to the door. *You drop your damn phone in the head?*

Even if he did, the Defever Pilothouse had a radio. He would have called for assistance.

If Abe was hurt, minutes could matter. Angry that he'd waited even this long when he suspected something might be wrong, Doc called the small, family-owned marina where Abe kept his tub of a boat.

"It's gone," the owner told him. "Been out since yesterday afternoon."

"You haven't heard from him?"

"Not a single sour note," she said.

That was it. He phoned ahead to Hayward to have

his plane ready to go. Then he climbed on his Ultra Classic Electra Glide. Before he started it he pulled out his phone and scrolled through his text messages. There it was—Abe had texted, *I'm going to go listen to elephant seals fart, it'll be an improvement over you*. He'd been headed for the Farallon Islands. Doc fired up the Electra Glide and sped to the airport.

Less than an hour later, he was headed west over the Pacific toward the Farallons. Seen from the air, the granite outcroppings were a jagged black curlicue of rock surrounded by churning white water. The highest of the peaks was 154 feet above the water on the Island of St. James, one of the total of three islands and four smaller, nameless rocks. Though he himself wasn't a sailor, Doc had always admired the pluck of Sir Francis Drake—reportedly the first human being to land here—for pausing during his 1579 around-the-world journey to collect eggs and seal meat from St. James, which the English privateer also named.

Doc didn't know whether to feel relief or concern as he neared the roiling coastline. There were only the birds and sea mammals that frequented the shores; he saw no sign of Abe or his vessel.

The westward-lying shadows were long and stark, and Doc flew low and wide around the island to make sure he wasn't missing anything. There were plenty of little inlets where a small vessel could have gone down.

There was no flotsam or jetsam that Doc could see, and the waters were opaque enough to hide anything that might be below the surface—including sharks, which was one reason they were able to prey successfully on the local fauna.

However, Doc did see something on Noonday Rock, named for a clipper ship that struck it in 1863 and sank in less than an hour. Doc looked back, saw the thin streak of light flash again. It looked almost like an old-school jeep antenna, one seen at night by muzzle flashes of an AK-47.

To each his own memory, Doc thought as he heard an imaginary Abe yelling in his ear, *"Does everything have to be a gun or knife fight to you?"*

Doc angled around for another look. Noonday was arguably the least welcoming spot in the national wildlife refuge, a desolate place that most of the tour boats avoided because of underwater outcroppings. But it was a natural, lonely, isolated place for someone as perpetually gloomy as Abe to visit, especially someone who knew these waters.

The sun was rising quickly, and the glint he had seen was no longer there. But something else was. It looked like part of the black rock surrounding it, but it wasn't.

It was a tarp. He had done enough recon from aircraft and hilltops to know one—even a good one like this—when he saw one.

Doc looked past the rock, across the horizon. That shallow part of the shoal was within sight of a lighted bell buoy—the only human marker in the region. His mind went where it had been trained to go: is there what the military referred to as a "casual or causal" reason for that?

And was that, in fact, an antenna he had seen?

Other than his natural wariness—what Abe bluntly called "unchecked paranoia"—there was no compelling reason to be suspicious of any wrongdoing.

Except for the fact that your friend had said he was coming out here and never came back, Doc told himself.

There was nothing Doc could do other than to avoid letting on that he had seen anything amiss. He circled again, ascertained that what he saw was indeed a well-secured artificial covering, not something that had washed up. Then he headed back to the airport.

He hadn't found Abe, but his gut told him that Abe's disappearance could well be linked to the presence on the island. Doc would check some of his friend's other haunts—a couple of bars, one or two old girlfriends, and even the disused Fort Mason Tunnel of the San Francisco Belt Railroad where he hung out with some old, homeless hippies. If Doc couldn't find him there—

Then you've got two options, he thought as he flew high above the local pockets of fog. Option number one was to notify the Coast Guard. If someone was out there, working with smugglers or a cartel, he would be prepared for such an eventuality. Mines, perhaps. Hand grenades. Automatic weapons. There was no reason to cause needless deaths.

Option number two was to come back after dark,

by sea, and approach unseen. That would not only be safer, it would give Doc something an official visit would not provide: a chance to ask whoever was out here whether they had seen his friend Abe.

And if so, where he'd gone.

Sausalito, California

Jack was awakened by one of the last phone calls he would have expected to receive.

"It's Carl Forsyth," the caller said. "I need to know if you've learned anything about Squarebeam."

There was no "Good morning, hi, sorry if I woke you." That and the urgency in the field director's voice caused Jack to sit up. Dover stirred next, followed by Eddie, who was between them.

"I had a late night," Jack said. "What happened?"

"A quarter mile of roadway outside Travis AFB was blown to hell a half hour ago, and we believe your hypothetical EMP device took down a police chopper."

Jack removed the TV remote from the shelf behind the bed and turned on the flat screen on the opposite wall. Ground-based cameras were showing flame and smoke rising from the road as if a hell pit had split open. Not surprisingly, there were no aerial shots. However, there was cell phone footage of the helicopter falling from about two hundred feet up.

Dover took Jack's hand.

"I met with Hawke, who was definitely playing *I've Got a Secret* but wouldn't say what it is," Jack told

Forsyth. He put the phone on speaker so Dover could hear. "But he only threatened *me,* not—not *this.*"

"Where did you meet him?"

"On his yacht in the Caribbean," Jack said. "He flew me down. He also threatened my associate, an intel officer who was furloughed for smelling a rat. He sent some mugs after her when she went snooping around the Squarebeam lab in Riverside County."

"Did he say anything about that technology?" Forsyth asked.

"Nothing we didn't know or suspect," Jack replied. "He refused to connect the dots between Squarebeam and China."

"That bastard," Forsyth said. "Jack, we need to find the guy who did this. I've got one agent on the ground up there. He just called from a gas station. The guy who did this was Chinese. He was apparently taken to Fairfield after being picked up at SF International. He's still on the loose up there."

"Your man lost him?"

"He only has two eyes, Jack. They had our target and a ringer."

"Fair enough. What's your game plan?"

"We've got the roads to and from Fairfield closed, all aircraft grounded. If he gets out, he's going to have to walk."

"Fairfield's a decent-size town," Jack said. "He could just hunker down somewhere and slip away when the roads aren't closed and aircraft aren't grounded."

"I know that," Forsyth said.

There was exasperation in the man's voice. Jack empathized completely.

"What we need to do is find out if there's a way to zero in on this device or the guy using it," the field director said. "We went over security footage of the airport. The man we think was the perp was wearing a hat. He knew we'd be watching. All we have is a chin and part of a cheek, which are no help."

Dover had already booted her laptop. She turned it toward Jack. It was open to a file on Squarebeam technology.

"The original handsets operated in a 1620.5 to 1660.5 MHz range—"

"We've got all that," Forsyth said.

"Have you asked Hawke?"

"Not yet. His exec told us he's out of the country. You confirmed that. He hasn't called back."

Jack didn't expect him to. The odd thing was, while Hawke had been unacceptably slow shutting down Squarebeam when it was proven to endanger the military, Jack had never pegged him as someone who would be openly antagonistic to America—even for a huge profit.

"Let us work on this," Jack said. "Stay in touch."

Jack was about to add, *"And don't beat yourself up over this,"* but he knew that wouldn't do any good. Forsyth had never been his strongest ally, but they both wanted the same thing: a safe and secure America. This one had to hurt.

"Jack, this is sickening," Dover said. "They're

estimating—look at that," she read from the crawl on the screen. "At least two hundred dead and scores more injured."

"You see where it happened?" Jack said. "Right outside Travis Air Force Base. Think about that."

"That was the intended target," she said.

"Right. Something got in the way of that. But what does it tell you?"

She thought for a moment. "If that's true? Two military targets, plus one target of convenience, the FBI car."

"That was a target of necessity, I'm guessing," Jack said. "They didn't want to be followed to Fairfield. So we have two military targets—the Chinook in Afghanistan and an attempt on Travis. Why?"

"It's not like the Chinese to take an offensive public posture like this," Dover said. "They're more like snakes moving through high grass, striking and then retreating."

"Yeah, I had that talk with Hawke," Jack said. He thought for a moment. "You speak Chinese, right?"

"Mandarin."

"You're still naked."

She shot him a surprised look. "So are you."

"I know," Jack said. "We need to get dressed."

"Why?"

"Hawke has an estate in Carmel. We're going up there."

"But—he's not home."

"Exactly," Jack said. He picked up his cell phone, dialed the last number.

"Who are you calling?" Dover asked.

"Carl Forsyth," Jack said. "I need a favor."

Fairfield, California

The explosions filled Sammo with a sense of validation unlike anything he had ever experienced.

This had to be what it was like to create art, he thought as he ran from the conflagration. Something lasting, something that affects so many others—yet it emerged from a small place in your mind, an idea that was part invention, part inspiration, part desperation.

He met up with the driver, who was standing outside the shoe store. He was alone, the employees having gone into the back, ducked behind a counter. Sammo could see them in the sharp, vivid glow of the flames.

"Let's go," Sammo said, pulling the driver by the shoulder.

"Your back," the man said.

Sammo turned so he could see it in the plate glass of the store. It was smoking. The driver darted behind him and slapped at the embers with his palms.

"That's good," Sammo smiled. "It will help us."

The driver, stunned and malleable, followed as Sammo walked south. They stayed on the main road, quickly joining a snakelike exodus of motorists and pedestrians, store workers and shoppers, who were moving away from the blast. Fire engines tore past them, running on the sidewalks as necessary to get through the traffic jam. All along the way drivers were trying to get onto side streets just to get out of the way; police were turning vehicles at the back end of the thoroughfare around, sending them away from the air force base.

You were responsible for all of this, Sammo thought proudly. It was not the primary target, the one he had been instructed to hit. But his colleagues would be pleased. It would have been unthinkable to come away from these last two days with empty hands. He would have irretrievably lost face, and the morale of the mission would have suffered grievously.

It was an hour or so before they met up with the men from the hotel: his consulate liaison and his doppelgänger. Sammo and the driver were supposed to have collected them by car along Don Wilson Creek, a tree-lined area well behind the hotel. After the explosion the two consulate workers had waited until their comrades arrived.

"Tear your clothes and cover yourselves with dirt," Sammo advised.

Though uncertain why, the men did as he had instructed, after which they walked along Central Way headed south, toward the entrance of Interstate 680. The freeway was packed with slow-moving vehicles looking to get out of the area, and Sammo had no trouble waving one down, a Caltrans bus that was happy to take them on.

"No charge," the young driver said as the men squeezed on board. "You folks look like you been through hell."

"Thank you," said the consulate liaison.

"We all pull together in times like these," the man

said as he shut the door. "Horrible stuff, man. I was stationed in Kabul, never saw anything like this. You see what happened?"

"Yes," the liaison said. "It was awful. Where are you headed?"

"My run is Sacramento to San Jose, but we've taken on a bunch of people who want to get off in Frisco so I'll be stopping there as well. What about you?"

"San Francisco is fine," the man said with a gracious bow.

"Make room as best you can, people!" the driver yelled back.

The thickly packed group in the aisle maneuvered to the sides to give the new arrivals space. There were reassuring smiles and a gracious air of support for these men who were scuffed and singed.

As the quartet maneuvered, Sammo made sure he had his own people on either side, giving him a small buffer. He was still wearing the device and did not want it damaged in the crowd. Although that was the only target he was supposed to strike here, Beijing might ask for another. The goal had been to strike the military and that had not happened.

But that lay in the future. Right now he was grateful just to have gotten his team out of Fairfield, away from the FBI. There had been a saying on the blackboard when he was in training, wisdom from Confucius: *It does not matter how slowly you go so long as you do not stop.* The essence of espionage was to have a goal in mind but to focus on one small step at a time. Beyond that, nothing was guaranteed.

He shut his eyes as the bus hummed and swayed slightly, the rubber floor covering vibrating beneath his feet. Withal, despite the challenges, it had been a good day.

He allowed himself a belated smile as he had in Afghanistan.

It had been a *very* good day.

Al Fitzpatrick reached the hotel around the same time as the thin tester of smoke from the fires. The staff was gathered in the lobby with guests. He heard the news streaming from a computer behind the counter, a small group gathered around it.

The bellman who had run after the agent was the first to spot him.

"Is this why you were here?" the man asked. "Did you—"

"I can't talk about any of that," Fitzpatrick said. "You got water?"

The man ran to the buffet table and came back with a plastic bottle. Fitzpatrick drained it as he walked to the desk.

"The man I was watching—did you scan his passport when he checked in?" Fitzpatrick asked the clerk.

"Yes, sir."

"Show me."

The woman looked at the manager, who nodded. She retrieved the image on the computer, printed it out. The black-and-white photo was washed out.

Magnesium overlay, he thought. It was common in forged documents. The picture would look fine to the naked eye but bounce back light in a scanner, obscuring the details.

He folded the page and slipped it in his jacket pocket. "All right," he said, regrouping. He turned, motioned toward the bellman, pointed to other employees he recognized. The group included housekeepers, shop clerks, waitstaff.

"You had a Chinese guest yesterday," he said. "Did any of you have any dealings with him?"

Three employees raised their hands. One was a housekeeper. He ignored her.

"You and you," he pointed at the others. "Are there security cameras where you work?"

The clerk, a Latino woman, said with a sneer, "Yes—they watch us."

The manager added, "It's standard. Internal theft is the only problem venues like ours typically face."

"I need a photo of this guy," Fitzpatrick said. He didn't even try to keep the exasperation from his voice. "*Anyone?* Do you know if he went to a cash machine?"

"I think there was a family taking pictures when he was here," the waitress said.

"When?"

"Yesterday at lunchtime. I remember because the soldier's folks asked me to take a photo of all of them. He might be in them—they were sitting nearby."

"Are they still here?" Fitzpatrick asked.

"I don't know," said the manager. He looked at the waitress. "Astrida, would you remember the bill? They may have signed with their room number."

She hurried to the adjoining restaurant while Fitz-patrick thought about his next move. Security-wise the city was a large, leaky sieve, and they might not be able to catch him here. But surveillance cameras in most of the airports, train stations, and bus terminals were run through law enforcement links that had fa-cial recognition software. If they could get an image of the man into that software—

"The Mihalkos, room 212," the waitress said as she came running back.

The desk clerk ran the name. "They are supposed to check out today—"

"Ring the room," Fitzpatrick said.

The woman obliged. When someone answered she put the agent on.

"Mrs. Mihalko, this is Al Fitzpatrick with the FBI. You heard about the attack outside of Travis—"

"We were just watching it on the television! We're trying to reach our son—"

"Ma'am, we have reason to believe you may have dined in the hotel while the terrorist was there. Would you mind coming to the lobby with whatever photo-graphs you took yesterday?"

The woman said she would be right down.

Fitzpatrick began writing on a pad of paper on the counter. "Here's a URL," he said to the desk clerk. "Please go to this site."

The clerk did so just as Mrs. Mihalko arrived.

"My husband is upstairs trying to get a call through to the base—" she said.

"It's going to be tough to get through to anyone

right now," Fitzpatrick told her. "What does your son do on the base?"

"He's in the 60th Air Mobility Wing Public Affairs Office," she said.

"Then he's fine," Fitzpatrick assured her. "I'm certain they would have sent operations personnel out to deal with this, not airmen from a support unit."

"That's what my husband said," she told the agent as he sidled over. "I hope you're right. Oh, the poor people who were out there—"

"Ma'am, may I see the pictures?" Fitzpatrick said.

"Yes, I'm sorry."

She began scrolling through slowly. He stopped her at the second picture. He couldn't be certain, but that might be his man. It would make sense they'd catch him in an early shot: when he saw the flash he would naturally have turned away.

"Can you zoom in?" he asked.

She fumbled for the function. "I'm sorry, I don't know—"

"Stop," he ordered. "You may erase it. Can you send it to the desk computer?"

The desk clerk gave her the e-mail address. Mrs. Mihalko typed it in, sent the photo. Fitzpatrick went around the counter. It arrived at the same time he did. The clerk opened the e-mail and displayed the embedded image.

He was there, a three-quarter view. Probably starting to turn.

Fitzpatrick looked at the clerk's name tag. It occurred to him he hadn't bothered to do that until now.

"Allison, would you clip the man's face, save the image, and go to the other website?"

"With pleasure," she said, smiling. Fitzpatrick tried to imagine the pride she felt being able to help an FBI agent on a matter like this. It was humbling to him—American unity, America's greatest strength at work, right here, right now.

When the Unified Law Enforcement Anti-Terrorism website came up, Fitzpatrick went to the keyboard and typed in his password. He dropped the photograph in a file that some programmer—a former military man with a sense of irony, he suspected—had labeled INCOMING.

"That's it," he said as he shut off the website.

He wasn't surprised to find a crowd standing around the counter, watching. His eyes swept across expressions that ranged from frightened to shell-shocked to hopeful.

"We're going to get the man who did this," he vowed.

"When you do," said the bellman who had run after him, "don't put him on trial like those 9/11 killers."

"Put him in Guantanamo and swallow the key," Mrs. Mihalko said.

"It won't be my call," Fitzpatrick replied. "But I know how you feel."

"Agent, I think I know how *you* feel," Allison said. "I watched you as you made this your post and waited. I watched you this morning, talking to those men. You did everything one man could do. I want you to know that."

That one went right to Fitzpatrick's throat. He tried to speak, couldn't, and just thanked her with a tight smile and a grateful little nod.

He turned to the manager and found his voice. "I'll need to set up a little command post with a landline. May I borrow your office"—he looked at the man's tag—"Mr. Devi?"

"It will be an honor," he said as he showed Fitzpatrick to the small room off the reception area.

The last thing Fitzpatrick heard as he entered was applause from the lobby.

Carmel, California

The estate on the appropriately named Scenic Road was on a piece of land the size of a small landing strip on Carmel's most expensive outcropping. Poised dramatically above the wild sea, otters could be seen in the cove below, lolling and tossing for fish. Great belts of kelp camouflaged the occasional cormorants whose slim, silky, black necks disappeared as they dived for food.

Jack and Dover could see the back of the mansion as they traveled along Highway 1, the Pacific Coast Highway, along the westward projection that ran by Rat Hill.

"Holy crap," Dover said. "I think I just changed sides."

"You wouldn't like the rental fee," Jack said.

"Sex for seafront?"

"No," Jack said. "Your soul."

He hadn't meant that to be a buzzkill, but Dover was silent for the remaining ten minutes of the ride. There hadn't been a lot of talking during the three and a half hours they'd already been on the road. Jack hadn't wanted to field a question from Dover about how he owned an SLR McLaren, so they'd taken a cab from the marina to Union Street. Feeling protective of his hideout, Jack went to Wilhelm's parking space alone, then met Dover around the corner. As she climbed into the Mercedes, he turned the radio on for updates about the situation in Fairfield. Dover was inquisitive about Jack's plan when they set out, but gave that up in the first twenty minutes.

"I don't see how we can pull this off," she told him. "And I'm not clear why we're even trying. Is it for information or for round two?"

"Both," Jack admitted. "I don't know what Hawke's hiding, but if we don't shake the tree we'll never know."

"And if he decides to shake back?"

"I expect he will," Jack said. "He'll shake us hard. I saw that kind of thing all the time on my TV show. You lean on some people, they break. You lean on others, like Hawke, and they get tougher. You saw it in Murrieta. But that's when you get your real story, when someone is upset, furious, ready to throw a chair."

"Sounds to me like that's when you get hurt. I almost got manhandled at HITV, and I wasn't pushing Hawke himself, just some flunkies."

"That's what makes life exciting," Jack said. "That's what makes this work special, unique—sacred.

It's one of the few places where you can't do your job by oiling the status quo."

"Jesus, I'm a researcher," Dover said.

"You studied to be a journalist—"

"In theory. In fact, what I do is pick over turkey carcasses. I don't shoot lions."

"You do when it's open season on civilized human beings," Jack replied. "And when that happens, you damn well better adapt. What would you be doing right now if we were back on the boat?"

"I should be—I don't know. Trying to find out more about what we're facing. Maybe Forsyth will get information from Fairfield, some additional data to crunch—"

"Forensics on the chopper that will confirm what we already suspect. At best, you get a tiny step forward." Jack shook his head. "I abhor baby steps. It's time to go to the source. And there's another aspect to this. It's 1 Samuel 17."

"You lost me. Again."

"The story of David and Goliath. 'When the Israelites saw the man, they all retreated before him, very much afraid,'" Jack said. "And what happened? 'David overcame the Philistine with sling and stone.' Even if we don't learn anything from Hawke, we need to put a rock in his forehead, drop him or send him in retreat. Stop him from doing more damage."

"Good idea," she agreed. "But it's not the objective that worries me. It's the plan. You haven't even talked to anyone about this, other than Forsyth. What if Hawke checks?"

"That's why we're going to light a very short fuse at his house—"

"Where he isn't. As far as we know he's still on his yacht."

"Right, but that's not important."

She shook her head. "Every tactical white paper I've seen in the course of my duties was the exact opposite of what we're doing. They laid out logical approaches to a situation."

"Chess moves," Jack said.

"Yeah," Dover said. "What's wrong with that?"

"Chess takes time to play. We don't have time. Anyway, there are school kids who could beat me at chess. But this game? It's for the few, the proud—"

"The crazy."

"The *committed*," Jack corrected her. "Soldiers, astronauts, volcanologists, deep-sea explorers—they all do one thing. A real journalist has to be prepared to do it all. If not, he has no business being in the game." Jack grinned. "Unfortunately for you, that's me."

Dover watched the ocean pass through the window beyond Jack. "It's funny. You protected me in Murrieta. Now you're risking me. And both of them make you sexy as hell."

"It's part of my master plan to confuse women," Jack said.

She smiled. "When I was a kid, my dad had this big reflector telescope. We'd use it to look at the planets and the moon. It had this little spotter telescope attached, like half a binocular. Before you looked into space, you'd pick a little target like the door of a house down the street. You'd get it in the crosshairs of the small scope and then you'd adjust the big scope until the door was in the center of that one."

"They used to call that master-slave alignment before the voices of political correctness infiltrated the military," Jack said.

"Dad called it a different kind of PC: 'precision calibration.' That way when you looked in space, whatever you saw in the crosshairs of the small guy meant the Martian ice cap or lunar crater would be right in the center of the bigger telescope. Dad's brother, my uncle Bernard, didn't have the patience to do the alignments. Whenever he'd go out on the patio with me, he just loosened the screws that held the big scope in place and swung it back and forth through the sky until he found something interesting. That's you. You're my uncle Bernard."

"What did he do for a living?"

"He was the manager of a local amusement park."

"And your father?"

"An electrical engineer."

"Yeah, I'm definitely your uncle," Jack said. "I'll bet your mother was in the arts."

"She was a singer. What made you say that?"

"You got your pluck from somewhere," he said. "It didn't come from a man who had to figure out which lights went on which breakers."

"It's called 'phasing,'" she grinned. "That kind of thinking helps with the kind of job I do—or did. There's nothing wrong with being able to open a specifications book and understand it."

"There's also nothing wrong with hiring electricians when I need work done," Jack said.

As they neared the house, Jack wasn't sure he had convinced Dover that this was a good idea. Despite the bravado, he wasn't convinced of it himself. He also knew himself well enough to recognize that round two with Hawke had been inevitable and that this, at least, would catch the man off guard.

Having researched Hawke in the past, Jack knew that the Carmel estate was also a veritable fortress. They went past a brass plaque that said PROPERTY LINE. NO TRESPASSING.

"We've just crossed into the first level of hell," Dover said.

A few yards beyond was a high iron gate with the expected hawk symbol in the center. Jack turned the car around in case he needed to make a quick getaway. Then he called a number Forsyth had given him, after which he phoned Hawke's office. He put the call on speaker so that Dover could hear. It took just a minute before he was speaking to Phil Webb.

"I'd like to speak to your boss," Jack said, ignoring the he's-my-coworker cant, of which he'd had enough.

"As you may recall, Mr. Hatfield, Mr. Hawke is out of the country."

"I saw a couple of Renoirs on the boat," Jack replied. "I'm guessing he can afford a phone?"

"My point is, he's on vacation," Webb said. "He does not wish to be—"

"I'm outside the estate in Carmel," Jack cut in. "I can send you a picture if you want."

"What are you doing there?"

"Phil, nothing personal but I'm done talking to you," Jack said. "Get Hawke on the line. There's something he needs to know."

The phone went silent. Jack was watching the driveway for any sign of guards, armed or otherwise. Hawke and this community had too much class to station armed guards up front, but Jack knew they were out there somewhere. He could feel Dover watching him. It was the longest minute-and-change he could remember in quite some time.

And then he heard the airspace open on the other end. He could almost smell the saltwater.

"What could you possibly want?" Hawke asked with annoyance.

Jack got right in the game. "Two quick questions, Mr. Hawke. First, why did you sell Squarebeam technology to China, and second, did you know they were going to attack Americans with it?"

"If you weren't so amusing, you'd be tragic," Hawke said.

"That's got nothing to do with Squarebeam," Jack said.

"Good-bye—"

"Before you go, you should know that a search warrant is about to be executed on your property."

"By whom?"

"The Federal Bureau of Investigation," Jack said.

"I don't believe you."

"You will, in about five minutes."

"Under what possible theory of inquest is my home

a legitimate target?" Hawke chuckled. "Something you concocted?"

"Here's how it went down," Jack said. "I didn't mention this yesterday, but I am an informant for the FBI on this matter. Seems they liked how I handled the Hand of Allah thing so much that they asked me to work with them on this Squarebeam thing."

"How nice for you to be wanted by someone."

Jack smiled inside. Hawke had attacked him, not what he was saying. That suggested he was listening.

"Late last night, after you dropped me off back in San Francisco, I made my report to my field office liaison," Jack said. "He whisked me to a judge's chambers where I was asked, under oath, to offer my conclusions as to why there is alleged criminal activity on these premises. I gave said testimony—which included research Ms. Griffith gathered using *her* contacts—and upon a finding of probable cause the warrant was authorized. As you can imagine, after eyewitnesses in Fairfield described the way a helicopter just plummeted from the sky, the judge did not hesitate to sign it. Field Director Forsyth also gave testimony, citing provisions of the Patriot Act that do *not* work in your favor. Anyway, Mr. Hawke, after explaining how your yacht was a nexus for information—but was outside U.S. jurisdiction—I suggested the next best thing would be your estate. The judge agreed, and they are on the way to come and get your computers. You've got about four minutes now. That's not enough time to scrub data from your hard drives, but it *is* enough time for you to answer my questions."

"Even if this were true, why should I care?" Hawke asked. "What do they—you—expect to find on a computer these days?"

"I know," Jack said. "Cloud technology, end user has no access to the physical location, which isn't here. Your secrets are safe. But what about security recordings? I see—one, two, three . . . six cameras on your property, just from here. Did the Chinese ever visit you here? Is that data stored on memory chips?"

"I entertain often and widely and, unlike Richard Nixon, I don't have my rooms bugged. Oh, and by the way—I can see you right now. You and Ms. Griffith. I'm watching you on my tablet. You didn't take the McLaren today?"

That brought both of them up in their seats. Jack was instantly and intensely angry at himself. He had been so focused on his offensive game, on moving the ball upfield, that he had neglected defense. He wondered how far down the road the bastard's video eyes could see. That could prove lethal.

"Good for you," Jack said. The bluster barely concealed what he felt: exposed and vulnerable. But what he had told Dover earlier wasn't just rhetoric. The hunter who flinched when the lion leapt was a dead man. "Speaking of video footage, I'm guessing that somewhere in your cloud files are recordings of your technology at work. That material may be saved somewhere else on your converged infrastructure but the FBI has some pretty smart tech people. I'll bet they could find it using your own hard drives. I'm not saying everything will be accessible, but there will be

enough to start sending out subpoenas—say, to HITV.
Maybe hold some committee hearings on the Hill.
Put an end to your absolute lack of transparency."

"I am a one hundred percent privately held corporation, Mr. Hatfield. I am not obligated to share anything with anyone."

"Yet. That may change once the boys and girls in
Kevlar get inside. People are dying by the dozens. If
you had *anything* to do with that, you're going to feel
like you were hit with a two-by-four."

"To hell with you!"

"Mr. Hawke, I go wherever the trail leads me."

The windows were rolled down. Sirens—not from
the FBI, as Jack had threatened, but cars of the City of
Carmel Police Department—could be heard coming
along Scenic Road. They had no instructions other
than to show up.

"No one covers their tracks absolutely," Jack continued. "Not even you. I'm betting my reputation—
what's left of it—that we're going to find something
when we get inside. That's all the Bureau needs—
something. A scrap, a crumb, and down your house
comes."

"You're stupid enough to do this, aren't you?"
Hawke asked.

"Not only that, I'm stupid enough to tell Forsyth
and his team that I was mistaken, that I withdraw my
testimony, if you just answer my damn questions."

There was another silence. When Hawke returned,
it was a voice Jack well remembered with a threat he
had been expecting.

"I should have dealt with you here," Hawke said. "I should do it now."

Dover tugged Jack's seat belt.

He followed her gaze, saw two men emerge from a side door of the mansion, behind an arbor. Their hands were not empty.

"No. You're too civilized for that," Jack said hopefully.

"Am I?"

Jack felt Dover's fingers pull on his seat belt again, but he refused to back down. He couldn't. He was wired for confrontation and that engine did not work in reverse.

"Even if you shoot us, the FBI goes in," Jack said.

"They're going in anyway, according to you. Besides, what do *I* have to lose? This surveillance will be erased. My security men shot trespassers who threatened me."

Jack suspected these men, these "coworkers," *would* take the rap for their boss. They would do a few years for shooting people who were, technically, trespassers. Hawke's influence would probably get them incarceration at "Camp Snoopy," any of the relatively cushy, low-security prisons. When they got out, they would be set for life.

It happens in the mob world all the time, Jack thought. *The world you once accused Hawke of emulating.*

"It doesn't have to go down this way," Jack pressed. "I told you I can stop it."

"Why would you do that?" Hawke asked. "To protect my interests?"

"Not *your* interests—*ours*. Don't you get it? America's under siege, and this attack may only be the opening salvo."

There was a pause in the call. The men near the mansion's arbor stopped advancing and stood still.

"What are you talking about?"

"The helicopter in Afghanistan—and what happened this morning, inland, in Fairfield."

"Those explosions? The reports said a car fire—"

"Mr. Hawke, we believe the Chinese were trying to hit Travis AFB but got stopped," Jack said. "This must have been Plan B."

The sirens were louder. The cars were just coming along a turn in the road. Jack flung off his seat belt, got out of the car, and held up his hands to stop them. To Hawke, that would play as if Jack were buying him time. In fact, he didn't want the patrol cars rolling into view.

More silence. Jack stared at the nearest surveillance camera. He could picture Hawke in the sun, on his bizarre custom hammock, his leathery face tense as he weighed the events that were happening half a world away.

"We don't agree on a lot, Mr. Hawke, but we're both Americans," Jack said. "If you're not a part of that—and God, I don't want to believe you are—then help me *stop* it."

Hawke finally broke his silence. "If I were to agree

to talk to you, this would stay between us? Your 'journalist's' word of honor. Both of you?"

Only now did Jack realize he had not bothered to breathe. He drew a long, uneven breath.

"That's fair," Jack said. "My word."

Dover nodded. She couldn't speak.

Jack waited again. In his mind's eye he saw Hawke, unhappy but resigned.

He hoped.

"I don't like you, but I believe you," Hawke said.

There was another pause, and Jack noticed the armed men by the arbor go back inside the mansion.

"The truth is," Hawke continued, "I'm not sure how any of this will help, because I *don't* know what is going on there. I sold Beijing the Squarebeam technology, because the DOD is killing the future."

"What does that mean?"

"The Air Force has been using their X-37C space plane to take down Chinese satellites—ones that I build for them," Hawke said.

"You were protecting a business relationship with American *lives*?"

"I said I didn't know about that, and—this isn't about commerce," Hawke said. "Since Obama killed NASA's manned space program, the Chinese are the only ones with an active, aggressive plan to build stations in Earth's orbit to colonize the Moon. By picking off their satellites in the name of national security, we're preventing that expansion."

"You think it's a *good* thing to have them spying on us?"

"They're doing it anyway, on the ground, in cyberspace."

"So you're saying we should let them put up their satellites because there are potential long-term humanitarian benefits?"

"That's exactly what I'm saying," Hawke agreed. "The human race needs to be up there, and the Chinese are the only ones pursuing that."

"So being a visionary trumps being a traitor?"

"Treason?" Hawke snapped. "Grounding our orbital resources is treason. Dooming zero-gravity research for new medicines is treason. Buying seats on Russian spacecraft—*that's* treason! What I did was necessary to get us *back* on the high road!"

"So you're saying you came up with a portable EMP device—and I'm assuming HITV did come up with it, right?"

"Yes."

"You came up with this thing and sold it to the Chinese so they could hit our military on earth, kill our boys, because we were zapping their unmanned satellites in space? Is that the big picture?"

"No! The Chinese weren't supposed to *use* it," Hawke said. "They were just going to let the Secretary of Defense know they had it, through channels. It was supposed to be a kind of mutual assured destruction if they kept taking out satellites."

"Genius move," Jack said. "Just like Moscow would have taken our word for it in '45 if we only *said* we had a nuke."

"Beijing is different."

"Yeah," Jack said. "Your elite Chinese will stab you in the back instead of in the gut. And you knew the Chinese *did* use it in Afghanistan. You *knew*."

"I wasn't sure," Hawke said.

"Did you suspect? Did you tell your bloody clients to *knock it off*?"

"I contacted the Minister of Defense," Hawke said. "He told me they had nothing to do with this. He was offended I'd even asked."

"So you immediately warned *our* Department of Defense, right? You told them about the EMP, warned them that this threat was real?"

Hawke's silence was his answer. Jack had already known the answer. Admitting collusion in an attack on the American military—that would have been a confession of treason.

"All right," Jack said, "that's secondary right now. What are the specifications of the damn thing? What's vulnerable?"

"Anything in a direct line of sight, three-thousand-foot range, one-hundred-and-ten-foot spread," Hawke told him. "Some macro porosity—beyond a fifteen-hundred-foot range it loses ten to twenty percent efficiency through certain kinds of soil, foliage, liquids. Metals, most kinds of natural rock will block it."

"But you're working on that," Jack said.

"Of course. Think what it could do to an enemy's nuclear power plant."

"I'd rather not. Is there any way to locate the device, home in on the pulse?"

"That's the beauty of it," Hawke said. "When it's

off, it's invisible. When it's on, it creates a dead zone over more than half-a-mile long, making it impossible to pinpoint."

"Beauty," Jack thought. *If ever that was in the eye of the beholder . . .*

A patrol car had stopped and was idling. A beefy, impatient sergeant slid from behind the wheel. Another officer, an African American woman, got out and remained behind the open door on the passenger's side. A second car was parked behind it. Jack held up his hand again. The sergeant waited, arms folded.

"You really think you can stop them?" Hawke asked.

"Who? The FBI or the Chinese?" he asked.

"I regret what has happened with the Chinese," Hawke said. "But in a way, we brought this on ourselves."

"That was the same crap a lot of Arab nations said after 9/11," Jack said. " 'We' didn't unleash this horror on Americans. You did."

"And it is on my conscience," Hawke said. "What about the search warrant?"

This was the moment Jack had been waiting for. Jack wasn't a gloater, but he hoped his expression reflected a little of the triumph he felt inside. "There isn't one, Mr. Hawke."

Hawke was silent once again. When he spoke, his tone was reserved, deflated. "Well done," he said quietly, before hanging up.

Jack ended the call and walked toward the patrol car.

"Good morning," Jack said. "I'm Jack Hatfield."

"Yeah. I recognize you from the news. I got a call from the FBI field office in Frisco saying there was some kind of emergency here, that an undercover team needed backup," he said. "Are you it?"

"We are," Jack said. "But things are under control now."

"I don't often get calls like that," the sergeant said. "In fact, that was my first one." The man looked from Jack to Dover then back again. "You two are Feds?"

"Undercover," Jack said. "Honorary."

"I would never have guessed," the sergeant said. "So we're done here?"

"We are," Jack said.

The sergeant returned to his car and the police drove away. Jack returned to Wilhelm and headed back down Scenic Road.

"That was a helluva job you did, Jack," Dover said with open admiration.

"Thanks, but it didn't really get us much."

"What are you talking about? You aren't going to tell Forsyth about Hawke?"

"We can tell Forsyth what he's dealing with, let his tech team chew on it." He handed Dover his cell phone. "You can text the details as we drive. But we gave our word to Hawke."

"You're serious?"

"Absolutely. Besides, prosecuting Hawke doesn't get us anything."

"Like hell! It puts other industrialists on notice!"

"No. Guys like Hawke will always find a reason, a loophole, a justification for what they do. The thing we have to watch out for isn't opportunists but a philosophy, the idea that there's no moral gulf between shooting down hardware loaded with software and shooting down hardware loaded with people."

"So then what do we do now?"

"There's something else that concerns me," Jack said. "Two other things that happened over the past few days involving Chinese. Both were relatively small and local, but the timing bothers me."

"What were they?"

"A suspicious attempt to buy a grocery in Chinatown and a deadly explosion at a Chinese clinic. The San Francisco area isn't usually a hotbed for this kind of activity. When you have these incidents on top of a Chinese terrorist flying in here and picking a local air base to attack—"

"It does seem a little more than coincidence," Dover agreed.

"Exactly. I need to think about this," Jack said.

Dover typed a text to Carl Forsyth as Jack got back on the Pacific Coast Highway. He was pleased his plan had worked. He had punched through Hawke's defenses and confirmed the existence and nature of the EMP device. But he hadn't gotten the magic bullet he had been seeking, and that bothered him—especially when he considered something Johnny had said back at the grocery:

"When Chinese seek something, they never want just that one thing."

There was another plot afoot. And it was up to Jack Hatfield to uncover it and stop it.

San Francisco, California

Liu Tang's plastic chess pieces were arrayed on their board in the center of a wooden card table. The magnets had been removed from the pieces, exposing the drilled holes in their bases.

"Lovely," Hu Kai remarked. He was bent over the pieces, his gloved hands on his knees, his smile wide, admiring. "You carried these, actually used them shipboard?"

"They are completely safe," Liu said. "The aerosolized *Yersinia pestis* cannot penetrate these sealed vessels."

Hu looked up at him. Liu was stoic. Hu himself was humbled. He had been informed that they would be spreading pneumonic plague bacteria through the old smuggling tunnels below the city. But to actually see the receptacles of the bacteria, hold them in containment—

"It is magnificent," Liu Tang added. "But if there were an earth tremor now, we ourselves might be in a rather unfortunate position."

"Yes, of course."

"The delivery system?" Liu asked.

Hu Kai straightened. He walked to the large locker in the back of the Eastern Rim office. They were alone, and the noise of the city sounded far away. The powdery white dust of the clinic operations came off his work boots in little puffs as he walked.

Hu opened the combination lock. He put on work gloves, removed an old fax machine, and carried it carefully, slowly, to the card table. He held it with his fingertips gripping the top, not the bottom or the sides. The interior of the machine had been hollowed out. Near the top of the fax machine was a plate with a series of thirty-two screws facing thread upward. Hu removed the white king from Liu's chessboard and set it aside. Carefully, he screwed the other pieces into place inside the machine.

When there was just one open peg, he said, "Once the king is inserted here and turned to the right, the explosion will occur fifteen minutes later."

"It is not triggered by cell phone?" Liu asked.

"That kind of detonator can be blocked. The environment and structural elements of the tunnel could interfere with reception. No," Hu said, looking at the king in his palm. "This device will be activated by hand. Sensors are attached by wire to the plate and to the other five sides of the steel container. The wires are held in place with an anti-seize paste. When the king is turned to the right, it will start a countdown to turn on a heater that will melt the paste. After fifteen minutes, the stripped ends of the wires will pop off and send a current to the bomb, which is under this." Hu tapped the plate with the screws.

"And the bomb will then detonate," said Liu Tang.

"Yes," said Hu. "If someone manually tampers with the device—which I assure you will not happen—we have a fail-safe: the sensors on the wires. Proximity of bodies, of body heat, will register on the sensors and cause the paste to soften."

"The gloves," Liu said.

"Exactly. They minimize my own heat. The bomb will detonate immediately if the temperature of the grease on the sides of the steel container rises. We have maintained the temperature in the office so that it matches that in the tunnel."

"Ingenious. What about the smaller blasts you will be using to ventilate the tunnel?"

Hu shook his head. "The contacts will not be broken by those vibrations. The paste can *only* be weakened by heat. It is my greatest design," Hu said. "In a way, I am sorry I must leave it behind. Either way," he went on, "once the king is in play, the game is over."

Liu nodded admiringly. "And you? Where will you be?"

"We will meet you and the others and Jintao *Zhǔxí* on the boat," Hu said. He had used a title of respect reserved for leaders of towering stature. "Together, from the sea, we will watch America die."

Liu laid a hand on his shoulder. "Jintao was right to select you," he said. "This is a great day for the new Chinese Empire."

Hu bowed humbly. It was a strange contrast, the rush of humility. For at that moment, with the chess piece in his hand, he also felt like the most powerful man on the planet.

Maggie Yu spent a restless day at the grocery, troubled by things unseen.

The attack on the helicopter in Fairfield had fueled fears of terrorism and business was brisk. Customers were using the grocery—as they used the nearby nail salon and bookshop and rebuilt electronics store—as an impromptu meeting place. Their discussions skittered nervously from hearsay to vaguely relevant anecdotes, but they always returned to the speculation of reckless newscasters, that what had occurred in Fairfield was not an accident.

Maggie half-listened and nodded in agreement with whatever was said. Her mind and soul were in the basement, lost in the labyrinth of the story she had been told by *Sifu* Qishan—

Not a *story,* she reminded herself. It was many stories linked by the tunnels and the strong reactions they generated—fear, pain, and violence. *Each girl who was pushed or pulled through those tunnels was a person who left behind something of what they were feeling.*

San Francisco had known many horrors over the centuries, but this one was right below her feet. Even if she had not heard those sounds, the tunnels should be opened and purged. She was waiting for the evening when the grocery closed and her father went to play mah-jongg and she could move crates and shelves to look for an entrance to the underground world.

When eight o'clock finally arrived, Maggie flipped the OPEN sign, kissed her father on the cheek, and shooed him to the door.

"I'll break down the cash register," she said.

"I don't mind counting out the drawer," he told her. "You seem tired—"

"No, I've been husbanding my energy all day for this task," she teased.

Her father grinned. " 'Husbanding' your energy? Is that a puzzle?"

She was confused.

"Never mind," her father smiled, hurrying out. "Your secret rendezvous is safe with me."

Maggie let him go on thinking that she was meeting some young civil servant. That was what he wanted for her, a holdover from the values of the old world: that a daughter's greatest security was to marry a member of the Nine Ranks, a system that originated a millennium ago in the Zhou Dynasty. It was a court hierarchy that reached from the Ninth Pin—county officials—to the First Pin, bureaucrats who answered personally to the emperor. Maggie would have been happy to oblige, but most men were intimidated by the fact that she could deflect unwanted advances with a finger to the windpipe. Those who were not were her fellow students, and they were more like brothers.

She counted out the cash, measured the sum against the receipts, and put the money in a deposit bag. She grabbed a water bottle, went downstairs, and put the cash in the safe. Then she looked around. Whatever she did, she wanted to return everything to normal before her father got back. He was not a spiritual man, but he believed in leaving the past in the past.

"It's better for the digestion to always look forward," he said.

The floor under the shelves was stuffed with things she rarely if ever touched: boxes of tools, dropcloths, cans of paint—some so old she doubted the containers could be opened—and cardboard filing cabinets that were stuffed with old ledgers. She had pulled those out, years before, to wrap the books in plastic to keep them from mildewing.

Maggie had not heard the humming the few times she had come down to check. But now that the store was empty and traffic was thinning, there were faint noises. The earlier sounds had been a whirring; this was more like hammering. It was coming from the same direction, the wall with the oak closet. She began removing the cleaning supplies: the broom, mop, squeegee, sprays, detergents. There was a clothesline her mother used down here before the cleaner opened down the street. Maggie used to jump rope with it. She smiled when she saw the old calendar hanging on the wall, from May 1996. That month's photo was a picture of the Huangpu River—coincidentally, the spot where her father had proposed to her mother. She ran her hand across it lovingly.

There is good energy here, too, she reminded herself.

The closet was bolted to the wall to keep it from falling during tremors. She didn't know how she would get behind it to see if there was a door. Perhaps if she cut a section from it, behind the calendar?

As she contemplated the problem she remembered something that *Sifu* Qishan had said: people came and went using trapdoors.

Her eyes drifted to the left, to the safe. The yard-high iron box sat flat on the floor next to the closet.

She didn't remember what was there before; she was just two years old at the time. But it was the perfect way to seal a trapdoor.

Maggie went to the small storage area under the staircase. That was where her father kept the dolly he used to move larger boxes around. He also had a crowbar he used to pry open wooden crates. She brought them over, and using a small mallet, she was able to knock the tapered end of the crowbar under the left side of the safe, away from the closet. That allowed her to slip the dolly under the raised edge. She kicked it in as far as it would go, then tied the safe to the dolly with the clothesline.

She pulled back on the dolly. Even with all her weight on it, the safe failed to move. She tried walking the safe back by shifting the dolly from side to side. She stirred dust, nothing more.

There's only one way you're going to move that, she knew.

Maggie got on top of the safe. This wasn't going to be pretty, but it had to be done. She braced her back against the side of the closet and placed her feet against the top of the dolly. Her knees were bent straight up. She placed her hands against her legs, against the quadriceps, so she could push them out toward the dolly. The young woman was used to drawing energy from the ground. Kung fu required a center of gravity that worked its way up from the feet, along the spine, channeled to the arms and hands. She rarely had the opportunity to train parallel to the ground.

You've done cartwheels and handstands, she told

herself. *The energy still comes from the ground. It's just entering at a different point.*

She took a moment to feel the closet against her upper back. She thought of the good memories represented by the calendar, the positive energy left behind by her father as he looked at that photograph over the years. She let that flow into her shoulders. And then, with a cry to focus that strength, she simultaneously pushed out with her palms and extended her legs.

The dolly leaned outward, and the safe went with it. So did Maggie. Even as her back left the side of the closet, she was pushing energy into her arms and legs. The roped safe-dolly combination fell over, tipping slowly enough so that Maggie was able to drop her rear onto the top, ride it down, and end up standing, facing away from the closet.

The dolly was bent by the weight of the toppled safe.

So much for returning everything to normal before Dad comes home, she thought.

Maggie walked around to the other side. She looked down at a piece of plywood that had been pressed so hard by the safe that it split into a series of slats. They weren't level with the concrete floor, flattened by the weight of the safe. She had to pry them up with the crow bar. Underneath were the rotted planks of a trapdoor. There was a large iron ring set in the side away from the wall.

The young woman knelt beside the door; it almost felt as if she was praying. Perhaps she should be. She needed the crowbar to lift the latch out as well. The ring creaked upright, shedding particles of rust; the trapdoor groaned with it.

Keep going, Maggie told herself.

She reached for the ring, pulled it, and moved her head back as the dust of a century wafted up. It was not quite the dry, musty smell she had been expecting but a smell of putrefaction, like damp soil and rotted leaves.

Water from the bay must have leached its way in, she realized.

The hammering was clearer, echoing from somewhere to the north. She left the trapdoor resting against the wall and got a flashlight. She squatted by the edge and shined it down. Four steep steps ended on a packed dirt floor.

She rose, took a long drink of water, then wedged one end of the crowbar behind the closet and slipped the other end in the ring. She didn't know where the tunnel would take her, but she wanted the light shining in so she could find her way back.

Maggie felt a chill. It was more than the cool air of the tunnel, but a sense that nothing good awaited her down there.

She also knew that growth required challenge, answers demanded effort, and that self-respect came from doing the difficult.

After taking several slow, cleansing breaths, she climbed down the ladder.

Jing Jintao stood alone in the conference room on the forty-eighth floor of the Transamerica Pyramid. Ordinarily the room was restricted to tenants of the building, but the consul general had only to mildly suggest that he would like a few minutes of undisturbed time in the room, to receive it.

The 360-degree view of San Francisco, so world-renowned that a trip to this floor was considered a cultural gift to visiting dignitaries, was not his interest. To Jintao, the city resembled sugar cubes stained by tea. He had once witnessed an American ambassador add sugar to his rare, triple-steeped *Anxi Ti Kuan Yin,* an offense so profound Jintao could almost taste it in his own tea. No, he was not here to marvel at the city, but at the sea in the late afternoon light. Soon Jintao would be on that sea, leaving this place at last, looking back only to see it dissolve.

The weaponized pneumonic plague, maximized for toxic potency and extended airborne motility, would be spread through inhalation. The city would send first responders to the bomb site but most of them would take breaks from wearing their cumbersome masks. They would be infected.

Wind would carry the plague to other residents. At first, people would think they had the flu—a fever, a cough. Not nearly enough of them would seek medical treatment. Even if they did, the necessary antibiotics would not be available fast enough or in sufficient quantities. Over the next few hours other people would be wondering why they suddenly couldn't breathe. Doctors would misdiagnose it as asthma, then they, too, would become sick after coughed particles of saliva infiltrated their nasal linings. Everyone the doctors treated after that would become ill. The social and medical infrastructure would quickly collapse.

Within hours, every person infected in the initial wave would start coughing up blood, in some cases vomiting. Septic shock would set in. Some people would wander in anxious confusion, their hearts racing, rasping for breath. Others, their blood pressure plummeting, would collapse where they stood. As airborne bodily fluids were inhaled, spreading the infection further, the panic would be well under way—the military sent in, the quarantine, the armed theft of vehicles to get out, the traffic accidents, the accidental shootings as people sought to protect themselves, the intentional shootings as people *did* protect themselves, the suicides off the bridges.

The death rate would be nearly one hundred percent above the tunnels and seventy to eighty percent in the rest of the city. There would be no escape—and anyone who did would infect more Americans.

Jintao glanced again at the small piece of paper that his deliveryman had brought to him just before he left his office. The source was unidentified but Jintao knew it was from the cell leader. Written upon the paper was only *mǎn yì.* "Satisfied."

When he exited the Transamerica Pyramid, Jintao passed the Mark Twain Plaza and smiled. That location had always pleased him, almost more than any other in the city. The bow of the *Niantic,* a triple-masted ship from the mid-nineteenth century, was still buried somewhere beneath the plaza. The *Niantic* had originally transported goods from China, the usual tea, silk, and most likely, opium hidden in the hold. The ship was then converted into a whaling vessel. Jintao considered that singularly appropriate as his harpoon was sharpened for this bloated behemoth that he was about to depart, forever.

When they were still an hour out of San Francisco, Jack got a text from Doc. He gave the phone to Dover to read.

"He says that Abe and his boat are MIA and there's something strange at the Farallon Islands. He did a flyover. He wants you to go out there with him as soon as possible."

"Tell him we'll take the *Sea Wrighter*. Ask him how fast he can get her to a marina on the San Francisco side to pick us up."

Dover started texting. Jack felt a twinge of guilt. He hadn't thought about Abe since he left Sausalito on his Defever. Their friend was an adult who was known to go off on mushroom-induced "walkabout" adventures from time to time. Still, the news about the boat was troubling.

Dover read a new text. "He says he can get to the side-tie wharf in the marina by seven."

Jack looked at the clock on the dashboard. It was six o'clock. They could make it if they went straight there.

"OK, that's good," Jack said. "Ask him to bring sweaters, since we're not dressed for nighttime boating."

"Will do. He should probably walk Eddie first," she said.

"If Doc's worried, we don't have time," Jack said. "Eddie will use the shower stall. Survival mode."

"You trained him to do that?"

"It was either that or a scrub brush and Simple Green," Jack said.

Jack fell silent then. His mind was still on the Chinese situation—more so than it was before. The picture was naggingly incomplete.

He said out loud, "The real story here is not what we've been looking into but something Hawke revealed."

Dover followed his thoughts. "The globalization of his interests? The fact that he sold weapons to China that could be used against us?"

"That's just a part of it," Jack said. "I believe him when he says he didn't expect the EMP to be used. No, the game changer is that an important threshold has been reached. The Chinese have achieved a level of technological advancement that has caused us to target their satellites and for them to retaliate, decisively, with wide-scale carnage on the ground. The China-America dynamic is no longer one of forbearance or diplomatic finger-wagging or sanctions the way it is with other wacko regimes like North Korea and Iran. Beijing and Washington are in a slow-motion, low-impact shooting war."

"You really think it's gone that far?"

"Yes, and I think it's going to get ratcheted up," Jack said.

"That much I got. Did you ever hear of that space plane he was talking about?"

Jack nodded. "It turned up when I was preparing a show, 'NASA After Obama.' Roger Boisjoly was going to be a guest, the whistleblower who'd been arguing for NASA to be shut down ever since the *Challenger* exploded. It would have been a great show, but then the network yanked the plug on *Truth Tellers*. Anyway, during our research Boisjoly made a suggestion, we followed up on it and found the predecessor of the space plane, the X-37B. It was built by Boeing Phantom Works, basically a robotic space shuttle about thirty feet long."

Dover shook her head. "That's the new China for you."

"What do you mean?"

"There was a time when they would have struck back with a kind of austere patience. They would have backed an enemy regime, the way they did in Vietnam—perhaps built up al-Qaeda in Yemen and applied pressure on us that way. Beijing doesn't have the time for that now. They have set grand goals in commerce, in science. They must meet them quickly and at any cost."

"Is it a question of face?" Jack asked.

"Very much so," Dover said. "They have reached a level of expectation both domestically and internationally that will not tolerate standstill and certainly not reversal.

"There's something strange about all this," Dover continued. "I don't mean about the politics but about the zen of it. I'm looking out at the setting sun, at that burning candlewick on the ocean horizon, and I'm thinking how alive it seems because of the impermanence of everything. What happened outside the air force base, what Doc is concerned about, everything with Hawke—it makes the beauty of the sunset, of this moment, seem much more special."

Jack understood that intellectually. But he was too angry at most of the Asian continent right now to share her carpe diem joy.

They reached the wharf precisely at seven. *Sea Wrighter* was waiting. Its big Caterpillar diesels were already warm for the trip.

"It's like I never left home," Jack said as he and Dover came aboard. "Where's Eddie?"

"Shower stall," Doc said.

It was dark, but the winds were at their calmest as Doc steered them out into the Bay, the three of them clustered on the bridge. Eddie came topside and hugged their ankles.

"Something's sour out there," Doc said. He explained what he had seen while Jack and Dover pulled on Berkeley sweatshirts he had brought. Abe had given three of them to Doc as a gag Christmas present one year. Doc wasn't wearing his; he had cut it into a little jacket for Eddie.

Jack agreed that the disappearance of Abe's boat merited investigation. Dover wasn't clear why Doc hadn't called the Coast Guard.

"I didn't see any trace of the boat or Abe over twenty-four miles of ocean," Doc said, handing the helm over to Jack. "There was no distress signal. That would have generated a search, and the marina would have known about it. That tells me he probably went down, and went down fast. If he'd gone aground on the islands, there would be some trace of the boat—the hull or at least wreckage. There's nada. Except someone hiding out. And I don't think it's Abe. He would have heard my plane."

"So what do you think?" Dover asked.

"I don't know," Doc said. "That's why we're going out there."

Doc was old school. When he went into the field on a mission, he always had paper maps and charts with him. He kept GPS devices as a backup, but he preferred to operate with a document in his hands lit by a penlight in his teeth.

He had spent the afternoon picking up a few supplies and studying nautical charts of the Farallons, and he mapped a course that would have them moving against the wind. As he explained to Dover, if there was someone out there he wanted the sound of the wind rushing against them rather than with them.

"Are we going into Fisherman's Cove?" Jack asked Doc.

"No, what I saw was on Noonday Island."

"Somebody really didn't want to be found."

"Exactly. There's a tiny temporary beach on Noonday right now," Doc said. "You're going to keep the *Sea Wrighter* about a mile off the island, lights out, while I go in on the Novurania." Jack had added a twelve-foot Novurania launch to the *Sea Wrighter* a few years ago, outfitted with a 40 HP Yamaha motor.

"While *we* go in on the Novurania," Jack corrected him. Doc eyed him, but what he saw there kept him from contradicting. Jack turned to Dover. "Will you be all right minding the *Sea Wrighter* while we're gone?"

"As long as I've got Eddie," she smiled. "Don't worry, I've steered a few boats around the Chesapeake."

"The water's a hell of a lot rougher around the Farallons," Doc said. "If you can't stay in one place, keep the throttle forward, 1,000 RPMs, and just circle. And watch the radar so you don't hit anything."

"I'll be all right," Dover said, "but it's sweet of you to worry about me."

Jack patted the boat. "She doesn't understand," he said to the *Sea Wrighter*. He grinned at Dover, and she winked at him.

Doc handed them two pairs of night-vision glasses, a third for himself.

"Are we going to be commandos, too?" Dover asked jokingly.

"Not unless you have to be," Jack said. "If somebody gets past Doc and me, you'll need to know how to use these." He didn't mention that if somebody got past Doc and Jack, Dover didn't stand much of a chance. He didn't have to. They kept up the pretense. "These binoculars can be disorienting if you're a novice."

"When and where did you learn?" she asked.

He answered, "I once spied on my ex. Long story." It was a commercially available model, not mili-

tary, which was the only kind Doc wanted to be
caught with abroad. Soldiers might not believe he was
owl-watching with these, but he might buy himself a
few minutes to get away while they called their base
for instructions. In many countries, mercs were shot on
sight.

The unit was a pair of binoculars with a large, cy-
clopean infrared generator in the top, center.

"There are five AA batteries in back. You just slide
this switch—" Jack showed her the plastic tab on the
side "—and nothing happens . . . unless you're looking through them."

Jack pointed her away from the shore so the lights
of the city didn't blind her. She switched them on.

"It's surreal," she said, gazing across the ocean
waves. "Like the surface of another planet."

Jack made no comment. There were times he felt
that way about everything outside of San Francisco.
Even Carmel had seemed strangely foreign, made unfamiliar by the hard, unpleasant truths he'd been contemplating there and back.

Dover was about to say something but Jack turned
her to look at the Golden Gate Bridge. She fell silent.
Jack put on his own binoculars and the world turned
into a green nebula. The towers of the bridge he loved,
the bridge he had saved, looked like cuts of old camera film in a haze of phosphorescence. *Remember,* he
thought. *Remember.* He was overwhelmed by emotion for his city, his home. The sight was both beautiful and—because of all his associations with that
color of green, courtesy of Iraq—a threat.

*   *   *

About five miles past the bridge, the lights of San Francisco disappeared. The *Sea Wrighter* was now in a black ocean, or green for Dover, who was still wearing her night-vision binoculars. The big Grand Banks yacht was as steady as a locomotive. Her deep keel and Naiad stabilizers kept her tracking without much roll. About an hour later they reached the islands.

Doc had gone wide to bring the yacht in so they were blocked from moonlight. With black ink he marked on a shoreline chart the point where he had seen the tarp and where he felt it was best to make landfall with the dinghy. There were two other marks, one in red, one in green.

"There's about five hundred feet of rock that will be slippery with sea water and guano," he said. "Slip on the galoshes I brought," he said, pointing to a locker. "You'll need them."

"What's the drill?" Jack asked as they pulled them on.

"Three minutes after I go ashore, you steer the launch here," he pointed to the green mark.

"What if he's armed?" Dover asked.

"I will already be here," he pointed at the red mark. "He shows himself, I take him."

Jack studied the shoreline chart as Doc and Dover maneuvered the launch into the water. Dover noticed the Walther P99 semiautomatic in Doc's belt holster on his right and the drop point hunting knife in a

sheath on his left side. He winked at her as he took a
length of nylon rope from a locker and wound it around
his arm. Dover grinned.

"We have a saying in the Spec Ops community,"
he told her. "If you're not living on the edge, you're
taking up too much room."

Eddie knew when Jack was about to climb into
the launch. The little guy had read his people and
knew something serious was going on so he didn't
protest, just licked Jack's hand. Dover gave the men a
thumbs-up, but Jack saw how tightly she was hugging
herself; he knew she wasn't that cold. He gave her a
big smile, and she visibly relaxed. Then he climbed
aboard the launch.

"Remember," Jack said to Dover, "if we don't return within two hours, turn her east and head toward
the Bridge. You can call the Coast Guard on Channel
16 with a 'Mayday' and they'll come get you in."

It was a choppy ride around to the target side of the
island. The throaty throb of the yacht's big diesels
drowned out any noise from the launch for quite a
distance, and even away from the boat the Yamaha
motor was beautifully quiet. But the slap of the waves
sounded like *ka-chunks,* heavy as footsteps in a horror movie. Jack cut the engine as they neared the
shore. There were no seals here, and it was as desolate
a spot as one could find in the Farallons. Slipping on
his night-vision glasses, Doc jumped out when they
were still a few feet away. He landed pantherlike on a
small, flat rock and hurried inland. Jack steered away

and headed for his own target. He was there in just under three minutes. Sometimes Doc's sense of time and space bordered on the supernatural.

Jack hooked his night-vision binoculars around his neck, stopped the inflatable boat, grabbed a flashlight, and went ashore. Doc had assigned him to a short stretch of what passed for beach, five yards of granite that sloped gently toward the sea. The smell of the seals thrust into his senses, but his eyes were on the surrounding slope, watching for any sign of movement.

Then he saw it. A dark shape in motion, fifteen feet up.

It fascinated Jack how everything was relative. San Francisco seemed windy until you were twenty-five miles out on the ocean. The old fish market used to smell until you came to a place like this. And the sky appeared very dark until something darker moved against it. Only one figure, and it wasn't Doc because Doc would never have let Jack see him.

The fact that that wasn't Doc meant that whoever was up there would soon be down here. It was all a question of how he'd be coming. Either he was going to investigate the launch or—

The figure fell—sort of. He descended a yard to Jack's left, gagging into his balaclava mask, clawing at a length of rope around his throat. There had been no drop so his neck hadn't snapped. Doc must have noosed him from behind, kicked his legs from under him, and lowered him over the side.

As soon as the man touched down, Jack went over

and punched him in the face. Then again. Choked and dazed, the man fell in a heap.

"We good?" Doc shouted from above.

"We're good," Jack answered.

Doc let the other end of the rope drop. Jack turned the flashlight on. He flipped the man on his belly, checked the man for weapons, found none. Then he picked up the other end of the rope. Without removing the noose, Jack tied the man's hands behind him—tightly, so there was still a tugging pressure on his throat. Then he removed the mask.

"Why am I not surprised?" he said as he looked down.

The man was Asian. His eyes were narrow, and his mouth was taut as he struggled to breathe.

Doc joined him, following a ridge that let him off in a pile of rocks to the west. He was holding his night-vision glasses in one hand and a Remington 700 tactical rifle with a night-vision scope in the other.

"Guess what he planned to do," Doc said. "I just took a quick run through his tent. He's got rations, a radio, and other electronics. He's also got a lunch box full of C-4."

"Another Chinese," Jack said. "Our girl talks his lingo."

Fifteen minutes later they threw the man on the deck of the *Sea Wrighter.*

"Oh, honey, you brought home a guest!" Dover grinned. "You should have warned me."

"No friend of mine, honey," Jack said. "Care to do a little interpreting?" Dover nodded. "Ask him if he's used the C-4 on any boats in the last twenty-four hours," Jack said.

Dover look shocked but just turned and spoke to the man. He didn't answer. Doc dragged the man to the edge of the boat. Keeping the man half on the boat, he kicked the man's legs out over the edge, took out his knife, and ran it across one of his calves.

"Tell him that any shark within a quarter mile will be having dinner if he doesn't talk," Doc said.

The man didn't need a translation. He started chattering.

"He says he sank a boat on standing orders from his group leader," Dover said.

"What is the group's mission?" Jack asked.

Dover asked.

"He says he doesn't know," she told them. "He says he is here to arrange a rendezvous."

"With whom?" Jack asked.

There was motion in the water less than two hundred yards away, and a fin. It wasn't out of the realm of possibility that a shark could take a leap and catch a leg. The man realized that and talked faster.

"He says he was supposed to coordinate a top secret emergency departure of a contingent of fifteen people from this spot."

"Names?"

"He's just getting to that," Dover said. "He swears he doesn't know any names. Only code names. And a company name."

"What company?"

"Eastern Rim Construction," she said. "He heard it mentioned. It sounds like a front to me. And he begs you, please, to pull him from the water."

Doc yanked him up. A few moments later a shark swam by, snapping at blood that had dripped into the waves.

"They're brave in the collective sense," Jack said. "Not so spunky flying—or dying—solo."

Doc raised the rifle and held it to the man's head. He screamed and gagged simultaneously. Dover gasped and half-turned.

"Find out what he did to Abe," Doc said.

Dover asked. She moaned as she listened.

"What?" Jack asked.

"He said he found something—he couldn't let the man leave. He shot him, and he went in the water."

"Eaten?" Jack asked.

She nodded.

"The boat?"

"Sunk with explosives. About fifty yards to the east of here."

Their prisoner was writhing, crying, trying to bend his hands in a direction they wouldn't go to release the pressure on his windpipe. Doc stood where he was, the gun barrel pressed to the man's skull.

"He still may be able to tell us things," Jack said.

"I'll talk to him on the way back," Dover said. "He may be able to identify other members in his group, or testify against them in a trial."

Doc remained there a heartbeat longer, then fired into the sea at the shark.

"That's for Abe, you dead-eyed SOB," he said as he shouldered the rifle.

Fairfield, California

It had been a long and soul-wrenching day for Al Fitzpatrick.

He had remained in Fairfield in case there were any clues to help with the search, or in the event the man had not fled the scene at all. There were enough hands in the field to grab the target if he showed up.

The office of the hotel manager was a small, mostly insulated pocket from the larger chaos of sound and destruction in Fairfield. But there were still the sobbing and angry oaths of those who came in and out of the lobby, both guests of the hotel and passersby who sought haven from the smoke and ash that still drifted from the sky. The explosions had melted the asphalt, adding the stench of melted tar to the noxious smell of burning rubber and plastic. Even in the lobby, there was a fine mist of particulate matter.

During one of his many short bathroom breaks, Fitzpatrick wondered how many of those motes had once been parts of human beings.

There was still no death toll, but estimates were placed at a minimum of seventy—which included those who were killed immediately after the blasts when pieces of automobiles and helicopter fell through stores and other vehicles.

Fitzpatrick spent the day monitoring feedback about the image of the terrorist. There were several false alarms. In a series of incidents that were disturbingly similar to the internment of Japanese Americans during World War II, nearly two dozen individuals of Asian descent who were tagged by the surveillance cameras at bus stops, train stations, banks, service stations, airports, and in cabs were tracked and interviewed by law enforcement personnel. The number increased exponentially as the day wore on.

The facial recognition software was calibrated to expand its circle of activity with every passing minute. Using Fairfield as ground zero, it added forty miles every hour, assuming the average rate of road travel by someone trying to escape the hub of a terrorist attack.

It was nearly seven P.M., when Fitzpatrick was on his fourth pot of coffee, that they got the first hit with a probability factor above eighty percent. It was at San Francisco International.

In less than three minutes of getting the HUA—heads-up alert—Carl Forsyth called Fitzpatrick.

"I think we have your man," Forsyth said. "He bought a ticket on Lufthansa and just showed diplomatic credentials at security. That's where we got the ping. He passed the x-ray screening but they took his word on the contents of his bag, as required."

"He didn't wait for a Chinese carrier," Fitzpatrick said. "In a hurry to get out?"

"Maybe. We've got people there and authority under the Patriot Act to detain foreign diplomats, but they have to be personally known by law enforcement to have committed or actively supported an act of terror. That's you. I'm arranging a chopper to get you out. Travis says they can pick you up on the roof of the hotel in ten minutes."

"I'll be there," Fitzpatrick said.

The agent finished his coffee and went to find the manager. He was in the lobby with his staff, a good general who had remained beyond his shift to support the beleaguered troops. Jack asked him how to get to the roof.

Before leaving, the agent took a moment to thank all the hotel employees. It was a sober parting, but with a trace of shoulders-back pride and the kind of unity that—sadly—only war and tragedy brought out in groups of citizens.

Two minutes later he was shaking the manager's hand before climbing into a Sikorsky HH-60 Pave Hawk helicopter of the 571st Global Mobility Readiness Squadron. It was a thrill to be on board, and an honor to be a passenger.

As they rose into the night sky, Fitzpatrick looked back at Air Base Parkway. It was lit with rows of high-pressure 400W sodium lamps, creating a quarter-mile-long island of light. It was a horrendous scene of fire engines and squad cars, soldiers and police, a handful of ambulances, and burned craters that were once vehicles and roadway. The smoke that had churned from the fires was mostly gone from the area, having risen on its own heat to spread across the rest of the city.

"I am taking you to San Francisco International, Agent Fitzpatrick," the pilot confirmed when Fitzpatrick had put on his headset. "I heard, sir, and it's just a rumor, that you may be able to ID the individual who did this."

"I can't say—"

"Of course not, sir, and it's not my place to inquire. I only want to tell you, sir, that if it's true, we only have one suggestion. Maybe it's more of a request."

"What's that, Lieutenant?"

The pilot replied, "Don't let the scumbag come to trial."

San Francisco, California

There was no evil here, no bad energy, nothing spiritually dark or frightening.

Whatever Maggie had felt in her basement was not a result of the traverse but of the destination. Emerging into the houses where they would be living and working as whores or laborers—that was what had evoked the fear, the terror. That was where it was strongest. It pained her to think that her grocery might have been one of those terrible places.

Maggie was not a tall woman, but she was forced to bend at the knees to fit in the tunnel. She never bent at the waist, which would leave her off-balance; she simply lowered her center of gravity. When she finally moved ahead, she did so in that same posture, her balance permitting her to walk with absolute silence.

The flashlight revealed the tunnel to be hard, compacted dirt below and stretches of rock with intermittent patches of old slime-covered brick for the walls. There were wooden boards along the low ceiling with occasional support timbers along the top and sides, like a mine. This particular passage ended in a sharp right turn that continued in a diagonal line. The route was leading her in the direction of the financial district.

The hammering was clearer here, a steady, echoing *chunk, chunk, chunk* against rock. The farther she went, the lower the ceiling became. After about five minutes, Maggie was forced to proceed on her hands and knees. Though the atmosphere was rank, she was surprised that the air in the tunnel was not stale. There was obviously an opening somewhere ahead.

During her passage, Maggie saw no other openings. That made sense. They were used for more than human trafficking. Any of the Highbinders fleeing through them would not want to risk being cut off by someone jumping down just ahead of them.

After nearly ten minutes, she noticed a glow ahead and turned off her flashlight. She moved slowly, feeling her way; she did not want to discover any sudden drops by falling into one.

The sound itself would stop for a few moments and then come closer, louder. The glow would be a little brighter. Whoever was down here was coming in her direction.

It occurred to Maggie as she went along that she should have brought her cell phone. The tunnels seemed sturdy enough—they had survived for well over a century—but they were still old, with seeping water somewhere beyond the walls. The actions of the people ahead, or even her own passage, any weight or pressure at all could do something to trigger a collapse. And she had no idea what *kind* of work was being done up ahead. She did not think it was authorized by any city department. What if it weren't geologists or archaeologists at work, which was what she hoped to find? What if she needed backup? That was a thought that had been growing since she had first learned of the tunnel, one that argued against work being done in the public interest. The man who had come to buy the grocery did not strike her as a man interested in civic-minded projects.

Was tunnel access the reason that man wanted to buy the grocery? If so, did he find another way in?

The tunnel had continued along its diagonal course until it turned suddenly to the left. Maggie stopped several yards from the corner. The sounds were clear here. The light was brighter. And she could see faint shadows on the wall—two of them. Their arms were upraised.

Then she heard the first voices that had been raised down here: the crackle of a radio with a Chinese speaker on the other end.

"We're ready here," the caller said. "Are you almost finished?"

"We're on the last one," a voice nearby replied. "Another two minutes."

The radio went silent. So did the men.

Being "finished" with something did not sound good, Maggie thought. She had to find out what it was.

Maggie was on high alert now, her senses sharp, her elbows automatically bending inward, toward her chest. That was the position from which forward energy was harnessed and projected. She raised her torso slightly so that she was resting on her fingertips. That would create the least amount of contact with the ground, generate the least noise. She inched ahead, her breathing shallow and silent but deep. That would give her the energy to strike if that became necessary. Her tongue was pressed to the roof of her mouth to moderate the flow of air and keep her from hyperventilating.

She turned her head around the corner and waited. She was still in the shadow.

There were two men: one had his back toward her, the other had his back to the wall nearest her. Both were working around a hole they had cut in the ceiling. The man with his back to her was working his fingers slowly, carefully around the excavation. She could not see what they were doing. A chisel and hammer lay beside a battery-powered lantern. The radio was resting against the wall to the right.

Maggie was still holding the doused flashlight. She laid it down and adjusted her position. She put her left hand against the bend in the wall and got on the balls of her feet. This was the Monkey position. Typically it was used to create a low target: an opponent would have to bend, giving the "monkey" a chance to throw out the hands, whiplike, to strike eyes or face or to deflect a grab or blow. In this case, however, it was the only style that would fit in the confined space.

She came around the corner with a low, bounding hop. She reached for the man whose back was toward her. Her right hand grabbed the collar of the sweater he was wearing: it was a tight grip that would hold him even if the fabric tore. She yanked him back, and as he fell she released her hold and drove her right elbow down into his nose. She immediately leaped forward, her left arm across her chest, and drove a stiff-armed back fist into the other man's face. That knocked his head hard against the wall. He fell face forward. The other man was still awake, pawing at his bloodied nose. Maggie turned, balanced low on her left foot, and planted her right heel in his forehead as he tried to rise. He flopped flat back.

Maggie checked both men by digging a fingernail into the cuticle of their thumb. If they were feigning unconsciousness, the pain would have roused them. Picking up the lantern, she held it close to the hole in the ceiling.

A thickish red stick was tucked inside. It looked—and smelled—like the gunpowdery Chinese firecrackers she had seen in New Year celebrations. Judging from the care with which the man had been handling it, she suspected it was a squib of some kind, though she didn't see a fuse.

The radio came on.

"Are you finished?" the caller asked. He waited a moment. "Chin, are you there?"

Maggie decided not to answer. She thought of going back but, as she held the lantern forward, it looked to her as if the tunnel was wider ahead. She would make better time in that direction. And there was still at least one person ahead: she wasn't likely to be in any danger as long as he thought there were still men at work back here.

She took the radio and pushed the lantern ahead of her, crawling behind it until she could waddle in monkey stance. Rounding a corner she was able to rise as she had before. She wondered whether the geography or a low foundation had forced the tunnel to narrow. The man had stopped calling to his comrades, was talking to someone else. Maggie couldn't make out what he was saying.

No doubt she would find out soon enough. After turning another corner she saw the longest tunnel yet, with a dim light at the other end. There was a faint, burnt smell in the air, like an old fireplace. She left the radio on the ground—it wouldn't do for the men to hear their own voices as she approached—and after ascertaining as best she could that there were no potholes or pitfalls ahead, Maggie switched off the lantern and hurried ahead.

Sausalito, California

The drive from the marina to Eastern Rim took less than five minutes. It was made shorter by Jack's desire to hurt someone.

It hadn't really registered that Abe Cohen was

dead, that the dialogues they had had over meals at Bruno's were over, that this *creature* had fed him to the sharks, because it was inconvenient to do anything else. Those were Hawke's egalitarian Chinese. *All for us and nothing for you, not even life.* Sitting in the backseat with the hog-tied prisoner, it was all Jack could do to keep from spitting on him.

Doc was at the wheel. He pulled up to the door of the small Eastern Rim office. He made no secret of his presence. He strode to the front door, gun and knife in his hands, with Jack and Dover running behind. He kicked it in, entered behind the gun that was held at his hip. The knife was in his right hand, blade facing ahead, ready to be thrown forward— not from the tip, like a knife thrower, but by twisting the body and pushing the knife through the air from the hilt. Doc had once explained that the forward throw covered a shorter distance, no more than six feet, but it did so more accurately and painfully, into the gut.

There was no resistance. They saw only one man in the room. He was smoking a cigarette and was halfway between the sofa and the door. He must have gotten up when he heard the car. Behind him there was a Chinese station on an old cathode ray TV.

"Knock, knock," Doc said as he strode into the room. He holstered the gun and grabbed the man's shoulder and put the knife to his throat. "You were expecting someone. Who?"

The man said something in Chinese.

"He wants to know by what right you come in here,"

Dover said as she and Jack walked through the door, which was swinging on just one hinge.

"Tell him we've got his pal from the Farallons in the car. We want the rest of the story, whatever it is."

Doc was talking as the Chinese man continued to speak.

"He says that whoever we are, we have no right to be here," Dover said.

"One more time," Doc said, pushing the knife at his throat. "What the hell is going on here?"

"I think I have a clue," Jack said.

Doc and Dover both looked over. Jack held up a work order that he had pulled from a bulletin board. "They're on the clinic job—excavation prior to demolition."

"So?" Doc asked.

Jack looked around the room. He walked to a closet in the back. The door had a padlock. "Doc, open this?"

Doc pulled the Chinese man with him as he sheathed his knife and took out his handgun. He put the barrel above the doorknob, angled toward the jamb, and put two rounds in the wood, shattering the lock catch. The padlock remained in place, but the door creaked open. Jack found the light switch, looked inside.

"As I thought—explosives."

"Meaning what?" Dover asked.

Jack literally sniffed around the room. "It may be a coincidence, but this closet smells just like the clinic did after it went sky high. Not a lot of places in the city are licensed for high explosives. Dover, ask this gentleman if these people had anything to do with the explosion, and if so, why? If he doesn't answer—Doc, start cutting off parts of him."

Dover swallowed as Doc put the blade above the man's right ear. She asked the question.

The man listened, waited, then put the cigarette between his lips. He puffed. There was nothing in his demeanor or expression that suggested fear.

"He's not going to answer," Dover said. "Please don't do this. Don't become like them."

Doc's eyebrows arched questioningly; there was a hint of amusement in his eyes. He looked at Jack.

Jack glanced down. "Jesus." He thought for a moment, then sighed. "All right. How about Dover and I go to the clinic and check it out?" he said. "We'll leave this guy and the other clown here with you."

"I'm good with that," Doc said.

Jack looked at Dover and shook his head. "That OK with you?"

She nodded.

"You're ruining our rhythm, girl," Doc said.

"I'm good with that," she replied

Jack went outside and got their prisoner, threw him at the feet of the other man. He watched for a reaction from either man. There wasn't one. Either they were well trained or they didn't know each other. Another piece of the puzzle that didn't quite fit.

Doc threw Jack his car keys. Jack hurried to Doc's car, Dover running after him.

"Thank you," she said.

"Sure. I like letting terrorists off the hook."

"We don't know that the other man did anything wrong," Dover said.

"Due process is a wonderful thing, and ordinarily I'm all for it. But there is something going down and that man may have been withholding essential information."

"That's possible, maybe even likely," she agreed. "But the same way you walked around that office and pulled together clues, I have a feeling you're better at fieldwork than torture. What you almost did in there—I think that was mostly about your friend Abe."

Jack wasn't sure whether his higher calling had been praised, his baser instincts condemned, or both. In any case, she was probably right.

The Eastern Rim van was parked outside the destroyed clinic. Jack saw a few work lights as he drove by, along with two police officers sitting in their patrol car. One was texting; the other was eating takeout. He didn't blame them: this wasn't what anyone would call glamour duty.

Jack did not want to get into a discussion with the officers about his business here, and risk being delayed or barred. Instead, he and Dover went to the back of Bruno's and climbed onto the Dumpster and over the wooden fence. The back of the clinic was only partly in ruins, and they were hidden from view as they went inside.

The ruins were lit on top by streetlamps but the lower half was in complete darkness. They moved

cautiously down a hallway, pushing their feet along
and feeling in front of them to keep from stepping on
broken shards of wall and ceiling or knocking into
furniture or cabinets. They were following the tap of
laptop keys from somewhere inside. One wall of the
hallway was gone; it used to separate the corridor from
a series of examination rooms. The ceiling was partly
intact, as was the wall on the opposite side. The
typing—and now the faint grinding of gears—was
coming from one of the exposed rooms toward the
front.

Jack neared the room and looked around the shattered wall. A man was sitting in a stool facing the
remains of the hallway. He was Asian. There was a
hole in the floor and a small, four-wheeled robot
beside it. An extension arm was inside the hole.

There was no way around this. Jack pulled a Doc
and walked boldly into the room.

"Hey!" he smiled, approaching the man.

"What do you want?" the man asked in English.

"We're with the California Department of What
the Hell's Going On?" he said as he stepped up to
the hole. A rope ladder covered the short distance to
the ground below. A camera attached to the robotic
arm was peering down what looked like a passage-
way. That was what had been making the grinding
sound.

Meanwhile, Dover entered and stepped behind the
man. He slapped the top of his laptop shut.

"That was damned suspicious," Jack said.

"You have no authority—"

"Oh, *Christ,* if I have to hear that one more time," Jack said. "What are you doing here?"

The man took out his cell phone. "I'm calling the police."

"Great," Jack said. He took out his own cell phone. "I'll call the FBI. Got 'em on speed dial now."

The man hesitated as voices came from below. They were shouts, in Chinese. The man in the chair looked concerned.

"Is that not supposed to be happening?" Jack asked.

The man continued to listen. The shouts stopped. Someone yelled from below in Chinese. The man answered. There was more shouting from below.

"Jack, someone told him to get out," Dover said. "There's a woman down there, attacking."

"Attacking who? Why?"

Dover shook her head.

The man jumped from his stool and started to run around the hole. Jack stepped in front of him, body-checked him, and grabbed him by the shoulders. The man was smaller than Jack but powerful. He ducked under one of Jack's arms and tried to drag him along.

"You're not leaving until you tell me what's happening!" Jack said.

"We have to go!" he cried.

"Why?" Jack demanded.

"Let me go!"

The man pulled hard, his jacket tore, and he would have gotten away if Dover hadn't hit him from behind with the stool. The man went down hard, face-first.

"You were saying something about *my* interrogation

techniques?" Jack said. He dropped to his knees, turned the man onto his back. The man was dazed but awake. "You tell me what's happening, and I'll get you out."

The man was about to answer when there was a series of loud bangs and the floor shook.

San Francisco, California

The Hawk landed just beyond the 747 at the international terminal. The pilot wished Agent Fitzpatrick "Godspeed" as he got out.

"Safe flight back," Fitzpatrick said, as the pilot waited for refueling.

An African American airport security officer who had the distinctive rigidity and alert eyes of a Marine MP was waiting for Fitzpatrick at the door of the mechanics' entrance just below the gate. Carl Forsyth was standing directly behind him.

"I'm Deputy Airport Director Cranston, Operations and Security," said the security officer, who looked about forty and had the grip of a weight lifter. "Field Director Forsyth has briefed me. It's an honor to meet you."

"You've got a fan," said Forsyth as he shook hands with his field agent. "Welcome back. The target is at the gate."

The men followed the security guard to a card-activated stairwell door.

"Has anyone figured out why he's here instead of at the consulate?" Fitzpatrick asked.

"That's one of the things we hope to find out,"

Forsyth answered. "Obviously we're watching for another attack. He's got a carrying case with him. Told the security agent it was ophthalmologic equipment."

"And they passed him."

Forsyth shrugged as they started up the concrete steps. "He's Chinese, not Middle Eastern. He's got diplomatic credentials. Not big draws on the profiling list."

The security agent opened the door to the gate area. He went in first, followed by Forsyth. The field director made sure their target was not looking in their direction before he moved from the doorway and let Fitzpatrick in.

Fitzpatrick recognized Agents Gailey and Kent. One woman was dressed as a flight attendant for another airline. She was seated at a gate across the way. The other was playing Scrabble on her iPad. She was sitting in the same row as the target. Between the two of them, they would see him wherever he went.

Fitzpatrick also saw Pan Kokinos, who was dressed as a janitor. He was the best shot in the field office.

"They're all going to move in as we get you closer," Forsyth said. "You need to be sure."

The man was sitting with his face to the big picture window, looking out at the dark tarmac. He was wearing a clean sweatshirt and baseball cap, both of which looked like they were fresh gift shop purchases.

As Fitzpatrick approached, he noticed two other men get up from different gates and, in unison, converge on the same spot. They were also Asian.

"Company," Fitzpatrick said.

"I see. Know them?"

Fitzpatrick was looking at one of the men in a rumpled business suit. "Yan Hua," the agent said. "He's the guy who kept me busy at the hotel while the other one got away. The other one was the ringer."

"Are they consulate?"

"Yeah."

Forsyth gave his head a small, slow shake. The other three FBI agents backed off. He and Fitzpatrick reached the seated man at the same time as the others. Both of the Chinese stood in front of the third man, blocking him from the front.

"It's good to see you again, agent," Yan smiled pleasantly.

"Would you step aside, please?" Forsyth said. "This is U.S. government business."

"What business would that be?"

"None of yours," Forsyth answered.

Yan Hua smiled. "Then we have nothing to discuss. Enjoy your evening, gentlemen."

"Go around," Forsyth told Fitzpatrick.

The agent did as he was told. The Chinese diplomats were standing shoulder to shoulder. The target was sitting absolutely still behind them, reading a newspaper that he held in front of his face. Fitzpatrick shook his head, indicating he was still unable to make a clear identification, and took a stance with his back to the window.

"We can detain the plane on some security charge,"

Forsyth said. "Are you prepared to stand here all night?"

"If that is necessary to protect the rights of our diplomats, we are."

"Diplomat? This man is a murderer!" Fitzpatrick yelled.

Other passengers who were waiting for the flight looked over.

"I do not think Lufthansa will appreciate you causing a panic," Yan remarked.

"Frankly, sir, Lufthansa is the least of our concerns," Forsyth replied.

Fitzpatrick wanted to grab the man and force him around. But if he or Forsyth did that, any detention would be a violation of international law. That question would have to be adjudicated before they could act on Title II, Section 218 of H.R. 3162, the USA Patriot Act.

The identification had to come first.

Forsyth motioned to the airport security officer, who had been waiting by the staircase. He jogged over.

"Sir?"

"What would happen if I told you that a bomb threat had been called in, against the terminal?" Forsyth asked.

"Aircraft in this section would be grounded, and we'd evacuate the building."

"Would the evacuation be voluntary?"

"No, sir. We would remove any individual who failed to depart."

Forsyth looked at Yan. "Will you step aside so we can determine the identity of this man?"

"We will not."

Fitzpatrick could see that his boss was struggling with the call. He didn't blame the field director. Even if they got their man, he would face arrest for making a false bomb report in a public building. The liberal press and their legal advocates would not give a damn about the circumstances. It could mean jail time and the end of Forsyth's career.

Most of the passengers at the gate were watching them. Some of the passengers at other gates were looking over and pointing. Forsyth looked at Fitzpatrick.

Suddenly, Deputy Director Cranston stepped over the row of seats, pushed Yan Hua aside, and ripped the newspaper from the hands of the third man that the two Chinese diplomats had been standing in front of, protecting him.

"Is this the guy who blew up Air Base Parkway?"

Fitzpatrick looked down at the face that he had seen on Central Place, in the lobby of the hotel, and since then constantly, in his mind's eye, etched there like acid on a copper plate.

"That's the man," he said.

The burning smell was the smoky residue of the health clinic. Maggie had realized that as soon as she saw the hole in the low ceiling and the rubble beyond it. There was a ladder leading to the opening and some kind of camera looking in on them. She had no time to dwell on that, however.

Two men were huddled over something beneath the low ceiling. They were crouched about four yards from the opening, wearing gloves, talking to each other in Chinese.

"Their radio *must* have died," said one. "They'll be here in a minute."

"You'd better go and check."

"What if the charges detonate?"

"I have the trigger!" he snapped.

"But there's obviously a problem—"

That was all Maggie had needed to hear. She scurried forward, in a crouch. There was no time for a slow, silent approach: if the men had weapons, she needed to be close enough to disarm them.

They looked down the corridor as she ran forward.

"Detonate!" one man cried as he ran for the ladder.

"Doing it!" the other man yelled.

A voice shouted down from above, "What's wrong?"

"Go!" the man in the tunnel told him. "I've already set the king!"

The first man was almost at the opening when the other rose to join him. Maggie was just a few feet from him as he turned a knob on his radio. She grabbed the front of his shirt, dropped on her back, tucked her legs against the man's waist, and cracked him hard against the low ceiling. She completed the somersault by hurling him back in the direction she had come—

As the tunnel exploded around them.

Maggie flipped onto her belly and covered her head as a series of blasts rumbled through the length of the maze. Most of them were behind her; one was between Maggie and the hole under the clinic. Dirt and rock fell in clumps, filling the air with a tawny mist. The sight faded quickly, however, as the pile of debris between Maggie and the exit filled the tunnel.

Her ears clogged by the blasts, her back covered with dirt, Maggie slowly got to her hands and knees. After a few moments she heard what sounded like distant laughing. It was faint at first, but grew louder as her ears began to clear. She pulled out her shirttail and covered her mouth to keep from inhaling dust.

"You have killed us," the man cried with a terrified expression.

Maggie crawled in the direction of the voice. She felt for him with her free hand, found his left arm.

"What are you talking about?" she demanded.

"The biotoxin," he said. "It cannot be shut down. All these preparations—I told Liu I should be sad to leave it. And I haven't."

"That box? Behind us?"

The man just laughed.

Maggie let her fingers move to the man's hand. She pressed her fingers to the palm, put her thumbs on his knuckles, and twisted away from his body. That forced the wrist in two directions it was not designed to go. The pain was awful. The man screamed.

"Talk to me," Maggie said. "What have you done?" She relaxed her fingers.

"You're Chinese," he said, laughing again. He said in his native tongue, "At least I will die with a countryman."

Maggie was about to twist his hand again when she heard a faint voice behind her.

"Hello! Who's down there?"

She released the man's hand, turned, and felt her way as she crawled to the wall. "My name is Maggie Yu!"

"Maggie? Maggie, it's Jack Hatfield!"

"Jack! Listen—there's a man here who says he's releasing a biotoxin!"

"Where? In there?"

"Yes! I can't see anything . . . there's a container of some kind! I hear it humming!"

"Stay still . . . don't touch anything." Jack pulled out his cell phone.

"It doesn't matter," the man behind Maggie sneered. "Leave it, we die. Touch it, we die. In less than fifteen minutes the entire city will die!"

Maggie had had enough. She spun and crawled back to the man, found his face, put the side of her index finger to his nostrils. She pushed up hard. He screamed again.

"I want it all, *now*!" she said. "Talk!"

"I'll tell you, I'll tell you!" he cried. "You have a right to know!"

She relaxed, and Hu Kai told her what he had created. When he was finished, Maggie snarled and drove her palm into his forehead, cracking it. She did not provide him with the dignity of death.

While Dover and Jack dug at the pile of rubble in the tunnel, Jack spoke to the woman on the other side.

"He says the container has multiple safeguards," Maggie said. "The explosions punched holes in the tunnel—the relative heat down here will carry the toxins up into the city."

"Did he say what kind?"

"Pneumonic plague, I think."

"Virulent lung infection," Dover said.

"They blocked the hole where you are so the bacteria would go out the other way, into the financial district."

"Sick plan," Jack said as he clawed at rock to get through. "Brokers are already at work dealing with the Asian markets. No thermal currents at night to carry bacteria up and away from the city. Maximum deaths."

"They gave themselves enough time to get away," Maggie said.

By sea, he thought. *That's what the Farallon station was for.* Jack pulled out his cell phone. "I'd better call Forsyth. He needs to know."

He went to the ladder, where the phone showed he had a few bars, and called the field director.

"Jack, good news! We've got the terrorist—"

"*Bad* news. We're at the clinic. The Chinese have triggered a bomb of some kind to spread pneumonic plague. We're trying to get to it, but they're saying it can't be shut down."

"How much time?" Forsyth asked.

"About eight, ten minutes," he said.

There was a short silence. Jack heard him say away from the phone, "Is the Hawk still there?"

"Yes, sir."

"Hold him!" Forsyth came back on the line. "Jack, do they have police on-site?"

"One car—they were just down here, sent for help."

"Have them pull as close as possible to the device, lights and sirens on. Tell them it's a Code 3 emergency, authorization FBI 746. I'll be there ASAP."

"All right, but—"

"Evacuate but don't do anything else. Out."

Jack closed his dead phone then hurried to the ladder.

"Where are you going?" Dover asked.

"Forsyth is on the way."

"Why?"

"I don't know," he said. "I have to talk to the cops. I'll be back in a second."

He disappeared up the ladder just as Dover broke through the dirt wall and pulled Maggie through. Beyond her Dover could see a prone form—and a fax machine.

"Is that the device?" she asked.

Maggie nodded. "It's active. You hear it?"

Dover nodded. "The FBI is coming to deal with it."

"How? There's no time—"

"I don't know," Dover said. She smiled at Maggie, like whistling past a graveyard. "What I *do* know: with about six or seven minutes to go, at least we won't die of suspense."

"Call the tower—tell them to turn the Hawk around."

Deputy Director Cranston was running alongside Forsyth and Fitzpatrick. He made the call on the radio as they reached the staircase. The three of them ran down. Fitzpatrick was cradling the carrying case with the EMP device in his arms. Forsyth had told him to take it, over the protestations of the Chinese diplomats.

"You will create an international incident!" Yan Hua warned.

"Ram it," Forsyth said. "I'm trying to prevent one!"

Between the actions of Cranston and Forsyth, Fitzpatrick had never been prouder to be part of a team.

"Clear the airspace over the highway, north," Forsyth told Cranston. "We're going to be breaking some regulations."

"You got it. G'luck."

"Thanks."

The Hawk had literally just lifted off and was back on the ground as they arrived. Forsyth got in front, and Fitzpatrick jumped in the back. The field director jabbed his finger up and north. The chopper rose quickly.

"Follow 101 north, *fast,* as low as you can," Forsyth said as he put on the headset. "Fifteen miles. How long at max?"

"We're rated at one hundred and sixty knots, one hundred and eighty-four mph."

"No good. We have less than five minutes," Forsyth said. "Can you push her?"

The chopper seemed to catch fire—literally. The cockpit dipped slightly, the fuel took on the scent of an oil blaze, and the helicopter ripped dizzyingly through the night. The fuel smell made Fitzpatrick slightly light-headed, and he heard his own heartbeat inside the headset. He was glad he had something to do rather than look out the window at cars so close he felt they were going to skid across the tops of trucks. Forsyth had not bothered to explain the plan, but Fitzpatrick had figured it out. He had taken the EMP device from the case and was trying to make sure he knew how to work it.

Forsyth ducked his head between the seats. "I'm told that thing is unidirectional!" the field director remarked.

"Damn well hope so," Fitzpatrick said.

"It has a fifteen-hundred-foot range before porosity becomes a factor," Forsyth told him. "When we get there, you'll see a cop car in the general target area. We'll try to get you above an open section of roof so you can aim straight into the ground."

The Hawk swerved left and right to avoid billboards as it sped lower and faster, the pilot obviously trying to cover as much distance as possible. No doubt he had figured out the mission listening to his passengers. He was pushing to get the helicopter as near to the target as possible.

"Lieutenant, I'm going to give you a half-mile warning when I see the target," Forsyth said. "We're looking for a blown-out structure and a cop car. There will probably be a bunch of cars and—"

"I see them," the pilot replied. "Three o'clock, fire engines, prowlers. Banking over."

Fitzpatrick put the device on the back of his right

wrist and strapped it in place. It was like wearing a watch with a spyglass attached. It was frightening to contemplate the power he had on his forearm.

Automatic weapons were deadly, but they were honest, he thought. *The sound matched their destructive power. This thing is sinister, evil.*

"I'm going to have to open the door," Fitzpatrick said as they neared.

"I've got about thirty seconds," the pilot told him. "I'm gonna swing around, point you there, and when I say 'open,' you yank on that handle and fire."

Fitzpatrick's heart was no longer just in his ears: it was in his jaw as well.

Don't screw the pooch, he told himself. His hands were trembling, and he tried to relax. He hoped this thing had some kind of spread in case his eyeballing aim was off. He put his left hand on the latch. The ruined building was about a quarter of a mile distant and roughly thirty feet below them.

The helicopter suddenly whirled, as though someone had stuck a pole through the heart of the rotor.

"Go!" the pilot shouted.

Jack climbed down the ladder and came over to Maggie and Dover who were huddled beside the opening in the wall. He hugged Maggie, saw their hopeful looks. Jack did not bother to discourage them. If the plague germs were released, chances were good no one would be getting out of this alive.

Jack had once done a program on dirty bombs and

weaponized bacteria. The natural heat generated by any city, and the winds that swept across most port cities, would spread radiation and toxins across a two-mile radius in under a minute. The toxins would go even farther, and faster, if there was some kind of detonation and not merely a release. He knew that these men had planned carefully. The area would be a dead zone within seconds.

Oddly enough, he considered going over to Bruno's for a last glass of Gaja Sori San Lorenzo. Jack wasn't big on wines, but ever since Bruno had introduced him to the '04, he had become a fan.

He hated the buzzing of the device on the other side of the dirt wall. It was like a mosquito in his ear, one he couldn't swat away. The only reason he didn't take the ladies to Bruno's was because he wanted to be here when Forsyth did whatever he planned to do, just in case he could help.

Jack did not bother checking his watch. Forsyth was probably already too late. They had a minute and change, at best. All that had happened was that the red-and-blue lights of a police car had moved closer. No one had come down here.

Maybe Forsyth changed his mind and was leaving town. He wouldn't blame him, especially if this was hopeless.

Jack heard, then felt, the helicopter as it arrived. The rotors beat hard for a few seconds and the ground literally shook.

And then the lights outside the hole went off.

"Holy shit," Jack said.

He couldn't see the women, but he heard Dover shift. "Jack, the device. Isn't it supposed to—"

"Blow up," Jack said, smiling. "Yeah!"

He took out his cell phone, tried it, and actually cheered when it refused to turn on. "Holy shit," he said again. "He did it. He used the EMP. Doesn't matter how you wire a bomb if you don't have electricity to run it. He shut it down!" The irony of Hawke's Squarebeam technology being used to save lives, including his own, was not lost on him.

The helicopter was still beating overhead. A light from above shined into the hole. Jack walked over to the ladder and climbed up. He went out what used to be the back door and stared into the most beautiful white light he had ever seen.

He couldn't see who was in it. The fact that it wasn't God made this a very, very good result.

Jack did not linger in the light. He realized that someone had better go back into the tunnel and secure the bomb and the men who had tried to trigger it.

"Someone" meant Jack Hatfield.

Go down in torn civvies that can't keep dust out, let alone biotoxins, he thought. *Keep things safe 'til the men in the hazmat suits get here.*

The story of my life.

After settling Dover and Maggie on a slab of concrete that had once been a piece of foundation, Jack turned back toward the hole. The helicopter was still hovering overhead, lighting the scene until the fire department and emergency services cops could arrive with portable spotlights. Enough of a glow spilled into the tunnel so that Jack could see the opening in the absolute dark that surrounded it.

His arms trembling, he started down the ladder.

Whoever said, "It's all over but for the shouting," had never actually fought a war, Jack thought. Or played a championship game. Or run a marathon.

When a hard-fought battle has been won, or lost, a sense of high energy lingers—sometimes for minutes, sometimes for an hour or more—followed by sudden, crushing exhaustion. It is not just weariness of the body but of the mind. All you can process are moments, events in your immediate vicinity. And for the warrior, "it" is never over.

Post-traumatic stress disorder, the shrinks call it, Jack thought. Before that it was *shell shock.* Neither term was really accurate. The condition was actually hopelessness, realization that the terrible aggression you threw your shoulder against had only been halted, not stopped. It would be back, in another body, with another terrible purpose.

That fear was what kept soldiers up at night. The fact that victory was temporary, fleeting.

Sometimes more fleeting than one had just imagined moments before—

Jack stopped at the opening in the earthen barricade through which he'd pulled Maggie Yu. There was a glow in the distance where there should be no glow. Everything inside and out had been hit by the pulse. There should be nothing darker on the planet than this tunnel.

Jack ducked through, saw an orange circle of light hanging near the roof of the tunnel. It was about ten feet distant and moving away from him. He put his hand against the wall to his right to make sure he didn't stumble over the bomb, which he knew was on the left. He felt his way along the pitted brick surface as he moved toward the illumination.

The light stopped and turned.

Jack saw a flickering flame—a cigarette lighter. In the ruddy illumination was a thin face looking back. The face was covered in blood from a wound on the forehead; Jack wasn't sure, but he thought he could see bone. Beside the face, at the very edge of the glow, the man was holding a chess piece. A queen.

The man was making for one of his targets, one of the holes nearer the financial district.

Jack didn't think. He ran toward the light.

The man dropped the lighter. It burned on the ground, casting its dull glow upward. Jack saw him reach for the chess piece with his free hand.

He was going to snap it.

Jack was on him in two great strides, grabbing the man's right arm with both hands, yanking it from the chess piece. He succeeded, but the man surprised him by putting the queen's head in his mouth.

"God *damn* you!" Jack yelled.

He was trying to bite the thing. Jack released the man's right arm and tried to grab the piece, realized that it might just as easily break in the struggle. Snarling with animal ferocity, Jack put his palm against the back of the man's hand, closed his fingers around those of the terrorist, and pushed hard. The chess piece was shoved into the man's mouth. Jack kept both his hand and that of his opponent against the man's chin, preventing it from opening. Teeth crunched, plastic cracked; all that stood between Jack and death was the man's closed lips.

Grunting, Jack dug his fingernails into the terrorist's flesh, squeezed, pushed him against the wall to pin him there. He bent the man's head back. He couldn't choke him, didn't want the man to lose consciousness. He had to *swallow* the damn thing.

His cheeks, Jack thought.

While Jack fought off the man's free hand with his own, he shifted his thumb and index finger so they pressed against his two cheeks. It was a trick he remembered from survival training: you could generate saliva by constricting the mouth.

The man shook his head violently as Jack pushed his cheeks in, hard. He could hear the man gagging. He was going to have to swallow or choke.

The man swallowed. He coughed inside his closed mouth, tried to retch, but Jack held him firm.

Within moments there was a change over the entirety of the man's body. He began to spasm, as though he were possessed. Jack heard bubbling sounds. They were not coming from the man's stomach but from inside his throat. His veins were erupting. Even in the dim light Jack could see the darkening of the skin on his neck. His limbs jerking helplessly, the terrorist was no longer resisting him. Jack put both hands against his mouth to keep it shut.

The man's cheeks bloated. He gagged, drowning in blood. It seeped from between his lips. Jack had a feeling that the airborne toxins were secure now, embedded in bodily tissues and fluids. Jack slid him along the wall to the floor, stepped back, picked up the flickering lighter. There was a spot of blood on his hand, and his first thought was to use the flame to burn it off. He stopped, realizing that that might aerosolize any bacterium, and simply wiped it on the man's shirt.

He looked down at the figure convulsing on the earth. Spots of blood were soaking through his clothes. They were beading on his forehead, thin streams were running from his nose, and there were ugly, dark blue lines under his face and in the whites of his eyes. The veins began to burst like hot dogs on a grill, some of them releasing blood under the skin, some over it. The man continued to twitch even after life had left him, the blood reacting to whatever pathology was feeding on it.

That medical minds, trained to heal, could conceive of and execute a weaponization project like this was the greatest horror Jack had ever faced. That wasn't just hate, like Islamic terrorists trying to explode a dirty bomb. It was cool calculation, the result of rational thought.

There is your fear, Jack thought. *There is hopelessness.* The fact that minds smart enough to create such a thing were cold enough to use it.

The cigarette lighter winked out. As it did, Jack became aware of movement and light to his left. He looked over at beams poking here and there in the dark.

Carl Forsyth shone a light on his face.

"Hi, Jack," he said.

"Hey."

"Everything secure down here?" he asked.

"It is now," Jack said, as he backed unsteadily from the dead man.

Several beams played across the dead man.

"You sure about that?" Forsyth asked.

Jack took a moment. He did a quick catalogue of his own bodily functions. He didn't taste blood. He looked at his hands, felt his cheeks, forehead. "Yeah," he said.

Forsyth stayed back as men in the white, Level A Positive Pressure Personnel suits filed around him. They looked like lunar explorers, their air cylinders and breathing apparatus inside the garments for protection. Three of them went to the bomb, one cuffed the other terrorist who was just coming to, and one came over to Jack carrying handheld electronics. He was testing the air, Jack's breath. Jack couldn't see his face in the dark behind the visor. It was like a medical exam where you didn't think you had anything to worry about until they actually started doing tests.

"Prelim AC," Jack heard from Forsyth's radio.

That was the technician, muted inside his suit, letting the field director know that everything seemed to be all clear.

Forsyth moved forward, shone his light on the dead man.

"What happened?"

Jack told him. He was in reporter mode, reciting facts concisely. In the telling, it felt as though the struggle had happened to someone else.

When he was finished, Forsyth nodded.

"We're just going to call this a suicide, OK?" Forsyth asked. "Saves me having to arrest you for murder."

Jack nodded, and an instant later he laughed.

There could *be* no other response to the absurdity of the truth Forsyth had just uttered.

Forsyth wasn't sure how to respond. He just backed away and motioned at EMTs to bring the oxygen over. Jack accepted the breather but declined a stretcher.

Unlike the genocidal son of a bitch at his feet, he had earned the right to leave here with his head high and upright.

The sun was warm on the window of Field Director Forsyth's office as Jack and Dover were shown in. Forsyth stood behind his desk and a young man rose, smiling, from a vinyl-covered couch against the wall.

"You must be Agent Fitzpatrick," Jack said as he walked in. "I hear we all owe you our lives."

"It was a team effort," he replied. "And that's not sunshine I'm blowing. It truly was."

"I can go along with that," Jack said.

He introduced Dover Griffith, then shook Forsyth's

hand. "Sorry that Doc Matson couldn't make it," Jack said. "He's out diving around Abe Cohen's boat with a speargun. Looking for something."

"I want to meet this man," the field director said. "Sounds like someone I should have in my Rolodex."

"Do you still use a Rolodex?" Jack asked.

"Now more than ever. You never know when the power will go out," he grinned as he sat. "Anyway, I wanted you all to meet. An official commendation will follow for Agent Fitzpatrick, but I wanted to thank him and the two of you for everything you did—and to tell you what else we've learned. Your friend Mr. Hawke came clean and named his contacts. As far as we can tell, he didn't do anything illegal, though the State Department has been in touch with Beijing about the attacks on military and civilian targets by Mr. Sammo Yang, who is presently in custody and will remain so at an unspecified location. Beijing has asked for us to turn him over, but in light of the other events of this week, they are not in a position to make demands. One way or another, we will find out who in the Chinese military authorized this program."

"We understand it was in retaliation for us attacking their satellites," Jack said.

Forsyth's mouth twisted. "Jack, we're doing good here. Let's keep the detente going."

"It's just a question."

"I know. But I'm liking you right now. Save the story-gathering for some other time."

"Fair enough," Jack said. His submission reeked of insincerity. "But here's a story you might enjoy. Right before coming over, I heard that the FCC is revoking the permission it gave for Hawke Industries to run its mobile broadband service. The FCC said its decision was based on a report from the National Telecommunications and Information Administration that 'there is no practical way to mitigate the potential interference at this time' caused by the global positioning devices that relay the satellite signals. They had evidence that it affected everything from aircraft landing gear to weather prediction technology."

"I saw the NTIA report," Forsyth said. "What does that have to do with the price of an EMP in China?"

"It supports what I was saying from the start," Jack said, "that Hawke was hiding the deadly facts about his technology. I'm going to expose that cover-up."

"Once a truth teller, always a truth teller," Forsyth remarked helplessly.

"What really ticks me off is that Hawke not only knew the danger, he had his scientists perfect it. What was the effective range of the device?"

"We were at twenty-one-hundred-feet distant with moderate-porous interference. Within specs. And that's for your ears only."

"Longer range than Squarebeam," Jack said. "The bastard. That's what he had them doing in Murrieta. Figuring out how to put more bite in those destructive teeth."

"Moving on," Forsyth said pointedly, "they've

promised to deal with whoever released the pneumonic plague specimens. They didn't deny that they have a germ warfare program, but it doesn't do anyone any good when those germs get out. Beijing said they know nothing about that part of it, and Washington believes them."

"Do we know who was behind that project?"

"We're still trying to get the lay of the land from the folks we rounded up, the ones from Eastern Rim and also the fellows Doc trussed up at their office. All fingers point to their consulate and to the ranking official in their consulate, Mr. Jing Jintao. Harbor patrol saw him in the harbor last night, on a powerboat, headed out to sea. They stopped him because the boat was traveling without lights. He turned around a few minutes later and went back to shore."

"He probably heard that his plan had failed."

"That's our guess," Forsyth said. "The Coast Guard spotted a yacht out by the Farallons around the same time. Before they could contact it, the vessel headed back out to sea."

"A hire?"

"Possibly," Forsyth said. "We don't have any ID on it yet. Now," he looked at Dover, "I also understand that you're currently between positions."

"You could say that."

"We've got a pretty good intel division, but we lack Chinese intelligence resources. I have a feeling that's going to be a growth market. Would you consider relocating to San Francisco and coming to work for us?

I think you'll find the city a little more exciting than Suitland."

"It hasn't let me down yet," she beamed.

"So that's a yes?" Forsyth asked.

"It is. Thank you, sir."

"Go easy on the 'sir,'" Jack said. "You don't work for him yet."

Forsyth regarded Jack. "You did great work here. Again."

"Thanks."

"What was the line in the movie? Something about this being the start of a beautiful friendship?"

"It was Humphrey Bogart to Claude Rains in *Casablanca*," Jack said. "And like I just told Dover, let's not get carried away. This is a big story. I'm going to cover it."

"You just can't help yourself, can you?" Forsyth asked.

"Hawke told me I would always be a lonely man, because ideals were more important to me than anything," Jack said. "Well, this is still a country with a government of the people, by the people, and for the people, as Mr. Lincoln so aptly put it. They have a right to know what has happened on *both* sides of the globe."

Forsyth stood and offered his hand. "To be continued, then."

Jack shook it. The handshake lasted a little longer than it needed to, and Forsyth's eye contact was unwavering. There was respect, at least, in that.

Dover did not hug Jack in front of her new boss; her broad smile was embrace enough. She stayed to fill out paperwork, Agent Fitzpatrick went back to work, and Jack walked alone into the beautiful San Francisco morning.

Not quite alone, he thought. And definitely not lonely, as Hawke had once described him.

He still had his big, vibrant, beautiful city.

Consul General Jing Jintao sat at his desk, thinking about pride and about disgrace.

The night before, watching the video images from the crawler on his cell phone, he was stirred by the risk and loyalty of his partners. He was on his way to the boat at the time, looking forward to joining them at sea, waiting for news of the impact of their work.

That had not happened.

The boat left without him, on his orders, against Liu Tang's protestations. As Liu Tang journeyed back to China, Jintao spent the night in his rooms at the consulate, waiting to see if any of the strands of the operation threaded their way back to him. He did not believe the members of the cell would talk. They were loyal. He did not think Sammo Yang would say anything about his own mission, which came from Beijing, not the consulate.

He had waited until the morning news reports spoke of a plot hatched by anarchists but thwarted by the FBI and informants—a plot to release a toxin through holes blown in the streets of the Financial District.

"They are said to be Chinese nationals," said one newscast, "but neither the Bureau nor the State Department will confirm this information, which was provided by controversial former talk show host Jack Hatfield. The Chinese consulate in San Francisco has not returned any of our requests for comment."

In fact, Jintao had his own plan for countering these reports. He had spoken with several ministers and fellow diplomats during the night, denying any knowledge of these actions. Today, he had called for a press conference at the consulate this morning to express outrage at the unfounded allegations and reliance on the word of a "disgraced" conspiracy theorist for information.

Still, the sense of loss and shame was profound. He had hoped that the destruction of this particular Financial District—perched, symbolically, on the edge of the Asian world—would lead to the final decline of the American nation and the natural ascendancy of China. That was to be his gift to his homeland, his legacy. Even if his colleagues never learned of his involvement, the failure would haunt him till death.

There was a gentle knock on the door.

"Come," he said.

Shing Wei entered. "Excuse me, Consul General, but there is a woman who would like to see you."

Jintao looked blankly at his personal secretary. "I assume she has a name?"

"Bu hao yi se," he apologized. "It is Maggie Yu."

"Do I know her?" he asked impatiently.

"No, sir, but I thought—"

"What does she want, Shing?"

"She says she has had enough of America and wishes to go home. I thought you might wish to see her."

The consul general felt a smile pull at the sides of his mouth. "Home." His eyes seemed far away. "I see."

The young secretary stood in the partially opened door, his head slightly lowered in respect, waiting patiently for his superior to speak.

"Bring her in," Jintao said.

The neatly dressed young man stepped back and extended his arm into the office. Maggie was dressed in a traditional costume, a floor-length red skirt and sleeveless, shoulderless white blouse in the style of a bamboo hat dancer.

She bowed respectfully to the secretary as she passed. It was protocol to leave the door open with all guests who did not come on official government business. These meetings were typically brief. Listening from his desk just beyond the door to the right, the secretary would know what was required without Jintao having to repeat it.

Jintao rose as the woman entered. He felt it was appropriate. He *needed* to do it: the gesture was less to honor the woman than to celebrate the idea of his homeland, the desire for an expatriate to be there.

Maggie approached the desk. "Consul General," she said softly. "You have disgraced yourself and the Chinese people."

Shing leaned across his desk to see into the room, frozen with surprise. Jintao was too startled to move.

Maggie did not have that problem. She tucked her elbows into her chest and pushed her arms straight out at the diplomat, across the desk, her hands open and facing him. The Dragon Palm strike hit him on the chest and sent him backward, off his feet, into his chair. She was on the desk with a single crouching leap. Her next jump had her legs tucked under her and her hands extended. She landed on the now-seated Jintao, her fingers grasping his shoulders, her knees landing hard in his belly. She was gripping him so hard that eight spots of blood appeared beneath his jacket, causing him to cry out. She released her right hand, curled the fingers into a tiger claw, and buried them in his eyes. His cry became a scream, which she smothered by putting her other arm across his mouth and leaning forward.

"If you want me, come and get me—if you have the courage," she said into his ear. "I'll be on American soil, the soil of my home."

Maggie rotated the swivel chair a quarter turn and stepped off backward. She turned toward the door. Shing was standing there, openmouthed and aghast. Without looking at Jintao, she formed a tight fist with her right hand and, with an arcing blow, punched Jintao in the right ear. He fell against the left armrest. A blow to that side sent him to the right.

"That was for treating your secretary with disrespect," she said.

She pulled the telephone from Jintao's desk and yanked it out, dropping it to the carpet as she walked to the door.

"I will hurt anyone who tries to stop me," she told his secretary.

"I—had no intention of doing so," Shing told her. He looked back at Jintao. "Though admitting you, I fear, will cost me my job."

"Yes. He cannot give a press conference with bleeding ears."

Shing looked at the panting heap sprawled in his chair.

"Leave with me," Maggie said. "I know people who can give you asylum, help you get a visa."

"But my home—my parents, my brothers, they are all in Hāěrbīn."

"You'll have a better chance of seeing them again if your fate is not entwined with what this man has done," she said. "He will be exposed. Disgraced."

The young man was nodding even as he considered what she had said.

"All right," he said, shutting the door behind him. "I should distance myself from what has happened here, at least for now."

"And it is fitting that we have met. You are at least a Third Pin."

"I beg your pardon?"

"Nothing," she smiled. "Come."

The young man took his overcoat from the rack and led the way from the office.

Bruno's was closed due to the rattling noise going on under the dining room and kitchen. Officials from the

Department of Public Works said they would need at least a day to finish work under this stretch of the tunnel system. But Bruno opened for his old friends when they came for lunch.

Doc sat in the outdoor area where the sounds and rattling were minimized. Work crews were coming and going from the wreck of the clinic, not only shoring up the tunnel but also sealing it off along its entire length with a series of iron bars. A roped-off hole two feet in diameter, blown by the terrorists, was a hundred yards to Doc's right, near a natural gas pipeline. A foot closer to the pipeline, the whole street would have gone up. And the hole was just one of a half dozen new potholes that stretched from the clinic through the Financial District.

Doc had arrived first, as usual. Jack had stayed up most of the night, making notes. Bruno came out with a pot of coffee and a cup when he saw him arrive.

"Salute!" Bruno said as Jack sat.

"Yeah, you did it again," Doc said, raising a glass of grapefruit juice.

"Stumbled through it," Jack said.

"We stumble through most things in life," Doc laughed. "The trick is not to fall and to recover intelligently, which you do."

Jack accepted that and took a sip of black coffee Bruno had poured before hurrying back to the kitchen. Jack's arms were huddled protectively around the cup and saucer. He noticed that since the last terrorist attack, from the Hand of Allah, he tended to do that more: protect his food. He wondered about the unmeasured, maybe even unrecognized, psychological tolls of living in watchful fear.

There was a third place at the table. Both men happened to look at it at the same time. Vintage love beads were set in a circle around a glass of herbal tea. Doc had retrieved the beads from the boat. The spotter had showed him the location on a map after some persuasion at the Eastern Rim office involving a soldering iron and a strand of melted lead.

"Nice of you to have done that," Jack said.

Doc shrugged a shoulder. "Abe's sailing token deserved to be here. Even if it does reek of hippiness. And nearly cost me my left foot in the getting."

"That would account for the shark bacon Bruno is preparing?"

"It would," Doc replied.

Both men chuckled and raised their respective beverages to their missing friend.

"At least Maggie Yu benefited from this," Jack said. "Her dad texted this morning—asked if I could put him in touch with our contact at the FBI. Seems Maggie not only beat the hell out of the consul general but came back with a young man who might want political asylum. Seems he knows enough to get the boss man in a sea of trouble."

"Hope Johnny appreciates that his daughter was instrumental in saving a hundred thousand lives."

"Enough to forgive her for going down the rabbit hole," Jack said.

The men fell silent as the colorful string of beads weighed heavily on them.

"He was a pain in the rear, but a good guy," Doc said.

"Aren't we all. So what's next for you?" Jack asked. "Sounded like you had something lined up."

"Texas," he said. "Bunch of folks on the border want to put together a merc army and go after the cartels."

"That will be interesting," Jack said.

"It was inevitable. Those suckers are recruiting kids in Victoria and other towns, kids as young as ten, eleven, paying them to get other kids hooked. Why don't you come along for a look-see? Helluva story in that."

Jack shook his head. "I've got a story I need to produce first. I don't know who will air it, since it implicates Beijing, Washington, and one of our biggest industrial powers, but I have to tell it just the same."

"Sounds like you *may* be safer in Mexico."

"Maybe." Jack grinned. "But it's like that Chinese kid Johnny was telling me about—the one who Maggie brought out of the consulate. Sometimes you just have to do what's right."

"I'll drink to that," Doc said, draining his glass.

Jack sat back and forced himself to move his arms away from the cup. It was a small gesture, but a significant one.

You can't let fear rule your life, he thought. *Not fear of terrorists or fear of criticizing your own leaders or foreign governments.*

"Truth tellers," Jack said.

"What?"

"Just thinking out loud," Jack said.

He smiled.

They had killed the show. But they could never kill the ideal.